MW01717550

HENRI'S ghost

Novels by Patricia L. Stebelton

SUSPENSE. MYSTERY. ROMANCE.

*

The Sleeping Matchbook

Watched!

Inherited Danger

Henri's Ghost

Uncharted Storm

The Forgotten Witness

HENRI'S *ghost*

PATRICIA L. STEBELTON

OAKTARA
www.oaktara.com

Henri's Ghost

Published in the U.S. by:
OakTara Publishers
www.oaktara.com

Cover design by Yvonne Parks at www.pearcreative.ca
Cover images © shutterstock.com: mysterious rock with a view/alsamua, 41154919; beautiful young girl enjoying the sunny freshness/Alyshyn_Andrei, 128301485; © thinkstockphotos.ca: abandoned wall/94009757
Author photo © Patricia L. Stebelton

The story on page 159 is taken from *I Remember Dahlonega: Stories about the People and the History of Lumpkin County,* Anne Dismukes Amerson (Dahlonega, GA: Chestatee Publications, 1997).

ISBN-13: 978-1-60290-202-2
ISBN-10: 1-60290-202-X

Printed in the U.S.A.

* * *

To our dear friends,
Curt and Sherry Mitchell

They were the first to tell me about the charming town of Dahlonega, hinting at the mysteries hidden deep in its colorful history.

"Do not fear, for I am with you…
for I am your God."
Isaiah 41:10

Acknowledgments

Special thanks to Jackie and Walton Peabody of Dahlonega, whose delightful hospitality and ongoing help with my research was invaluable to my story.

I also want to give special acknowledgment to Robert Lepage, Master Mechanic, Paul Marks, Retired Crime Scene Investigator, and Vanessa Stebelton, BSN, RN. My faithful readers, Kelly Vollmar, Dick Stebelton, and Anne Garris. Last, but not least, to Ramona Tucker, my editor, and the whole OakTara crew.

Note: Guest appearance in the book of Jackie and Walton Peabody is by permission.

1

The Inheritance

IN AN AGED, COMFORTABLE NEIGHBORHOOD on the fringe of New York City, a thin, medium-tall, sharp-featured man slipped silently into the lobby of an apartment complex. His dark, ill-fitting apparel gave him the appearance of a street person. Pausing briefly, the ominous visitor scanned the lobby before proceeding to the apartment mailboxes, pulling a dirty-brimmed, black hat low over his eyes. Shielding the movement of his hands, he worked clumsily on mailbox 312-B.

While rifling through its contents, he was interrupted by the jerking sound of the lobby elevator settling to the main floor and its subsequent door release. Replacing everything, he tugged his floppy hat lower and stepped swiftly back in the direction of the outside doors.

An older woman holding a small dog exited the elevator, laboriously moving toward the walled mailboxes. Her shrewd eyes followed the dark figure exiting the lobby. As she turned back, her finger ran down the numbers to her mailbox, number 314-B. She hesitated, frowning at the evident scratch marks around the key opening on the mailbox next to hers, 312-B.

"Well, I never!" she exclaimed, her eyes lifting suspiciously to the empty doorway.

*

Leslie Weldon slid, agitated, into a tall restaurant booth across from her long-time friend Diane Risner. "Sorry I'm late...last-minute details."

Diane smiled knowingly, her light coloring glowing a soft peach in the dim lighting. "So what's new? I ordered water and salads for us to begin. It will give you time to decide."

"Wonderful! You know me so well." Leslie briefly closed her eyes to catch her breath. "Well, it's final! Everything in my desk is contained in two boxes, which now sit in the back seat of my SUV. The entire culmination of my career—four years of devotion and overtime without pay." Her eyes flew open, flashing anger. "For what? So my removal will serve the company's efforts to save money this quarter—a token to make them look good at the stockholders' meeting." Her words denied any attempt to conceal her bitterness.

Her friend shook her head in sympathy. "You're a good worker, Les. They'll miss you, whether they know it yet or not."

Leslie pursed her lips to hold back her emotions. "The office staff presented a cake and served diet cola in paper cups. Shirley even taped three balloons to my desk. Everyone in both offices made an appearance to wish me well…except Torri. She was conspicuously absent. Rushed for a deadline was the excuse, I heard. Whatever!"

Diane lifted a brow. "Torri was probably busy packing up her desk to move into your office. I think she started her campaign to undermine you after you dated the heart-throb of the office. I saw the way she looked at him when I came by the office one day."

Leslie made a face. "That man is such a waste of skin. Torri is welcome to him. Our first and last date was a disaster—the worst ever! I swear, the man is an octopus!"

Diane leaned in close. "What did you do?"

"After I got his attention," Leslie smirked, "I threatened to expose him at work if he didn't back off."

"And did he?"

"He did—not happily, but he did. I received the silent treatment at work the next day, but that was actually a relief." She rolled her eyes.

"Do you have any leads, or will you have to contact a head hunter to find a job?"

Leslie shrugged. "The company didn't give me time to send out my résumé. Naturally, I've thought about a head hunter. At least until..." Lowering her voice, she continued, "Yesterday I received a curious letter in the mail. It's bizarre, really! I've inherited 350 acres in north Georgia, outside the town of Dahlonega—some distant cousin of my father's. I met Wayne Riker maybe twice, when Dad took me there on vacation. He was a nice old fella who never married."

Leslie conjured a vague recollection of that day. "His place was a bachelor's nightmare. I don't think he ever hung up a thing, and all the dogs…I was afraid to sit down. He said a housekeeper came in once a week—poor woman!" A smile tugged. "At any rate, I thought I might go down and check it out."

Diane's mouth dropped open. "What are you saying? You're going down there—to Georgia? Are you going to sell or what?"

"I don't know, but now I've got time to figure it out. The truth is, Diane, I'm tired of this rat race, and all the rats that go with it, if you know what I mean." She chuckled dryly. "I need some time to regroup. My apartment is paid up until the end of next month. I can come back if I don't like it and pick up the pieces. It's not like I'm attached to anyone," she added soberly.

The persistent ringing of a phone interrupted whatever Diane planned to say. She fumbled in her purse, withdrawing two phone-like apparatus, and reached for the vibrating one. Finishing her short call, she returned it to her purse before extending her hand toward the other mechanism.

"What's that?" Leslie stared at the weird-looking device.

Diane laughed. "One of those hearing amplifiers you can order off TV. This one now belongs to young Drew. My dad bought it, hoping it would enable him to hear better in crowds. His hearing aids were ineffective in large gatherings. Unfortunately, he hated the way it looked. Dad said it made him look like he had some kind of fungus growth on the side of his head and refused to let his friends see him wearing it."

"But if it helped him hear..."

"Dad said most people weren't worth listening to anyway. He told Drew he could have it. I knew it was a bad idea at the time and should have said something, but didn't. When I caught the little scamp listening at our neighbor's fence when they had company, I gave him an ultimatum: Use it only at appropriate times and places—or else. I should have known that twelve-year olds don't have the common sense God gave them. Next I caught him listening at our bedroom door. That settled it!"

"So you took it away from him?"

"Among other things," she emphasized with a dark look.

"Ouch!" Leslie said, grinning. Picking up the odd-shaped apparatus from the table, she found it was actually made of two separate parts.

Diane took it from her and separated the pieces. "This is the amplifier section." Pushing a slide switch on the side, she lifted the silver, comma-shaped piece to Leslie's ear, attaching the fitted portion around the back of the ear. Softening her voice to a whisper, she asked, "This other portion is the charger unit. Can you hear me clearly?"

Leslie scanned the room. "I can hear *everyone!"* she whispered back, afraid to raise her voice.

Giggling, Diane murmured, "You better be careful, or someone will catch you."

Enjoying herself, Leslie leaned her head against the thick wooden structure of the tall booth, curious whether the amplifier had the strength to penetrate the partition wall. She pressed her ear tight and turned up the volume, stunned to hear the voices of two teenagers on a date, giggles and all. She smiled, hearing the couple prepare to leave, and would have turned off the device, but for a sudden compulsion to remain in place. She kept the apparatus in position and waited, wondering why her sense of mystery was still kicked into high gear.

The restaurant was busy, and the booth was cleared quickly. With her pressed ear, the shuffling of feet in the booth and the voice of a cheerful waiter came through clearly. *This thing is amazing!* Leslie was impressed.

Then she glanced at Diane, and pangs of guilt struck her sharply. Listening to conversations wasn't ethical. But before she could turn off the amplifier, the harsh, ominous words of two men grabbed her attention, alarming her. Something was very wrong. She felt frozen in place and continued to listen, her heart racing.

The more she heard, the more nervous she got. Suddenly, Leslie pulled the device from her ear and hurriedly concealed it within her hands. Her breathing came in short puffs; her eyes locked downward on the tablecloth.

Diane's hand grasped her friend's arm. "What is it? You're white as a ghost! Did you hear something?" she asked anxiously.

"Ssshhh," Leslie said in a hurried whisper.

One of the men exited the booth behind them and rushed past their table as both women pretended to concentrate on their salads. Leslie raised her eyes in time to catch the profile of the fast-receding figure. His thin face highlighted his sharp features, though his eyes were shadowed by a black felt hat.

Leslie suddenly realized she was holding her breath and forced herself to exhale. "He's gone!" she said hoarsely.

Diane stared at her. "Leslie, what did you hear?"

Placing a quick finger to her lips, Leslie leaned close. "Later," she said, pointing toward the booth behind her.

Diane seemed to understand, her expression mirroring her concern.

For the rest of their hastened meal, the conversation between the two women was stilted, both afraid of saying something that might possibly be overheard by the remaining man in the booth behind Leslie's seat. After paying, they walked quickly toward the parking area.

Leslie rushed her friend out of sight before attempting to explain. "One of those men in the booth is planning to kill someone."

Diane frowned. "Who? Did he say?"

"No…all I could hear was clipped sentences. One said, 'He wants her dead.' The other one argued that he was interrupted from getting something or other the day before. That part was vague." She shrugged. "He must have lowered his voice. But I did hear him say that he knew where *she* lived and had the '*mark'* in his sights. He seemed to think this comment was hilariously funny because he kept laughing. It was eerie and weird. The other man said the boss wanted *all* obstacles eliminated. The first one answered that he'd removed all but one, and *she* would be no problem."

Diane's face paled. "*She?* A woman? Oh my! I didn't realize how well that amplifier worked. Do you know those booth partitions are at least four inches thick? I couldn't hear a thing through my side."

Leslie shivered. "I wish I hadn't!"

The friends stood by Leslie's car, each momentarily lost in thought.

Then Diane's worried eyes searched Leslie's. "Are you going to the police? Maybe they can stop that man."

"Neither actually said the word *kill* or *murder.* Oh, I clearly understood their intentions, but it won't be clear enough for the police to do anything. The woman's name was never even spoken and…" Leslie heaved a troubled sigh. "I don't know which man said what." Pulling the hearing amplifier from her purse, she tried to hand it to Diane.

"Keep it! I don't want that thing back in my house." She gave Leslie a quick hug. "Call me and let me know what you are planning. And, for heaven's sake, don't leave for that strange-sounding Georgia town without keeping in touch. You've kept to yourself far too much lately. Don't close yourself off. Forget Kevin." Checking her watch, Diane added, "I gotta run. Call. Don't forget. I mean it!"

"I won't. I promise." Leslie waved, feeling suddenly at loose ends and very lonely. Her thoughts went to her father. She still missed him. Dad would know what to do. *Why did he have to die? It happened so fast. I didn't even have time to make things right.*

Opening her car door, she climbed in behind the wheel. On impulse, she shifted to glance back at the boxes filled with the remains of her career. Leslie knew she was being morbid and feeling sorry for herself, but right now she felt justified. Dad would say a crisis meant a "crossroads"—a time for choice, an opportunity. This choice was forced on her, and she resented being placed in the position.

"God will supply all your needs." How often had she heard her father quote that verse? Turning back, she gripped the steering wheel and grimaced.

"Tell me, Dad, will God supply my rent money after next month?" she muttered.

Uncomfortable, she felt guilty for her thoughts and grudgingly admitted there was a tidy amount in her savings—her reward for living frugally. Jutting her chin upward, Leslie pushed the ignition. "But that money won't last long. Then where will I be?"

It had been years since she'd trusted in God's promises. She remembered clearly the night she stopped—the night her world came crashing down. *I quit believing in most things that night, including faithfulness, honor, and the justice of life.* Standing on the balcony of the Tropical Paradise Hotel, she had watched the soft shades of early evening settle across the ocean waves. *My heart pounded waiting for Kevin to arrive, to join me at our appointed rendezvous. When the telephone rang, I had no idea it signaled the end of our love. And that was only the beginning of my woes....*

Pulling into traffic, she frowned, trying to decide if leaving everyone she knew in New York to go to the strange town with an Indian name was worth the time. Perhaps she would do better using that time to find a new job. With the economy so bad, it could take awhile. How long would her savings hold out? She had serious concerns.

*

A rapping sounded on Leslie's door and a simultaneous ringing. Leslie grinned. It could only be Alberta Maybourne, her gray-haired, wrinkle-faced neighbor just across the short hallway. She opened the door and flashed a warm smile at the only neighbor she'd grown close to since moving in. "Bert. I was about to come over to your place."

"I was afraid I would miss you before you left."

Leslie waved the woman into the room. "Don't be silly. I would never leave without saying good-bye. After all, you were the first person in this whole apartment building who bothered to speak with me."

Bert rolled her eyes. "Oh yeah, I *spoke* to you all right. I stomped across the hall, banged on your door, and yelled at you. For what? A petty grievance like playing your music too loud. Some welcome that was!" She lowered her eyes as if it hurt to remember her actions.

Leslie laughed. "Well, it made me feel noticed, and I *was* playing my music too loud. Bad habit from college days."

Alberta gazed up at her with adoration. "I'll never forget it. You were so sweet about it, and then you asked me in for coffee and cookies."

"Stale, store-bought cookies at that."

"Stale or not, they were the first sign of hospitality anyone in this building had ever offered me. It touched me. I'll surely miss you." The old lady's voice quivered.

Leslie cleared her throat. If they kept this up, both of them would be bawling. "It's not as if I'm leaving forever. But before I'm comfortable about selling this property, I feel I should at least see the place firsthand." *Is that really why I'm going?* It wasn't the first time she'd questioned the motives behind her decisions.

"That's understandable, and quite practical. Though I've never heard tell of this town you're heading to...and so far off the beaten track. I don't know." Bert frowned. "They say those woodsy places can have some pretty strange ways. I'll worry about you."

"I have no idea if the place is woodsy or not." She'd never given it a thought.

"I looked it up on a map, and it's a long way from an expressway, dear. I've heard some odd people live back in the hills. You see it on TV all the time. You be careful! I won't rest easy until you're back safe," Bert said curtly.

Leslie shook her head free of fear's shadow as an uneasiness passed over her. "Listen, Bert, don't you worry yourself with wild tales and made-up TV stories. It's not as if part of the country lives back in the frontier days. Technology is everywhere!" *Am I trying to convince Bert or myself?* Sighing, she checked her watch, worried she wouldn't reach her first night's destination if she didn't get a move on.

Alberta patted her arm. "I won't hold you up, dear. I just wanted to say good-bye."

Placing an arm around her thoughtful neighbor, Leslie walked her to the door. "Bert, would you keep an eye on my place for me while I'm gone? I'd really appreciate it."

Alberta leaned in with a conspiratorial whisper. "You don't even have to ask. Especially after I discovered those scratch marks on your mailbox and that scruffy-looking bum hustling out of the building. I knew he was up to no good."

"It was probably just a drug addict or some homeless person hoping to find money in the mail."

Alberta didn't look so sure. "I'll keep a sharp eye. If I see so much as a whisker of that bum back here, I'll call the cops pronto."

Leslie squeezed the woman's arm. "Just don't tackle him yourself."

The older woman smiled. "You might be surprised what I could do. I might surprise myself."

After a long, lingering look, the women parted. Alberta shuffled sadly across to her apartment.

Leslie closed her door, her face tightening as she considered the uncertain weeks ahead. Would they prove to be an adventure or a nightmare?

*

Leslie parked her SUV in front of a brightly lit convenience store in northern Georgia. The sky was growing dark. She hated to think about driving strange roads in the midst of a thunderstorm, especially two-lane winding ones leading into the foothills of the Appalachian Mountains. Turning off the car, she held her map to the window.

Had she made a wrong decision by going out of her way to visit with an old college friend? It had seemed like a perfect opportunity to honor her long-standing promise, but now Leslie experienced second thoughts. The short visit had been great, but the added miles had extended the drive to Dahlonega into an eternal road trip.

"There is no direct route leading to Dahlonega!" she muttered. It was tense driving, threading her way across to this elusive town. Leslie had driven with butterflies in her stomach all afternoon, ever since she'd left the expressway.

These two-lane winding roads dragging her through every small town in six counties kept her on the ragged edge. One wrong turn could get her lost and into real trouble. Worry settled in. *I know absolutely no one around here. Who would I call if I got into trouble?* The memory of her silent desire for adventure now served only to irritate her. Leslie slammed her car door and carried her map inside the store for helpful directions.

*

It was late afternoon when she navigated the wet, dangerous curves toward Dahlonega. Her white knuckles were cramped from gripping the wheel so hard. The last directions assured her that if she kept to this road, it would lead her into town, but she'd driven anxious and uncertain for hours.

A glance at her watch told her that finding lodging in town for the night would be her best bet. It was Sunday; the lawyer wouldn't be at his office. And the next day was Labor Day—a second lost day. It was poor planning to arrive on a long holiday weekend. As enjoyable as her brief stay with her friend had been, she now regretted the timing. So far the trip had been a fiasco.

The last she and the lawyer had talked, he hadn't sounded pleased with her decision to drive down to look over the property. His echoing words mocked her tired, irritated state: "*It's far too much trouble for you to come all the way down here when I can easily arrange the sale on your behalf and send you the money.*" His whole manner indicated it wasn't worth her time or effort to drive halfway across the country.

Sighing, Leslie squinted through the rain-blurred windshield. *Now I wish I'd listened. This trip is proving a big waste of time and money I don't have. I should have put my efforts into finding a new job.* The doubts stacked up as she drove. Adjusting the wiper, she turned on her lights to see the wet road ahead. *The first decent motel I see I'm pulling in for the night.* She was drained to the core and ready to cry.

*

Hearing the mattress squeak when she rolled over in the bed, Leslie stretched, drawing the blankets closer. She clung to her warm valley of twilight sleep, until a shaft of light fell across her face, urging her eyes open to greet the sunshine. It was morning. She scanned the area for the motel clock. It would be a long day to spend alone entertaining herself. Staring up at the ceiling, she planned how she might do that.

After a quick shower and a change of clothes, Leslie checked out of the motel to look for breakfast. A short drive took her inside the town limits, where she discovered a charming coffee shop that amazingly was open early on this Labor Day. Stunned at her good fortune, she slid into a padded chair at a small table.

Slipping out of her lightweight trench coat, Leslie looked around, pleasantly surprised at the warm, cozy atmosphere and tantalizing aromas. Relaxing, she picked up the menu, prepared to enjoy her breakfast. How long had it been since she didn't have a tight schedule pushing her into a mold? It seemed almost unnatural.

Sipping her coffee, she pulled the lawyer's letter out of her large handbag and smoothed it out across the tabletop. Roger Galbraith had given her specific directions to his office, listing his hours. Further down the letter, he'd included the address of the inherited property. Beside the address was an asterisk, indicating she was supposed to check in at his office for direction and keys before trying to go out there.

Leslie mused over the clipped legal instructions. *Unfortunately there's no way I can stop at the lawyer's office when it's closed, but I see no reason why I can't drive out to the property and get an idea what it's like. What could it hurt?*

She reached for her pastry, accepting the offer of more coffee. Suddenly prospects were looking up. The day might prove more interesting than first imagined.

*

Armed with the waitress's instructions, Leslie threaded her way through the side streets of Dahlonega and out of town. At 10:30 a.m., the charming town was just coming alive. The tourist and specialty shops were opening their doors in droves, and Leslie promised herself a second look at the unique shops when she was through with her trip to Wayne's ranch and had faced her dusty childhood memories.

Would her cousin's place look the same as when she and Dad last visited? She chuckled, thinking of the pack of dogs Wayne kept as pets. They had scared her silly at first, running up in force. Their worst attack was their wet, slimy tongues, reaping welcome upon unsuspecting visitors.

Morning sun danced in speckled brilliance on last night's raindrops, sparkling across fields and trees. The landscape was touched with the beginning blush of fall's changing color. While the distant mountains and winding roads had threatened her last night in the wake of the dark storm, they now seemed playful, almost beckoning.

Passing only a few cars, Leslie found her tensions unwinding. She actually enjoyed her drive, gazing on the full fields and rambling homesteads. This was beautiful country. Granted, the twisting roads would take some getting used to for this city girl. Coming to a crossroad, Leslie slowed and checked her instructions before turning right. The homes were far from the road, acres apart in individual farms. She passed a large poultry farm on the left, and directly across the road, a horse ranch stretched out endlessly. Hopefully, the ranch wasn't far.

Cruising slowly around a large sweeping curve, Leslie stared at fences in a gross state of disrepair lining both sides of the road. Beyond the fields looked wild and rangy. Still she saw no visual sign of the ranch house. Was her memory failing her? Could this be part of Wayne's property? It all looked so different. She kept driving, searching for a familiar sight.

A double twisting turn took her eastward toward the blinding, high-rising sun. Her right hand shot up to shield her eyes just as a large, dark shadow darted in front of her car. Leslie slammed on her brakes. The car wheels skidded sideways; her heart pounded wildly against her rib cage. *Did I hit something?*

Squinting against the sunlight, she frantically tried to identify the dark form she'd seen. Could that be a dog at her left front bumper? It didn't exactly look like a dog—not any dog she'd ever seen. After fumbling inside her oversized bag, Leslie shoved her sunglasses in place. She slammed the transmission into park and hurriedly opened her door. The hairy beast lunged at the opening. She yanked it shut. Denied access to her person, the dog now reared up, placing his huge paws on her side window, snarling and barking. Leslie instinctively pulled back from his attack, crunching low inside the car. Her heart was stuck in her throat.

Once it dawned on her she was safe from the animal's reach, she shifted into gear and jammed her foot on the accelerator, spinning off down the road, leaving the snarling dog in the dust. "Please don't follow my car! Please!" she cried, checking her windows.

Spying the roof of a distant ranch house, she turned left on the weed-edged drive under the swinging, broken sign. Leslie backed up and tilted her head to read the faded name on the sign: *Riker Ranch.* She slumped in disappointment. The lawyer told her Wayne had been ill for several months and was unable to keep up the ranch. The sign left her with no illusions about what the ranch house itself would look like.

Reflecting on an earlier thought that it might be fun to spend tonight at the ranch, she frowned. *That's not likely.* Lately her life had been one disappointment after another. She slowed her speed so she could glance at her surroundings on the curved drive leading to the ranch house. Her ranch knowledge was minuscule in portion, but it almost looked as if the fields had recently grown hay.

*

Standing on the aged front porch of Wayne Riker's rambling house, Leslie's thoughts traveled back ten years when she'd last stood on this porch. Dad had been with her then. More paint had been on the siding, and the fields had been cultivated, sectioned off from the modest herd of beef cattle Wayne had proudly driven them out to see. She raised her hand to knock on the door before she remembered. *Wayne is dead.*

Lowering her hand, she looked around, not quite sure what to do next—now that she was here, having no key. Leslie tried the door, amazed to find it swing open for her entry. *Odd!* She stepped inside with trepidation, feeling like an intruder. Her eyes roamed across the large, open living room to the beautiful stone fireplace and around to the spacious, country kitchen beyond, complete with a breakfast nook and bay window.

She remembered the fireplace and bay window. The rest of the place had been badly littered with worn clothing and multiple pairs of shoes beneath old newspapers. Leslie hardly recognized it tidied up. The furniture was clean and comfortable looking, though the leather recliner had several unseemly tears. *The dogs' work, no doubt.*

Someone had given the place a thorough cleaning. Walking into the kitchen, she rested her hand on the slightly dusty counters. Not a dirty dish in sight. The cupboards could use a facelift, but a little hard work would do wonders for this place. Who had taken the time and care to clean this home? The layout of the main rooms allowed for maximum light. *Dad would have loved it here,* she mused with a stabbing sadness.

Shivering, Leslie briskly rubbed her arms. The house was chilly, holding the cool morning temperatures. Making her way to the bay window in the kitchen, she stared outside. The large barn was up a hill off to the left. She should look over some of the outbuildings while she was here. It would provide her with needed information before she checked in with Wayne's lawyer, Mr. Roger Galbraith, tomorrow morning.

Looking around, she was suddenly sorry to be leaving this lived-in room. It was welcoming, as if she'd come home. Instantly she chided herself. *What am I thinking? My life is in New York!*

Leslie closed the door behind her and walked in the direction of the barn. In so doing, she passed a very old outbuilding on the left of the path. The outside temperature was rising, creating mist in the area of the mountains with a hazy sun radiating through the clouds. Partway up the path to the barn, she paused to peer behind her down the drive toward the road. She worried about that gigantic, hairy dog. Here she was out in the open with no visual protection. What if he had followed her car?

Hastening her steps, Leslie covered the remaining distance to the huge structure set to the right of the path. Her forehead was damp with perspiration. She wrestled with the latch, pushing the gigantic sliding door open. It was enormous inside and smelled as if cattle were still housed within its vast confines. Curiously, bales were stacked in the hayloft, making Leslie question why they remained.

She wandered from stall to stall, noticing partial pails of water and scatterings of hay in the feeding troughs, as if cattle had been simply moved out to pasture for the day. This added to her questions. Walking out into the main area of the barn, she noted the stored machinery. They too looked like they could have been parked yesterday.

Leslie looked beyond the hayloft to the large opening on the side of the upper barn. It allowed air and light throughout the barn. It was a solid barn with modern features. She found that strange for someone as old and settled as Wayne Riker.

What do I actually know about Wayne? I only met the man twice. She smiled, remembering his laughing, kind eyes and the way he'd ruffled her hair. *He said he wished he had a daughter just like me.* "I liked him," Leslie said softly, suddenly sad he was no longer here. *I wish I'd paid more attention to what he told Dad about the property on that last visit.*

Backing to the right, she felt the floor give way. Leslie screamed as her left foot crashed through floorboards splintering outward. Her right foot followed, pushing her further down until her hands caught on jagged edges and held tight. She braced her body from plummeting to the cellar below.

On and on she screamed as pain pierced her body. Then, suddenly, she stopped, hearing only her own breathing. There was no one to hear her—to come to her rescue. The vastness of the barn's interior was stony silent. Dust motes floated, settling to the floor, as fear seared her body like lightning.

Her one foot ached fiercely somewhere beneath the splintered surface of the barn floor. *It must be broken!* She calmed her rising panic with the realization there was nothing she could do about the situation at this moment. *I'm alive. That's what's important.* Whatever was wrong could be fixed. *Think, Weldon. There has to be a solution!*

Leslie bit her lip. The pain was increasing. *Remain calm,* she told herself over and over, but her composure was fragile. Her arms were the only support keeping her from crashing through to whatever lay below. Leslie doubted they could last much longer. Her muscles and tendons ached, bulging from the sheer intensity of holding up her entire body weight. The weekly workouts at the neighborhood gym were worth every monthly fee she'd paid out over the last three years.

Long minutes passed before her elbows began to shake. She couldn't see her watch from her position. *How long have I been here? No one knows I'm even on the property.* Her gaze roamed the interior. *Alone in this secluded barn on Labor Day. How stupid I am!* Her calm cracked as her panic rose. *"Help!"* Her voice sounded so small in this huge facility. "Oh God!" she cried.

It was the only prayer she could manage.

Leslie shifted her weight to one side and tried to push up with her one elbow, but it slipped, and her upper body grated against jagged wood, dropping deeper through the floor. Wetness seeped through her shirt.

I'm bleeding! She felt sick as a warm sensation crept over her. She couldn't afford to pass out.

"Hello! Is anyone there? Answer me!" a loud voice demanded from outside the barn.

2

Friend or Foe?

"HERE...I'M IN HERE...HELP ME!" she cried weakly, not sure the distant voice could hear her.

The terrifying snarl of the large dog blasted adrenaline through her body. Leslie braced herself with renewed strength. She stared upward into frightening, bared teeth. It was the wild-haired beast she'd met on the road. Her breath caught in her throat.

"Boris, back! Back!" a harsh voice commanded.

Heavy footsteps pounded toward her, but her eyes stayed riveted on the dog, relieved to see the fierce animal back into a nearby stall, his light-yellow eyes glued to her face. Leslie gulped, and her focus shifted to the long-legged man standing above her to the right. He looked like a giant from the floor...and not a very friendly one at that.

He knelt in one swift, fluid motion, and his muscular arms grabbed hold of her upper arms, relieving the strain. "Take hold of me, and hang on. Don't let go until I tell you!" he ordered. His tone was no different than when he spoke to the dog.

The hair on the back of her neck bristled at his arrogance even as she took hold of him. Stretching her fingers around his forearms, her muscles cramped in agony. "Your compassion is compelling." She gritted her teeth.

"You don't need compassion. You need someone to help get you out of this fool mess before you get yourself killed. I was afraid of something like this when I saw your SUV speed past my place. An old barn is a good place to get hurt. Just what are you doing trespassing on this property anyway? I almost called the cops, lady," he barked.

"Ouch!" she shrieked, her breath catching as the man lifted her upward through the jagged wood. Silent tears streamed down her face with no way to brush them aside.

He stopped lifting and stared down at her blood-soaked shirt. "How badly are you injured?" he demanded, his brow wrinkled in a deep frown.

"I'm bleeding," she said tersely. "That's all I know."

The tall stranger cast a glance toward the door. "I can see that, woman. But there's no other way to get you out. I can't leave you and get help. I doubt you've got strength left to hold yourself up for much longer. You're going to have to cowboy up until I get you out of there. Are you ready?" His facial muscles had grown tight.

Leslie blinked away the tears and nodded.

"Good," he said, his voice softer. "Now take a deep breath and hold it. I'll be quick." He lifted her straight up through the expanded hole, carrying her off to the side before lowering her down to a flat surface, where he waited while she caught her breath.

Kneeling beside her, he carefully lifted her right foot, rotating it slowly while feeling for broken bones. She winced only slightly. When he moved her left foot to the side, Leslie couldn't contain a sharp intake of air at the sudden pain.

"I think you've got a bad sprain. I don't feel anything broken." Lowering her foot, he said, "But you might consider getting it x-rayed. I'll carry you up to the house where Wayne has some ace bandages and you can get washed up. Can't tell how badly you're scratched until then." Without giving her a chance to respond, he gathered her up in his arms and marched out of the barn.

Leslie was speechless for the first ten yards. Her abdomen and stomach burned like fire. She bit her lip to keep from crying out and giving this uncaring man the satisfaction of hearing her whine. *I may have to accept his begrudging help, but I don't have to melt into a pathetic puddle and let him think I'm weak and incompetent.*

Leslie could feel his dark eyes studying her. She braced herself against each painful, jarring movement.

"It's not much further. Still okay?" he asked, more gentle than before.

His changed tone took her aback. "I'm—I'm ok-ay," she stuttered.

"Good girl. I'll hurry it up." His steps lengthened. In his haste, his gait became jerky, increasing her discomfort.

Closing her eyes, Leslie sucked in a big gulp of air, wincing in pain. She cried out, "Stop! Please! Slow up!" Her breathing came rapid and shallow.

"Sorry," he said huskily, halting briefly. Starting up again, his steps eased into a soft, loping gait, lightening the pain.

Leslie wondered if this torment would ever cease. The sun was high, drilling straight down on her head. Between the heat and loping gait, she experienced an unpleasant woozy feeling in her stomach. *No! I can't get sick—I just can't!*

"Clive! What happened?" a woman called out from a short distance.

Leslie's closed eyes flashed open, unable to connect the voice with the source.

The stranger's head snapped to the side. "A barn accident, Mona. You better come along and give a hand. I don't know what all we've got here. She could need a doctor, but you'd know better about that than me."

"I'll get the door," said the feminine voice answering to Mona.

Leslie saw the back of a petite, brown-haired woman race ahead onto the porch and open the door. Leslie's queasy stomach lurched as Clive stepped on the porch and entered the cool large room. He whisked her over to a faded, flowered couch, where the woman placed a random throw, and lowered her onto its soft fabric. Leslie rested her head back and closed her eyes.

Standing, the man named Clive cleared his throat. "This is your area of expertise, Mona. I'm out of my depth here. I had almost decided to drive her to the hospital."

"Then back up and let me help the poor woman," Mona directed. Pushing ahead of him, she sat down gently on the edge of the couch. Her warm, discerning eyes scanned Leslie's bedraggled form. "Get me a basin of warm water, some soap, and a washcloth. When you get back, I'll give you another list."

Clive started to turn when Leslie's eyes slowly opened. "My name is Leslie Weldon," she said, her voice shaky and thin.

"Leslie Weldon?" Mona's head lifted, shooting Clive an indiscernible look. Her focus returned to Leslie. "Ooooh...Wayne's young cousin."

"Perfect!" Clive muttered, stalking off.

Leslie sighed, reclosing her eyes. *Not exactly a warm welcome.* At the moment she really didn't care. All she wanted was to lie so still her pain would lessen. Yet the gentle caress of a light comforter upon her battered body felt like a soothing balm. She knew it was Mona's doing.

"Lie still. We'll soon get you cleaned up and find out what the damage is." Mona pulled over a large ottoman.

Leslie heard footsteps.

"Good," Mona murmured. "Clive is back."

The big man answering to Clive set the water basin down with the soap and a hand towel. He fairly growled, "Now what?"

Leslie peeked through one eyelid and saw the corners of Mona's mouth turn up. What could this woman find humorous in this rude man's abysmal attitude?

"Check in Wayne's medicine cabinet for some Peroxide, Neosporin, and bandages of all kinds," Mona directed. "We'll use what's available."

Clive's frustration showed. "And if I can't find any of that stuff? This isn't my line, Mona. Can't we take the princess here in to the hospital?"

Leslie pushed the comforter aside and lifted her head. "Look!" She labored to speak. "Just leave! Whoever you are! Everything you've done, you've done begrudgingly. And your snide remarks aren't exactly helpful! Leave and take your horrid dog with you." Her voice dropped off as she flopped backward on the pillow.

Clive startled. "What dog? Boris doesn't belong to me."

Mona sighed deeply. "Clive—really! Now is not the time."

"All right! I'm sorry, Miss Weldon," he said. "When you're feeling better maybe we can start over on a better note. I'll just go look for those things you asked for, Mona."

"That would be good." Mona's gentle hands sponged off Leslie's face and arms before carefully undoing her shirt. Pulling it off to one side, she began to examine the gouges and scratches down her side and stomach area. "Oh, my! You, young lady, are going to move easy-like for the next week or so. I guarantee it."

As Clive's heavy footsteps returned, Mona hurried to cover Leslie with the comforter. "Just set them down here next to the basin," she directed the big-shouldered man.

He stood to the side while Mona examined his stash of medical supplies. "That's the best I could do," he said, sounding frustrated.

Mona studied the contents. "I'm going to need some stronger meds than Wayne kept on hand. I want you to drive over to my place and ask Henri O' to round up some items and package them up for you. And tell her to hurry." She stared down at Leslie with concern. "While you're gone, I'll clean out Leslie's wounds and apply some ointment. Oh, and ask Henri O' for some pain medicine. She'll know." Pulling out a pad, Mona waited as Clive handed her his pocket pen.

Lifting his hat, Clive ran his hand through his longish dark hair and smoothed it backward while Mona finished writing her list. He obviously was uncomfortable in this situation, but Leslie could muster little empathy. When his eyes connected with her curious gaze, he looked away. "Almost done?" he asked, sounding impatient.

Mona tore off the top sheet of the small pad, handed it to him, and slipped the pad back in her jeans pocket. Leslie gave her a closer look. Mona's small figure was flattered by the cut of her Western jeans. She was an attractive woman in her thirties who was clearly comfortable with being in charge in a crisis situation.

Clive glanced down the list and back at Mona. "O—kay. I'll call if I have questions." He spoke with a measured degree of uncertainty.

Mona rolled her eyes. "Fine. Now git a move on. This girl is hurting!"

His eyes lingered on Leslie's face. "I'll do my best," he said, shifting into high motion. "See you shortly."

As Clive exited the door, Mona tucked back the comforter and resumed work on Leslie, her fingers gentle and quick. "I'll try to not hurt you any more than necessary. I think these will heal up nicely, but they'll take time and will not be comfortable."

"You seem to know what you're doing."

Mona chuckled. "I've had some practice. I'm a Registered Practical Nurse, mostly part time anymore because of farm duties. They require a lot of time and my husband, Ray, can't do it all. Besides, I like working with the chickens. Guess I'm just a country girl at heart. Hold still now. There's a splinter I need to extract."

Leslie winced at the sharp barb. "Wooo…that smarted. It's been quite a day so far. I'm grateful you came by. Otherwise I would have spent the whole day in a hospital examining room."

"I was handy. We live at the farm next door—the one closer to the highway. Wayne's place is the last property on this road. I saw your car go by earlier and was curious. Then, when I saw Clive drive up the road, I thought I'd better check it out. We've been overseeing your cousin's ranch ever since he died. Clive owns the horse ranch across the road just down the road a piece. We all were pretty close to Wayne."

Shifting on the couch to find a more comfortable position, Leslie regarded Mona. "I guess it was my lucky day when you happened to drive in and rescue me."

Mona leveled a look. "Clive rescued you. You'll like him better when you get to know him. When you get to know me better, you'll learn that I don't believe in luck." She flashed Leslie a confident smile. "Steady now. I need to clean this area."

Puzzled by Mona's comment about luck, Leslie was too uncomfortable to pursue it. Her ordeal had depleted her energy. Moistening her dry lips, she looked toward the kitchen, wishing for a drink. Leslie didn't want to ask the woman to wait on her more than she already had. "What now, Mona? After I'm fixed up, am I good to drive out of here? I need to line up a motel for the night."

Mona studied her curiously. "What? Now? Well, while we wait for Clive to return with the bandages, I'm going to get you a tall glass of water to keep the liquids flowing. You've some pretty deep scratches that need to be protected from infection." Standing, Mona crossed her arms. "About that motel, I'm not even sure you can walk without help at this point. I want to examine that ankle myself."

While Leslie relished the coolness of the cold water, Mona tenderly rotated her foot and ankle from side to side.

"Ouch," she cried, flinching from the pain.

"It's pretty swollen. I'm going to make an ice pack to wrap it in. That ankle should be iced on and off most of the night, then reassessed in the morning. I wouldn't recommend driving anywhere until tomorrow, maybe longer."

Leslie's jaw dropped. "Mona, I don't have a choice. I'm on my own here in Dahlonega with nowhere to stay. I don't even have legal title to Wayne's place yet. I *have* to drive. "

"Nonsense! You can stay at my house. My rambling old place has four bedrooms, two of them downstairs, which is exactly what you need tonight. It's the best of a bad situation. I will be close by to keep an eye on you. If your ankle is no better by morning, I'll take you in for x-rays."

Mona's generous offer had taken her aback. "But you don't even know me." Leslie's vision clouded with confusion. Her constant pain made her acutely conscious of her need. And she was in a bind—in the awkward position of being forced to depend upon strangers.

The sound of a truck skidding to a stop in gravel drew the women's attention. "Clive's back. We can get you finished up in no time. My housekeeper knows where I keep all my medical supplies. She's a wonder!"

Clive discreetly waited on the front porch while Mona worked with Leslie. As Leslie buttoned her blood-stained blouse, Mona called him in. "We're going to need your muscles to get Leslie into my car. She'll be staying with me overnight."

Clive's frown told Leslie that he disapproved. What did this guy have against her? Was he always this hateful? As he carried her outside, she heard Mona's whimsical murmur, "Nice hair, Leslie. Clive has a *thing* for redheads."

Clive shot Mona a stabbing glare. He grunted something indiscernible in the wake of Mona's soft laughter. Leslie wished she were back in New York.

*

Her first glimpse of Mona's home surprised her. Mona and her husband had turned a spacious farmhouse into a comfortable, updated home. It was decorated in soft greens and creams, except for the oversized, dark green recliner situated happily beside a natural stone fireplace. It looked as if it might belong to Mona's husband, complete with an old copy of *Field & Stream*. The enormous fireplace, spanning the entire back wall, held Leslie's attention. Whoever constructed it was a gifted craftsman.

Before she had time to observe more, Clive reached the couch. He fairly dropped her to the waiting cushions and hurried toward the door, almost as if he couldn't wait to leave. She gritted her teeth, murmuring a forced, "Thank you."

Clive pivoted back to face Mona. "I'll call you tomorrow. I've got work to do," he said in parting.

"That man acts like he hates me," Leslie blurted as the door closed behind him.

Mona's eyes darted to the fast-diminishing form of Clive's back. Without a word, she disappeared down a long hallway off to the left, leaving Leslie to fume alone. Leslie was literally a prisoner.

There was no way she could get up and walk out of here on her swollen ankle. It had been a long time since she had felt so dependent on anyone…actually, since Kevin disappeared, breaking their engagement via the telephone. Kevin had taught her a valuable lesson. All it had cost her was raw heartbreak and weeks of bitter tears.

In a matter of seconds, she fell asleep on the butter cream couch.

*

Leslie awoke to the coldness of an ice pack on her ankle. Mona lowered a cotton blanket over her.

"Oooo, what was in that pill you gave me back at Wayne's?" asked Leslie.

"A painkiller. It sometimes makes people sleepy. Why don't you rest awhile longer? You've taken quite a shock to your system. I have some work to do outside. If a large man with a blond crew-cut wanders in and asks who you are, that would be Ray. Tell him to call me on my cell. I'll be out with George working with the chickens."

"I have a different need," said Leslie tersely, hating to be put in this situation.

"Sorry, I should have thought of that earlier. Let's get you up. It's not far, and you can lean on me. I'm stronger than I look."

When Leslie was back on the couch with blanket and ice pack, Mona scanned the area with efficiency and turned to leave. Pausing, she seemed to ponder her words before speaking. "Clive doesn't hate you, Leslie. He's just angry and frustrated. We all are... he perhaps more so than the rest of us." She hurried through the kitchen to the back door.

"Why direct it at me?" Leslie shouted to her back.

Mona stopped. Her head snapped to the side. "Ask Clive."

Leslie lay there, more confused than ever. *What is going on? Why is everyone angry? What's it got to do with me?*

Gradually, the pain medication clouded everything in her mind. She allowed herself to be swallowed up in the relief of sleep...no pain to deal with...no frustrating questions without answers.

*

"Hello there! What do we have here? I had to check again to make sure I was in the right house. Finding a strange, pretty girl asleep on our couch doesn't happen every day. I assume you're a friend of Mona's?" He looked around, clearly bemused at the situation.

Leslie blinked upward, staring owl-like at the blond, crew-cut giant standing to her right. *Isn't there a normal-sized man on this road?* she wondered, thinking of Clive. "You would be Ray. Mona said you might have questions." Leslie blinked again, trying to clear her head from the heavy logy feeling. "I would answer them for you, but Mona gave me something." Shaking her head, she added, "She said you were to call her. She's out with the chickens." Leslie pointed vaguely.

Ray chuckled, staring at the floor in front of the couch. Bending, he lifted a limp ice bag, laid it on the coffee table, and nodded. "Okay, I'll call her. What should I call you, Miss?"

She looked up at him. "Leslie. Leslie Weldon."

He cocked his head. "Seems like I should know that name, but I can't bring it to mind. I'll just wander out back and call Mona. You rest," he said, seeming at a lack for additional words. Ray started off toward the door.

Everyone seems to know me—strange. She winced at the burning pain under her bandages whenever she tried to move.

*

After eating her dinner from a tray on the couch, Leslie silently watched Mona and Ray Schiller finish up in the kitchen. Ray's attitude toward her had noticeably changed from their earlier meeting. When he and Mona came inside, he had skillfully avoided any eye contact with her. *Maybe I have typhoid and no one's told me?*

Her thoughts smoldered in the strained silence. As soon as Ray and Mona were seated in the living room, Leslie pushed her body up on her one dependable leg. "I appreciate everything you've done for me. Mona, you gave me quality care and fed me a great meal. But there's no way I'm staying in this house tonight with all of your silent hostility. I've asked what's wrong, but no one will give me the courtesy of telling me anything." Her swollen foot touched the floor, making her wince in pain, but she refused to cry out.

Leslie continued, "It's obvious you know something I don't. I feel the antagonism from all of you. I arrived in Dahlonega yesterday and know nothing—only what Wayne's lawyer told me initially. I have yet to even meet the man." Pursing her lips, she added, "If someone will drive me back to my car, I'll manage somehow without bothering you further." She steadied herself, holding to the couch arm.

The couple exchanged glances. Mona stood, nodding at her husband before crossing the room. "Leslie, you're in no shape to go anywhere. We do apologize for our rude attitude. Hearing the situation from your perspective makes us realize how unfair we've been with you. Please lie back down on the couch and let us explain."

Leslie's leg started to give. She had to sit whether she wanted to or not. Easing herself downward, she glanced from Mona to Ray. "All right, tell me what gives? Why am I being treated like the ugly stepsisters in *Cinderella?"*

Mona sat next to her on the couch. "We loved Wayne. Clive, Ray, and I tried to help him out the last few years. In fact, we've been leasing some of his back acres to raise hay. Ray and I bought some of Wayne's beef cattle when he auctioned them off a couple of years back. We all did what we could." Mona glanced at her hands. "Wayne loved the ranch. He felt a part of the land and its history. The property has been in your family for almost two hundred years. He dearly wanted it to stay that way."

Leslie was more confused than ever. "I had no way of knowing how he felt. We weren't close. We've met maybe twice a few years ago. I think I understand what you're telling me. What I don't understand is why I'm the bad guy all of a sudden. I received the letter from Mr. Galbraith, telling me of my inheritance less than two weeks ago. I don't even know what I'm doing yet!"

"You're not selling the property?"

Leslie stared at Mona. "What are you talking about? I arrived yesterday to look the property over. I haven't had time to make any decision."

"We were told it was all but a done deal, that you'd sold the property to some investors and wanted no part of it. We're expected to give up all rights to our leases—with compensation, of course. But Clive has been counting on that hay harvest. Galbraith practically hung up on Clive when he asked for the name of the main investor, and all Clive wanted to do was work out a fair solution. Every time we call, Galbraith is always too busy to talk. We've been totally shut out."

Leslie stared at Mona, dumbstruck. She groped for the right words. "But I never...I mean, Mr. Galbraith has been pressing me to sell, but I..." She thought back on her earlier conversations with Roger Galbraith. "He said the property wasn't worth my time to come down and look it over. He mentioned having a ready buyer offering more than a fair price." She frowned. "If I hadn't lost my job, I might have taken him up on his offer. But, you see, I suddenly had the time and opportunity to come down and look things over."

No one said anything as long seconds passed. Finally, Ray cleared his throat. "It sounds as if our Mr. Galbraith has a different story for different people. I'm going to make us all some coffee so we can talk."

"And I'm going to get Leslie a fresh ice pack for her ankle." Mona made her way to the refrigerator while Ray walked to the coffee maker, leaving Leslie to ponder the things she had just heard.

"What would Galbraith have to gain? Why would he lie to us?" Leslie called out, louder than she meant. She was too perplexed to wait for coffee.

Mona came back with a new ice pack, eyeing her strangely. "I don't know, Leslie. You'll have to ask him."

As Ray reentered the room, Leslie could hear the sounds of perking coffee in the kitchen. She inhaled deeply, savoring its invigorating aroma. "Maybe our Mr. Galbraith has some special deal of his own?"

Mona made no comment on that. Leslie sensed the woman wasn't sure who was telling the truth. "When are you supposed to meet with him?" Mona finally asked.

"I was supposed to call or stop by his office as soon as I arrived in Dahlonega." She now saw the irony in the timing. "I was supposed to check in with him before coming out to the property, but I arrived on Sunday and today was Labor Day. I had the whole day with nothing to do, and frankly, I was curious how the place looked. The last time I was here, I was with my dad. And there were all these memories..."

She fought her sadness. Blinking away her thoughts, she added, "I was planning on going to Galbraith's office tomorrow morning." She glanced down at her throbbing ankle.

"Your ankle could be a lot better in the morning if we keep up with the ice packs. I could drop you off to meet with him and bring you back afterward," Mona offered.

"It might be smart not to mention that you were here, or that you had spoken with us," Ray inserted.

Mona glanced at him without comment.

"I can't enter his office leaning on someone's arm," said Leslie, realizing the difficulties of her being injured. She had a sudden thought. "Mona, do you by chance happen to have a cane or a pair of crutches?"

"We have a cane that will work for you. As for now, we should all turn in soon. Leslie, I'll get your bed ready. There's a bathroom right next door to your room. You'll get practice using that cane tonight. I'll leave a small bell if you need me during the night. Ray, would you bring in Leslie's overnight bag from my car and put it on the guest bed?"

After Mona switched on her lamp next to Leslie's bed, she turned to leave. Something in the woman's manner—the negative vibrations—disturbed Leslie. Was Mona not sure whether or not she could trust Leslie?

What else can I say to convince her? Leslie wondered. *Nothing,* she decided. *She doesn't know me, and I don't know her—or Galbraith for that matter.* Leslie surveyed the strange room feeling lonely. *Who can I trust?*

"Thanks Mona. I'm sorry I've been such a problem." Thinking back on her frightening episode, she asked, "How long has Wayne's barn flooring been in a dangerous state?"

Mona turned with a quizzical look. "Wayne's barn has been kept in good condition in most every respect. Clive has seen to that. He's spent hours of his own time working on Wayne's place, though obviously he can't attend to everything."

"Then how do you explain my accident?"

Mona shrugged. "I can't, unless the boards rotted through without Clive realizing. I've left your window open for air. This room is a little stuffy. Ring the bell loudly if you need us. Ray and I are right down the hall, but I'll warn you, we're heavy sleepers. I'll bring in an ice pack about 2:00 a.m. Good night, Leslie."

Long after Mona left her, Leslie stared at the ceiling, her foot propped on a pillow. A pain pill lay next to a glass of water, but Leslie was holding off. She didn't understand how the accident occurred if the structure had been kept up, and she didn't doubt that someone had been working in there. All the machinery looked to be in good condition, the barn tidy—a fact she'd noticed upon entering. It was all so very strange. And what about the story the

Schillers related about Galbraith? Why would Galbraith lie…if he did lie? Someone had lied! *Maybe tomorrow I'll learn the truth.*

Something else puzzled her. *Why did this woman and her husband, who clearly distrust me, go out of their way to take me in, nurse me—even feed me? All they had to do was drive to a hospital and drop me off.*

Groaning, she reached for the pain pill.

3

The Barn

CLIVE LAID HIS WORN LEATHER BAG of tools alongside a sack of wood pieces on the barn floor and knelt next to the splintered, gaping hole. His fingers followed the break line. Squinting, he leaned to examine the area that gave way, discovering a series of deeply indented heel marks at various stress points. It troubled him. His hand roamed up to his chin, rubbing the dark beginnings of beard stubble. Pulling a small camera out of his plaid shirt pocket, he clicked a series of pictures.

Replacing the camera, Clive took out his hammer and broke off the damaged wood in preparation to repairing the hole. He peered downward into the dank cellar below. The deepest area of the cellar lay beneath these broken boards—was that a coincidence? It was amazing the redheaded woman survived. *If she had not clung to the flooring...*

It was clear Leslie had been protected that day. His brow deepened in thought as he picked up his tape measure and went to work.

*

Hobbling with the aid of the cane into the kitchen area, Leslie looked around. There was evidence of dirty dishes on the counter and a place set at the table. Was it set for her? Mona told her she had early chores but would be ready to take her wherever she wanted to go by 10:00 a.m.

Turning, she found herself face to face with a tall, well-proportioned woman who had slipped inside the back door so quietly Leslie hadn't heard her. The woman's long, sleek jet hair was gathered at the back of the neck with a silver clip. She appraised Leslie in a sweeping glance.

"Are you ready for your breakfast?" the woman asked curtly.

"Ah, I don't want to be any trouble. A piece of toast would be fine. My name is..."

"I know your name. I've worked for the Schillers for several years. Fixing breakfast is my job. Now what would you like, Miss Weldon?"

The woman's abrupt manner took her aback. Leslie carried no illusions. This intimidating person had formed the same preconceived opinion as everyone else.

Leslie sighed in frustration. "Toast and coffee will be fine, thank you."

Mona burst through the back door, her face flushed with the morning sun. Walking briskly across the kitchen, she smiled warmly at Leslie. "Good. I see you made it to the table with your cane. What's your pain level?"

Eyeing the inviting chair, Leslie edged closer. "About half of what it was last night," she answered, lowering herself with relief.

"But I notice you're not applying much weight to that ankle yet. After you meet with your lawyer this morning, I think I'll drive you to our local clinic. They're equipped with an x-ray unit. We'd both feel better once we know for sure if there is a fracture." Pivoting, she addressed the striking, sloe-eyed woman next. "Henri O', whip up a breakfast for Leslie so she can get to her appointment."

"I'm working on it, Mrs. Schiller. She's only having toast."

Mona frowned. "Leslie, I wish you'd try to eat an egg at least. Your body needs the extra protein."

When Leslie nodded, Mona turned to her cook. "Add an egg to that order, Henri O'."

"Yes'm, one egg coming right up."

Mona sat in the opposite chair facing Leslie. "How are those scrapes?"

"Sore is an understatement! I'm breathing pretty shallow, afraid to move my chest and stomach muscles any more than necessary."

Mona chuckled. "Your body took quite a beating yesterday. After breakfast, I'll take a look at them and change your bandages."

"Mona, would you point out property lines to me when we leave for town? I'd like to have some idea of the extension of Wayne's property before I meet with the lawyer this morning."

"Let me think. Wayne's property extends to both sides of the road and across the back quite a ways up into the woods that you see from the road when you first drive up. I'll try to point them out once we're on the road."

"I had no idea it was so big. It truly is beautiful country."

"Yes," Mona murmured. Gazing down at the tablecloth, her finger followed its intricate pattern. "I, ah, talked with Clive this morning. He's already been down fixing that hole in the floorboards in the barn."

"That was very nice of him," she mumbled. "Had the boards rotted through?"

Shaking her head, Mona looked troubled. "That's what was strange. Clive said none of the boards were rotted, but he didn't explain. Curious. Why would the floor collapse, if the boards hadn't rotted?"

From her position at the stove, Henri O' glanced up sharply in the direction of the table. "The property is *cursed,* that's how! Ever since that dead child's ghost returned and began calling out in the dead of night, bad things have been happening, like Mr. Wayne riding that tractor over a hill and killing himself."

Leslie's head jerked to the left. She stared blankly at the cook.

Standing abruptly, Mona spun about. "Henri O'! That's enough of that kind of talk. You know how I feel about your superstitions. Is Miss Weldon's breakfast ready?"

"Yes'm, I'm almost done." The frozen-faced cook walked over to their table and set the plate silently in front of Leslie before returning to the counter.

Leslie stiffened, staring after the woman. "What is she talking about? What's all this business about the ghost of a child?"

Mona shot Henri O' a dark look. "Nothing but wild imagination and silly superstition! Henri O' claims she has heard weird sounds coming from the area of the woods, and she attributes the night noise to an old rumor about a child who disappeared from an area ranch almost two hundred years ago—*your* ranch, Leslie. Apparently, no one really ever knew what happened to him. It's an old tale, revised each time by the teller."

Staring at Mona in a dazed-like fog, Leslie tried to push away the frightening declaration. "Has anyone else heard these noises?"

"Our ranch hand, George Truitt, but he sometimes drinks a little too much on his off times, especially on the weekend, so we haven't put much stock in his ramblings. A few others have reported hearing something, not sure actually what it was they heard." She lowered her voice. "Henri O' is part Cherokee, and her mother's side believes in the spirit lore from the old days. She now believes in Jesus as God but constantly battles the beliefs of the old ways, as many of us do. Don't be upset. There is nothing to the stories, Leslie."

Henri O' frowned. With a shake of her head she turned back to the sink.

Pushing the egg around on her plate, Leslie wondered at the situation she found herself in. Her trip had been filled with mishaps and catastrophes. Reaching for the homemade jam, she found her thoughts a jumbled heap of conflicting input, now overshadowed by a new fear. Superstition or not, it made her uneasy.

Leslie poised her coffee in front of her. "So far this inheritance of mine has been nothing but a hassle. I ache all over. Everyone in two counties hates me, and now I hear about the ghost of a child haunting *my* property." Her eyes filled with moisture. "Have I stepped into a bad movie or what?" Lowering her coffee, Leslie buried her head in her hands.

Mona motioned Henri O' out of the area. "Leslie, everything is going to work out, trust me. Take each step slowly, examining all of your options," she encouraged in a softened tone. "But before you make any decisions, just promise me you'll bear in mind the incredible history lived out by generations of your family before you were ever born. Many of them lived through the most exciting history making events of the time—right here in Dahlonega, at that ranch down the road. In the process, you may even discover your own heritage."

Raising her head, Leslie eyed her critically. "What history? I know nothing of any history pertaining to our family."

An animated excitement surged to Mona's features. "There's history all right! Get ready for an earful. But first..."

*

"Ouch!" Leslie winced, glaring at Mona. "I thought you were going to tell me how my relatives are involved in Dahlonega history?"

"I will. Just hold still. This is the last bandage. I can't do two things at the same time, and we'll never get you to Galbraith's office at this rate."

"What history?" Leslie repeated bleakly, like a dog with a bone.

"Gold, honey! The yellow stuff people dream about and travel thousands of miles to find. Dahlonega is the home of the first gold rush in America—before anyone heard of California, and Alaska belonged to Russia. The name *Dahlonega* comes from the Cherokee word *Talonega,* meaning 'yellow' or 'golden'!"

"I never heard of Dahlonega gold," said Leslie, perplexed.

Mona helped her put on her lightweight sweater. "I know. A lot of people haven't. Did you notice the yellow dome when you came into town?"

Breathing out against the restrictive bandages around her middle, Leslie thought back to yesterday morning when she drove through town looking for breakfast. "Yes, the tall pointed one. It's made of gold?" Her eyes widened.

"Well, covered with gold leaf anyway. They call it the Price Memorial Hall...built on the foundation of the original U.S. Branch Mint that operated back in the mid 1800s, at the height of the gold rush in Dahlonega. And the old courthouse in the town square is now our Gold Museum. We'll pass it going through town. Why, our town still boasts active gold mines," she said, grinning. "Of course, they're basically for tourists, where people can pan for gold."

"So were my relatives part of the gold rush in Dahlonega?" Leslie asked, beginning to lose interest in bygone tales.

"It's rumored they registered one of the first mines in this area."

"Really?" She brightened with new interest.

Mona checked her watch. "It's almost 10:00 a.m. We'd better hurry."

With Mona's help and the aid of the cane, Leslie made her way to the car. As they pulled out of the driveway, Leslie looked from point to point as Mona indicated the land lying on both sides of the road. The rising sun cloaked distant hills in a yellow haze. The sight took her breath away.

She swallowed hard at the thought of all that property belonging to her, until the fear of responsibility and the prospect of dealing with the long-distance hassle of ownership became brain numbing. *It will never work,* she told herself. Yet the thought of not owning it suddenly made her feel oddly depressed.

Shifting uncomfortably in the adjoining front seat, Leslie found it painful to ride with the seatbelt pulled around her. Her troubled thoughts didn't improve her disposition. "Mona, I don't know what to do about the property. All this is beyond what I bargained for. I had no idea there was so much involved, and everything has happened so fast. I didn't even know I was mentioned in the will until a week and a half ago."

Mona hesitated. "I believe it was no accident that the property was given to you. God does everything for a reason. I will pray for you to make the right decision."

Leslie blinked at the petite dark-haired woman behind the wheel. Her words could have come from her dead father's mouth. "You're a Christian," she blurted, jolted by the awareness. Hearing this woman speak so confidently of God caused her chest to tighten. Reminders were everywhere she went.

A soft smile played upon Mona's lips. "Yes, I am. Are you?"

Leslie stared out the window as memories swarmed her mind. "At one time, I-I thought so."

"And now?" Mona gently pressed.

"Now I don't know. It's been a long time." Her words fell off. *There's so much more involved.*

Uncertain silence filled the confines of the car. Mona pressed her lips as if holding back unspoken words. As they reached town, she maneuvered through the busy streets teeming with people. Steering down a second side street, she pulled into a parking space and pointed to a small office front down the block. The office was tucked two doors down from a gaily decorated window headlining *The Christmas Shoppe.*

Staring at the lawyer's office, Leslie wanted more information about this stranger who held her future in his hands. "Has Galbraith been in Dahlonega a long time?"

"About three years. I figure he must have a powerful contact in town because his list of clients rose absurdly fast, like high tide in a fish bowl."

The analogy made Leslie smile.

"It normally takes a new lawyer in town twice the time to establish himself and make contacts in good standing. Galbraith, on the other hand, has been ushered into the inner ranks in record time."

Puzzled, Leslie asked, "Is that good or bad?"

Mona opened her door to come around and help Leslie out. "I'd call it at the least very curious." Opening Leslie's door, she added, "Galbraith might be a man to bear watching, considering the supposed mix-up in communication—too many verbal mix-ups to be a coincidence."

Undoing her seatbelt, she labored to maneuver out of the car. Mona's words reminded her that Galbraith had informed everyone she was selling the property to out-of-state investors. Leaning her weight on the cane, Leslie shifted to step up on the curb of the sidewalk and pushed her wavy, auburn hair over her shoulder.

"If you think you can handle things," Mona called, "I'll be back in an hour and pick you up. It might be better for all of us if you didn't tell Galbraith you've been staying with us, at least not right out of the box. It's just a feeling. When you come out, look for my car down the street. Call if things get rough." She indicated Leslie's foot.

Leslie nodded, suddenly unsure about everything. "Thanks, Mona," she murmured.

After Mona drove away, Leslie drew her shoulders up, proceeding toward the office front. Something told her the next few minutes would be very important, and the decisions she made could decide the rest of her life. An involuntary shiver raced through her.

*

Leslie's fingers drummed the side of the vinyl padded chair in Galbraith's compact waiting room. The very attractive young secretary glanced up at her every few minutes, smiling in reassurance. "Mr. Galbraith will be with you shortly. It's been a busy morning for him after the holiday weekend."

It was the same speech she'd been given fifteen minutes ago. Leslie gazed down with little interest at the magazine on her lap. Hearing the office door open, her eyes lifted for her first glance of Wayne Riker's lawyer. Could she tell anything about the man's character in a first impression?

A brown-haired man of medium height backed slowly through his office door, indicating he was still talking to someone within the office. When he turned, Leslie was taken aback by his mild, gentle bearing. He was an attractive man who obviously had much on his mind. His focal attention went first to his secretary and the clipboard in her hand.

Glancing upward from the clipboard, the lawyer widened his flecked amber eyes. Clearly, Galbraith was pleasantly surprised with his first visual of Leslie, though his gaze dropped in a shy counteraction. "Miss Weldon, I'm so sorry to keep you waiting. Please come into my office." As an afterthought, he turned back to his secretary. "Hold all my calls while I'm with Miss Weldon, Stephanie."

Stephanie's eyes melted at his words. Was that devotion Leslie saw, or something more? "Certainly, Mr. Galbraith," she said softly.

The lawyer appeared not to notice Stephanie's overt attention. His eyes rested solely upon Leslie. Reaching downward, Leslie picked up the cane lying beside the chair and pushed up, avoiding pressure on her bandaged foot.

Galbraith looked startled, rushing forward. "Miss Weldon, you're injured?"

Avoiding his gaze, Leslie shifted her position to reach for her purse. "I clumsily tripped and fell down some motel steps," she lied. She couldn't very well tell him the truth. Too much was at stake.

"May I be of help?"

"I think I can manage, thank you." She forced a smile.

He waited patiently for her to make her way through to his inner office. Its roominess surprised her, compared to the waiting room area. She looked around, vaguely wondering about the person Galbraith had been talking to in his office, until she noticed a rear exit. Her eyes gravitated back across his walls, covered with warm cherry wood bookshelves and lined with what Leslie assumed were law books. A matching cherry-wood desk sat at an angle with expensive padded chairs positioned to face the desk.

Mr. Galbraith's office spoke of position and prestige for so young a lawyer. He was either a remarkable lawyer or…

She tried to keep an open mind.

Once situated in the front chair, Leslie relaxed and waited for Roger Galbraith to lower himself to his leather swivel chair. He smiled shyly across from her. "I must say, I had no idea you were so..." His lack of immediate, adequate words was quite charming. It disarmed her.

She almost replied, "You aren't what I expected, either." He seemed less self-assured than he'd sounded over the phone. But she held her tongue, feeling she stood on uncertain ground. It all added to her unsettled state.

Galbraith opened a file folder on top of his pristine desk. Leslie's late uncle had been a Lieutenant Governor of the state when Leslie was quite young. She remembered her uncle's worn office and oversized messy desk. This office was sterile in comparison. Galbraith's manicured hands hypnotized her as he turned the pages in the file.

Glancing up with hesitation, Roger Galbraith placed his fingertips lightly together. "Your cousin, Wayne Riker, was worn out by the time he died, Miss Weldon. He'd worked hard all of his life, but it had finally become too much for him. Even the day he died, he was still trying to tend to his ranch. You might say the ranch was the death of him—too large an enterprise for a man his age." He shook his head. "It was sad, really. He might have lived longer had he not clung to the land so fiercely."

Leslie thought back on what Henri O' had said earlier. "How exactly did Wayne die, Mr. Galbraith? I just assumed he'd died of old age. He wasn't a young man when I met him a few years back."

Galbraith lowered his head. "It happened only a few days following the settling of his will. The sheriff assumed Mr. Riker had an attack of some sort and was temporarily confused. They found him at the bottom of a small ravine, his old tractor upside down beside him."

Leslie willed herself to close her mouth. She settled back against the comfortable chair, thinking back to that afternoon she and Dad shared with Wayne Riker. The man's exuberance for his ranch filled her with such excitement that she was induced to ride an old, rusty tractor. Never in her life had she been on such a huge contraption.

As the lawyer watched her, his hooded expression tightened. "Miss Weldon, is something wrong? Are you all right?"

"I'm fine, thank you," she replied. "It's just that I wouldn't necessarily assume Wayne was unhappy with his life. He absolutely loved his ranch—it's all he talked about. Dad once said it was Wayne's reason for living. So, no matter how he died..." She allowed the lawyer to fill in the blanks.

Roger Galbraith drew back, slightly offset by her words. He cleared his throat. "Well, I only knew him for a few hours, you understand, but yes, Wayne did appear to have rather strong feelings for his ranch. I'm sorry if I misspoke."

Leslie chose to change the subject. "Did Wayne know that my father passed away a couple of years ago? I mean, did he know that the ranch would come to me if something happened to him?" Leslie found it hard to believe that Wayne had purposely left everything to her. She also thought it strange he didn't tell her.

The lawyer's smile formed slowly. "Yes. Mr. Riker was well aware of the situation with your family. He set up the will as it stands, naming you specifically. He knew everything would come to you. As you know, there are no other living relatives. All of it has been thoroughly investigated." He cleared his throat again. "Miss Weldon, may I call you Leslie?" he asked, with the slightest hesitation, as if afraid of offending her.

She nodded.

"Good, but I'll call you Leslie only if you address me as Roger." He smiled, then continued. "As you know, Wayne's will gives you the house, everything, including farm vehicles, the land, and the entire amount of his small savings after inheritance taxes. If you sign here, that part of our business will be concluded." He stood and came around so she could sign the documents. On completion, he handed her one set of the signed copies and a set of keys with nametags.

Returning to his side of his desk, Roger slipped the remaining set into his folder. He looked at Leslie, a boyish grin in place, and lifted out a separate set of documents to hand her. "This is the proposal to purchase your ranch and the surrounding acreage. When first we talked over the phone, I informed you about this group of investors. They have a wealthy client who believes he can breed excellent prime beef on your land. This looks to be a good opportunity for all concerned."

She glanced at the legal documents in her hands, finding their words and meaning blurred in her mind. Lifting her gaze to Roger, she grew even more unsure. Suddenly this shy, boyish lawyer appeared altered in presentation, more confident and self-assured. Who was this man? The in-charge lawyer who now smiled back at her, or the shy lawyer who often hesitated to meet her eyes? Leslie's earlier doubts returned.

She shifted uneasily, her gaze gravitating toward the door.

"Leslie?"

Her focus returned to the papers in front of her. She rested her hands on top. "I'm puzzled, Roger. When I arrived early yesterday, I used the time to drive out and look over Wayne's property. En route, I met a neighbor who seemed to think the sale of the property was already completed. Why would he think that?"

His suave smile froze; his eyes registered alarm. *Is he surprised that I drove out there, or surprised at the mix-up over the sale of the property?* She was unable to determine what was behind his reaction.

His eyes dropped; the shy, confused smile was back. "That is puzzling. I spoke with the neighbors, but only to mention there was a sale pending. Perhaps in my excitement I made it sound more settled than it really was, but that was only because this proposal is gigantically huge!" His features came alive with enthusiasm. "It offers well above market price for the property. I admit Mr. Masters' offer to purchase the property was untimely. I'm afraid I didn't consider his offer to be in the same league as the investors." Galbraith arched his neck above his tie nervously. "It's amazing how things can get all mixed up. That's one of the reasons I wanted you to check with me before driving out there. It's pretty much of a mess—quite run down, I'm afraid. Did you see those front grasses?"

Deciding Roger Galbraith was clearly pressing his own agenda, Leslie became wary. It was true, he'd overstepped his authority. But, then, neither Clive, Ray, nor Mona had bothered to mention Clive had also offered to buy Wayne's property. *Why? Are they hiding something too?* Her fingers drummed the papers. *Who can I really trust*?

Experiencing increased pain, she straightened on the chair, steeling herself for one more question. "Did you tell the neighbors that their leases would be canceled?"

Roger's facial muscles tightened. He drew in a long breath. "I admit I was a little premature in telling them that, but I was only trying to give them a heads-up to look for other avenues for their crops and animals. I would feel terrible to have them left in the lurch at the last minute. After all, this is a small community, and we're all neighbors."

His forced smile left Leslie unconvinced. Her hand rubbed her temple. "Roger, I'm afraid I'm not feeling very well right now. I should get back and rest for a while. May I take these papers with me to think it over? I'm going to need some time. This is the biggest decision I've ever had to make." She wanted to leave.

The lawyer nodded. "Of course. How inconsiderate of me. May I drive you to your motel?"

"I have my car," she said swiftly, wincing at a twinge of guilt.

Well, I do. I just can't drive it right now, she reasoned. She didn't want Roger to know she had been staying with Mona, not until she knew more about what was really going on. "I'll call you soon," she said, pushing up on her cane to stand.

Roger hurried around to help her, offering his arm. Her foot pain drove her to accepting. Together they made their way toward his office door. "Leslie, I'm concerned about you being on your own in this condition. Is there any way I can help? I have an extra room at my house. My housekeeper lives in, and she's a great chaperone on occasion as well," he said shyly with a small nervous chuckle.

Leslie bit her lip. "That a very kind offer, but I'm good, and I think I could use the time alone to think through this proposal."

Stepping ahead, Roger opened the door and hurried back to assist her. His secretary, Stephanie, stood by her desk watching, her lips pressed in a hard line.

Roger ordered Stephanie to hold the outside door for his client. From the edge of her line of vision, Leslie observed the blond secretary stiffen before striding across the room to the exit.

When they reached the opening, Roger gently restrained Leslie's arm. "Call me if you need anything," he insisted, his expression earnest.

Leslie was briefly touched by his overt sincerity. He made believing easy. She watched his eyes for variation, finding none.

"I'd hate for you to get saddled with a rundown ranch in Georgia, Leslie. Paying taxes a thousand miles away is a pain. I've been there." He spoke as a caring friend. "You are a lovely young woman. You don't need the stress and burden of property in this economic setback. It's a miracle these investors happened along. I'm afraid if you take too long, they might look elsewhere. Just think about these considerations." He patted her hand before allowing her to continue through to the door. "Remember, call me for anything, anytime. And if you'd like me to accompany you around the property, I'm available. Just let me know."

Leslie smiled wanly, giving the smoldering-eyed secretary a wide berth at the door. Outside on the uneven sidewalk, she could still feel his eyes on her and slowed her steps to discourage his gaze from lingering. One swift backward glance assured her Roger was gone and so was the jealous secretary. Feeling slightly dazed from her encounter, she scanned the parked cars up the street. Mona's car awaited her.

*

Following an x-ray scan of Leslie's ankle and a short consultation, the women drove away from the clinic, neither inclined to talk. Leslie's sober manner brought probing looks from the tanned, dark-haired woman behind the wheel. "You're awfully quiet since leaving Galbraith's office. Is it the ankle? I know it's a setback to find out it's fractured."

Leslie was unsure of anyone and anything, least of all her own situation. Her gaze was drawn downward to the unattractive, boot-like cast on her left foot. Lost in her thoughts, she hadn't even heard Mona's running monologue. *Maybe Henri O' is right. The ranch is cursed. I've had nothing but trouble since I inherited the property.* Immediately she berated herself. She had never believed in curses. Though God hadn't passed out any blessings her way lately. *And why would He?* Guilt stabbed her. Her heart was heavy.

Leslie refused to be a burden to people she hardly knew. "Mona, with this boot on my foot, I should be able to manage nicely. I'll collect my things at your place and find a room in a nearby motel until I feel I'm able to drive back to New York. I noticed a nice bed-and-breakfast right in town that would be very accessible."

The words felt unnatural even as they left her mouth, as if each word was at odds with her actual feelings. Yet she stammered on, "It's not fair for me to keep you away from your work. You've spent far too much time on me already." Jabs of reservation continued to strike at her. She visualized herself sitting alone, in pain, in a bleak, affordable motel. The bed-and-breakfast was only a pleasant idea. Her emotions betrayed her. She didn't want to leave the comfort of the Schillers' home, yet she'd known these people less than a day. *How can I impose on them further? It will be best for everyone if I leave,* she told herself with new forced conviction.

Mona frowned at her watch. Her eyes flickered in sudden dismay even as her foot pressed on the gas pedal. Leslie gritted her teeth as Mona zipped out and around a slow-moving, rusty truck. The jolting car spiraled her pain, adding serious doubts to her ability to care for herself. She rejected the impulse to retract her offer to leave the ranch. Somehow she would manage.

After studying the winding road for a lengthy time, Mona sent Leslie a probing look. "Look, my work is getting done. I have help with chores. George, our handyman, covers for me when I'm working at the hospital. Leslie, right now you are a prior commitment. In worst-case scenarios, Clive's assistant, Evan, comes over and lends a hand."

Did Mona want her to stay?

Mona's chin bobbed, as if she'd settled something with herself. She gave Leslie a glancing professional appraisal. "You do realize that boot isn't going to eliminate the pain. You are still going to have a very difficult time, at least for the next few days. And those deep scratches are going to be almost impossible to re-bandage by yourself, not to mention meals."

Calmly, she added, "Ray and I spoke, and we feel your place is with us until you are stronger. Unless you are unhappy and would prefer to go it alone, stay put a few days longer."

Leslie felt a little blown over. This quiet-spoken woman had out-flanked her. Inwardly, she was relieved. Caught in a situation of needing help, the thought of being alone was depressing. The nagging doubts about who was telling the truth didn't seem as pressing in the wake of other advantages, like remaining with these people. They had been Wayne's friends, or so they said. *Perhaps it might be easier to determine the truth if I can observe the Schillers firsthand and ask questions.*

She found herself saying, "I just don't want to be a burden any longer than necessary. I am a virtual stranger, after all."

Mona whipped around a farm wagon to make a sharp turn down their private road. "God doesn't look at you as a stranger, and neither do we," she stated matter-of-factly.

Grabbing hold of the car strap, Leslie held on tight, closing her eyes until the motion of the car was steady once more. She opened her eyes just as the Schillers' farm came into view—none too soon. While Mona seemed unrattled by the hectic ride from the clinic, Leslie held her side.

Opening Leslie's door, Mona eyed Leslie with alarm. "Oh, I'm so sorry about that ride. What was I thinking? I was worrying about relieving George so he could go home early today, but I should have taken your condition into account."

Leslie grinned up at Mona's concerned face while sliding slowly to the edge of the car seat. "I'll be fine. I've had worse rides in New York traffic."

*

A few hours later, Leslie was seated at the dinner table with Mona and Ray when Clive rapped on the back door and entered, not waiting for an invitation.

A look of bliss encompassed his features. "It smells fantastic in here!" He strode briskly toward the table, his face sobering as soon as he spotted Leslie.

Mona stood. "Pull that extra chair over, Clive. I'll get you a plate. As you can see, we have plenty."

Clive glanced longingly at the piled platter of BBQ ribs. "I thought that's what I smelled coming in the back door. If I remember correctly, Henri O' has a wonderful way with ribs." He slid into a chair between Mona and Leslie.

"Yes, she does," Ray said, laughing. "I'm surprised the aroma didn't carry across the road, or is that why you're here?"

"Actually…," Clive began, the lines around his eyes crinkling in mirth.

Mona pushed a plate and silverware in front of him. "We've already prayed; you're on your own." She returned to her chair.

Leslie stared at Clive with open curiosity. When he met her gaze, she quickly looked down at her plate, but not before she saw him incline his head in silence.

Was Clive a Christian? Somehow she had trouble imagining him in this role. He didn't fit the profile—a man like her father. Could Mona have only been goading him? Things weren't always as they seemed, but still? Leslie cast her speculations aside. Why should she waste her thoughts on a man who clearly detested her?

Most of the bantering across the table occurred between Ray and Clive. Mona watched with amusement, occasionally contributing a comment. These three were obviously friends as well as neighbors.

While Mona served up the cake Henri O' left for them on the counter, Clive grew quiet. Leaning backward in his chair, he zeroed in on Leslie. "Who wants you dead, Miss Weldon?"

Mona spun about, a plate of cake suspended in her right hand.

Ray leaned on the table, his line of sight drilling Clive for an explanation. "What are you talking about, Clive?"

Clive dragged his chair up close to the table. "I went up to the barn today to repair that hole in the floor and found something very interesting."

Mona set the cake down and slid into her chair. "You already said the boards weren't rotted through. Is there something else?" She eyed him quizzically.

His lips thinned into a hard line. "Rotted—not hardly! All the boards around that area were staved in with hard heels from a boot. No small guy could have done that kind of damage. It took mass power."

"You're saying that a big man deliberately smashed in those boards to weaken them?" demanded Ray.

Mona frowned. "Still, I don't understand why you think it was meant for Leslie?"

"I think the odds add up to it looking that way."

Mona walked over to stand beside Clive's chair, her anxiety evident.

Leslie watched each of them, awestruck by what she was hearing.

At that instant Mona hit Clive on the shoulder. "Don't say things like that. You're upsetting her. How can you know the boards were staved in so that Leslie would be hurt?" Mona waved her arm. "For crying out loud, Clive, you and Ray have been in and out of that barn and the outbuildings on a daily basis for months, ever since Wayne had his heart spell. It could just as well have been one of you it was set for."

Clive stood and began pacing. "I would've agreed with you up until one week ago. Remember?"

Mona stared at him strangely. "You mean when Galbraith and those two associates stopped by to talk to us about the property?"

Ray glanced at his wife. "Was that the day I arrived just as that lawyer dude pulled out of the drive in his fancy Porsche?"

She nodded as Clive pointed his finger in Ray's direction. "Galbraith drove to my place first. He said he knew I was interested in purchasing Wayne's property from the estate, and he'd come by to let me know the property had already been bought up by a holding company from up north."

Jamming his left hand in his pocket, Clive walked over to the counter. His right hand idly picked up the cake knife, making patterns in the icing until Mona removed it from his hand. Grimacing, he turned and leaned against the counter. "That slick lawyer smiled like a Sunday preacher and thanked me for taking such good care of Wayne's place the last few months. Gibraith's words dripped with sugar.

" 'You and the Schillers will be reimbursed, Mr. Masters,' he said, 'but I should give you a heads-up. With the estate sale pending completion, it would be better if you stayed off the ranch and away from all outbuildings. None of us would want the unpleasantness of a trespassing charge cited between neighbors.' "

Clive's jaw tightened. "Would you believe he waved when he drove off? I couldn't believe the way those words rolled off his tongue, like he was doing me a favor, when in plain speech, we were being threatened from entering any of the buildings."

"He gave us the same speech," said Mona. "But don't forget the part about our leases being cancelled. We're allotted only so much time to get our livestock out of the fields. Plus we were banned from entering the buildings."

Leslie shook her head in disbelief, torn between the conflicting stories. Roger had seemed so sincere, but hearing this.... "But you did enter the buildings yesterday. Clive ran in the barn to save me, and then you both took me inside Wayne's ranch house to patch me up."

Clive exchanged looks with Mona. "When I saw you headed for Wayne's, I couldn't ignore it. I'd told him we'd take care of the place."

"And we had no choice when we found you. You were hurt bad," finished Mona.

Leslie remembered how they'd rescued her, but she was still trying to sort out the serious implications of Clive's words. "So you're saying, either Galbraith or someone who knew about the new ground rules arranged for the broken floorboards?" She felt like she'd entered the Twilight Zone.

Clive moved from the counter and slid into the chair next to Leslie, holding her gaze. "We are not saying anything, Leslie. We are stating the facts. The boards were deliberately weakened to the point that someone would either be badly hurt or killed."

"Roger Galbraith has no reason to arrange anything so sinister. He is in line for a hefty fee for handling Wayne's estate whether I sell or don't sell."

Clive inhaled. "Then why is he pushing this sale proposal so hard? It's as if he's their personal spokesman!"

Leslie narrowed her eyes. "I'm not sure, but I'll find out. Maybe he believed it would mean more money for the estate, or perhaps he had doubts about you being a good investment." She shot Clive a wry smile.

His eyes flickered and met hers as a challenging grin tugged at his mouth.

Mona hurriedly shoved a plate of cake in front of him. "Eat up," she ordered, darting a warning glance at Leslie.

4

Trial Run

REPOSITIONING HERSELF IN BED with the extra care an injured person is forced to practice, Leslie felt encouraged. Her pain level was lighter; she was healing. The clinic had praised Mona's quick, skillful treatment to her injuries. Why then was sleep so evasive in coming tonight? She couldn't seem to forget the uncomfortable feeling she was left with when Clive finally said good night. Over and over, she replayed the scene. Leslie knew he believed she was gullible and short-sighted, swallowing Galbraith's persona, hook, line, and sinker, and it bothered her. Why she didn't know, but it did. In the darkness with only the moon's brightness reflecting shadows through the window, she clinched her jaw in defense of her position.

"I didn't defend Roger," she muttered. *All I said was, Galbraith gave a plausible answer about the pending sale mix-up, and I needed a chance to question him about the rest before I accused him.* Could it be that Roger Galbraith was that deceitful? Had he truly ordered these people off Wayne's buildings, and if so, why?

Lying there, she pondered the troubling situation while watching a shaft of light reflect across her quilt. With the window open, she could hear the muted night sounds of bird calls and branch movement in the nearby woods. The memory of Clive at the back door was stamped on her memory, his words shouting in her mind.

"While you're listening to Galbraith's explanation, Miss Weldon, remember that those floorboards were deliberately staved in—just waiting for someone to walk across them...and it wasn't any of us."

Mona and Ray's worried expressions had only alarmed her more. Every time Leslie thought on the possibility of someone actually trying to harm her, it seemed ludicrous. What possible reason? *No! There must be a plausible explanation.*

She turned her head toward the window. There was a shifting in the night sounds. She strained to hear strange whisperings through the window screen. Her breath caught in her throat as the sounds faded, only to be followed by an eerie woebegone murmur that sent spiraling chills throughout her body. Were the sounds human? Her mouth went dry.

Moving her legs to the side of the bed, Leslie slowly pushed up to peer outside into the blackness beyond the window. It had been a long time since she'd slept out in a rural setting. *There's nothing out there,* she reasoned. In the middle of night, when all other sounds of active society were hushed, it was only natural to hear the more obscure sounds of nature.

Relaxing, she shifted to tuck her legs back under the covers and was leaning on her pillow when a muted child's scream shattered all previous thoughts of nature. *What or who is that?* Henri O's ravings sprang to mind. *A child's ghost crying at night...*

Nonsense. Wind sounds, she kept telling herself, refusing to give in to her imagination. *Perhaps it's the effects of the pain medication?*

Eventually, she slipped into an uneasy slumber.

*

Awakened all too soon by morning kitchen sounds, Leslie roused and labored down the hall. With no pain medication left in her body's reserve, she made a major effort to work her way to the kitchen. She pondered whether Henri O' would speak of last night's eerie sounds.

Reaching the kitchen, Leslie found that, once again, both Ray and Mona had breakfasted early and were busy with farmwork. She alone was left to brave the dour countenance of Henri O'. "Good morning, Henri O'," she called brightly.

"Mornin,' " the woman muttered. "What will you be havin'?"

"Whatever Mona and Ray had this morning will be fine," she said sweetly, schooling her voice to sound like imitation sugar.

"Blueberry pancakes and sausage," the cook said in a bored tone.

Ignoring the woman's offensive attitude, Leslie forced a smile. "Sounds great. If they taste even half as good as that dinner I sampled last night, I can hardly wait. Mr. Clive raved about it."

Easing into a kitchen chair across from the east window, she felt the warmth from the rising sun. Leslie shifted, chancing a covert glance in Henri O's direction in time to see the rich, facial coloring of the Schillers' cook crinkle with pleasure. *Finally!*

Somehow Leslie had known the cook would be flattered by any compliment Clive Masters had to give, as most women probably were. The thought surprised and irritated her. When had she admitted to herself that Clive Master was an attractive man, whose energy-forced personality had the same effect as a sharp, strong wind—powerful and breathtaking? Immediately, she pushed aside her musings.

Some females might be easily swayed by such a powerful man, but a woman with a strong, intelligent mind, like I have, will not be so quickly predisposed, she determined with pride. She lifted her chin at the mere thought of Clive Masters affecting her.

Henri O's manner improved. It was visibly mellowed by the time she carried over Leslie's breakfast. "Mr. Clive raved about my ribs, did he?" Her voice was smooth like warm chocolate.

Leslie flashed a smile. "Yes, he did. His exact words were, 'Henri O' has a way with ribs.' He could hardly wait to pull up a chair," she quickly added.

Henri O' nodded. "Good! Mr. Clive is a fine man. I'll fix ribs again next week and whisper to him the day so he can drop by at the right time."

Leslie stared at her breakfast, anticipating the first bite. "I'm sure he'll be thrilled," she murmured, her mouth watering at the sight of the bursting blueberries nestled inside the hot buttered, golden-brown pancakes. If Henri O' didn't leave soon, those beauties would get cold.

A final nod accentuated Henri O's decision as she moved away with purpose, leaving Leslie to hope the cook's new attitude would last.

As Leslie picked up her fork, aiming it at a plump sausage, Henri O' swiveled to glare at her. "And don't you go telling Miss Mona what I'm planning for Mr. Clive...you hear me?"

Holding the speared sausage high on her fork, Leslie retorted, "Of course not. How could you think that I would do such a dastardly thing?"

"Just as long as you understand," declared Henri O', spinning back around. She marched to the stove.

So much for improved relationships, thought Leslie, chomping down on a mouthful of sausage.

*

Leslie leaned her head against the stacked pillows in the easy chair, happily situated near front windows in Mona's light-filled, living room. She glanced around restlessly. Her boot-enclosed ankle rested comfortably on a matching ottoman. Yet she balked against the feeling of being trapped.

Magazines lay strewn across her lap, but her body and mind craved action. Mona had lectured her royally before they'd said good night, and while

Leslie saw the need for her foot to have time to heal, every aspect of her personality fought against the inactivity. Her fingers drummed erratically on the forgotten magazines.

Squinting, she leaned forward to make out the reason for the cloud of dust rising at the end of the long drive. Clive's dust-coated truck slowed to a fast rolling stop. His door swung open in record time, and then he slammed the truck door behind him. Without a glance in her direction, he glided with long strides past the fence and on toward the huge chicken pens and elongated coops behind the ranch house. *Will he take the time to come inside? And what will I say if he does?*

Their awkward parting the night before had left her uneasy.

Long minutes went by. Thoughts of Clive held her captive, her eyes drifting from his dusty truck to the kitchen area and the back door. When her cell phone rang shrilly beside her in the chair, it took her unaware. She raised the phone to her ear.

"Roger," she exclaimed in surprise, trying to recover the shock in her voice. "I'm doing quite well at the moment—thank you for asking. But my situation has taken an unexpected turn...in what way? Well..." She told him about having her foot x-rayed and the dismay of discovering it was fractured. But when she mentioned encountering Mona Schiller and subsequently accepting her invitation to covalence at the Schiller house, an uncomfortable sound ensued at his end, followed by a stretch of dead-air space.

Leslie took this advantage to relate part of the conversation that took place the night before at the supper table. She asked him point-blank, "Roger, did you order the Schillers and Clive Masters to stay off my cousin's ranch and any of the buildings? I heard you also took it upon yourself to cancel their leases. Didn't you know they have been working to improve the buildings? I need a few answers here."

She listened to him stumble over compound words and inverted sentences. It was obvious he was taken aback, not only by her staying at the Schillers, but also by her directness. He was now on the defensive.

She pressed her point, cutting him off. "I'm sorry, Roger. Whatever your so-called reasons of protecting my interests in lieu of the impending sale, I feel you've overstepped your authority. These are good people who were very close to my cousin. From now on, I don't want you making any decisions without conferring with me first. Consider the Schillers' and Master's leases reinstated from this point until I decide differently."

She listened as Roger accepted her rebuke with surprising grace. He rushed to offer his sincere apology. His staggering elastic personality continued to amaze her, knocking her off center. "I appreciate your attitude, Roger. No, I wouldn't be averse to having you stop by soon. That's very kind of you."

Leslie ran her hands through her hair, feeling out of her depth. "Yes, I will continue to think about the advantage of selling to the investors, but I warn you; I'm not going to make any hasty decisions. My foot has pretty much decided that for me. I want a chance to look over Wayne's place as soon as I'm able." She listened to his persistent pressuring. "Yes, I know there is a lot to consider. I'll talk to you soon, Roger. Good-bye." The conversational bantering had tired her.

Leslie stared moodily out the front window, focusing on a bumble bee flitting from flower to flower. It was impossible to tell if Roger was guilty of no more than being overly aggressive in selling what he wanted, or if there was something more sinister behind his actions. Then there was the matter of the barn flooring staved-in prior to her arrival. Had someone truly set an evil trap intending to injure her? Why had she kept that information from Roger?

She heard a stirring near her.

"You surprise me, Miss Weldon. I didn't think you had it in you to stand your ground that way. Frankly, I thought I was the only one you troubled to bad-mouth."

Startled, Leslie snapped her head to the side. Clive's lanky form leaned easily against the facing connecting the kitchen. She drew herself up. "I'm surprised you noticed anything, since your mode of operation is normally nasty!" she retorted, hating the sound of her own words. *Why did I snap at him like that?*

He pulled his Western hat low over his eyes. "Ouch! That smarted. Say, how about a moment of truce? A chance to start over?" he entreated.

Her conscience took another jab for her sharp tongue. The Bible had spoken about women like her. *That isn't the real me—or is it?* She hadn't been normal since she first arrived. Why did this man make her so mad? Bringing her hands together in her lap, she said softly, "Fair enough."

Sitting on the chair opposite her, Clive removed his hat, placing it on the floor. Raking his fingers through his slightly rumpled hair, he leaned forward and rested his elbows on his knees. "So...what are your feelings on how or why the boards were set up for someone to crash through? Any ideas?"

Her head drooped. "I honestly don't know." She hadn't been able to tell much from Roger's words. There could be an underlining motive for him overstepping his authority, or it could be nothing more than ambition and human greed. Unwilling to speculate, she clarified, "I don't know enough yet to make even a good guess. You mentioned Roger Galbraith last night as if he might be a suspect. But after speaking with him today, all I can tell you for sure is the man is decisively gung-ho on this estate-sale transaction. But where's the motive in that?"

"Greed. It's possible they've offered him big money. People don't usually work that hard without some kind of inducement."

She blinked at the word *greed.* It echoed her thoughts. "I don't know yet."

"By not yet, does that mean you have a plan?" His voice held a hint of suspicion.

Lifting her eyes to check on the bumble bee, she answered slowly, "I'm not positive the boards were deliberately set up to harm me. But if that is the case, then I need to know who and why." Her chin firmed in determination.

Clive eyed her with interest. "It's been my experience that life is filled with unsolved puzzles. Having said that, I agree about finding out answers. But don't forget how close you came to being killed!"

Her lip quivered as she relived those fear-filled moments in the barn.

Clive's hand drew her chin around until their eyes connected. "You are safe here with Mona and Ray. You can trust them. I know we all got off to a bad start, but they are reliable, good Christian people." Staring down at her boot, he added, "And with that foot, you will probably be here for a few days. That's good! We can protect you, plus it will give you time to think things through. You might even think of a reason why someone might think life would be better without you."

"Thanks. That makes me feel warm and fuzzy all over." Wiping her eyes with the heel of her hand, she shivered, even as the sun warmed the room.

"I'm sorry to be blunt, but the situation exists. It's good for you to bear that in mind whenever you're out of this house. It will keep you alert."

Leslie studied her propped-up foot with dismay. "Well, as you stated so eloquently, I'm basically stuck for a few days." Her lips went taut. "But trust me, I'm going to get back on my feet as soon as possible."

Standing, Clive picked up his hat from the floor and placed it back on his head. In so doing, he extended his height by several more inches. Leslie had to crane her neck to view the top of his hat. A wry grin inched across his face. "Don't be in too much of a rush, Princess. Might as well enjoy the soft life while you can."

"Princess!" she flung back at him, sparks shooting from her eyes. "Do you think I enjoy lying around like a trapped hamster having people wait on me? And what is this 'Princess' business you keep laying on me?" she sputtered. "I don't appreciate being labeled a pampered priss!"

Clive chuckled, striding toward the front door. "It's good to keep your blood moving like that, Princess. You won't get too sedentary that way. Later," he called, allowing the front screen to slam shut behind him.

Leslie gritted her teeth, her eyes following him down the path all the way to the truck. After swinging inside the cab with fluid ease, he gave a cowboy wave with his hat before closing the door. Leslie seethed. *He knew I was watching him!* She didn't know who she was more furious with, Clive or herself. As the dust settled in the drive, her thoughts flitted like that bee on the flowers, touching on everything that had happened to her.

As she leaned her head back, memories of last night's eerie sounds haunted her. They'd sounded so real...a small child crying in the dark!

Biting her lip, she tried to dispel her anxious feelings. All her attempts to convince herself it was only the wind moving through the trees had failed. There was no chance it was a ghost, of that Leslie was certain. She might not be a Christian in good standing at present, but she did know what God's Word said about the dead, and it wasn't that they roamed the earth once the spirit departed the body.

The years melted back in time in the hazy afternoon sun. She closed her eyes and drifted off to sleep, transported back to that fearful night as a young child when she had run to her father. He'd told her what happens to a believer in Christ after their last breath is drawn in this world. Had they been discussing Mama?

*

Less than twenty minutes later, Leslie's head thrashed against the back of the chair and her eyes flashed open, remembering her father's words of encouragement: *"When a spirit is absent from the body, they are present with the Lord...a believer is with Jesus."* She suddenly felt cold as the words replayed in her mind. *But, I don't know if I'm a believer anymore, Daddy. Not after what I've done.*

Her father had said no one could take her out of Jesus' hands, but had she ever *really* been in His hands? Lately there were doubts. Recalling where the Bible said nonbelievers went after death, she decided it wasn't a thought she'd dwell on. But how long had it been since she'd felt the presence of God...years?

She yanked her despondent thoughts back to her original problem—the eerie, childlike sound. But if it wasn't something supernatural, and it wasn't, then what could it be? *What would sound like a child? Was there an animal out there that sounded similar?* If there was, she didn't want to meet it. Leslie made a goal to find out what it was.

*

After a light lunch, and a short walking attempt outside the house to watch Mona work with the chickens, Leslie succumbed to the throbbing pain in her ankle and made her way back to the house, anxious to sit once more in the chair by the window.

Eyeing the uninteresting magazines, she returned them to the coffee table and hobbled over to the bookshelves lining the side wall by the fireplace. She scanned the titles advertising a variety of subjects until finally resting on a small book about Dahlonega, a fairly recent book on the history of the town written by a local resident.

Leslie carried it with her, relying increasingly upon the support of the cane. Once settled, she lifted her aching foot to its lofty perch on the ottoman and leafed through the history book. *I might as well learn something about this infamous gold rush.*

Flipping the easy to read pagers, she was fascinated by the authentic photos depicting those rough and ready times. Leslie gradually felt her eyelids growing heavier, not noticing the book fall to her lap or the actual second her head slumped in sleep.

*

"Leslie, wake up, or you won't sleep tonight," Mona's voice said gently. "Come on, open your eyes. Dinner will be ready in a few minutes. I hurried in to clean up."

Leslie blinked. Glancing at her bare wrist, she recalled her watch was on the dresser top. "What time is it?"

"Five-fifteen on the dot." Mona threw the words over her shoulder as she disappeared down the hall.

Lifting her eyes to the kitchen, Leslie watched the silent figure of Henri O' move about the room, her competent hands completing the evening meal. Had she actually seen the exotic-looking cook cast a furtive glance her way? Henri O' was not one to trust easily—something they shared in common and yet another mystery to deal with. The sloe-eyed woman was a curious blend of cultures, and though her features were definitely more European in form, her eyes were undetectable and secretive. Leslie wondered if Henri O' had heard the same frightening noises as she had the night before.

Doubting the cook would dare speak of ghost noises again in her presence, Leslie determined to question her at the earliest opportunity. From what she'd be able to determine, the Schillers' housekeeper was unmarried. *Why would a fairly young, handsome woman with the obvious skills she possessed remain unmarried in this section of the country?* Henri O' was a puzzlement in a growing list of unknowns.

After dinner, Leslie made her way to the privacy of her bedroom to catch up on her personal calls. "Alberta, I've missed your sassy comments. How's everything going up there?"

Listening to all the local news in and around the apartment building, Leslie debated how much she should share with the older woman on the happenings over the last few days. Trying to spare her friend, who had become the grandmother she'd never known, Leslie left everything out of the news about her foot, except the injury itself.

"I appreciate your concern, Bert, but I'm being well taken care of by my cousin's neighbors, and the food is terrific!" Laughing, she kept her voice light. A similar call to Diane put her in good standing with everyone of importance in her meager circle. Why did it sadden her to recognize the truth of her thoughts? Ever since Kevin's unfaithfulness and her father's death, she'd pulled her life into a shell, so close no one could break through the barrier. Busyness had filled in all the cracks, of which there'd been more than a few. Only recently had she begun to relax her guard and experience the presence of loneliness on an escalating scale. Would the pain be too great?

Holding her phone in her hand, she mused on her empty life the last few years. Her business major had opened the door to money and more busyness. Now it was gone—her job, her busyness. That vacant space had brought her face to face with her grief, anger, and ever-present guilt, but even worse was the vast hollow feeling inside.

Leslie laid the phone on her night table and reached for her cane. Suddenly she was eager to return to the living room filled with light and the comfort of Mona and Ray's company.

5

Putting Out Feelers

MONA WAS NEEDED AT THE HOSPITAL the next day, leaving Leslie at loose ends. Breakfast and lunch passed without incident. Each time Leslie thought she had the perfect opportunity to engage Henri O' in a conversation, something would happen. Either the phone would ring, or Henri O' would slip through the back door for some reason known only to herself.

Leslie drummed her fingers on the chair arm. Feeling totally useless, she was staring mindlessly at the sun-bleached driveway when the midnight-blue Porsche drove slowly up the drive, parking in front of the house. She watched, fascinated, as Roger Galbraith climbed out of his shiny car and brushed off his designer jacket. He carefully adjusted his hair and clothing before turning in the direction of the front door.

While Leslie was still in the process of extricating herself from the chair, Henri O' opened the door to Roger. Catching only a word or two of their brief exchange, she waited while Roger was directed into the front room. Leslie smiled as he moved toward her, but her gaze held to Henri O', observing her open disdain for the lawyer. Watching the cook back away like a shadow, Leslie was filled with new doubt. *Is Henri O' conveying the feelings of the others, or does she know something more?* The thought weighed even as she put out her hand to welcome Roger.

"It's hard to believe you were just passing by, Mr. Galbraith." Leslie smiled a little too brightly to counteract her negative thoughts.

He lowered his head. "I thought we had progressed to the Roger point at least."

"Make yourself at home. It was kind of you to check on me." She eased back in her chair.

He seemed pleased with her reaction. "A fractured foot is nothing to laugh at. If you're interested in suing the motel, just say the word." He grinned.

She was at a brief loss to comprehend what he was talking about until she remembered telling him she'd injured her foot on motel stairs. That was the trouble with lying. Her father always said the truth was easier; it never came back to accuse you. *You're so right, Dad.* She fumbled for the right words. "Ah, that's all right, Roger. I don't need the hassle. I have enough to worry about."

The lawyer within Roger jumped on the opportunity. "You, of all people, should have no worries, outside of your foot, I mean. You've just inherited the answer to all your money problems. As far as hassles go, there would be none if you would only accept the profitable offer on the table." His eyes were eager.

Her resistance rose. "Roger, speaking of tabling something..."

Inclining his head, he held up his hands in submission. "Sorry. Consider it tabled for a brief while, but not forgotten, I hope." His charm was turned on full force.

"I could hardly forget it," she said dryly. "But I want the opportunity to learn more about the ranch. I've barely even seen the place, let alone toured it at length." It was a partial truth, but the best she could do at the present.

Perching on the opposite chair from Leslie, as if flight was imminent, he took but an instant to consider her statement. "Are you able to walk in the boot?"

"Very short distances."

"Well, if you feel up to it, why don't I drive you up to Wayne's house? We'll see how you do."

Leslie widened her eyes. "Now?"

He shrugged. "Why not? It's up to you. How do you feel?"

"Bored!" she exclaimed, her thoughts racing. Though she'd already seen the ranch house, she couldn't reveal that to Roger. It was a chance to get out of the house.

Her response had made him laugh. "Then I think we should take care of your boredom. May I help?" He rose from his perch.

She allowed Roger to help her to her feet. Once she had the cane in her hand, she pushed away. "I'm good now, but you can get the door."

"I can do that," he offered eagerly, striding toward the entryway.

"There's no need to rush." Her tone was filled with mirth, even though she spotted Henri O' covertly watching their actions. Raising her free arm, Leslie nodded in Henri O's direction. "I'm going up the road to the property. Tell Mona I won't be long."

Leslie was sure the woman heard her. She also had a feeling Henri O' didn't miss much of anything. *I need to find a way to tap into that resource.* Turning, Leslie redirected her attention to Roger. If there was a chance he might say something that would give her insight into what was going on, she wanted to catch it.

Clive thought Roger was a part of what happened in the barn. What if there was a way to find out? An idea formed. For it to work out, Leslie's ankle had to be able to walk further than yesterday. She wasn't sure that was possible. A fleeting thought of prayer was pushed aside. That side of her had been unresponsive for so long she wasn't sure how to bridge the gap. She moved forward.

"Are you hurting?" Roger asked. He must have observed her pensive expression.

"I'm fine, Roger. It feels good to be out in the sunshine."

While holding the door for her to slide inside the luxury car, he grimaced. His manicured fingers had lifted dust accumulation from the shiny finish. "I wish all these roads were black-topped."

Restraining a giggle, Leslie replied, "You sound like a city boy."

Entering the car, he replied, "I was a city boy."

"So, what brought you out here?"

Turning the ignition, Roger rotated the wheel with care, easing out of the long driveway before answering. "Oh, a friend of a friend suggested I'd do well in the charming town of Dahlonega."

"Was she a pretty friend?" Leslie asked coyly.

He chuckled. "Oh, no, nothing like that. Strictly business."

"Oh." A flash memory of Mona suggesting Roger had a contact in Dahlonega came to mind. "Could that friend be anyone I might have heard of?"

"Who have you heard of?" Roger laughed, obviously enjoying himself. It was as if she'd never confronted him earlier. Was it a charming ploy, or might he really like her?

An uncomfortable thought niggled. Maybe she could use that advantage to get more information. The idea made her squirm. Leslie didn't like using people's emotions. Kevin had been an expert in that art—especially for money.

So she shook her head sadly. "Not many people, I'm afraid. If I hadn't stumbled over Mona and Ray and..." She'd almost said, "Clive."

"Who else did you stumble over?"

"Ah...you." She grasped for any answer but the truth. "I basically stumbled into your office two days ago—remember?" She flashed him a smile.

His eyes warmed, resembling a Bassett Hound in a pet shop with his nose to the window. It made her uneasy, not knowing how to respond.

After the laborious walk to Wayne's door, Roger slipped a set of keys from his pocket and fumbled to unlock the door.

She frowned.

He flushed, as if embarrassed. "You're wondering about these keys? That's actually one of the reasons I drove out to see you. I found this other set after you left." He looked back to the lock.

She nodded. But the doubts Clive had planted caused her to immediately suspect there was another reason Roger was in possession of an extra set of keys.

He turned the knob and pushed the door wide for her to enter. Once inside, Leslie's eyes darted immediately to the couch, where Clive had first laid her when he'd carried her wounded from the barn. Someone had returned and cleaned up everything. Was it the same someone who locked up the ranch—Clive looking after the ranch?

Wrenching her focus from the area, her eye caught the glint of a hair clip on the floor by the couch—the one she'd worn the day of the accident. Leslie spun her body about with her good foot, directing Roger toward the kitchen. "What a charming breakfast area—a bay window with lots of light!" Her heart raced in double time.

Roger nodded, scanning the spacious living area and kitchen. "Wayne told me he'd done some remodeling a few years back. It must have cost him a fair amount. The siding needs to be redone. I wish all the outbuildings were in as good condition." He glanced down the hall. "Would you like to see more?"

"Yes, I think I would." While Roger proceeded her down the hallway, she hobbled off to the side and scooped up the hair clip.

"Leslie?" his voice called from the hall. "Anything wrong? Are you coming?"

"I'm coming." She slipped the clip into her pants pocket.

After a general tour of the area, she declared an official rest time, situating herself in the nearest chair. "Give me five," she said, panting from pain and exertion.

"Of course. Take as long as you need," encouraged Roger. "When you're ready to go back to the Schillers, let me know."

She had a decision to make. For her plan to work, she'd have to push her endurance beyond this point. Leslie gritted her teeth. What was the term the guys liked to use—*Cowboy up?* "Roger, I'd like to see the big barn before we return to Mona's." *It's now or never,* she told herself.

The lawyer was slow to agree. "All right, if you're sure, I'll make it as easy as I can. We'll drive."

Roger parked his fancy car as close to the barn entrance as possible. Their arrival stirred up clouds of dust. "I'll have to use the spray and wash when I get back to town," he said unhappily.

Balancing her weight on the head of the cane, Leslie closed the door on the pretty little car. "Have you considered trading the Porsche in on a Jeep?" She grinned.

Roger gave her a sharp, wounded look. "Not exactly my style, but if Jeeps interest you, there is one of your own in the garage down the hill."

"A Jeep...really? Where's this garage?" asked Leslie, not remembering taking note of a garage. The idea of owning a Jeep was exciting.

"Yes, the Jeep was included in your cousin's inventory. You must not have read through the list. All the papers are in the folder I gave you. That old wooden structure next to the tool shed serves as a garage. Wayne told me he'd always planned on doing something different." Roger pointed down the hill. "The Jeep is in there, such as it is. The old Jeep runs when it has a mind to—Wayne's words, not mine. You might consider taking it in for an overhaul before attempting a drive. Wayne talked about upgrading to a newer model before the accident, maybe even a comfort car. Then there's a truck parked in the back of the barn with a bad transmission that needs an overhaul. Wayne had so many plans that never materialized."

Most of what Roger said barely registered. Leslie was gazing in the direction of the wooden garage, wondering about the Jeep. Sometimes she thought herself in some kind of make-believe world. Her life was so incredibly altered from last week, it was hard to fathom. She stared ahead at the huge barn as Roger worked to open the sliding door. Forty-five minutes ago, she had thought this a good idea; now she wasn't so sure. Was it wise to enter this gigantic building with a man whose integrity was in question?

"Talk about a white elephant." Roger extended his hand upward in the vast interior. "I suppose a farmer would find this building of value, but a business girl from New York—not likely. If Mr. Masters hadn't kept it from falling into rubble the last few years, it would be a pile of lumber today. Even so, this place still needs work." He sighed, moving into the center of the room, scanning the interior with obvious doubt.

Leslie moved slowly, one step at a time, her focus fixed on Roger. Would his eyes go to the scene of the accident? If he'd known about the staved-in boards, he was a good actor, because his vision never veered to the area as natural curiosity might dictate. She watched him look to the upper level, where mounds of stored hay waited for use. He walked further until he stood directly under the swing trap door above and stared at it with curiosity.

The misty memory of Wayne demonstrating the process came to mind. The trap door was designed to allow a portion of bales to drop to the lower level whenever the heavy cord was yanked from below. At the time she had thought it ingenious and quite entertaining. She walked toward Roger, eager to show him how it worked. Hearing a sharp click, she froze, her eyes traveling to a distant spot on the floor where he now stood. Too late the sound of a mechanized release from above drew their attention. Her jaw dropped in horror, watching the trap door above him fly open.

"Roger! Move!" she screamed at the top of her lungs.

Instantly, Roger reacted to the sounds. Seeing the bales plummeting from the gaping hole, he jumped sideways in time to miss the initial impact of the first bale striking the floor but faltered in his balance. Recovering quickly, Roger scampered to safety, avoiding most of the main thrust of the following bales tumbling on him.

Seemingly fixed in the one spot, Leslie called, "Are you all right?"

Roger's face was a mask of shock. He kept looking from the hole above to the huge pile of baled hay inches from where he stood. It was the first time Leslie had ever seen his hair mussed. As if hearing her thoughts, he yanked hay from his hair, slicked it back, and pulled his ruffled clothes in line.

"I'm alive!" he said curtly, making his way in her direction. Standing by her side, he fixed his focus on the scattered bales, as if mesmerized by the scene.

"Wow! That was close!" exclaimed Leslie, her voice breathy. "You could've been directly under that—maybe unconscious, Roger!"

Inhaling deeply, Roger's hands rested on his hips. "That is a prime example of why it's not safe for you to own this place." He released a vent of pent-up air. "That accident could have happened to you when no one was around. I'd hate to imagine what might have occurred, had that been you." His labored breathing eased.

Realizing the significance of his statement, she thought of her own injury in that same barn. Her eyes gravitated to the place where she'd crashed through the floorboards two days earlier. Slowly, she backed toward that area. Roger, slightly dazed, followed her directional lead.

Leslie steered their footsteps over the repaired area of the floor, dismissing her slight apprehension. In lieu of what had just occurred, would Clive's repair job hold, or would both she and Roger plunge through the floor?

There was a noticeable difference in the coloring between the old and repaired section. She backed further yet. Roger did the same. His focus gradually shifted from the unsettling scene to the flooring beneath his feet.

"That's odd. Look at these boards." He pointed at the lighter paneling. "Wonder what occurred here?"

Following the direction of his pointed finger, she knelt. He knelt also, frowning at the repaired area.

Leslie studied his expression for any clue to foreknowledge of the trap. *Is that honest surprise? Whatever he's a part of, he didn't seem to know about the caved-in flooring, and he obviously didn't know about the trap door.*

"Maybe the old boards rotted through?" she said, baiting him.

Roger moved his hand across the wood from the old boards to the new. "Maybe. Though Wayne told me he'd had solid oak plank flooring put in this barn only ten years ago. You were right when you said he was proud of his ranch. I would've thought oak would last longer than that." He straightened. "Well, it's clearly been mended—Masters, no doubt. Wonder what the charge will be for that?"

Leslie shot him a sharp look. There was definite animosity in his quip. As aggravating as Clive could be, she knew differently. Besides he didn't appear to be that type of person. Of course, she recalled she had judged wrongly in the past. "What does Mr. Masters usually charge for his repair jobs?" she asked, masking her cynical feelings. Inwardly it angered her that she felt a need to protect a man she hardly knew. If it wasn't for the fact Mona had told her about Clive's generosity...

"I-I don't remember right off the cuff. I'd have to look it up," he murmured, then added smugly, "I can't help but wonder how Masters overlooked that problem with the trap door."

Leslie rolled her eyes and started for the door—men! She'd found out what she wanted to know in Roger's reaction to the repaired floor. It didn't solve the puzzle, but it was one piece. There were more problems to worry on now. Was the trap door incident only a malfunction, or was it planned? The thought scared her, intensifying her confusion. Suddenly the barn felt cold and ominous, and she was anxious to leave. Limping from the mouth of the barn, she directed her painful steps toward Roger's shiny car. Her plan to uncover information had backfired. Roger's nervous state added to the gloomy atmosphere. Not able to think of a thing to say, she stared outside.

Clearing his throat loudly, Roger began, "Ah, if you're feeling up to getting out a little more this week, how about having lunch with me on Thursday? I would pick you up and promise to practically deposit you inside the restaurant."

She was amazed at his quick emotional recovery. Roger's enthusiasm to be with her was not only flattering but inviting, and she agreed without the slightest hesitation. This boyish lawyer had the kind of natural charm that carried her away in its wake. She would have to guard herself.

They said good-bye at the door.

As she labored from the entry into the front room, Leslie searched the kitchen for any sign of Henri O', curious to find it empty until she recalled viewing the interaction of two people outside the house when she'd driven up with Galbraith. She'd caught a glimpse of the attractive cook talking with a sandy-haired man in Western garb. When Roger had pulled up in his Porsche, the couple had abruptly disappeared behind the house. Their physical closeness caused Leslie to wonder about the relationship.

*

There were no unusual sounds that night to alarm Leslie, but neither had she found time to discuss them with Henri O' and purposed to watch for future opportunities. She had told Mona about the barn incident with Roger, but her new friend wasn't pleased.

*

Following breakfast the next morning, Leslie made her way out the back door to seek Mona's whereabouts. After a stop-and-go lengthy process, she spotted the energetic woman cleaning chicken roosts, her face moist with perspiration. Upon Leslie's arrival, Mona removed her gloves. Her smile welcomed a visit. As the two sat on the edge of a convenient structure, Mona asked, "How's the pain level today?"

"I made it all the way out here," Leslie said proudly.

"I noticed. I also noticed the effect it had on you."

"I'm walking further each day."

Mona nodded thoughtfully. "Your pain level should guide your activities. As the pain eases, gradually increase your distance. I don't believe you mentioned how you came to be with Galbraith yesterday in the barn." She waited for Leslie to elaborate.

Leslie chuckled. "I figured Henri O' had filled you in on all the particulars."

Mona grinned. "Henri O' is very loyal to Ray and me. She's been with us ever since her father became ill. She quit school and returned home to care for him. In spite of everything, I've never heard her complain."

Shared information about the cook gave Leslie an opening. "How old is she? I first thought somewhere in her twenties, but it's hard to tell."

Mona leaned against the structure support. "Henri O's bone structure makes it difficult to judge her age. Actually, she's in her late twenties. She's been a Christian for only six months, but she's been coming out to church pretty steady. God is doing a good work in her."

The direction of the conversation made Leslie uncomfortable. She changed the subject. "The other day in the car, you mentioned a handyman named George. Is George a tall man with light hair?" She wondered about the man she'd seen with Henri O'. Mona looked puzzled. "No. George is medium height and slightly bald. Your description sounds like Evan Robinson. He's Clive's assistant. Where did you see him?"

Glancing away, Leslie replied vaguely, "Oh, I think I saw him talking with someone when Roger drove me back yesterday. I was just curious."

Mona nodded. "Was he talking with Henri O'?"

Leslie shrugged, unsure how much to disclose.

"Ray and I have noticed a certain interest there, and as I said, Henri O's church attendance has increased. We think Evan is an added inducement." Mona's gaze searched Leslie's features. "So tell me, is there an attraction between you and a certain lawyer?"

Leslie shook her head in amusement. "I think he's trying to make a sale, but it is nice to get out of the house. I was going stir-crazy. He's taking me to lunch Thursday."

Seeing Mona's eyes narrow, she asked, "You don't approve?"

The pretty, petite woman extended her hands palms up. "Leslie, I don't have a play in any of this. But I do have a question. What are your reasons? Am I to believe you accepted Roger Galbraith's invitation simply for something to do?" Her dark eyes probed for a deeper reason.

Turning from Mona's scrutinizing stare, Leslie watched the brainless birds roaming at will in all directions. Ray and Mona believed in the natural system of raising chickens and all of the mess that went with it. Leslie observed the contented animals while trying to condense her true reasons for spending time with Roger Galbraith.

"I'm grateful for everything, but the truth is, I'm stuck here with nothing to do but watch the dust settle on your winding driveway."

Mona moved in front of her, forcing their eyes to connect. "I'm not buying that as your only reason. Considering Clive mentioned your determination to find out what was going on, it makes me wonder. Are you by chance investigating on your own, Miss Weldon?"

Leslie tried to hide her smile. "Unguarded information has been known to be casually dropped over a bowl of soup, or perhaps even a glass of wine."

Mona's lips parted in surprise, and both women erupted in laughter.

*

Clive Masters was finishing a piece of pie when Leslie entered the house through the back door. Watching her favor the injured foot, he gestured toward a kitchen chair. "Can we interest you in a piece of fresh apple pie and a glass of milk? Henri O' just baked a beauty." He pointed to an inviting pie on the counter.

Leslie looked first at Clive's deeply tanned face, then lingered briefly on the warm pie, and moved lastly to Henri O's flint-like features as she stood at a nearby counter. Shaking her head, she giggled. "Clive, I would bet that pie was intended for special company, like yourself. The rest of us peasants will have to wait until supper. Right, Henri O'?" Her mirth-filled eyes rose to challenge Henri O's stoic stare.

Clive lowered his fork. *Whoa! What's going on here? A feminine standoff?* Caught in a potentially explosive taffy pull, he darted a covert look to the cook, expecting a curt volley to Leslie's comment.

Surprisingly, Henri O's veil of sullenness lifted as her gaze interacted with the spirited, red-haired woman. Clive watched, amazed, as Leslie's challenge extracted one of the few smiles he'd ever seen on the housekeeper's face. Henri O's mouth curved upward, and the rare smile moved slowly into place, completely transforming her features.

During the last few months, there had been a gradual blossoming of personality traits in the stoic cook. Yet, for some reason known only to Henri O', the sudden existence of Leslie Weldon in their midst had clearly roused feelings of suspicion in the exotic woman. It was obvious she didn't trust Wayne's young cousin, so Clive was now baffled by her sudden change in attitude. *I don't understand any of this.*

Clive wasn't sure where to go with the pie issue, so he changed the subject. "I've got a better suggestion, Miss Weldon. How about a drive out in the country? I thought perhaps you might be tired of sitting in the front room and staring at butterflies or whatever and are looking for a change."

Having made her way to the chair nearest him, Leslie eased into it, eyeing him critically. "So, because I'm bored, you're willing to take time out of your busy schedule and take me on a sightseeing journey? Am I understanding this rightly?"

He flashed a dazzling smile. "That's about it. Nice guy that I am." His amused expression dared her.

She cocked her head. "Well, Mr. Nice Guy, I don't know that I trust your reason, but I'm going to take you up on your offer. I would love a drive in the country."

Her answer was a surprise. Clive had anticipated having to goad her into going with him. They hadn't exactly gotten off on friendly footing. Their first meeting had set them both on edge. *My fault,* he admitted to himself. Everything about her had thrown him off balance. Gradually the impact of her accepting his invitation sank in. Standing, he said, "All right then. Let's do it now. My truck's out front. Henri O', if you would be so good to get us a couple of water bottles to go?"

"Coming right up, Mr. Clive." Her answer was as swift as her movements. The water was waiting by the time Leslie rose from the table.

As Leslie grabbed a bottle from the counter, her eyes connected with Henri O. Clive felt the electricity flow between the two and watched with interest. *Is this a moment of truth between two strong-willed women?* He paused, fascinated to observe the outcome.

Leslie nodded at the cook. "Thanks. This will taste good on the drive."

Henri O's low voice replied, "Why, you're quite welcome, Miss Weldon."

A slow smile moved across Leslie's features. Turning, she beamed with confidence toward Clive.

He shook his head, wondering what had just transpired, and led the way to the door. *Women are a dark mystery,* he mused. He likened them to a new chemistry set. *You never know what weird thing might set them off, or when they might blow.*

*

Leslie reached out to brace herself as Clive's truck headed down Schillers' drive. Stopping briefly at the road, he surprised her by turning left. Knowing left would lead them to the dead end, empting onto Wayne's property, she frowned. "I thought you said we were going for a ride in the country?"

"We are. You now own 350 acres. I'd call that countryside. Most of it is valley or prairie land, perfect for both crops and animals. I thought it was time you saw some of it." Clive shifted the truck into low as they neared the entrance to the ranch drive.

She looked up to the right where the land gradually mounted until it joined with deep woods, visible from the end of the county road. She wondered if today's property tour would include those woods. An involuntary shiver ran through her as she thought of the night sounds, where a child's cry penetrated the night.

Though last night had been free of the troubling sound, yesterday's episode at the barn had triggered another restless night of sleep, and Leslie hoped her lack of energy wouldn't spoil today's outing.

Clive slowly drove by the front of the ranch house and separate wooden structures and then from there up the lane where they passed the massive barn and two other pole buildings.

"I keep forgetting the property now belongs to me." She scanned the ever-widening landscape.

The sandy ranch lanes were every bit as rough and bumpy as her original ride in Clive's truck. Her hand continued to clutch the door on her right. "I thought you said this was valley land. Doesn't that normally refer to flat—as in less rocky?"

"Quit your whining. You sound like a city girl," Clive rebuked her lightly, a ring of laughter in his tone.

Leslie swallowed her ready remark. Thinking back to the day before, she chuckled. "You're right. I do. Only yesterday I accused Roger Galbraith of that same thing." She instantly wished she hadn't mentioned Roger's name.

"Ah yes, Galbraith. I heard about his near calamity in the barn yesterday."

Swallowing against her cotton-feeling mouth, Leslie reached for her water bottle. "It was a little frightening, not to mention the big mess in the barn," she said, soberly remembering how close the man had come to being buried by hay bales.

"Tell me everything that happened, step by step. It might make it easier to determine what triggered the trap door."

Leslie had just begun to absorb the serene quietness of the flowing countryside. It irritated her to intrude on these few moments of relaxation. She groaned softly. Returning her thoughts to the unpleasantness of the day before, she related the entire episode, from the moment she and Roger entered the barn to when Roger first wandered across the floor to the far side of the building. Leslie tried to remember everything. "Right after I heard the click…"

"What click?" he demanded, not waiting for her to finish. "Describe the sound. Did you see anything or anyone unusual?"

"The click had a quick, definite sound, but it was muted, as if happening a distance from me. And no, I didn't see anyone but Roger. Thinking back, I remember that when I heard the click, Roger stared at the floor seconds before the trap door released above him, and then all those bales shot out of the hole in machine-gun fashion."

"And Galbraith was standing directly below the trap door at that time?" Clive questioned.

"Yes." She nodded. "Of course he jumped aside when I hollered at him to move."

Clive's mouth thinned. "I'll clean up in the barn first chance I get."

By the set of his jaw, Leslie couldn't tell what else he was thinking and decided it was better not to ask. She tried to reconnect with her initial relaxed mood, but several ruts in the road jarred her head back and forth. "This ride reminds me of the first time I rode in your truck, the day of the accident."

"Accident?" Clive shot her a challenging look.

She held her retort, waiting until they were beyond the bumpy section. "I said *accident* for want of not knowing what else to call it. One thing I do know. If it was planned as you say, Roger wasn't involved. His reactions yesterday were unrehearsed. In fact, he was curious. He asked me why oak flooring would cave in."

Clive made an indiscernible sound in response to her comments and reached for his water bottle. When strained silence followed, Leslie sighed, chiding herself for bothering to defend Roger Galbraith. *It's not my job to keep peace between those two.*

As the dusky lane straightened out, Leslie relaxed, impressed with the healthy looking crops on either side. "Is this your leased land?" She studied his rugged and handsome profile, partially hidden under the worn Western hat, and couldn't help wondering why he wasn't married. She guessed him to be around thirty-two, give or take.

"Yes," he answered, "this is my crop." And then, as if he'd felt her eyes perusing him, he shot her a glance. "What?"

Warmth rushed to her face. "Nothing—just random wonderings." Her gaze immediately shifted to the semi-blurry landscape flowing by her window. The truck wheels kicked up a mounting cloud of dust that rose and dispersed into the wind. The whole effect was a muted haze over crops and distant hills. It was a wild, exciting adventure to bump along these dusty lanes with Clive. "Where are we going?" she shouted above the truck noise.

Coming to a sudden fork in the road, Clive swung the wheel to the far right. "Sorry, I always forget about that sharp turn." He swung the wheel to the right again, taking a lane that led between two fenced-in grazing areas scattered with beef cattle. The field on the left butted up against a low-slung mountain, rich with more grazing land.

Leslie pulled out her sunglasses to block the blinding glare from obscuring her view. She watched several of the steers raise their lazy, cud-chewing heads to stare curiously at the noisy truck racing along the rugged ranch lane. The air caught in Leslie's throat. She was savoring every second of this wild, midday ride on her extensive estate. *I've been locked inside an office for far too long,* she admitted, strangely feeling as though her essence was merging with the rolling scene beyond the window.

"You're enjoying this, aren't you?" Clive threw the unexpected comment over his shoulder.

Leslie turned her head in time to catch his mocking smile. Clive's sunglasses partially hid the threat of more unspoken questions. She restrained her oncoming smile and tossed her head like a spring colt.

The bumps in the road no longer bothered her. Her breathing deepened in the thrill of the day. It was like an unbridled ride on the back of a wild mustang. Her upturned face angled in Clive's direction.

"It sure beats napping in a window chair." She flung her saucy reply. Her head swung back toward the window, exhibiting her new exuberance. "Can we open the windows?" she asked, desiring the wind and sun on her face.

Grinning, Clive reached to push buttons on the side, admitting a hot rush of wind and sand flurries across their faces. It was the high temperature of the day, and heat waves wavered across pastures to the far right. Beyond that, Leslie made out the beginning of a steady rise of ground, its top cloaked in dense woods. She pointed out the window, shouting to be heard, "Are we going up there?"

"If you want to?"

Leslie turned and nodded. "I want to." Shifting back, she rested her arms on the open windowsill and lowered her head, her hair lifting behind her head in a film-like cloud. For some reason she felt an excitement building.

Clive's eyes locked briefly on her, as if mesmerized. Then he jerked his gaze back to the road ahead. Reaching the end of the lane, he turned right again, taking the road leading to the distant woods.

6

The Woods

"IS THIS WHAT YOU WANTED TO SEE?" asked Clive as they both stared up the rocky hill to the woods beyond.

"Oh, yes." Leslie pushed the truck door open and started to inch herself to the edge of the seat.

"Hold it. If you want to get out, just ask. I'll come around."

Leslie gritted her teeth. "I hoped I could do it on my own." She waited for Clive to round the outside of the truck.

"Well, next time try it when the truck is parked on ground level—and not on my watch. Mona will kill me if I let you stumble out of my truck."

"Gracious as ever," Leslie came back with a wry smile, allowing Clive to help lift her from the seat to the ground.

They both turned to face the imposing hill above them. The exhilarating air that had stung her cheeks riding over the lanes now laid still and heavy. Perspiration gathered on her forehead. "Everything is *so quiet*—like a church or something," she whispered.

Clive regarded her strangely. "Interesting analogy. What were you expecting to see here?"

Leslie's gaze returned to the woods at the top of the hill.

"Wait. Don't tell me. Does this have something to do with the ghost cries Henri O' has been talking about?"

"You've never heard them?" It was as much a statement as a question. "If you'd heard them, you wouldn't act so smug." Stepping around him, she tested the ground under her boot and positioned her cane to move ahead.

His hand stayed her, resting lightly on her shoulder. "I take that to mean you have? What exactly did you hear, Leslie?"

"Whispering noises at first. I took them to be the wind moving through the trees. It was my second night at Mona's. My window opens on the west side of the house." Leslie moved past his hand, stepping forward, still trying the steadiness of the ground.

Clive took his place alongside her on the left, his lifted arm ready to catch her if she stumbled. "And after the whispering noises…?" he pressed.

Leslie swiveled slightly toward him. "It began like the low murmurings of a child crying and gradually increased to a faint, eerie whine resembling a child's scream. Whatever it was, it was not rustling tree leaves on a windy night!"

"You're saying it sounded like the ghost of a child?" Clive eyed her critically.

Shaking her head in frustration, she spoke slowly. "No! I don't believe it was a ghost. I don't believe in ghosts, but it did sound like a child's scream, and later came the sobbing. I'd like to walk closer, maybe even upward of the top of the incline."

His instant frown was hard to read. "You're the third person to mention the night sounds. It's evident you heard something, but exactly what, it's hard to tell." Shifting, Clive regarded the rocky hill ahead and pointed. "That is more than an incline up to those trees. I doubt you'll be able to scale that grade. I have even greater doubts it would be a wise action." He seemed to wait on her decision.

"I want to go up there," Leslie said quietly.

Heaving a deep sigh, Clive fell in line beside her as she moved forward. In all honesty, Leslie wasn't sure she could manage the hill now facing her, but she felt driven to try. *"One step at a time,"* Daddy would quote, *"whether a yard or a mile."* She moved ahead. The closer they came to the hill, the stronger the wind felt. They started up the incline.

Leaning on her cane and holding to available rocks, Leslie allowed her breathing to level out. They'd gone only a quarter of the way. Higher up, the rocks became boulders. She fully expected Clive to order her back to the truck. When no order was forthcoming, she moved ahead with renewed determination.

The pain level in her foot had been fairly light during the ride out. Was she pushing things with this stunt? *But it's not a stunt. I want answers,* she reminded herself. When next they stopped to rest, only a third of the distance remained. At this height, the heavy smell of pine was strong in her nostrils and her labored breathing was the loudest sound in her ears.

"Take your time. It's very difficult from here on out. See that plateau. There's a ridge to sit on when we reach that level."

Leslie took strength in his encouraging words. Feeling the support of his hand under her elbow, she eased some pressure off her foot by leaning against his chest. "Thanks." She panted softly in the thin, cooler air of the hillside.

"How's that foot holding up?" he asked.

Leslie chuckled. "Not as good as it was ten minutes ago. Let's just say, I'm counting on the downhill trip being easier." She moved her booted foot ahead, only to wince and draw back in sharp pain.

"How badly do you want to do this?"

"I want to reach the top! Maybe if I rested a few minutes more?" she said with intensity.

Clive rolled his eyes. "I should pick you up and carry you straight down to the truck." He frowned, eying the plateau. "All right. Slip your arm around my waist and hang on to the belt edge of my jeans—and hold tight. I'll lift you over the hard places," he ordered, as if angry with himself as well as her.

Sensing his conflict, she quickly did as she was told, waiting as Clive brought his strong arm tightly around her waist and lifted her off the ground to clear rocks in the foreground. The pressure pushed a breathy *oomph* through her pressed lips as Clive's powerful motion and long legs stretched upward. Her free hand clasped his arm with all her might. They moved higher, her heart pounding. Was it the effort to breathe in the heat and thinner air, or the closeness of their bodies? She was afraid to examine her feelings.

In a few strides they were there, on the plateau. After he released her to rest on a jutting rock formation, she held her injured ribs, breathing gently. Clive withdrew two small apples from his denim jacket and handed one to her. "I grabbed them before I left my place. They're the first of the season." He crunched down, still breathing heavy.

"Thanks," she murmured between bites. "This is lunch." Nothing had ever tasted as good as the crisp apple at this particular moment.

From this height, they could view the valley for miles. Behind them to the right stood a copse of trees, the edge of the forest line, some of which looked hundreds of years old. With his hands on his hips, Clive surveyed the landscape while Leslie scanned the shadows among the tree foliage.

Her lungs filled with pine-scented air, reminding her of childhood camping days. She tried to tune out the increased throbbing in her ankle. *What was I thinking to push myself like this?* Her impulsiveness had always caused her pain and remorse. *Will I ever get it right, Daddy?* Her mind echoed his accusing words, *"Leslie, your headstrongness drives me to prayer each and every day!"*

She wished her father were here to direct her now. *I don't know what I'm up against, and it scares me.* Turning with effort from the tree line, she squinted to make out shapes against the horizon and pointed a finger. "Is that Wayne's barn way in the distance?"

Clive shifted his position to stand behind her. "Yes. This wooden area follows the high ridge, extending to the end of the county road. Wayne used to go up often into that section of the woods. He wore a trail up to the top with the tractor after his legs grew too weak to walk it. He said it was his special sanctuary."

"I'd like to visit there sometime," she said softly.

Clive turned her shoulders to face him. "You talk as if you planned on keeping the ranch. I say that, because the chances of you going up into that end of the woods will only happen after your ankle is well. I'm not carrying you up that hill too."

Even as she smiled, she recalled the pending decision. Roger was pressuring her to make a quick sale, but she didn't know now if that was really the best way to go. How long did she have to decide? What if the investors found a new area of interest before she made her decision? Their offer was more than she expected or ever dreamed. *If they want it that bad, will they wait? I know what I want to do.*

Leslie experienced an unexplainable resolve. "I'm staying long enough to look over the ranch on two good feet." The words flowed from her mouth almost without her realizing. "So I guess my decision is tabled for a few weeks, if my ankle is any thermometer."

"Will the investors wait?" chided Clive.

"I guess we'll see, won't we?" She stared past his left shoulder to a curious portion between the trees. "What's happening up there?" She pointed to some churned ground.

Clive stared in that direction. "Stay here. I'm going up and have a look."

Leslie seethed at her immobility. This had been her idea, and she hated being left behind. She was acutely aware her limitations had been reached, though. She'd pushed her body to its limit—maybe beyond. If she had done more damage to her foot, her recovery time could be extended. Gritting her teeth at the frustrating thought, she watched Clive climb the hill to the left.

Clive didn't stop at the crest of the hill. Leslie watched until he dropped out of sight on the other side of the ridge top. Resting her weight on the rocky ledge, she waited—not patiently, but she waited. The top of his worn hat was the first sighting of his return.

The curious look on his face told her there was something of enough interest to bother Clive Masters. "So, are you going to fill me in? I think I have a layer of moss growing on my backside just waiting for you."

"Moss? Surely not." He shook his head, clearly amused. "Moss doesn't grow on that side of any tree."

"Cute. What did you see up there?"

He looked back in the direction of the crest of the hill. "Nothing unusual for a farm, I guess. There are a lot of tracts that look like one or two tractor type machinery has been messing around up there. Truck tracks too. The ground is all roughed up as if deep holes had been dug and filled back in. Could have even been a back-hoe." His brows were knit in thought.

"But what does all that mean? What was Wayne doing up here?" When he didn't answer, she stared up at him. "Clive?"

"It's nothing, really…only some of those tracks look as if they were made recently. Wayne's been dead almost a month. Still, it's hard to determine the exact time. The color of dirt can change depending on rain or temperature, so we can't use that as an exact gauge."

"You don't look convinced," Leslie stated, studying his expression.

"That's because I'm not, and since there's no one here to ask, I'd say it's time to leave." He stared at her ankle propped up on the ridge. Without a word, he walked to her side and bent, cradling her in his arms. Standing and lifting her in one fluid motion, Clive descended the hill.

Before Leslie could offer a different solution they were halfway to the truck. "I feel like last week's laundry slung over your shoulder," she sputtered in irritation.

"Would you prefer if I did sling you over my shoulder?" he asked curtly. "A thank you would have been nice."

"It was only a figure of speech. You could have at least warned me what you planned to do. I might have tried walking partway. It's easier on the downside."

"It's too late, and I'm too tired to hobble you downhill just so your pride won't be tweaked. I should never have brought you up here to begin with. If I'd listened to my gut…" His jaw tightened.

"Mr. Charming. Well, I for one am glad we came. It's wonderful looking down from up there."

His expression softened. After long seconds passed, he murmured, "It's like you said. There's a special quietness, almost like church during prayer time."

On the return drive, Clive's countenance took on that distant vagueness that told her he was lost in his thoughts. *Something bothered him on that ridge. I wish I had seen what was there.* A new thought nibbled, something she would check out when her foot was better.

When Clive carried her inside Mona's house and deposited her gently in the window chair, Mona stared open-mouthed. Even Henri O' left the busyness of her work to observe their grand entrance. She stood discreetly at Mona's side, her eyes filled with question.

"What happened now?" Mona demanded.

Clive pushed up the brim of his hat. "Nothing to get excited about. Leslie had a bigger outing than either of us planned, and she was on that foot longer than was probably good for her, so..." He shrugged.

Mona's eyes blazed. "So that's all the information I'm to expect. What did you two do—climb a mountain?"

Leslie and Clive exchanged a glance.

Mona gave her head one quick shake. "Oh, don't tell me..." In a flash, the petite woman was at Leslie's side where the two of them gently worked to pull off her boot before propping her swollen foot on top of the ottoman.

"Henri O', get me the blue wraparound ice pack," she ordered.

Throwing the dishcloth over her shoulder, Henri O' moved quickly and efficiently.

Clive backed off to the side, watching. "If you two don't need me any longer, I have work to do at home."

"Hold it!" Mona stood. "She was in your care. What happened?"

Clive pulled down his hat brim to cover his eyes. "Nothing happened. Leslie simply wanted to see some of the ranch."

"Didn't you take the truck?"

Clive's rough hand rubbed the side of his jaw. "I couldn't drive my truck up Rocky Ridge. Those rocks would have ripped out my muffler or maybe my oil pan. That truck isn't three years old, Mona."

Leslie spoke with weariness. "Any blame for this afternoon rests solely with me. I was the one who basically begged to scale that...relatively moderate hill."

Mona regarded each of them with narrowed eyes, like they were small children caught in a mud-throwing fight. "So do I have this right...you badgered Clive into escorting you up Rocky Ridge, and he caved without a fight. That's a first!" She eyed the large man with new interest.

Leslie interjected, "I thought I could do it, Mona. It was that simple. I guess I'm not as strong as I thought. I figured the boot would protect me. Sorry if I made more work for you." She rested her head on the back of the chair.

Clive turned from Mona's probing gaze and waved on his way out.

Henri O' discreetly returned to her kitchen work as Mona settled in the opposite chair from Leslie. "There's no way of telling if you delayed your healing until tomorrow. Worst scenario, you might find yourself occupying this chair instead of exchanging information with your Mr. Galbraith. Isn't that when you're scheduled to have lunch with him?" Mona stared at the puffy ankle cocooned within ice.

Leslie nodded. "Mind if I take my supper here? Maybe if I'm real good…?" She raised her eyelids only enough to focus on Mona.

"A little prayer wouldn't hurt either. If you know any, now would be the time." Mona stood and walked down the hall to the ranch office.

Once again, Leslie felt inadequate. Except for the clatter of pots and pans in the kitchen, the house was weighed with that oppressive stillness that sometimes impregnates the air during the sleepy time of afternoon. Leslie had almost drifted off when a deep growl low in her stomach reminded her of a missed lunch. Her outing with Clive had cost her more than she'd gained thus far. Instinct told her it would be better to endure hunger pangs than approach Henri O' for a snack.

Her stomach growled again, jarring her further awake. The enticing aroma of roasting chicken in the oven didn't help her condition. Squirming in her chair, Leslie reached to reposition her ice pack on her foot and spied Henri O' with a broom.

When the housekeeper came in clear view of the front window, Leslie tried to keep her voice casual. "It was a beautiful day to look out over the valley. We could see Wayne's barn, the ranch house, and the copse of trees ending the forest line across the far rim. Clive found something curious over the crest of the hill. It looks like either Wayne or someone else has been working up the dirt on the hillside."

"What was happening over that crest?"

Leslie shifted in her chair to see the woman clearer. "I don't know. I saw only a little dirt discoloration from the plateau. I couldn't walk any further, but Clive walked on up. He said tractor tracks and mounds of disturbed dirt showed recent activity. Was Wayne working in that area?"

"Mr. Ray might know about that. I don't. Mr. Clive didn't know?" she questioned, looking puzzled.

Leslie came alive. "Of course! Clive was as close to Wayne as anyone—even Ray or Mona." If he didn't know of any reason for the tracks, that greatly reduced legitimate options. No wonder Clive was deep in thought on the way back from Rocky Ridge.

Henri O' silently regarded her, as if expecting Leslie to share her thoughts.

Leslie took courage, almost desperate to know about the night sounds. "I've heard the cries, Henri O'."

A flicker of an expressional shadow crossed Henri O's features. "When?"

"Two nights ago. It began as a faint whispering, then a clear child's cry. The last I heard was faint sobbing."

A single nod was Henri O's only response. Tension-filled silence occupied the following space. Leslie held her breath wondering and hoping for more. The cook's question came as a surprise. "What do you think, Miss Leslie?"

"I don't know yet. Except I know it isn't a ghost."

Henri O' took a step forward. "How do you know?"

From somewhere in the recesses of her earlier years came a deep confident report. "Scripture. God's Word says differently."

Henri O's features were unsearchable. "You know Scripture?"

"I do. At least certain portions, primarily because of my father."

"What does it say?"

Leslie could tell the woman was troubled, looking for a way to ease her thoughts. "It's been awhile, so I'll have to paraphrase the wording, but God's Word promises that children go directly to the arms of Jesus. They don't come back and cry out in the night. King David of the Old Testament said his dead son could not come to him, but someday he, the king, would go to his son. God cares for children. If a child's death needs avenging, God will do it."

Henri O' stepped closer. "How do you know that?"

Leslie rubbed the back of her neck. "Again, God's Word. Jesus said it would be better for a man to have a millstone hung around his neck, and to be drowned in the depth of the sea than to offend one of His little ones."

It was the largest Leslie had ever seen Henri O's eyes. "Jesus said that?"

Leslie nodded, not sure Henri O' was convinced. "Still, I admit those night cries creeped me out." She shivered again. "Let me know if you hear any more of them. I'm determined to learn what is causing those noises."

Henri O' studied her oddly before turning away. The inscrutable woman continued her sweeping on the other side of the kitchen while Leslie stared out the window. *What made me say all that? Why should I care if that woman believes in ghosts?* Irritation raked at her comfort and confused her even more. She was involving herself in the affairs of these people—allowing them to get to her. It would hurt to leave.

She challenged her unprompted eagerness to quote promises in the Bible. Was it possible she still believed in these promises, in spite of the long separation from worship and personal prayers? Her very words mocked her. Yet, even now she resisted turning to the God she had just quoted. *If I believe, what's preventing me from turning to Him?* Leslie's heart rate increased. She didn't want to think on those troubling questions. *I'm not ready. Yet I was quick to share God's promises!* Her confusion mounted.

Every step she took the rest of the night throbbed with pain. Mona kept up a continual flow of ice packs, her serious looks telling Leslie more than she wanted to know. *I have to go to lunch with Roger tomorrow, especially now that I know about those tractor tracks. Why would someone dig on Wayne's property?*

Taking the pain pill Mona offered plunged her into a deep, troubled dream. She heard a child crying but couldn't reach the child. The crying continued.

Leslie awoke, startled. Had there been actual cries, or had she only dreamt them? A painful trip to the bathroom and she fell back into deep slumber.

*

When morning rolled around, her head was logy and her thoughts uneasy.

Did I really hear those cries last night? The line between dream and reality was blurred in her mind, with nothing tangible to hold to. She went looking for Henri O', but no one was in the kitchen area when Leslie stumbled out into the front room. Disappointment clouded her morning. She'd hoped to confer with Henri O' about last night's noises.

Freshly baked coffeecake waited for her on the counter with a ready cup set up by a fragrant pot of steaming coffee. She helped herself and watched the morning sun slowly bleach the landscape beyond the window.

Mona burst through the back door like the miniature dynamo she was, her eyes bright with morning energy. "Good morning, Leslie. Thank you for making do for breakfast this morning. I'm utilizing Henri O' outside with me on a project. How's the foot?"

Leslie smiled at the way Mona rushed her ideas all together. "Good enough. This coffeecake is yummy. I wouldn't call this making do."

Striding quickly toward her, a slight glistening of perspiration on her face, Mona bent, tenderly examining Leslie's ankle. "The swelling is better, but not down where it was before yesterday's brouhaha on Rocky Ridge. It's not like Clive to let a female talk him into something his head is telling him not to do." Her raised eyebrow made Leslie uncomfortable.

"It was my fault, like I said, and we did learn something. What, I don't know yet. But something is going on up there on that ridge."

Sliding into the chair across from Leslie, Mona leaned forward, resting her arms on her jean-covered thighs. "You are showing an awful lot of concern for a ranch that you're interested in selling, aren't you?"

"Right now that ranch still belongs to me, and I want to know what's going on." Her chin firmed in determination.

"So do I, Leslie. If you have a plan, fill me in."

"I'm working on an idea." Leslie smiled.

"Good enough." Mona stood and started back through the kitchen. Pausing by the counter, she cut off an ample-sized piece of coffeecake and started for the door, shoving her mouth full. "You're right," she mumbled.

*

Amazed her foot was cooperating, Leslie frowned at the unfamiliar landscape. "I thought we were having lunch in town?" she questioned Roger Galbraith's evasive plans.

"My surprise. I figured you hadn't been out to one of our prize vineyards. This place has a particularly fine menu. Just relax and enjoy our outing. We couldn't have a more perfect fall day."

"Uumm," she murmured in response, feeling the heat of the sun through the car window. Roger's shiny car purred like a sleepy cat around the winding roads. There was something deep inside Leslie that desired nothing more than to do just that, but there were questions to be answered. Besides, eating lunch in a fine restaurant with a handsome man beat wasting an afternoon in Mona's window chair. And just maybe Roger would be talkative after a couple of glasses of wine. She was counting on it.

Roger's fine-featured face appeared pleased with life. He'd obviously gotten over his brush with danger. No mention was made of the accident with hay bales in Wayne's barn. Today he had an air of a man having everything in life he wanted. His quality clothes, impeccably tailored to his slender frame, gave credence to his confident attitude. Shooting her a dazzling smile, Roger looked every inch a little boy on holiday. One minute he was the dandy man; the next a youth looking for approval. The latter was the most dangerous.

When a second smile was thrown her way, she smiled back. "I can't deny the day couldn't be more perfect, Roger. I'm amazed you can get away from your busy practice. You appear to be in great demand as a lawyer."

Leslie could almost see his esteem puff up in her presence. "I admit I have done all right. My friend was right. Dahlonega has been very friendly to me."

"Tell me," she asked wistfully, "who is this special friend you keep speaking of? He was clever enough to invite you here." She covered a tired yawn.

An uncertain frown cloaked Roger's features. "Ah," he stalled with a forced laugh, "my friend is an important man, very careful to keep his personal life to himself—somewhat shy as well. He wouldn't appreciate my talking about him. I'm sure you understand."

Leslie stretched in her confined space. Roger's description of his shy friend didn't ring true. Self-made important men generally weren't shy. Yawning again, she reached to turn up the AC. The sun load through the windows was lulling her into a sleepy haze. She needed to remain alert. Last night's dreams had drained her of needed rest and left her senses dulled. She blinked as her eyes followed the rhythm of rolling vineyards in dazzling sunlight.

*

Leslie was comfortable in her sage green shirt jacket. A colorful scarf of interwoven rust and varied greens flattered her flowing pantsuit. She knew the outfit suited her by the amount of admiring glances in the restaurant. They held importance only to the point of reassuring her choice of clothing for today's outing. Nothing could dress up the ugly black boot on her left foot.

The restaurant ambiance was amazing, a quietly soft, elegantly subtle atmosphere. The cool temperature inside invigorated Leslie, clearing her mind in short order. Roger was correct. It was a fine establishment. He guided her through the crowded tables, waving at several occupants as they threaded their way to a reserved table with a wonderful view of the vineyards.

Lifting the wine list, he scanned its contents. "May I order you a particular favorite of mine?" he asked with confidence.

"Roger, I'm on medication and don't want to risk any reaction. I'll stick with a glass of water, but please feel free to order." The instant disappointment in his expression made Leslie feel awkward. Reacting to the unease, she reached for a complimentary bowl of almonds. "Nuts?" she offered brightly.

He shook his head, his thoughts obviously elsewhere. "No, I'm allergic. Leslie, I'm sure a little wine wouldn't prove to be a problem, but whatever you think would be best," he replied in a wistful voice.

Leslie smiled. "Thank you for understanding, but please enjoy it. It all looks so appealing," she said, surveying the interior with unmasked admiration. "This is very lovely, Roger. I'm glad you invited me."

Seemingly mollified, he hurried to match her enthusiasm. "The food is superb here! Everybody says so." Lifting his hand, he smiled at a passerby, looking around as if he wanted everyone to see Leslie with him.

She shifted, uncomfortable with being on display like some prize trophy. Leslie was happy to see their waiter approach the table until she learned Roger had not been dissuaded concerning the wine issue. When his rich-colored glass was lowered in place, the waiter also set a miniature glass in front of her.

Roger urged, "Forgive me. I had them bring you a tiny tasting glass—nothing more. Just sip a little," he coaxed playfully. "You'll love it! This wine is known across the country. In fact, I'm considering investing in it myself," he said proudly.

Leslie lowered her gaze so Roger couldn't see her rising flash of anger. Pasting a small smile in place, she lifted the tiny glass with sheer force of determination. Sampling barely a sip of the dark red liquid, she set the tasting glass firmly in front of Roger's plate with definite, quiet finality. Immediately, she reached for her water glass and menu.

Roger looked dumbfounded, as if he wasn't quite sure what had just taken place in her quiet, defined gesture. He downed a large gulp of wine and hid behind his menu.

While appetizers and more wine were served, several professional-looking people passed their table. Many stopped to exchange comments with Roger. Occasionally he would introduce her with obvious pride. Names and faces became a blur. At first she tried to identify each one's name with their image but found it altogether overwhelming. Noting the boy-like lawyer was clearly in his element, Leslie found herself tuning-out those occasions that didn't apply directly to her. She centered her concentration on the lovely view, leisurely enjoying the appetizers lined up on her plate.

Roger's energetic voice broke through her wandering thoughts. She turned to give him her full attention, taking mental note of two men standing on either side of his chair. Both were older, finely dressed in suits and ties. She forced a pleasant smile.

"Leslie, I'd like to introduce you to the president and vise-president of the National Pride Bank of Dahlonega, one of the town's newer established banks. Hamilton Longworth, Jonathon Hager, I'd like to introduce you to Leslie Weldon, the new owner of Riker's Ranch, at least at this point of time." He winked at Leslie.

Leslie smiled at the men. The large, flushed-faced man with a bulky build and booming voice stepped forward. "Hamilton Longworth, ma'am, my pleasure, I'm sure."

Gesturing toward Roger, Longworth continued, "Here sits one of our best new boys in Dahlonega. Yes, ma'am, he's a hard-working fella who knows what he wants, and he's not even wet behind the ears yet." The man laughed heartily and everyone joined him, drawn into the spirit of his natural exuberance. Looking at Leslie with admiration, he added softly, "And this lady is a true beauty, Roger. Don't let her slip away from you."

Roger's youthful look returned. "I'm working on it, sir," he said shyly.

The big man laughed. "Good man!"

The second man, dwarfed in size by the big man, was quiet, with a gray mustache and wire-rimmed glasses. He edged closer, extending his arm timidly toward Leslie. "Jonathon Hager at your service, ma'am. I hope you're enjoying your stay?"

She gave him a tongue-in-cheek expression. "It's been interesting, Mr. Hager."

His eyes strayed to the surgical boot on her left foot, and he frowned. "Not serious, I hope?"

Roger intervened before Leslie could answer. "It happened just prior to her arrival. She didn't know she'd broken it." He shook his head. "It has certainly slowed up her visit."

Hamilton Longworth leaned forward, his forehead wrinkled in concern. "I'm sorry to hear that Miss. Weldon. Was it a bad accident?"

She groped for the right answer.

Once again Roger stepped in. "Steps. Would you believe she fell down motel steps? I begged her to let me sue."

Everyone laughed, allowing Leslie to relax. That lie was getting more coverage than she ever thought possible. Still, it made her cringe whenever she heard it replayed.

Longworth nudged Jonathan Hager. "Come along, Johnny. We need to finish our lunch and get back. Have to make it look like somebody works in our bank." Laughing, he extended his hand once again. "A pleasure. I hope we see more of you."

Roger fairly beamed, seemingly basking in their approval of her.

When the men were well out of earshot, she soberly said to Roger, "They certainly think a lot of you."

From his expression she couldn't have said anything that pleased him more. He lifted his wine glass and downed the entirety, his eyes lingering in the bankers' direction. "Mr. Longworth has been very good to me. He has given me a lot of business since I came to Dahlonega and has been quite pleased with my results. He's a good man to know in town."

Jarred from her relaxing lunch, Leslie recalled Mona's comment two days earlier concerning the possibility of Roger having a prominent backer paving the way for him. *Could Hamilton Longworth be that man? Is he Roger's important friend?*

Their main entrée was fantastic, the view marvelous, the quiet unruffled by the murmurings of other patrons. When the waiter refilled Roger's wine glass a third time, Leslie knew the time was ripe for questioning.

Leaning her forearms on the table so no one else could hear, she whispered, "Roger do you really think those investors are interested in doing something worthwhile with Wayne's ranch? I wouldn't want to see the place mishandled or not kept up." It was a leading question she hoped would guide Roger into giving her more information.

Roger's mellow expression lit up with the mention of the property proposal. He leaned forward eagerly. "I have been assured they have big plans for the ranch property. They plan to breed only the finest of beef cattle, selling to some of the country's biggest ranches out west, even Florida." His eyes shone with enthusiasm. "I'm glad you've been thinking the proposal over."

She nodded. "I'd really like to meet some of these investors and talk with them before considering their proposal further. Could you arrange a meeting?" She gave him her most engaging smile.

Her request had the same effect as a shock treatment. His eyes blinked and he licked his lips. "I'm not sure that can be arranged. I'll check, but these are busy northern businessmen who are looking for a side venture to invest their assets. I was given specific instructions to handle the entire transaction on their behalf." He cocked his head, begging her understanding.

"I really wish you'd approach them on this matter, Roger. It's very important to me." Then she added, "Is there any chance these investors are doing soil testing on my property?"

The startled, blank look on Roger's face was immediate, a reaction of total confusion. "*Soil* testing? No...as long as the property belongs to you, nothing is going forth. Why would you ask?"

Leslie watched his reaction carefully. "Unusual tractor tracks have been found on one of the ridges on Wayne's property."

Roger tensed. "Was any unauthorized person seen in the area? Have you called the authorities?" Leaning back, he grew suddenly pensive. "I remember that Wayne's accident was the result of riding his tractor over a ridge. I didn't see the place myself. Could those tracks be some of his work before his death?"

Hearing the reference to Wayne's death brought a quick catch in her throat. "No. It was at the opposite end of that same ridge. Neither the Schillers nor Mr. Masters know anything about the tracks. They are just as confused."

"Perhaps it was work Wayne didn't tell anyone about? It happens," Roger offered.

Strangely, his words were a consideration. Maybe Wayne was spending time on his tractor that he purposely didn't mention. Like any aging, active man, he would naturally see the restrictions of age as an irritation, maybe even a blow to his manhood. She bit her lip. "I don't know."

Roger had no further suggestion and Leslie felt at a standstill in her attempt to uncover the truth. The rest of the meal was spent in small talk, ending in a pleasant return drive. Leslie went straight to her bedroom for a rest. She needed to think. Where could she go for the answers she was seeking? What would be her next move?

7

A New Wrinkle

LESLIE WAITED FOR MONA TO FINISH HER MORNING CHORES. Staring thoughtfully out the front window in the padded chair, she repositioned her foot on the ottoman, her expression somber. After a fitful night's sleep, she'd come to an uneasy decision. Along with that decision came a mind full of doubts. *Can I really make it work?*

So deep were her thoughts that she never heard Mona's approaching footsteps. "Henri O' said you wanted to see me. What's up?" asked the steady voice behind her.

Startled, Leslie snapped her head to the side. "Ah, sorry, I didn't hear you come in."

Seeking out the nearest chair, Mona wiped off her glistening face. "I'm not surprised. What put that frown on your face?"

Leslie chuckled. "Nothing really—just thinking."

"You must be having some pretty heavy thoughts. Did you find out anything when you lunched with Galbraith yesterday?"

Leslie's thoughts flicked back to the day before and her time at the Vineyard Restaurant. "There were interesting moments, but nothing I could pinpoint as a real clue, which brings me to my decision."

Mona inched forward in her chair. "What decision is that?"

"I want to move into Wayne's ranch house. Perhaps if I stay there on my own, I'll be able to look through his papers and poke around more thoroughly."

Mona's dropped jaw was her first reaction. "You? Stay by yourself at Wayne's?"

Leslie nodded. "I'm better now. Even you said so earlier this morning. With you and Ray right next door and Clive across the road, I feel help would be close at hand. Cell phones make for almost instant communication." She rested her hands in her lap, waiting for Mona to cipher through her proposal.

Fingering the ring on her hand, Mona raised her head. "Leslie, you're a grown woman. I have no control over whether you stay or go, and only you know how you feel, but I'd caution you to wait a few days longer."

Leslie gazed out the window, where she could see the top of Clive's red roof across the road. "I think it's time I go there," she said, quietly. "Did you ever feel like something or someone was nudging you onward?" The same questions she saw in Mona's eyes had kept her awake the night before.

Mona sighed. "Yes, actually I have. Only I would call it the hand of God guiding me in a specific direction."

Mona's unexpected statement jarred Leslie. Was it really possible? How long since she had sought God's guidance or even wanted it?

"Well, I can't tell what it is, except a strong feeling that refuses to be dismissed," she said with resolve. "I'll drive into town and get some groceries for the ranch before returning for my clothes."

Whatever was out there, she needed to face it.

"Good idea," Mona interjected, "except I will drive you in to get groceries, and together we will get you set up over at Wayne's. Let me do this, Leslie. Don't blow your energy on unnecessary actions. Conserve it, because you're going to need it later."

Considering Mona's proposition, Leslie nodded. "Agreed! When can we leave?" she asked expectantly. Now that the decision was made, she was eager to put it into action as soon as possible.

*

With sacks of prepared dinners and essential staples, Leslie and Mona made their way out of the store and into the spacious parking area. Once they were loaded up, Mona steered the car out to the main road.

A short ways down the highway, she struck the side of her temple with the palm of her hand. "I almost forgot that you need a new yard light. Trust me. It's pitch black without a yard light out there. We'll swing by Sonny's Hardware before heading out of town so you can pick up the light. Clive mentioned it the other day, and I clear forgot."

With reluctance, Leslie took note of Clive's thoughtfulness. Why did his actions annoy her more often than not? Was it his directness that grated like sandpaper? Clive never pulled his punches. She, on the other hand, was used to a gentler approach. Her father never raised his voice to her in his life, even in his most frustrated state, and Kevin had treated her like a princess from the first day they'd met, until…

She sighed, remembering her impulsive romantic flight to the island to meet Kevin. It was supposed to be their engagement weekend. Her thoughts filled with wry humor. Yet, where was Kevin today? With clenched fists, she thought back to that humiliating night at The Tropical Paradise Hotel.

My heart beat so loudly I could hardly think. I waited in that elegant, exotic room. Kevin was coming to meet me. Yet I couldn't shake the uneasiness that was stealing my joy. Knowing Dad didn't approve of my actions, I'd tried to shed myself from nagging guilt without success. How his words haunted me: "You're throwing away God's best."

I watched the door expectantly. Kevin had arrived the week earlier, but time passed, and he didn't come. Where was he? Why wasn't he there to greet me as promised?

At the first sharp knock, I flew to the hotel door. I was greeted by a bellboy and a huge flower bouquet instead of Kevin. I read his note with disbelief:

Dearest Leslie,
I beg you to forgive me. Try to understand that I've met someone new.
It's better this way. In the end I would only break your heart.
Kevin

He'd met someone new in one week and thrown away everything they had planned. It hadn't helped any to later learn the woman was wealthy. *And to think I almost...*

She burned with shame at what she had been willing to sacrifice.

"Leslie, did you hear me? I said you needed a new yard light," repeated Mona.

Her thoughts were shattered into a thousand pieces. "Sorry. Yes, we need to stop for a new yard light. Where is Sonny's Hardware?"

"Close. We're only a short distance away."

Leslie followed Mona into the popular hardware, its crowded aisles teeming with patrons. After they paid for their purchase and filed through the outside doors, Mona lingered to exchange friendly words with an acquaintance while Leslie made her way back to the car. Pausing on the sidewalk, she viewed the main road that led directly to Dahlonega square, marveling at the differences of small town versus big city.

Small-town friendliness amazed Leslie. In New York, people existed side by side without uttering a single word. The attractive charm of Dahlonega's side street was dotted by groupings of people greeting one another. Something familiar drew her attention to a certain grouping of three men not quite two blocks away. One profile struck her heart with instant terror. She denied her own eyes. How could it possibly be the same profile she'd seen in that New York restaurant with Diane?

Squinting, yet still disbelieving, Leslie wished for a pair of binoculars. This man was wearing a black, corduroy jacket and a leather Western hat. Surely she was mistaken, but that other man had been wearing a similar hat. She blinked, her eyes watering. Sensing that Mona was standing near her, waiting, Leslie felt an urgency to leave—yet she couldn't move.

The large man standing beside the slight, sharp-featured man was wearing jeans, a plaid, long sleeve shirt, and cowboy boots. He too was wearing a Western hat, as Leslie had noticed many others chose to do in this area. Leslie couldn't see the third man's face. He was blocked by the others. All she could see was the back of a business suit.

"Leslie? What are you looking at?" Mona nudged her.

Just as Leslie would have turned, the sharp-featured man shifted his stance. Then, almost as if he'd felt someone's eyes on him, he stared directly toward Leslie.

Her heart froze. Whirling about, she hurriedly climbed inside Mona's car. *Maybe he didn't see me. It can't be the same man anyway. My imagination is running wild. It has to be the nightmares working on my subconscious.* She could hear her heart pounding as Mona headed the car away from town.

"Leslie! Are you going to tell me what happened back there? You look as if you'd seen a ghost."

Leslie tried to laugh, but her mouth was too dry. "It's too strange to believe. I could have sworn that I just saw the same man who sat behind me in a restaurant booth in New York City. It makes no sense."

"Could it have been a lookalike? I see people all the time who look like my cousin or friend from high school."

A forced deep breath helped to ease Leslie of some of her discomfit. "I know. I do too. I tell you, Mona, that really shook me! This man's profile has been drilled into my conscious mind these past weeks."

With a sidelong glance, Mona asked, "Why would a man you saw once in passing at a restaurant be drilled into your consciousness? You're beginning to worry me."

"Because either this man, or the man he was with, was talking about killing a woman," murmured Leslie, her voice so low it was hardly audible.

"What?" The car swerved to the side of the road, quickly corrected by Mona's steadying hand. "Do you want to tell me about it?"

Leslie related her lunch with Diane Risner, including the episode with the hearing amplifier. Nothing was said in the following interim, until Mona turned down the road leading to the ranch. "You say, the man in town resembles the man in the restaurant?"

"The spitting image!" Leslie was finding it hard to think two individuals, outside of twins, looked identical to one another, but she dearly wanted to believe it was possible, because if it wasn't... She refused to finish the thought.

"How far away was he when you saw him today?" questioned Mona.

"Not quite two blocks."

"And what happened to the hearing amplifier?"

"I still have it." Leslie grinned at Mona's inquisitive glance. "My friend refused to take it back. I could've pitched it, but frankly it intrigues me in a weird sort of way. It's a clever device."

"So far, I can't see that it's improved your life," said Mona, frowning.

Having no easy comeback, Leslie took refuge in the passing landscape. There was no solution to the mystery of the sharp-featured man.

*

Mona and Leslie pulled into Wayne's ranch in a somber mood, but poured their frustration into direct action. Working in tandem, Leslie and Mona were able to air the bedroom Leslie would be using before they tackled the cupboards to put away the groceries.

When Leslie favored her left ankle, Mona exclaimed, "Sit! I can't stand the way you're hobbling around this kitchen. If you overwork it, I guarantee, you will reap the pain later. Just talk to me while I finish up here. If you watch carefully where I put the stuff, you'll have a better chance of finding things tomorrow."

Leslie grimaced but obeyed with little protest. "It's hard to believe this house is as large inside when you're looking at it from a distance. Amazing!" Her head swiveled from side to side from her bar stool position in front of the counter, giving the living room a concentrated appraisal.

"Wayne's furniture is in far better condition than I expected, all except that recliner. It's ripped to pieces!"

Placing a box of cereal on the second shelf of the pantry, Mona turned and reached for the peanut butter and two cans of soup. "That probably happened when Wayne was working with Boris. Wayne told me that dog was the most aggressive animal he'd ever attempted to tame."

The name *Boris* touched a memory nerve inside Leslie's brain. "Is Boris that multi-shaded, wiry-harried beast I saw in the barn?" She peered out the kitchen windows for a glimpse of the fearsome dog.

"Is that dog still hanging around?" Mona shook her head. "After Wayne died, Clive arranged for his dogs to go to different farms around the area. An extra dog on a farm is not a big deal. They're good watchdogs and usually earn their keep by managing the varmint population. The thing is, he could never catch Boris. He'd run off whenever Clive got near him. Wayne was the only one Boris ever really trusted. He was a wild dog that Wayne worked months to try and gentle."

A mental picture of the snarling breast manifested itself. Leslie slowly repeated the words, "Wild dog? Why would Wayne want to tame a wild dog?"

Mona laughed. "Yep, a wild dog. Boris was hurt and starving, and Wayne took a liking to him. After several weeks of setting out food, the dog finally ventured near. The first time I saw him, I froze in place. He used to scare me half to death whenever I came to check on Wayne. He's not for the timid of heart. If Wayne wasn't there, I never got out of the car. Talk about a watchdog!" She lifted her eyebrows.

"That has to be the same dog I almost hit on the road the day of the barn accident! He tried to attack when I opened my car door, and later after I crashed through the barn flooring, I saw him again." As late afternoon rays filtered through the windows, she could almost visualize the snarling beast inches away. Rubbing her arms, she shivered. "If Clive hadn't ordered him back..."

"If you see Boris, I'd recommend you give him a wide berth. Keep in mind he was a wild dog. I don't know if you can ever really tame an animal like that." Distancing herself from the opened pantry, Mona scanned the shelves. "I know you spent a lot of money, but you still don't have much food here. You've got the basics—that's all." Her look said she wasn't satisfied.

"I'll be fine, Mona. I have five frozen dinners in the freezer and a jar of peanut butter. What more could I ask for?" She chuckled. "I appreciate everything you've done for me. Staying with you and Ray has spoiled me. I can well understand why Wayne was so close to you. You're a hard act to follow." Leslie grew pensive. "But now it's time for me to find out what ranch life is all about. I have a big decision to make, and I can't do it sitting in your lovely front window. I've felt a growing restlessness to do something—whatever that is."

"I've watched that restlessness build in you. I'm just not sure it's a good thing for you to live here alone, especially with that bum ankle. But I know your mind is made up and..." Folding the last paper bag, Mona stored it inside the pantry. "Paper bags always come in handy in the country. Well, it's time we get back to the house. Supper should be about ready."

Closing the pantry door, Mona leveled a look at Leslie. "Look, I wasn't going to mention this, but our handy man, George Truitt, told Ray today that he wasn't sure, but he thought he saw lights flickering in Wayne's big barn two nights ago."

Leslie sat upright on the stool. "What does that mean, flickering lights? That was right after the trap door incident. Could someone have been setting another trap, or removing evidence?" Her anxiety rose.

"I have no idea, but if George was right, and he did see lights shining from inside the barn, I guarantee it was not for good reasons." Mona hesitated. "There have been two serious, or near serious 'accidents' in that barn, and that is reason enough to pay heed. Be careful and alert to anything out of the usual. Keep your cell phone handy."

Before Leslie could comment, Mona raised her hand. "Now for a more pleasant subject—food! You'd be downright daft to pass up a hot meal at our table before launching out on your own. After dinner, Ray can help you transport your luggage up to the ranch. That way, he'll be available to show you where the essentials are, water heater and fuse box. The rest you can learn as you go. As you said, we are right down the road. Are you ready to leave?"

Looking around at the cold, empty kitchen, Leslie heaved a sigh. "I know I've imposed far too long and I should refuse, but I'm much too weary and hungry to argue against a hot and ready meal. I accept. It sounds great."

*

Standing in the graveled drive, Leslie waved good night to Ray and Mona, rubbing her chilled arms as she watched their car swallowed up in the inky blackness of the brisk, autumn night. Only the reflective glow from the kitchen spilled out into the side drive, providing barely enough light to make her way back to the door. Ray had promised to replace the outside lamp tomorrow. She looked forward to enjoying the secure feeling its brightness would add.

She paused, experiencing a sudden sensation of being dropped into a foreign land, alone and separated from human contact. Her fingers groped for the security of her cell phone in the pocket of her bulky cardigan. *Mona told me to call about anything,* she reminded herself, *and they're only down the road.* Staying her emotions, she forced a calmness she didn't feel.

Lifting her eyes upward to the murky skies, she searched for even a hint of the zillions of stars she'd seen nightly at Mona and Rays, but the heavy cloud cover moving in was far too dense. She wondered if it would rain, not anxious to spend her first night in an inherited ranch house enduring a thunderstorm.

Hearing a small sound in the direction of the garage, she turned, peering into a solid wall of darkness. Seeing nothing obvious, she started to turn back to the house entrance when she spotted two yellow eyes watching her from the safety of night. *Boris!* Her throat went dry.

Leslie's eyes darted from the menacing eyes peering at her to the back door of the ranch, and back to the yellow eyes, calculating the distance between. *If I run, can I make it to the door before Boris reaches me?*

She thought back to the day of the accident and the image of the mammoth-sized dog—and his long legs. She stared back at the area where the eyes pierced the darkness and challenged herself with a new question. *Will Boris attack me whether I run or not?*

Her gaze dropped to her orthopedic boot, knowing her dash to the door would not be fast or pretty. With her heart in her throat, she dropped to one knee and struggled to find her voice. "Boris, Boris, come Boy, come," she called with a squeaky edge, her body trembling as she squinted at the shadowed area for any movement.

When none came and the eyes continued to glare back at her, she called again and waited. One last time, she called his name, but the dog chose to remain within his safety zone. Leslie rose slowly from her kneeling position and slowly turned her back on the dog, taking very easy steps toward the door, unsure what the dog's response would be. *Does he view me as an intruder? Will he attack?*

Leslie couldn't tell if the next sound was thunder vibration or the low growl of a dog about to spring. Her breath caught in her throat. Reaching the door, she yanked the handle, throwing the door wide to scurry inside. Closing it quickly, she locked the bolt. Her heart raced. Pushing the curtain aside, she stared out in the direction where she'd last seen the yellow eyes.

Seconds passed. She stood fixed on the spot, watching—waiting, as if she sensed something was about to happen. Then, seemingly on cue, out of the shadows slinked Boris, his head low, his eyes on the house. Tonight he resembled a wolf. Leslie swallowed hard, knowing the animal couldn't get at her, yet fascinated by this fierce, wolf-like dog staring back at her. Could he see her? While she didn't think it was possible, a part of her believed it was so.

Allowing the curtain to return to its original position, Leslie backed away from the door, making her way into the kitchen and living area. She turned on every light she came across, fanatically wanting to dispel all dark areas that might spook her imagination on her first night alone at the ranch. She went next to the TV, turning it louder than necessary, sheepishly feeling like a child ousting all monsters from the bedroom closets. Inhaling deeply, she tried to slow her pulse rate.

Staring across at the wide expanse of front windows, Leslie felt suddenly exposed and vulnerable. Hobbling from window to window, shutting each of the blinds, she attempted to laugh at the blatant silliness of her fears. After openly denying she believed Clive's theory that someone meant her bodily harm, then dismissing Mona's warning about lights in the barn, everything she'd done upon entering the house only confirmed she believed their concerns. That fact alone angered her.

I can't afford to allow my fears to gain the upper hand. I'm not going to buy into that ridiculous idea. There is no reason for anyone to harm me. Even as she reasoned with herself, she thought about the night noises.

After a restless forty-five minutes of forcing an interest in a re-run sit-comedy, Leslie rose from her position on the couch and switched off the dial. Her body was exhausted from the day's activities, but her nerves were on high alert. *Perhaps an hour or so of reading in bed will calm me enough to sleep.*

Before advancing toward the hall leading to her bedroom, she retraced her earlier pattern, turning off all lights, save one. Leslie decided to leave the light in the kitchen on—more for comfort than necessity. Mona had thoughtfully placed a night-light in the bath nearest her bedroom so she wouldn't trip or stumble in the night.

Leslie flicked on the bedroom light where Ray had deposited her suitcases in the evening. This room had obviously been Wayne's guest room. The crisp, bright-colored bedcover and accessories had seen little use. The windows faced the front of the ranch. Leslie purposely left on one tiny bed lamp. Drawing a stabilizing breath, she stood by the side of the largest window, carefully lifting the mauve-colored blind to peer outside.

Nothing seemed amiss. At first glimpse, everything looked quiet until she noticed there were more reflections on the drive than could possibly stem from the light off the kitchen. Where was the extra light coming from? She saw no movement of any kind, human or animal. Boris had disappeared back into his shadows, and the landscape was still and silent.

Leslie traced the light's strongest point back to a directional source. *Something or someone is creating that light behind the massive foliage. Could it be reflections from headlights or strong flashlights?* She wondered if she should venture outside.

Her left hand probed the inside pocket of her sweater and drew out her cell phone so quickly she almost dropped it to the wood floor beneath her feet.

Her fingers jabbed at the numbers, misdialed, and started over again, more in control this time. Her lip was mostly numb from biting by the time Mona answered her call.

"Mona, listen close. I think there's someone outside in my drive. I didn't hear anyone drive in, but I saw light on the gravel, coming from the road direction. I hate to ask, but could Ray check it out for me?" She tried to stem her trembling. *First night on my own and I call for help...Fantastic!* She despised being so vulnerable.

"Relax, Leslie. It's Clive parked in your drive. He left here twenty minutes ago. Once he learned that you'd decided to move into your own place, he made up his mind to watch the house tonight and make sure you didn't have any unexpected company. Ray told him about the barn lights two nights ago. I told him to call and let you know, but he said it would only start an argument, and he was brooking no opposition on the subject."

"Clive! I should have known. He's pigheaded and obstinate! Argument...I have a good mind to walk out there and..." She stopped, remembering how scared she'd been over the light in the drive.

Before Leslie could continue her tirade, Mona interjected, "He's spending the night sleeping in his cold truck because he's worried that you might be in danger. Think about it, Leslie, before you march outside and say things you'll be sorry for. You can never take angry words back."

Mona's soft voice cut her like a knife. All her anger deflated like a crushed water balloon. Leslie's free hand rubbed the back of her neck. "My father used to say that exact same thing. I was forever apologizing for words I'd spit out before thinking."

"I think I would like your dad. He sounds like a thoughtful man with deep convictions," Mona said.

Leslie's words were so low it was hard to make them out, "He would have approved of you...more so than he did me." Her fingers went to the window and gently lifted the window blind again, peering out at the directional light. Without the excess noise of the TV blaring, she strained to hear what she could now barely identify as the low murmur of a well-tuned engine.

"He really plans to sleep in his truck tonight? That's ridiculous. The temperatures are dropping to a record low. Wait. I think Clive just turned off his engine," she added quietly. "The lights are gone."

Saying good night to Mona, Leslie readied herself for bed. She experienced the release of her earlier nervousness. As much as she wanted to ignore the thought, Clive's physical presence outside in her driveway gave her a comforting sense of being safe.

*

Less than twelve miles away, fifteen year-old Meg McDonald slipped outside of a cramped, smelly trailer that reeked of fried fish—three-day-old fish that Cleary had swapped for hooch. It was past 1:00 a.m. and already damp with chilled dew. Heavy boughs from imposing pine trees pressed in on her, pricking her skin, so close she had to push them aside to make her way out of the wooded area. She tiptoed down to the edge of the narrow creek, an off-shoot of Yahoola Creek. Kneeling down, she splashed her face, again and again.

The cold, needle-like effect soothed her hot cheeks, still stained from endless bouts of crying. It had begun with yet another shouting match between her and her stepdad, Cleary Norton, and ended in a resounding slap from his powerful hand. Her fingers went from her stinging face to her badly bruised arm, where she protectively tugged her sleeve to cover its shame. Cleary was surly when sober, and downright mean when he drank. His drunken periods had run rampant since her mother's death three years ago.

I miss you so, Mama. Sometimes, I wish I'd died too. Why didn't you take me with you?

Meg heard a sharp noise down the hill. She stared at the rundown, tiny ranch house, situated in the clearing at the base of the incline, unafraid. With no stars and miniscule moonlight, she felt secure in the murky darkness, knowing she was practically invisible. At first she had protested against Cleary pulling their trailer up in the tree line, but now she guarded what little privacy she could call her own.

Cleary's employers, the Vanook brothers, were encamped within their own swill inside that ranch, liquored up to a right fine lather. Hopefully they would pass out soon, and it would be safe to go to sleep. Those men frightened her with their leering looks and lurid laughter. Cleary would be no help if they ever moved against her. He had the nature and backbone of a dead rodent.

She'd long ago determined she was no beauty. Meg knew she was painfully thin with limp, pale hair, but still their stares made her uneasy. She wished Cleary had never taken this job and moved them from North Carolina. At least there she had one friend she could run to. Here she had no one. When Meg visited Mama's grave shortly before they'd left, she'd cried, knowing there was no kin left to bring flowers to her mother's grave site. Mama loved flowers.

Meg was all alone in the world. Cleary didn't count. If he'd taken his wife to the hospital when she'd first asked, Mama might be alive today. Meg knew she was wrong to hate the man like she did, but she couldn't help it. Mama always forgave him. She said that's what God wanted her to do. Forgiveness or not, Meg couldn't understand why Mama never left him when he'd repeatedly beat on her. Surely God didn't hold with people being treated like that.

The first chance I get, I'm out of here...once I know of someplace I can hide out until Cleary gives up looking. She believed God was with her, but she wished she could feel His presence. *Why am I here in this mess, Lord? Help!*

Money was another obstacle she had to overcome. Mama had taught her the ills of stealing, but if Meg saw an opportunity to get her hands on Cleary's stash.... Whenever that thought surfaced, it gave her a guilty twinge, no matter how often she told herself that she'd earned most of that money. Cleary worked her like a slave and treated her no better than a cur dog.

Feeling the chill of the cold mountain temperature penetrate beyond her skin, Meg looked up the hill and the meager warmth she knew existed inside the back cabin bedroom. Wretched as it was, it remained her only refuge. Cleary would have passed out on the front gaucho by now, yet she despised having to go back. Her thoughts wandered to an ideal place where love existed. *Will I ever find such a place?*

Regarding the decrepit, rusty trailer, she remembered her earlier curiosity over why the Vanooks insisted they set up camp in the woods. Meg had waited until the predictable moment when Cleary was half soused. After alcohol loosened his lips, she'd timidly asked why they hadn't pulled the trailer closer to a hook-up for electricity. Asking stupid questions was never tolerated. Mostly he said it was none of her business.

Once asked, Meg had held her breath, unwillingly tensing her body as she waited for the inevitable slap. Stumbling to the gaucho at the front of the trailer, Cleary had waved his fat finger in front of her, his rubbery lips slurring his words, "Incon-spic-uous! You hear me, little miss busybody...incon-spic-uous to pryin' eyes who don't need to know we're even up here." He'd given her a hooded sly wink.

It was then she had known for sure. Cleary wasn't here to do real work—honest work. He was here to make moonshine—back hills hooch. Part of the reason he'd jumped at the idea of moving to Georgia was to get away from those ATF agents who'd been asking questions of all their neighbors. When Mama was alive, she'd kept him from selling it around, though she'd never been able to stop him from making it. Now that Mama was gone, Cleary did as he pleased, with no apologies.

What bothered Meg even more was his other job, the secret one that he'd run off to whenever the top boss called, whoever he was. Cleary and the Vanook brothers would pile into the pickup in the dead of night and load up a tractor, not getting back until almost morning. Meg squared her shoulders and trudged up the hill to the old trailer. *Someday,* she promised herself.

*

Streams of peach and lavender-tinted light pierced though the sides of the blinds when Leslie blinked her eyes open the next morning. She labored to sit up and slip her foot into her orthopedic boot, hobbling over to the window. She peeked between blind slits. Was Clive still out there, or had he left before dawn?

After dressing and drawing a brush through her wavy hair, Leslie made her way to the kitchen and peered through the back window, trying to see if Clive's truck was still parked in the gravel drive. The overgrown foliage between the ranch and the road completely blocked her view. She had no visual confirmation one way or the other. Looking at the empty coffee pot, she had an idea.

Ten minutes later, Leslie pulled on one of Wayne's old jackets from off a hook near the back door. Exiting the house, she experienced a rush of brisk air while slowly making her way along the coarse gravel drive. Her cane dug through the stones to stabilize her steps. Pausing, she listened to the bird song of a morning dove before continuing down the drive.

Gazing upon the crunched form asleep against the cold window glass, Leslie smiled gently. She hunched her chilled shoulders deep inside Wayne's jacket, and stood undecided beside Clive's truck with her knuckles poised inches away from the glass. Still reluctant to wake him, she rapped twice, as softly as possible.

Clive's head jerked away from the glass, and he blinked at her. She held up a large thermos cup of coffee and smiled. He blinked again and extracted his body from his pretzel-like position. Turning on the ignition, he opened the truck window and stretched in his confined place.

Leslie handed the cup through the open window. "Would you like to come inside for a doughnut or something hot?"

Sipping the steaming coffee, he shook his head. "No thanks. I think I'll head home if everything is all right here. I've got a barn to check out this morning." His eyes rested on her. "Any problems last night I don't know about?"

"No," she said, slapping her one arm to keep warm. "Unless you count Boris staring me down outside my own house." It was irritating that a mere dog threatened her on her land. "It was a toss-up to whether I would make it inside the house last night after Ray and Mona left."

"I don't think he'd really hurt you, but I'd keep your cell phone handy in case you're away from the house and get frightened. Wayne told me once that the dog was crazy about butter-flavored popcorn. Wouldn't hurt to keep some handy."

Leslie rolled her eyes. "Butter-flavored popcorn? I'll try to remember that. I have to be honest. The dog freaks me out. I have no way of knowing whether or not he will attack me. Why is he still hanging around? You'd think he held the deed."

Slurping a large gulp, Clive took his time answering. "Personally, I believe he's just missing Wayne. He tolerates me—even obeys me on occasion, but he doesn't trust me enough to come close enough for me to cage him." Clive scratched his head, his mussed hair falling over his forehead. He rubbed his rough, shadowed jaw. "Even if I can manage to cage Boris, I don't know any farmer around here who would take him. They're all afraid of the dog. The other alternative is the pound, and we both know what that means. But if he frightens you too much..." He left his statement open-ended.

Leslie nodded that she understood. It wasn't fair that she was the "heavy" in the situation. "I'd hate to be the one who sends the dog to his death. I'll see if we can cohabit." She looked toward the area where she'd last spotted Boris.

"Call if you need me." Clive shoved the gear into reverse. "I'll get your cup back to you." The truck started to roll backwards.

"Wait, Clive! Listen, I-I appreciate you spending the night outside my ranch, but I really don't see a need. Besides, it made me feel terrible seeing you all huddled inside that cold truck. You must have spent a wretched night."

Clive took another drag of coffee. "I've spent worse." Grinning, he placed his hat on top of his mussed hair. "But thanks for worrying about me, Mother." Tipping his hat, he backed out of the drive at top speed, leaving Leslie to stand open-mouthed in a cloud of dust.

"Mother, is it?" Her tongue rolled the words with an acid flavor. "I try to show kindness and that's what I get," she sputtered. Turning, she picked her way back over the gravel toward the house and her own hot cup of coffee.

8

Getting Settled

LESLIE WAS SEATED ON THE FLOOR, lost in a sea of papers inside Wayne's cluttered office. The file cabinet was in a total mess. It looked as if someone had torn it apart on purpose. Her eyes roamed the tight confines of the compact area. An intricately carved oak gun case was lined with hunting rifles. Wedged between the corner of the room and the gun case was a long, aged mahogany bookcase, approximately three and a half feet high.

Groping for her sandwich plate buried somewhere beneath the debris, she paused when she heard the click of the front door opening. *I locked that door before I came in.*

She used the chipped, old desk for support, pushing up to a standing position. Searching the desk top for the cane she'd placed earlier, Leslie grabbed it in the middle, raising it high to use for a weapon. There were only a handful of people who had keys to the ranch, unless more were out there than she knew about. She remembered Roger handing her an extra set she hadn't been aware of. *There could be others!*

Moving silently toward the French-styled doors opening on the hallway, Leslie walked to the main area of the house, her body ready for action, yet hoping the occasion didn't arise. Seeing no one, she scanned the front room.

Then she heard the clattering of a pot. Edging slowly into the kitchen area, she spotted Henri O' squatted in front of the stove front. Leslie watched the woman remove a large pot from the drawer.

Expelling a long breath, Leslie allowed the cane to slide through her hand to a useable position. "Henri O', you gave me a terrible start! What are you doing here?"

Pushing the drawer closed, Henri O' stood, looking striking in a multi-colored, Indian-styled top. It favored her rich ethnic coloring. "Mrs. Schiller sent me over to fix something nourishing for your supper."

"Something nourishing? Mona Schiller saw all the food I bought yesterday. Does she now think I'm going to starve?" Leslie asked wryly, amused at Mona's overt concern.

"Did you already have lunch, Miss Leslie?"

Leslie's hand ran through her disheveled hair. "It's somewhere in the office. I was looking for it when you came in."

Henri O's expression was indiscernible. Her curious gaze lifted first to the kitchen clock registering 2:00 p.m. and then to the sink with unwashed breakfast dishes.

Seeing this, Leslie winced and hurried to explain. "I planned on putting them all in the dishwasher after lunch," she said, suddenly feeling defensive and cross.

"Yes'm. I'll get started on the vegetable soup I planned on making, if there's nothing else?"

Leslie stammered, "Ah—ah no. Actually vegetable soup sounds great. I'm just sorry you're forced to do double duty, Henri O'. Especially when there's really no need."

"No problem, Miss Leslie. I have an easy roast on right now, cooking away at Miss Schiller's, and the truth is, I work a certain number of hours each day, no matter what I do."

"Fine. Let me know if I can be of help. I'll be in Wayne's office sorting out a few things." She leaned briefly on her cane before making her way back to the office where she stared down at the paper collage, trying to remember where she had previously been sitting. It was her point of organization.

Once she was back on the floor, she parted the papers until she found the forgotten sandwich. Scanning the doorway like a fugitive, Leslie wolfed down her sandwich. All too vividly, she remembered Henri O's condescending manner in respect to her kitchen abilities. Finishing, she wiped her mouth on the sleeve of her purple sweatshirt. She knew Mona was thinking of her health, but Henri O' cooking for her was over the top. It magnified Leslie's feelings of ineptness and made her indebted. She would have to find a way to convey her feelings, without offending Mona's generosity.

In an absentminded gesture, she lifted the empty sandwich plate to the edge of the desk, centering her thinking on Wayne's papers. Roger Galbraith had given her every deed and official document that belonged to Wayne, but Leslie was looking for something deeper—anything that might shed light on some of the odd occurrences happening on site. She desperately wanted to believe they were harmless accidents. It would ease her mind, if she chose to sell.

The selling part wasn't as clear in her mind as when she first arrived. Everything seemed more complicated. She bit her lip in consternation, not wanting to delve too deeply. Leslie never heard Henri O's footfalls entering the office. The brooding presence of the young woman was no more than a few inches away when Leslie first noticed her.

"Have you found any of the family journals yet? Mr. Wayne was right proud of all his family's writings. *'This is history in the making,'* he used to say," quoted Henri O'.

Leslie probed Henri O's impassive features. "I wasn't aware you knew my cousin so well."

"Not nearly as well as my father. Mr. Wayne would spend hours talking about all kinds of stuff with Pa."

Leslie smiled up at the woman, momentarily stunned that they were actually having a conversation. "I didn't know that. It's very interesting."

Nodding silently, Henri O' turned as if she meant to leave the room. Stopping after a few steps, she swiveled back. "Miss Leslie, I don't think Mr. Wayne's death was an accident. I just thought you should know that."

"Why not?" Leslie's voice was a mere whisper.

Henri O's dark eyes smoldered. "Because it makes no sense. Mr. Wayne's back and legs were hurting him so bad, he could barely climb into the Jeep. He would never have climbed up on that tractor of his, let alone drive clear up that small mountain of a hill that sits back of his big barn. My pa doesn't think so either."

Rising up on her knees, Leslie asked, "Did you mention that to the sheriff after my cousin died?"

"The sheriff." She waved in condescension. "He'd already made up his mind about what happened. He wrote his ideas down in his record book and left. Pa said we had no proof that Mr. Wayne didn't die from an accident, so I kept my mouth shut."

Leslie was flooded with questions. "Why are you telling me this now?"

Henri O's features closed back up. For an instant, Leslie thought she might leave without answering, but the slow voice finally spoke. "Because you are Mr. Wayne's only family. At first I wasn't sure about you. Truth be told, I still haven't fully made up my mind. But when I heard about you checking into the weird happenings, I thought you ought to know about Mr. Wayne."

As she turned, Leslie called out, "Henri O', wait. Do the Schillers and Mr. Clive believe that theory about Wayne's death too?"

Henri O's hooded eyes stared back at her, but the hint of a smile formed on her mouth. Nodding silently, she walked back to the kitchen.

Sitting amidst the volley of papers, Leslie's shoulders slumped. Her thoughts went crazy tying to assimilate the idea that Wayne's death was not an accident. It made her cold all over. *If what Henri O' said is true, the accidents didn't begin with my arrival. Why didn't Mona or Clive tell me their thoughts on this?*

Even as the question arose, the answer was evident. Leslie had repeatedly vocalized her refusal to believe a planned attempt had been made upon her life. Had that kept her on the outside of their confidence? Even now, with this new information about Wayne, she still fought the idea there was actual danger directed at her personally. *I just don't see a reason. Things don't happen without a reason.*

As her thoughts returned to the mess she'd created, Leslie formed new plans. Her original goal had been to discover the truth—to uncover anything that would give rational reasons to unanswered questions and make her world comfortable...but what if there weren't any? She also wanted Roger to prove to be nothing more than an aggressive lawyer. He had a pleasing way about him. Thinking of all the lawyer jokes she'd heard, Leslie might have smiled if her thoughts were less serious. She resolved to make new goals. The first was to keep an open mind and see where her searching took her...whatever the results. Hurriedly, she gathered the loose papers into a neat pile. These were areas that could wait. Hefting her body to a standing position, she used her cane to walk into the kitchen.

Henri O' was cutting carrots up into the boiling mass swirling in the pot.

"It smells good," Leslie said, pointing to the stove.

"Not yet, but it will be in a few minutes. Wait until I add my herbs and spices."

The cook focused on her chore as Leslie moved closer, leaning against the counter. "Henri O', you mentioned the family journals. Do you have any idea where they might be found?"

Reaching for a stalk of celery, Henri O' shifted to regard Leslie with new interest. "He told Pa he'd bought a special bookcase to keep them all together. I think he kept it either in his office, or maybe his bedroom at one time. I don't know about now."

"That's where I'll begin my search." The impassiveness on Henri O's face lingered, causing Leslie to speculate what the woman might be thinking. Was there more she wasn't telling? It was like she was pointing her in a specific direction, like one would give a dog a scent to track.

Instinct told Leslie that pressuring this quirky personality for answers wouldn't gain the right results. The woman didn't fully trust her. Leslie was learning there were times when it was best to remain silent and observe. Retreating from the kitchen, she directed her steps down the hall leading to Wayne's bedroom—the first area of search.

*

Later that night Leslie sat in bed, a stack of old journals situated beside her, some of them so old they were encased within new leather sleeves, the edges taped together. If the brittle condition of their covers was any indication of age, they could be the oldest of the lot. The newer books were labeled by year and author. Not all of the previous ranch owners had kept a journal, but those predisposed had written prolifically. Leslie flipped open the last red-covered, leather-bound book, finding Wayne's name clearly inscribed inside the cover. First date listed was late fall, the year Wayne arrived in Dahlonega to take over the ranch from his dying brother.

Wayne had written several accounts recounting his ongoing shock over the staggering amount of work required to run the ranch. Sore and exhausted every night, he'd come close to throwing in the towel. As a retired Detroit policeman, Wayne had no idea what it took to manage a ranch the size and caliber of Riker's Ranch. It was hard for Leslie to imagine this was the same man she'd met a few years earlier, who ran this ranch like a finely tuned watch.

Leslie skipped several pages, noticing her cousin's gradual change of attitude. He'd thrown himself into the throes of operating the cattle ranch, from management level down to the stable boy. In the evenings, Wayne spoke of sitting with his brother, gleaning whatever the poor man was up to sharing.

Closing the cover, Leslie rubbed her eyes. Finding out that Wayne, like she, had come to the ranch as an absolute stranger out of his element, was a comfort. She blinked at the closed journal, trying to decide whether it would be more beneficial to read a few of the earlier records before concentrating on the latest legacy. There was too much input.

Her eyes gravitated to the clock on the night stand. 9:00 p.m. was an acceptable time to retire in the country, if only her restless spirit was ready to retire as well. She'd had a full day to adjust to living in the ranch alone, but it would take longer to adjust to the total silence at night. She was tempted to turn on a radio to fill the void.

In the end it was her curiosity that motivated her out of bed, through the large house to the back breezeway beyond the kitchen. Pulling the curtain to the side of the door window, she peered outside, her focus centered on one particular area.

True to his word, Ray Schiller had changed the bulb in the outside lamp, its beams of light extending up to a thirty-foot radius. Leslie was interested mainly in one section under the roof extension of the tool shed beyond the garage. Was the dish of food she'd placed there for Boris still full? Would he approach when he thought it safe?

Why do I even care? she asked herself. Did she hope it would make him less of a threat, or did she really have a soft spot for this dog? *Ridiculous!* She was a kind person at heart, that's all. Boris had lost his only connection to human affection when Wayne died; yet he still hung around. *Is he hoping to connect with someone else?*

At that moment Leslie spied a reflection of light through the overgrown foliage between the ranch and the road. It wasn't a headlight—more like the yard light bouncing off something shiny, like a chrome bumper maybe? *Is Clive sitting out in my driveway again tonight?*

Her hand reached for the doorknob. "This has got to stop. He can't stay up every night guarding my house. There's no reason." But instead of turning the knob and walking out into the night to confront the man, Leslie stopped. Instead, she walked back through the house even as she drew out her cell phone.

"Mona? Is Clive's truck babysitting my house again? Someone is out there."

Leslie paused in the long hallway listening to Mona's reply through the speaker phone, "That's not Clive out there, Leslie. It's one of his ranch hands, working overtime. You might as well give up convincing Clive that there is no unseen danger. He believes otherwise. Let it go, Leslie! If you've got a plan to figure out what's going on, you'd better be trotting it out soon. Now get some rest and quit worrying."

Leaning against the wall, Leslie remained in the silent shadows as long minutes past. Mona was right. Something needed to be done. Not knowing what, if anything, of a dark nature was going on at the ranch placed everyone in the neighborhood at a disadvantage. For some reason Clive felt a need to protect her, while Mona insisted she have nourishing food. It made Leslie uncomfortable, reminding her of things she'd worked four years to forget. *Those years after Mama died when everyone protected and coddled me.*

A small smile played upon her lips. "They act just like you, Dad," she murmured. They also reminded her of the members of the small church she'd grown up in. *"A church family takes care of one another."* How often had she heard those words spoken?

Leslie brought her thoughts back to the present.

Tomorrow, she'd take a ride in the country. Ever since that day on Rocky Ridge with Clive, she'd had a nagging question. Maybe she would find an answer when she explored tomorrow. It was also a good time to try out the Jeep in the garage. Leslie went back to her room and bed, pitying the ranch hand stuck outside in the cold truck.

*

Still in her nightshirt and striped pants, Leslie maneuvered her hot coffee in one hand, while making her way to the backdoor in the breezeway. She squinted through the morning light to the tool shed. The dog's food was still there. She thought she'd heard barking earlier. Was that what had awakened her so early? She couldn't be sure.

Leslie turned in frustration. Staring at the dish wasn't going to make the dog materialize anytime soon. *What if putting out food didn't work? Maybe Boris doesn't like what I left for him?* How was she going to connect with this fierce animal and live in the same space? Leslie hobbled back to the kitchen. The ankle was stiffer in the morning.

Even in the short time she had been around Dahlonega, the mornings had grown increasingly cooler. Leslie dressed in jeans and layered a sweatshirt over a long-sleeved top. After breakfast, she gathered her large bag and her long-range camera. She found the Jeep keys on the back board in the breezeway, alongside the various tractor keys. All other keys had been handed to her by Roger on the day she signed the legal papers.

Roger's late-night call the night before had been awkward in several areas, leaving her unsettled. He wasn't thrilled about her being at the ranch by herself, citing her injured foot as a major reason. She had to draw on her resolve to stand her ground, giving him almost the same speech she'd given Mona, keeping her personal reasons just that—personal. When the ranch wrinkle was worked out, their easy talk centered mostly on daily affairs, though Leslie felt it escalated far too fast into a personal nature. It made her nervous and wary.

It alarmed her that Roger's attentions were becoming more intense. She was uncertain exactly how to balance their relationship. In all honesty Leslie didn't know her true feelings concerning the lawyer—or trust his. There was a certain amount of attraction, but she'd been unable to allow herself the luxury to discover where the attraction could lead. Besides, her life was too uncertain to even contemplate romance.

There was way too much unknown gray area about Mr. Roger Galbraith. *How can I maintain a safe balance until I find out the whole truth about Riker Ranch?* Her thoughts were troubled as she locked the back door.

Embracing the brisk morning air, she pulled the sweatshirt hood over her free-flowing hair. Protected against the stiff wind, Leslie now centered her attention on the garage, a ripple of delight racing through her. She'd always wanted her own Jeep, ever since her teen years. She'd even considered purchasing one while still living in New York. The closed garage was a short walk from the house, and a hair's breadth from the tool shed. The garage structure was ancient but solid looking.

Lifting a separate keychain from her sweatshirt pocket, she was surprised to find it unnecessary. The door lock hung loose. "Strange." Leslie lifted the lever and swung the heavy wood door far enough open that she'd be able to back out the Jeep. Whoever ended up with the ranch would no doubt replace this structure with a modern garage. "But until then..." She gave the heavy door an extra hard shove.

Leslie glanced over at the wooden tool shed to find the dog dish empty of food. She was elated. "Well. Well!" *Boris snuck out and cleaned up the food while I dressed.* Whether she'd be able to establish a coexisting relationship remained to be seen. She wondered if Boris was somewhere near and braced herself against a sharp gust of wind.

Centering her focus back on the garage, Leslie ventured inside its darkened interior. She switched on the weak fluorescent overhead, scanning the rough walls. This structure was barely large enough to house one car. It had been on site a long time—perhaps as far back as the early part of the twentieth century. There was no evidence what its original function might have been, except at some point, it had been turned into a garage.

Shifting, Leslie's warm gaze rested on the vehicle itself. "Oh my!" This old motorized veteran had seen a great deal of use—at least thirty years or more. Her red finish had long been dulled by harsh weather and cross-country use.

She patted the dingy canvas cover. "Well, old girl, it's you and me now." It had been a long time since Leslie had driven a manual transmission, and never one straight out of the archives. Hopefully the experience would come back to her sooner, rather than later. Her eyes ventured to the cracked upholstery, obviously patched with a great amount of care. *Wayne must have loved this old Jeep.*

Sliding behind the wheel, Leslie's whole attention focused on the outdated dashboard in front of her. This adventure wasn't going to be easy. Maybe she should have had Ray Schiller walk her through a crash course first.

She made sure the gear was in park, wishing the garage had windows and better lighting. Next she examined each knob, trying to acquaint herself with its specific function. After squinting at the gear shift, Leslie drew the key from her pocket.

I have a perfectly good car sitting out in the drive. Why am I even bothering? She smiled to herself, fingering the key. *Because this is my private adventure and worth the challenge. And where I'm going, I'll need a four-wheel drive.*

The ignition was behind the wheel on the steering column, entirely different from what Leslie was used to. Cranking it to the right, she found it stubborn and uncooperative. The motor was sluggish, not wanting to turn over. *Maybe I should have followed Roger's advice about a tune-up.* She tried again. This time the engine sputtered encouragingly. On the third try, it roared to life. Savoring this slight success, some of the tension left her neck and shoulder muscles. Easing her foot off the pedal, Leslie leaned her head back and tried to be patient. Dad always allowed an old engine, especially one that had sat dormant, to warm up before attempting to drive it. Said it worked out the kinks.

Pulling at her sweatshirt collar, Leslie was suddenly overly warm. The stuffiness in the garage was stifling. There was no telling how long this Jeep had sat unused. As the engine idled, she grew impatient, imaging what it would be like driving those back trails on the ranch in her own Jeep. The afternoon she'd spent in Clive's truck had been thrilling, whetting her appetite for this moment. Her throat felt scratchy. She coughed.

Anxious to leave the garage, Leslie sat forward to shift into reverse. Clearing her throat, she swallowed hard, sensing an unnatural closeness that hadn't been present before. She coughed again, tasting exhaust fumes—even more alarming. She blinked, finding it difficult to read the dials. *Where had all the light and cool air gone?*

Suddenly fearful, Leslie glanced in the rearview mirror, feeling an alarm resound in her head. The garage door was shut! How and when had that happened? The wind. Seeing the rising fog of exhaust around her, she knew there was no time to lose.

Leslie was angry and resentful about the delay the closed door represented. She awkwardly climbed out of the Jeep and hobbled back to push it open, even more irritated to find the ancient door stuck. *It won't budge! The timing couldn't be worse!* With the exhaust growing heavy inside the garage, she didn't have time to spare working on it now. *First things first. I'll turn off the Jeep and allow the air to clear.*

As she rushed back to the Jeep, her ankle ached in protest against the hard pounding across the cement floor. She reached across the seat, grunted, and yanked out the key. With the key in her hand, Leslie stood staring in disbelief at the shuddering vehicle. The engine was still racing! "Impossible!" she exclaimed. She covered her mouth to suppress repeated coughs. Her heart beat wildly, choking back the bile of panic.

Leslie slid all the way inside the Jeep and reinserted the key, twisting it back and forth, but nothing seemed to disconnect the engine. There was no explaining it. She didn't believe it; yet it was happening! How could it be? Her hands flew to her head in stark terror. Tension gripped the muscles in her neck in a stranglehold, and her throat felt full, like it was closing off. *I've got to get some air in here fast—the door!* Somehow she had to open that door. It was her only hope.

Hopping out of the Jeep on her one good foot, she raced to the door, ignoring the pain. Leslie pushed and yanked on the handle with her whole weight. She even tried rocking the massive door inward and outward. Surely it would give way. *Why won't it budge?*

Horrified, Leslie remembered the outside latch. Had it somehow slipped back in place? *Am I locked inside this tomb?* Her coughing was coming in convulsive spurts. She couldn't stop, and her thoughts seemed murky. Pounding on the door with her fists, Leslie tried to scream, but the coughing wracked her throat. *Get a grip. Keep calm...try to think.* She was losing hope. *Who will hear me?*

Despairing as she watched the rising fog, Leslie had her back to the door when she heard something on the other side of the thick panel. Had someone heard her pounding? But as she pressed her ear to the door, her hopeful expectancy crashed in disappointment. *Barking?* That dog was outside. Her numbed mind was close to tears. She needed a human, someone to help her.

Pushing her body from the door, she forged back toward the Jeep. *If I could get the car in gear, maybe I could back straight through the door. Why didn't I think of it before?* Doubt clouded the feasibility of that action even as she moved forward. Where was her strength? Her arms and her legs weren't acting right. They felt rubbery. Leslie could barely see the outline of the Jeep. She would die inside this structure! *Did God know? Was He here? Would He help her?*

"Why should He?" an accusing voice hissed. Her thoughts were a pitiful jumble making no sense.

Her fists tightened in a feeble attempt to clear her mind of this paralyzing feeling. The whole garage was a gray cloud. *I'm losing control!* Her body suddenly went rigid with panic, causing a short burst of energy. Leslie stumbled back to the door, pounding and screeching.

The sound choked in her throat. Her ankle throbbed. She slid to the garage floor, still battering against the rough, dense wooden barrier. Seconds passed, and her fist grew limp, followed slowly by the rest of her body. As Leslie slipped helplessly unconscious, she heard a faraway clanking and the ever persistent barking of a dog.

*

Leslie gasped, striving to breathe, feeling wet and so very cold. Shivering, she blinked against a blinding brightness—the sun. Her blurry eyes made out a murky image. Henri O' frowned down at her. She winced and drew her head away.

"Wake up, Miss Leslie. Breathe deep," the cook ordered, shaking her shoulders gently.

Inhaling only brought about more coughing. Leslie pushed her body upward, still coughing, but now able to see Henri O' clearly. "Why am I all wet?" she asked hoarsely.

"Whew!" Henri O' rubbed her forehead with the back of her wrist. "You're all wet because I emptied my water bottle over you, trying to get you to wake up. I also gave you CPR."

Leslie groaned softly and regarded the woman kneeling in front of her. Her brows narrowed. "Why are you here?"

"Miss Mona sent me over with those fresh eggs she promised you. When I drove up, that big ugly mutt was scratching and barking furiously at the garage door. I wasn't sure at first if he would let me get near enough to find out what he was barking at. I heard pounding on the door and smelled fumes coming from underneath the door. You scared me big time. That crazy car is still running! Why did you turn it on with the door closed?"

Leslie struggled to clear her throat, coughing. "I didn't close the door. The wind…must have blown it closed." She felt the cold wind stabbing against her wet clothes.

Henri O' stared at the garage, her face scrunched in doubt. "That's a pretty heavy door to blow closed."

The truth of the statement lay heavy in an unspoken look between the women as Clive's truck roared up in the drive. It barely slammed to a sudden stop before Mona jumped out of the passenger side. Clive was yet climbing out of the driver's side.

"Bring that oxygen unit with you, Clive," Mona called back to him.

Leslie stared up at Henri O'.

"I called Miss Mona once I saw you were breathing again," said Henri O', standing to her feet, answering Leslie's unasked question.

"Is someone going to tell me how this happened?" Mona knelt beside Leslie. Pulling out her stethoscope, she placed it on Leslie's wet shirt. "Breathe."

"I am," said Leslie. "And I don't need that—that oxygen 'thingamajig.'"

"I'll be the judge of that. I keep it on hand for special home assignments."

Coughing, Leslie murmured, "You haven't had many of those lately."

Mona placed the mouth apparatus in place. "No, I've been a little busy."

Twisting her head to speak, Leslie tried to laugh but was unable to quit coughing. "Surely, not with me around," she said dryly.

Mona put the apparatus back in place. "Lie still and inhale a few times."

After waiting to learn of Leslie's condition, Clive rushed by them into the garage. When he returned a few minutes later, the motor had ceased running and his jaw was tight. "I had to go under the hood and pull the distributor coil to turn it off. I'll call someone and have the Jeep towed into the shop."

Mona continued to listen to Leslie's chest. Nodding, she reached up and removed the breathing apparatus. "Well! I'm still waiting to find out what happened."

Leslie raised a limp arm. "Like he said…the engine wouldn't turn off." She coughed, her voice gaining strength. "I pulled the key, and the Jeep kept running." Her hand unconsciously felt her jean pocket for the outline of the key to reassure herself.

"Henri O' said you were unconscious. Did you sit inside the car too long, or what? " Clive's gaze roamed from Leslie to Henri O' in obvious confusion.

"The garage door was closed and latched when I arrived." Henri O' retold the story she'd related to Leslie. "That dog barking his head off by the door got my attention. He was telling me Miss Leslie was inside." She shook her head. "I wouldn't have believed it from that wild beast. Then I smelled the exhaust coming from the garage and heard pounding on the inside of the door."

Clive's hands were jammed on his hips, his jaw ridged. He pierced Leslie with a look. "Don't you know anything about a car? Remind me to give you a lesson before your next brush with death. Did you see anyone around outside this morning—anything?" Scanning the surrounding area, he squinted as if prying into crevices.

Leslie ignored his remark about her lack of car technology. Nothing made sense anyway—the door, the engine that wouldn't stop. "All I know is I suddenly noticed how dark it was inside the garage. When I looked in the mirror, I discovered the door had somehow closed. I thought it was the wind and the door was stuck, but when it wouldn't open..." She frowned. "The bizarre fact the engine didn't turn off when I pulled the key blew my mind!" She coughed again. "I panicked when that happened. Somehow I made it back to the door and kept pounding. That's when I heard the dog barking on the outside. I can't remember much of anything else."

Leslie scanned the area. "Speaking of Boris, where he'd go?" The fact this wild dog alerted help was beyond her, yet why else had he continued to bark? He'd smelled the fumes. Her hands went to her fuzzy feeling head. She was tired of thinking.

Mona placed her finger over Leslie's mouth. "Enough for now. The rest will keep."

"I saw no one but the dog when I arrived, Mr. Clive," Henri O' offered. "Miss Leslie suggested the wind blew the door closed while she was in the Jeep."

Mona stared at them. "Clive, why couldn't Leslie push the door open?"

Clive pursed his lips. "When you shut that old wooden door, the latch sometimes falls into place. It's unlikely, but that could have happened...if the wind was incredibly strong, if the door actually blew closed."

All eyes went to Clive. Mona stood. "You don't think that's what happened, do you?"

Clive heaved his bulky shoulders and walked over to the garage door, its wood weathered from age and neglect. He took hold of the door, moving it back and forth in place. It moved with some resistance. Turning back to face the group, he called back, "I can't say for sure. I'm no engineer. The Jeep engine is another matter." He shook his head as if he wasn't convinced.

Returning to the group, he told Leslie, "It could be just a series of major malfunctions—or not. Nevertheless, I think we should let the police know what happened today. There's been a lot of 'accidents' lately—too many for comfort."

Leslie deflated in disappointment. She'd had such exciting plans for the morning. As Mona and Clive helped her to her feet, she winced. After a few wobbly steps, she felt secure enough to walk on her own.

"How do you feel about going to the clinic to be checked out?" Mona offered her suggestion as if she already knew the answer.

"I'm fine." Leslie cleared her voice as if to prove her point.

Clive herded them toward the ranch. "Then let's get inside. We'll have to wait for the police to arrive anyway. Henri O', if you'd make us all some coffee I would deeply appreciate it. Meanwhile, I'll get a hold of Evan and have him take over that project I'd planned on working on this morning."

Leslie shook her head. "There's no reason for you to waste your entire morning on what was probably an accident. Make a few phone calls and go home."

"Ah yes—*another* accident?" He held out his hand. "Your house keys, Leslie. Mine are home on my dresser."

She looked around, and her hands went to her head. "Oh. My keys must be inside my bag still in the Jeep, along with my camera and what all."

He shot her a questioning look. "You were planning quite a morning."

"I'll get them. You help her inside," offered Mona, sprinting back toward the garage.

The rest of the group started toward the breezeway door. Mona rejoined them with Leslie's bag. Clive took the keys and opened the door for the others. The three women filed inside in sober silence. Reaching the kitchen first, Mona pulled out a chair and indicated for Leslie to sit. "Before coffee, would you please fix Leslie a strong cup of black tea, Henri O'? It will help open up her lungs."

Turning aside, Clive pulled out his cell phone. Leslie couldn't help but hear him speaking with the police department. It gave her mixed feelings. While she had doubts about the wind closing the heavy door, she didn't want to spend hours answering questions she didn't know the answers to.

One emotion was still fresh enough to make her relive those moments. The fear she experienced when she couldn't get the door open, and the helpless feeling of losing consciousness. She shuddered, trying to reconnect her thoughts to Mona's latest comment. "Yes, thank you. I would like some sweetener in that tea, Mona."

*

Leslie sat in the same kitchen chair in a near stupor while Mona saw the sergeant out to the garage. Rarely in her life had she felt more misunderstood—even stupid. At some point she'd lost track of how many times she kept saying, "I don't know."

The Dahlonega sergeant seemed to find it hard to believe that she hadn't noticed the door was closed sooner.

"Because I was trying to figure out how to operate the Jeep," she'd explained.

"Why would you simply allow the engine to run inside the garage?"

"Because I wanted the engine to warm up. It was hard to start. I wasn't anticipating the door closing."

The entire inquisition replayed in her mind. Near the end, the sergeant had gone so far as to ask if she had been depressed lately. Thankfully, both Mona and Clive had rushed to her defense, citing two other "questionable accidents" prior to the garage incident.

"Were these incidents reported?" Sergeant Ford asked.

Glances were exchanged.

"No," Clive admitted. "Although I've since had serious doubts about the first barn accident. It happened the day Leslie arrived on the property and was injured." He pointed to her fractured foot. "I found suspicious markings, staved-in boot indentations in the area where the boards supposedly broke through."

"But you didn't report it?"

"No, I informed Miss Weldon, but she believed it to be an accident at the time." He glanced at her.

"I see. And the second barn incident?"

"From what Leslie told me I had suspicions about how the hay trap door would release in such a manner, but when I went the next morning to investigate, I found nothing to indicate foul play," he explained.

"Our handyman, George, told me he saw a strange car drive down this way right after dark that same night," Mona offered. She looked at Clive. "I forgot to tell you."

The sergeant's writing hand paused briefly as though he were considering what she'd said. He finished writing and summed everything up with a shrug. "I'll write up a report and keep it on file in case anything else is uncovered, but I have to be honest. There isn't enough evidence here to push through an investigation." He turned to Clive. "Give me a call when the mechanic is through going through that Jeep. I'd be interested in knowing why the ignition wouldn't shut off. I've heard of such things happening to Jeeps of that vintage but never experienced one myself. I'd like to know if I'm right. Never did like loose ends." His smile was reserved. "I think I have all I need today.

"Miss Weldon, you've had a very rocky start on this ranch. I understand you're new to the area. I can't urge you enough to go carefully from now on. Your neighbors here seem willing to help. I'd take them up on their offer. Serious accidents happen on ranches all the time." His brows narrowed. "Is this the same ranch where the old man was found at the bottom of a ravine alongside his tractor two months ago?"

"That was my cousin, Wayne Riker," Leslie said tiredly.

The sergeant's stare seemed locked in place. "Interesting." He put on his hat before starting for the door. "I'd like to look over the accident scene now."

Nodding, Mona accompanied him outside.

Leslie pushed up from the chair her body had felt glued to the last half hour. To Henri O', she murmured, "If you hadn't come right when you did..."

Henri O's stoic expression softened. "Miss Mona would say that was God's timing, Miss Leslie. I'm glad I was here today. I only wish I could have been there the day Mr. Wayne..."

Clive caught Leslie's eye. "God sent His angels to keep you safe more than once the last two weeks. He must have definite plans for you. If I were you, I'd take the time to ask what they might be. I'll wait outside for the tow truck before I head home." He turned to leave, then pivoted back. "If you want to take a ride, call me, okay? I mean it, Leslie. This was too close for comfort this morning."

Clive's words made her uneasy. Leslie was still thinking on what he'd said, about God having plans for her, remembering that moment in the garage when her life was in question. *Maybe God was there today...and maybe...?*

Mona burst into the kitchen with her usual energy. "Well, ladies, I say we celebrate life today. I vote we call our own personal holiday. Leslie, you were going to take Wayne's Jeep for a ride. Would my little truck do for a substitute? I can ride back to my place with Henri O' and come pick you up with my truck. Henri O', when you get back to the ranch, take a few hours off today. Do anything you want, as long as we have dinner tonight." Mona's chin firmed as she glanced at Leslie. "And Miss Leslie will be joining us." Her expression conveyed no arguments.

Leslie's head whirled with the speed Mona's ideas came spilling out. Though still feeling more than a little shaky, she didn't want to be alone. "Okay, it's a deal," she said brightly. "Can that truck go across country? I'd offer my SUV, but it isn't a four-wheel drive. It just looks good."

Mona grinned. "No problem, we'll take my truck. It's no mountain goat, but it will go across country within reason."

"Fine. I'll go put on a fresh pair of jeans. I feel a little grubby after that garage ordeal." Reflecting briefly, she was suddenly glad for the distraction of the outing. The fear of the locked garage was still too close for comfort.

Mona shot her a parting warning. "Lock your doors, Leslie."

Leslie felt the impact of her friend's message. She was trying not to be paranoid. *Like the sergeant said, accidents happen every day on a ranch.*

9

Back Trails

LESLIE'S ANKLE PAIN SHOT UP HER LEG when she hopped up into Mona's truck. Gritting her teeth, she determined to keep that information to herself. She refused to give Mona a reason to cancel their outing. The goal for the day remained the same, to satisfy her nagging question, and not think about her earlier brush with death. Straightening herself in the seat, she noticed a covered basket on the floor behind the driver's seat. "What's that?"

Mona laughed. "Check your watch. I don't know about you, lady, but I don't plan on missing lunch. Henri O' packed us some sandwiches before she left."

"What were her plans?" Leslie was curious about Henri O's private life.

A smile spread across Mona's face. "She didn't exactly say, but I noticed she was packing a separate lunch in a smaller basket. My guess would be that Henri O' was going on a picnic of her own."

Leslie raised her eyebrows. "What? Do you think she and this Evan, the one who works for Clive, are having a picnic together?"

"Could be? Clive has a cozy, park-like area at one corner of his ranch. It even has a small waterfall and pond. You should ask Clive to show it to you sometime."

Leslie threw her a warning look. "Don't start, Mona. Just drive on."

Mona grinned. "I'm waiting for instructions. I gather you have a destination in mind?" Her eyes probed for a deeper answer than a direction to drive.

"Yes I do." Leslie stared at the lane leading up by the barn and beyond, to the back trails of the ranch. "Do you know how to get to Rocky Ridge?"

"Certainly, I've been there often. Don't tell me you're planning on walking back up that hill, because this little truck and I will have no part of that plan," Mona said sternly.

"No, I just want a second look at the country in that area. Will that be acceptable, Nurse Mona?" she asked with a wry grin.

Mona shook her head. Shifting the gear into reverse, she turned the truck upward of the lane toward the barn. "What's so interesting out there?"

"That's what I want to find out." Leslie studied her friend's face. "Did you really want to play hooky with me today and go for a ride, or is it a devious plan to keep an eye on me and make sure I'm all right?"

"I can honestly say I wanted to play hooky today. Of course, while you're with me, I know you're out of trouble for a short period."

The sun had nearly reached the vertical position in the sky, bathing the countryside in warmth and vitality. Once again, the rugged beauty of this land incited Leslie's emotions. Her body was revved, ready for adventure.

Mona's truck hugged the curving trails all the way to Rocky Ridge. As they climbed out of the truck, Leslie remembered the day she and Clive had stood in almost this exact place. The memory of Clive lifting her from the ground and climbing that rocky hill still caused her to catch her breath.

"I have to park back a short distance. This truck is built low. Can you walk to the base of that hill?"

Mona's voice scattered Leslie's thoughts about Clive and realigned her purpose for coming here. She nodded. Spotting a good place to sit down, she helped Mona gather the lunch fixings. Once Mona had mentioned the thick-sliced ham sandwiches resting in the bottom of the basket, Leslie's mouth had started salivating in expectation. Her morning toast and coffee had worn thin after the scary episode in the garage.

Throwing extra jackets on the ground, the women sat in the sun, letting the gusty wind blow free through their hair. Holding her half-eaten sandwich in her hand, Leslie squinted at the landscape directly across from Rocky Ridge. "Do you ever get tired of watching the changing color across the valleys and mountains?"

Mona stopped eating and regarded the young woman next to her. "Either this country is beginning to get to you, or you have the heart of a poet, Leslie Weldon—maybe even an artist. They see the world through colored lenses and descriptive words."

Sitting straight, Leslie cleared her throat. "Once maybe…a long time ago, I was interested in art. But there's little security for a steady paycheck in that line, unless you start at the top, so I chose computers. My last job was for an advertising agency. I would never have made a good nurse, like you."

"And how did computers work for you?"

"I made a living…or was making a living until I was let go a few weeks ago." Her tone was matter-of-fact. "Advertising contracts were at an all-time low, and our finance manager wanted to show a profit on paper to the boss, so…"

Mona frowned. "Are you going to look for another computer job when you get back?" she asked, ending a bottle of water.

Leslie took her time answering. "I suppose..."

"So, is there a reason you wanted to drive way out here?" Mona eyed her with interest.

"Do you know what's on the other side of this valley stretching to that low line of trees?" Leslie pointed across from Rocky Ridge.

Picking up a plastic bag filled with celery and baby carrots, Mona squinted against the bright sun. "Honestly, I can't tell you what's on the other side of that small ridge past the tree line." Twisting her head to the side, she followed the landscape line, pointing off to the left. "But I know a little of what's over there."

Leslie leaned closer, her interest growing. "Can we get there with the truck? If we reached that point, we could follow close to the tree line and find out where it leads."

"What? Across country?" Mona stared in the direction with a troubled expression. "We could try…if we take it easy over the rugged parts. But if it gets too rough, I'll have to turn back. Like I said, my truck is no mountain goat."

Leslie nodded. "Understandable! I don't want you to tear up your truck. Let's finish up here and get started."

"Not until I eat that leftover coffeecake I saw Henri O' stick in the basket for us."

Laughing, Leslie reached out her hand. As she chewed the yummy cake, she surveyed the valley in the area they'd be traveling. No longer hungry, and anxious to get inside Mona's truck and underway, she began cleaning up their sandwich wrappings. "Almost ready?" she prodded Mona.

"I guess I'd better be." Mona pushed the last of her cake in her mouth.

While buckling up their seatbelts, Mona gave Leslie a discerning glance. "Am I wrong, or do you have a plan rattling around inside that active brain of yours? Tell me there's a reason my little truck is going for a rocky ride."

Leslie tried to organize her thoughts. "Remember when Clive and I returned from our trek up Rocky Ridge? He found machinery tracks high on the ridge, but I don't sense he told me everything—probably didn't want me to worry. I know something has been happening up in that end of the wooded area, and I want to know what."

Her thoughts were coming fast. "It didn't make sense to me that Wayne made the tracks, especially after learning about his painful condition this last year. If those accounts are true, there's no way he could've ridden up there on his tractor without Ray or Clive knowing. It's much too far from the ranch. So I've been trying to figure out how anyone with a tractor got up there. That's why I wanted to see what lay across the valley. It seemed the logical point to begin."

Mona inhaled. "If it will make you feel better, Ray and Clive have been talking on that theory too. Unfortunately, they've had little time left over after long days of work. And that big rain we had a few days ago pretty much blurred anything except what Clive found the day he was with you on the ridge."

"Why didn't anyone tell me they were checking things out?" Strangely, it bothered her more that Clive had kept those things from her than Mona.

Mona shook her head. "Come on, Leslie, you've wanted to believe everything was an accident."

"I did, I know," she said slowly. "It's all been so very confusing! Why, even this morning could have been an accident. There has been no real proof! And if I can't find a motive, I'll never get a handle on what's happening. That's what bugs me most! I know of no reason why someone would want me dead," she added soberly.

"Yet, with all those unresolved issues, you've mounted this investigation of your own. That's pretty gutsy for someone who isn't convinced." Mona's voice rang with obvious admiration.

"Just because I'm not convinced doesn't mean I don't have a healthy curiosity. I have to know! Wayne's journal hints there are longstanding mysteries at the ranch."

As the soil beneath their tires grew bumpy, Leslie held to the edge of the seat.

"Hang on." Mona maneuvered over the body jars and grating sounds of metal against ground and small rocks. "It's too rough! I can't drive any faster."

"This is fast enough," yelled Leslie, her teeth hitting together, her ribs aching.

Midway across the expanse of the valley, they came to a closed gate. Putting the truck in park, Mona climbed out to open the gate to allow entrance into the fenced area. Within the next stretch of land roamed close to fifty head of cattle, many of them eying the Jeep intruder with suspicion.

Leslie maneuvered her body across the bench seat into the driver's position. Shifting, she drove through the opened gate far enough for Mona to refasten the lock behind them and slid over in time for Mona to climb inside the truck. "Whose cattle are these?" she asked, wondering what the beasts might do if they felt threatened.

"Ours. The last of Wayne's herd. Ray bought them last year. Clive has a small herd closer to the ranch itself." Mona sighed. "Wayne could no longer take care of the animals. His cash reserve had dwindled after his age and health began to fail him, leaving him insufficient funds to hire ranch hands. The cattle are added work for everyone, but we try to think of it as future steaks for the grill. Of course, if God blesses, and beef prices don't crash, they might even be an investment."

Leslie continued to eye the unfriendly looking cattle. On the far side of the range, she spied a rough-looking wooden structure. "What's that?"

"A place to store hay and needed supplies for the herd. It saves multiple trips for Ray and George."

"How do they bring supplies in?" Leslie scanned the area for an outlet.

"I've only been up this way a couple of times, as I said. If I remember correctly, I think it depends whether Ray brings hay from Wayne's big barn, where it's stored, or whether he carries in water to supplement during dry spells." Her focus centered on a section of trees to the right of the wooden structure. Turning the wheel in that direction, Mona pointed down a would-be path. "I think we can get to the county road by driving this path. It's been so long that I'm not sure. We'll go as far as we can."

Easing the vehicle down a small, ditch-like depression, Mona gunned the engine for extra power. She grimaced when she heard a grating sound beneath the truck. Racing tires dug into the grassy earth, and the truck shot upward onto a two-lane county road.

"Oof!" Leslie expelled air as the tires impacted the cement coating. Mona allowed the truck to idle in the middle of the road while they got their bearings. No traffic was evident in either direction.

"Next time we take your Jeep," Mona muttered. Then, almost as if she anticipated Leslie's next question, she pointed to the left. "I do know where this road leads. If you think of a map from this point, there is a three-sided box course that will take us back to Dunn Road, the road our ranches are on. It's almost the same distance if we were to drive cross-country back to Wayne's ranch. The road, of course, is easier on truck tires than the way we came."

Pointing to the right, Leslie asked, "And where does this lead?"

Mona shook her head slowly. "I've never driven that direction before."

"It looks like it follows the property line across the valley from Rocky Ridge. Do we have time to follow it?" Excitement thrummed in Leslie.

Mona raised her arm. "We've got an hour, no more. There are chores that have to be done. There's no time to waste. If we're doing it, we need to go now."

With the truck in motion, Leslie felt the vehicle sway to the left. She looked out the window at the slight discoloration in the sky. "Is it going to storm?"

Mona gripped the steering wheel. "Sixty percent chance of heavy weather, but not before 9:00 p.m. tonight. The wind is picking up, though."

"You make the call. If you think we need to go back, just say the word and we'll take that course home." Leslie could see tense lines in Mona's features.

"Let's see where the ridge line leads us."

Knowing their time was short, Leslie peered through the trees at the raised mound adjacent to the county road. She was searching for a glimpse of Rocky Ridge across the plain. When it was in sight, she signaled Mona to slow down and concentrated fully on the ridge to the right. "Stop, Mona!" she shrieked.

The sudden screeching of brakes slid the truck into a three-quarter turn. Mona's heavy breathing was the only sound in the truck cab. "Tell me there is a reason why you screamed, and we stopped on a dime?" whispered Mona in a breathy voice.

"Did I scream? Sorry, didn't mean to. I saw something move—something that might be important. I couldn't let you drive past it," she said, observing Mona's trembling hand. "Guess I got a little carried away."

Mona ignored her apology. "Just be thankful, there's no traffic." She turned back to the area of interest. "Where's this something important?"

"Hopefully important," Leslie corrected. "It's back a few feet more. By the time I spotted it, we'd almost driven past. I was studying the berm when I saw it."

"I'll coast back slowly. Tell me when you see your something—softly please."

As the truck crawled backward, Leslie grabbed hold of Mona's arm, pointing across the road on the ridge. "Pull off to the side! I think this was where I saw my something."

Mona eased the truck to the edge of the opposite side, her wheels partly on the pavement. "What exactly did you see?"

"We'd better get out. I can't show you from here." Together, the women climbed out of the truck, walking in the direction of the ridge. "See how the ditch is filled in across this area. Wide enough for machinery to drive across, you think?"

Mona peered at the weed covered rough ground. "I don't know, Leslie...maybe. Is that all you saw?"

"Help me up this incline."

"Leslie?"

"Just a short way, promise," Leslie begged. After the first few steps up the mound, she balanced herself on Mona's arm. "I'll wait here if you'll go up and pull back some of those dead-looking bushes." She pointed upward to a wide cluster of brown bushes. "Notice how the berm is lower in this area?"

Mona looked at the mound and back at Leslie. "Will you be all right here?"

Sifting her weight to the good foot, Leslie smiled. "I'm fine. I'll be better when you check out those bushes."

Shaking her head, Mona took several steps upward the slight incline and reached to pull back the dry bushes Leslie was pointing to. A part of one bush came up in her hand, roots and all. Turning, she stared back at Leslie with surprised question.

"The ground. Look at the ground under the bushes," Leslie directed.

Mona parted more bushes that were merely stuck in the ground. "There are tracks of some sort under here. They're partly washed away and hard to read, but they're here." Her forehead wrinkled as she stooped to study the tracks and the partially leveled berm.

Leslie's body arched higher to see. "Remember that dry bush that blew in front of the car? When I looked up at the berm, a sharp wind separated the other bushes and I saw those tracks. That's when I screamed. I was afraid we'd totally miss them." Studying Mona's stoic features, she hurried on. "What's the odds of that happening? It was freaky the way the bushes parted at that exact instant we drove past." She stared at the berm. "The brush is thinner here, and there's less grass to camouflage beneath the trees. I could have so easily missed it." Leslie stayed her balance to offset gusts of wind. "Whoever drove over this ridge attempted to cover it up with bushes stuck in the ground—like the one you pulled up."

Her chin rose as she scanned the tree line across the ridge. "And I think if we scaled the other side, we'd not only see deeper tracks, but we'd find some of the trees have been removed to clear the way to drive equipment over the berm. This has got to be where they came in," she murmured thoughtfully.

Taking it all in, Mona stood quietly pensive. Abruptly, she turned, climbing the short distance to the top of the berm. Looking back, she called, "Right on, Leslie! Two trees have been removed that I can see." Descending the incline, she added, "I'm not sure I understand, but everything is pointing to your theory proving correct…except Wayne's property is on the other side. And I know for a fact that all of his land was newly fenced a few years back."

"Mmm," said Leslie, considering Mona's words. "It's possible we might find that fence over the berm has been cut. Has it recently been checked out?"

Checking her watch, Mona sighed. "I think it would be better if the guys checked the fence and took over that part of the investigation. Where do you want to go from here? We've still got a half hour or more."

"Let's see where that side road leads."

Mona glanced from Leslie to the narrow gravel road connecting to the county road. It lay directly across from where they stood on the incline. "You don't think?"

Leslie shrugged. "I don't know, but it's too much of a coincidence, and too close to the tracks to pass checking out."

"All right. The side road it is. But I say we tread carefully from this point forward. Some of this sounds a little dicey. Look at me." Mona spread her arms wide. "I've got goose pimples and this weird warning in my brain. I'm not so sure about this investigating business."

Excitement pumped through Leslie's veins. Her senses were on high alert. "Don't you see? All of it has to mean something!" she cried. "That bush blew across the road at the right time to show us where the tracks are...and now this road!"

Back in the car, Mona backed up and swung the wheel to the right down the one-lane road. Shooting Leslie a glance, she smiled at her friend's exuberant outburst. "I admit this is kind of exciting, Leslie. But you need to meter your expectations."

"Really? I don't believe in coincidences. This means something!"

Mona looked upward, toward the sky. "I don't believe in coincidences either."

Leslie instantly comprehended her meaning. Mona had brought her awareness back to God. In the flicker of an eye, she considered everything from her timely rescue in the garage to these amazing discoveries.

At that moment, she experienced an all-over sensation unlike nothing before, the first in a long dry spell. It was like someone switched on a bright light, interlocking all of the events. Sitting in the front seat of this truck, Leslie was aware of being in the presence of someone bigger than herself—someone who had been there the entire day—a Power working through a plan. The sensation caused a catch in her throat, and left Leslie slightly dazed. An unexplainable moment she would never forget.

Mona pointed. "Leslie! There's a small ranch off to the right. See if you can see anything suspicious as I drive by." She reduced her speed to 20 mph. The mailbox had a rural number posted on the outside, and the modest white house without shutters was set back from the road. A miniscule vegetable garden off to one side was dried and yellow from frost damage. Various children's toys were scattered broadly across the front yard, and one lone young tree was planted in the front of the house.

The second-generation truck in front of a large pole building, a good distance from the back of the house, was the only visible machinery. "Nothing too suspicious here…just a young family struggling to get on their feet."

Leslie turned her head to the opposite side, where an old farmhouse with red shutters had laundry whipping on the clothesline. A standard red barn was situated on a low rise far to the right. Behind that, she could glimpse cattle grazing in a fenced area. She was losing interest. Acres of untended ground, long overgrown with weeds and scrub bushes, stretched out as far as she could see.

"Maybe we should find a place to turn around? There isn't anything out of the ordinary that I can see down this way. Is this a dead-end road?" she questioned aloud.

"We'll find out." Mona peered at the desolate road ahead.

Almost a quarter mile down and around two curves, the road bottomed out at the base of a foothill heavily wooded with pines. As Mona attempted to back up and turn around, Leslie saw a narrow dirt drive partially hidden with thick brush.

"Mona?" The unspoken question hung in the air between them.

"A driveway is private property, Leslie."

"It wouldn't hurt to drive in a ways and ask the people if they'd noticed anything out of the ordinary on their road."

Mona eyed her doubtfully. "And if they aren't receptive?"

"We leave—quickly!" Leslie wasn't nearly as confident as she pretended, yet she was determined to pursue the gains they'd made earlier.

Easing her foot off the brake, Mona guided her truck through the encroaching foliage of the long drive until they came to a ramshackle, plank-sided ranch, no bigger than a two-bedroom house with draped sheets in the windows. Empty liquor bottles lay at the base of two plastic chairs situated in the front yard of the badly mowed yard. Off on a second drive to the left sat a dingy semi-van with lettering *Vanook Hauling.*

Mona rolled down her window but kept the motor running. Leslie stepped out of the small truck, searching for anyone she could talk to. She spotted the ribbon-like stream meandering down the hillside on the right. At the tree line a small, vintage trailer was parked, tucked behind three pines. To the right of the pines sat a rusty backhoe parked in a tall stand of scrub brush.

Her focus returned to the trailer and the pines, narrowing her eyes as the sun reflected off a white shirt. Standing alongside a pine tree was the thin figure of what appeared to be a young girl wearing a baseball cap. Most of her face was shaded by the large bill of the cap and her torn, faded jeans were a size too small for her. Yet even from that distance, Leslie was struck with concern. The slumped stance of the girl indicated an air of hopelessness.

"What do you want, lady?" demanded a sharp voice with a threatening edge.

Whirling about, Leslie faced a tall, skinny man dressed in black jeans and a black T-shirt with a shiny gold chain about his neck. His gray-toned beard was unkempt, as was his whole appearance. A bald head, reddened from the sun, glistened with sweat and old dirt with wild, wiry wisps sprouting above his ears

"Now, now, Zeke, when a purty lady like this one comes a-callin', you shouldn't make her feel unwelcome." Mr. Oily Voice had a carbon copy physique of the man next to him—a brother perhaps—with one exception. He had plenty of hair. It hung to his shoulders, interlocking with his sideburns.

Leslie felt his leering appraisal glued to her body. Everything within her wanted to run, but she forced an unnatural bravado. "I'm sorry to bother you gentlemen, Mr....ah..." She stalled, hoping they'd volunteer their names.

The bald-headed one stared at her with venom, but Mr. Oily countered with a light chuckle. "My brother, Zeke here, ain't ever been any too friendly with strangers." He mockingly bowed low. "I'm Fred Vanook, ma'am. How can I be of help? Do you need a ride somewhere?" He leered gleefully.

Leslie's smile felt like it would crack. Her eyes strayed to a mud-spattered lime green truck at the back of the house. Flustered, she groped for a question. "No, thanks, our truck is running just fine. We were wondering if either of you have ever noticed any heavy machinery moving down your road on a regular basis?" Immediately she remembered the backhoe on the side hill, and her next words froze in her throat.

Thankfully the glaring sun gave cover to the creeping warmth now encompassing her neck and face. It was obvious they owned heavy machinery. Not only did she feel like an idiot, but she suddenly felt like a rabbit under chase by wild dogs.

"Have you noticed any machinery, Zeke? I can't say I have. Of course, Sweet Cheeks, if you and your purty little friend inside the car there would come inside, we could talk real friendly like, and just maybe we might remember something."

Hearing his invitation made the skin on the back of Leslie's neck crawl.

"No machinery!" Zeke growled, adding a string of profanity so vicious it singed Leslie's ears. "We're too busy to waste time on such nonsense. It's time for you to leave. We've got a business to run." He pointed at the lettered semi.

"Sorry to have bothered you." Leslie edged toward the open car door. Sliding inside, she made a point of locking the doors. Mona, having heard the entire conversation, quickly put the truck in reverse, backing to a place she could turn around and rip down the rest of the drive. They heard laughter in the background.

"Well, that was pleasant," murmured Mona, sounding nervous.

Feeling as if she needed a bath after five minutes in the presence of the Vanook brothers, Leslie stared straight ahead of the truck. "They were creepy! Did you see that backhoe up on the hillside—the old one? They could be the ones that have been digging on Wayne's property."

"That's a far jump, Leslie. As uncouth as those hillbillies are, they are businessmen. At least they have a persona of being businessmen with that semi in the drive. And that rusty backhoe on the hill is so old, I have doubts it even runs. All that and the fact they live on a road across from some washed-out tracks adds up to very little. Sorry, Leslie, I don't like them either. Their accent isn't from around here."

"It's heavier than anything I've heard. Let's go back to the ranch, Mona. I need to do some thinking. Those two are guilty of something—I know it. Did you see that young girl up on the hill, back in the pines? She made my heart ache just looking at her. I wonder if she's family?"

"I couldn't see her very well from inside the truck, but I'd say she's undernourished. I'll never understand why people like that are given children when..." Mona's mouth drew tight.

Shifting in her seat, Leslie regarded her friend with gentleness. "When what, Mona? Do you want children?" It was a subject Mona had never discussed before.

"Ray and I have wanted children ever since we married. Unfortunately, that hasn't happened. Our names are on an adoption list, but it takes forever. There is so much red tape and too few babies. So many aborted babies." She sighed sadly. "And my heart aches daily to have one of my own to care for. I pray for God's will and I wait." The sadness in Mona's face made Leslie wish she'd never pressed the question.

Leslie's cell phone erupted inside her purse. By the time she fumbled around and found it, the message clicked into voicemail. She hurriedly spoke. "Roger? Don't hang up. I'm here."

"Leslie, I tried your home phone. Where are you?"

Looking around, Leslie suppressed a giggle. "You could say I've been taking a sight-seeing tour of the area with Mona this afternoon. What's up?" She listened for a minute, then replied, "No, I didn't drive the old Jeep like I first planned. It didn't work out, so Mona drove me around instead." There was no way Leslie wanted to rehash her ordeal of the morning. She rushed to continue. "I've learned a lot just riding around the countryside with Mona today."

"Really!" said Roger, "you'll have to tell me all about it. How about at lunch tomorrow, in town? If you could meet me at my office about 11:30 a.m., we could leave from here." His voice was filled with youthful earnestness.

It made Leslie smile and encouraged her to answer impulsively, "That sounds great, Roger. I'll meet you there, 11:30 a.m. Thanks for calling. Bye."

Mona shot her a sidelong glance. "Roger Galbraith? Our young lawyer is quite taken with you it seems." Her statement invited a follow-up.

Leslie giggled. "I don't know how taken he is, but he sure is persistent, and it provides me with male companionship and occasionally even a little information. More and more I'm becoming convinced that Roger has had nothing to do with any of the 'so-called' accidents on the ranch." She felt sure of it as she thought about her luncheon date for the following day.

"Answer me something, Leslie. Did Roger know you planned on taking the Jeep out for a drive this morning?"

Instantly, Leslie paled, recalling an earlier conversation. She searched for words as the diabolic idea attached itself to all that had happened. Finding her voice, she answered, "Yes, we talked briefly last night on the phone—just chit-chat about nothing, really. But I did mention how excited I was about taking the Jeep out for the first time alone." She stared, unseeing, at the road. "There's no way Roger deliberately would have tried to hurt me. I can't believe that!"

The very fact Mona remained silent troubled and irritated Leslie. She wanted a chance to defend Roger with everything that had proved false in her observations, but as the miles stretched out in strained quietness, she finally relented with a measure of acceptance. "Okay. You're right! I need to be extra careful until I know more about him. I'll try to probe for more information tomorrow."

"I didn't say anything, Leslie," said Mona quietly.

"Maybe not in words, but I knew what you were thinking." Leslie cocked her head with mild irritation.

When Mona laughed, Leslie joined her. As late afternoon sun splashed through the window glass in changing patterns, the women enjoyed quiet camaraderie. Though their earlier laughter had provided an emotional release from their recent experiences, yet Leslie was left with a real, new concern about Roger. Sobering, she murmured, "You know, today's little jaunt through the back trails has provided us with possibilities, but no real answers."

"Still, you need to tell Clive what we found today," Mona urged. "He'd be your best bet for checking out some of those possibilities you feel strongly about. You'll get your chance at supper tonight. Henri O' is cooking ribs the way Clive likes them."

"Clive's going to be there tonight?" Leslie pictured his rugged, tanned face and felt her pulse rate increase. Hating the way her body betrayed her emotions, she reigned in her enthusiasm. "Fine. Dinner will be a great place to air some of our findings. I personally intend to ask him why he's been holding back on everything he saw up on Rocky Ridge that day. I'm not a child who needs to be spared." She lifted her head in defense of her clipped words.

"You'll get more out of Clive with a gentler tongue," Mona said, flashing Leslie a discerning look before turning back to watch the road. Her sudden grin flashed like a spotlight had hit her brain. "Leslie, you're afraid of what kind of response you'll get from Clive with gentleness, aren't you? You've seen that look in his eye when he's around you, and you don't think you can handle the reaction," she said smugly. "It just came to me! Both of you are afraid of allowing your true feelings to show. That's why you pick at one another all the time. I can't believe I've been so dense and not seen it before now!" She chuckled, mischief dancing in her eyes.

Leslie expressed an exasperated sigh. "Mona, you've been out in the sun too long. You're getting fantasy mixed up with reality. Reality is: Clive and I just rub each other the wrong way—it happens."

As the scenery flashed by, Leslie steeled any thoughts of Clive Masters from her mind. Never again did she want to feel so totally vulnerable, as she had that day Kevin betrayed her. She'd responded to her true feelings that day and was made to look like a fool. Well, never again.

When they arrived at Wayne's ranch, Leslie climbed with effort from Mona's truck. She glanced back at her friend with a new awareness of her warm character. "You give of yourself and your time, Mona Schiller. Dad always said that was one of the greatest gifts a person could give. Thanks for this afternoon. It kept my mind off the garage incident."

Mona grinned. "It was fun to drive across country with you."

Patting the side of Mona's little truck, Leslie said, "This little honey may not be a mountain goat, but she did everything we asked of her today. I'll drive over for supper in a little while. What time is the gala event?"

"Six-thirty p.m. ought to be good. See you later, Leslie. Today was good for me too. It's important to stop and celebrate life now and then, but even more important to know you're living within God's plan, under His umbrella of protection." Her eyes lingered on Leslie before putting the truck in reverse.

Leslie could feel herself perspiring. *Pop was under God's umbrella of protection, yet He took him all the same. I wasn't ready, Dad. I wasn't ready for you to go.*

Watching Mona's truck disappear in a windy, dusty haze, she couldn't fight the memory of that instant awareness of God's presence. *I did experience His protection in the barn and again in the garage. Why now, after all this time, and why me?* Then there was the unexplainable finding of the tracks on the low ridge. She swallowed hard, slowly making her way toward the breezeway door, not ready to embrace the deeper meaning for all the happenings. It was threatening—even harder to believe that God might still know her name after so long an estrangement. What did He want from her? She hurried her steps, trying not to think.

*

Supper was a wild rush. Ray was clearly running late, hurrying to get cleaned up before Henri O' rang her miniature dinner bell. Leslie arrived in time to dodge Mona's husband in the hallway on his way to the shower and still aid Mona in setting the table. When the dinner bell actually sounded, Clive was midway of the back door, following the aroma of BBQ ribs from the stove all the way to the table.

Following the table blessing, a hubbub flow of heated comments and counter remarks saturated the air between Clive and Ray as they bantered ranch issues. Leslie was secretly pleased with no mention of her near-fatal barn ordeal that morning. Barely listening to things that had no bearing on her immediate life, she relaxed and enjoyed the camaraderie of friends.

After the ribs were devoured, a cream pie was downed with all the *oohs* and *aahs* accompanying such a delight. Mona nodded to Leslie, an obvious nudge for her to introduce their afternoon excursion from Rocky Point. Leslie was reluctant. Not ready for a tongue-lashing from Clive about venturing into dangerous places, she concentrated on scraping her pie dish, pretending not to hear Mona's exasperated sigh.

Raising her focus to Clive's face, she found that he too was watching her with curiosity. "I thought maybe you were trying to scrap the wildflowers off that pie dish. How did your afternoon go with Mona?"

When Leslie shot Mona a censored look, he explained, "I spoke briefly with Mona before you left this morning. So, where did you two go?"

Leslie prepared for probable reprimand. Beginning with their picnic at Rocky Ridge, she described each leg of their adventure up to their uncomfortable encounter with the Vanook brothers. She carefully skimmed the highlights, trying to downplay some of the Vanooks' offensive behavior.

Both men leaned forward, exchanging troubled glances. She went on nervously. "We came back on the same route Ray uses to tend the cattle. That's how our day went." She flashed a weak smile, hurriedly downing a glass of water.

Ray centered his concern on Mona, who returned a sweet, serene smile. Clive, on the other hand, leaned back in his chair lost in deep thought. Leslie stared at him, feeling unexpected disappointment. He hadn't so much as raised his voice at her for encouraging Mona to drive up in the Vanooks' drive. *Clive probably thinks I would have deserved anything that might have happened,* she thought crossly.

Then, all of a sudden, Clive settled forward in his chair, resting his elbows on the dinner table. "Leslie, you and Mona are sure that this gravel road comes in directly across from the area you spotted the camouflaged tracks on the roadside berm?"

Leslie nodded

"I'll second her assessment," Mona added. "The Vanook brothers are the only farm that has any equipment—at least visible equipment of a type able to do the kind of digging you described to Ray and me earlier."

Clive looked first to Leslie before nodding in Mona's direction. "That's a good lead. But, equally possible, is that someone could have come from the opposite direction on that road alongside the berm edging Wayne's property."

"That's Ryman Road," volunteered Ray. "And you're right, Clive. Ryman Road circles around the Mojave ranch and a dozen other smaller farms before winding its way into town from the east. Anyone could pass those ranches at night with a backhoe, or even an amphibian landing party, and who would notice?"

Both men stared at Leslie, who now felt as if someone had popped all of her birthday balloons. "So what you are saying is, we don't really have any more leads than we had before?"

"Not necessarily." Clive's finger tapped on top of the covered butter dish. "The Vanook boys may be more than just obnoxious, nasty residents. Ray and I'll check out those tracks you discovered and nose around a little. That being the case, you realize there's no reason for either of you to go back there.

Actually, that was very good work, ladies," he encouraged, his eyes resting on Leslie.

Leslie basked briefly in his compliment. Clive Masters was certainly unpredictable, and his words left her without comment. Smiling with hesitation, she nodded and began to help Mona clear the table. Henri O's workday ended after the dinner bell was rung and the meal ready to serve. Leslie and Mona left Ray and Clive to speculate and work out possible scenarios while they scraped plates and loaded the dishwasher.

When the group was back around the table, Mona was eager to jump into the discussion with the guys, but Leslie held back, feeling out of sorts. Not wanting to rehash the unsolved episodes at the ranch, she quietly borrowed one of Mona's farm jackets off the pegs at the back door and slipped outside, under the cold, clear, star-studded night sky. At some point during supper, the clouds had dispelled.

Favoring her aching ankle, she slowly made her way out to the wooden fence bordering the small patio area behind the house. Resting her injured foot on the bottom railing, she leaned her weight against the top edge of the fence. The vastness of the heavens made Leslie catch her breath. How many miles extended into the unknown nothingness beyond our own galaxy? More than she could fathom? It was mind-boggling! Staring upward, she was instantly lost in its endless dimension.

Where is God in all of this vastness? Everything is so huge, it's scary! At some point today her faith had started to leaf out. After a long dry spell, there was a single bloom. Could it survive in her sea of doubts?

From behind her a resonant voice spoke: "O Lord, our Lord, how majestic is Your name in all the earth. Who has displayed Your splendor above the heavens!" The timbre of the quotation gave her chills. It was so tender and reverent—so unlike Clive. Or, at least, the Clive she thought she knew.

Half turning, Leslie faced him, surprised to hear him recite a psalm. The glow of the yard light etched his strong profile against the velvet of the black night.

"I remember Dad telling me that God named each of the stars in the heavens." She felt doubtful. "I accepted those words as a child. But looking up at the zillions I see right now, I don't know how anyone could name all those, when I can't even see them."

Her breath was frosty in the night air as she eased back against the fence. Scanning the sky from east to west, she continued to marvel at the unending expanse. With Clive behind her, she didn't feel quite as small and insignificant.

He moved forward to lean against the railing next to her. "At home I have a large book, almost an inch and a half thick. On every page are multiple pictures of intricate, varied-colored seashells from all over the world—so many, they soon begin to blend into a kaleidoscope. I can't begin to keep them straight. Yet not any two of them are the same—incredible sight!"

He breathed deeply of the crisp air. "I've also been told there are not two snowflakes alike in all the blizzards. And when you think about the complicated nervous system in the human body, and the inner working of the brain that man is still trying to figure out, well..."

Leslie waited while Clive paused. *Where is he going with all this?* she wondered. Her one hand covered the other. She'd never heard Clive talk like this before, and it unsettled her.

"I have but one question, Leslie. Why would a God who could do everything I've just mentioned have any difficulty naming zillions of stars?"

She turned to look at him. "I'm not sure I understand what you're trying to say."

He stared upward. "Thinking back, I can't count the times I've tried to judge or understand God by what I can do or can't do. Then I realize how ridiculous that is. It's like putting God in a matchbox and molding him like putty into what I want Him to be. If God is that small and incapable, why would I ever need Him? Looking at those stars, I can proudly say, my God is an awesome God and He made those stars, and named them, every one."

Leslie picked out one star to gaze upon. "There is so much I don't know or understand..." The night air crept in, and she shivered. "Dad never questioned."

"Everyone questions, Leslie. Faith is both a gift and a choice. God knew that at some point in your life you would trust and choose to believe. What's different now? What's blocking that trust you once had? Sometimes angry questions are only an excuse." His piercing gaze probed the depths of her soul and she recoiled from it.

"You do things every day that demand faith of some kind. You ride in a car, believing it will get you where you want to go. You board a plane, flown by a pilot you've never met. How often do you check the legs of a chair before sitting down? Like the label says, 'There are no guarantees.' Getting out of bed every day is a gamble—a gamble of faith. Who knows? You could trip and break your ankle at any given moment or fall into a manhole." He smiled, turning her to face him. "Look at you."

His analogy only troubled her more, but the gentle humor and tenderness in his approach overwhelmed her. It had been a long time since she'd read anything in her Bible. Staring up at his shadowed face, she was astounded at this in-depth side of Clive's nature she'd never seen before. Her gaze locked in on his strong features. Had it been four years since Leslie had last felt such a strong attraction for a man?

The fact that it was deeper than physical attraction didn't help in this close proximity, standing under soft starlight. Frankly, it scared her. She didn't want to deal with these feelings—not now, maybe not ever. Swallowing hard, she refocused her thoughts on his challenge concerning trust and faith issues.

"Don't you see," she murmured, "with all those ifs in life, how can I grab hold of anything solid and know I am truly safe?" A small gasp escaped before she could call back her words. She hadn't meant to show her weakness—the need to feel safe with someone. Ever since her parents' deaths and Kevin's betrayal, her emptiness had become a bottomless pit.

She was afraid to meet Clive's eyes. Too much emotion was written in her own. What if he asked her something so personal, she might unwittingly reveal more than she could bear?

"Leslie, how would your father have answered your question?"

His words took her completely off balance. Instantly, the answer blazed across her mind. It shocked her, especially when she connected it to the supernatural happenings of the past day. Like a robot, her memory recited one of her father's oft cited verses, *"The Lord is my rock and my fortress and my deliverer."* Had God truly been her deliverer today? She rubbed her neck.

The words of Scripture were like a slap in the face, reminding her that she should be seeking her security in God. Turning abruptly, Leslie started back toward the door. She filled her lungs with the chilled air to revive her numbed feelings. "I think it's time for me to head home," she said blandly. "Thanks again for all your help this morning."

"Someday, Leslie Weldon, you're going to have to make that choice about faith. Hopefully when you do, you will discover the peace and security you seek."

There was no censure in Clive's tone or words, yet Leslie felt as if she'd disappointed him in some way. *Why not? I disappointed my father for years.*

10

A New Outlet

CLIMBING INTO BED, LESLIE REMEMBERED too late she'd failed to talk to Clive about his nightly stakeout in her drive. Putting out food for Boris and brushing her teeth was a major effort. She'd been too exhausted to notice if someone had pulled in the drive after lights were out. When she woke in the morning, she discreetly pulled the blinds aside but saw no evidence to indicate that a truck had been parked there. Gathering her clothes, she made her way to the shower.

Leslie had more troubling issues. Instead of the relaxing luncheon with Roger she'd first anticipated, she now had a cloud of distrust to wade through. The fact Roger knew about her planned outing in Wayne's Jeep would cause new uneasiness in his presence. As much as she'd defended him to Mona, she still had unanswered questions.

As Leslie drove into Dahlonega to meet Roger at his office, her thoughts jumped from last night's starlight talk with Clive, to the mysterious tracks on Ryman Road, even to the unanswered sighting of the sharp-featured man on one of Dahlonega's side streets talking to unknown people. *Was that only my imagination? It's hard to believe it was the same man I saw in the New York restaurant. I saw him only an instant.* The longer the time from the sighting, the stronger the doubts became. Pulling down the car visor to block the late morning sun, she made the turn into Dahlonega.

Choosing a parking place down from Roger's law office, Leslie grabbed her cane before exiting the car. Frowning, she thought about having to encounter his secretary again. She labored up on the curb in front of the brightly decorated Christmas Shoppe and checked her watch. There was time. Allowing her instincts to lead her, she entered the charming little store that smelled of cinnamon and apple spice. Soft strands of a Christmas carol was playing as a round-faced woman in her sixties approached her.

"Good morning, I'm Georgia McCray. Is there anything I can help you with—a special ornament, a Christmas keepsake, or perhaps a Christmas layaway account?" the white-haired woman offered cheerfully.

"Oh, I'm just browsing. But now that you mention it, I might find something special for an elderly friend of mine back in New York. She's always loved Christmas." Glancing around, Leslie was delighted with the stunning ornaments and unique articles, all relating to Christmas. Her focus was drawn to one in particular. "I think I'd like to get her that small nativity set with the exquisite features. There isn't much room in her apartment," she added, thinking of Alberta's tiny living area.

Georgia McCray led her down a center aisle. "I've been thinking about selling my own big house and moving into an apartment. There's just too much room for a woman living alone. I can't seem to get accustomed to the feeling."

Noticing the cloud of sadness pass across the woman's features, Leslie was reminded of Alberta's lonely life. Leslie fingered a box of bulbs while the pleasant-faced proprietor carefully wrapped each piece of the nativity set. "I see you have some plain, frosted bulbs. I've always wanted to try my hand at painting scenes on a few for presents—you know, for special people. But unfortunately I brought no supplies with me," she added wistfully, turning back to the counter.

The older woman regarded her brightly. "You know, it's almost providential, you mentioning hand-painted bulbs. My Robert tried his hand at painting the last year before he died. Nothing fancy, little pine trees and snowmen, but people liked them because they were personal and artsy. I'm not the least artistic, but if you were interested in painting some bulbs, I'd take a few of them in payment for paint and brushes. That is, if you work in oils?"

Leslie had to admit the idea interested her. It was a chance to edge her way back into what she loved. Surely the small bulbs wouldn't require a lot of work. She turned back. "I-I'm not sure how long I plan on staying in Dahlonega, but if you're not expecting advanced artwork, I could probably try a few simple bulbs for each of us. And, yes, I work in oils."

The white head bobbed up and down. "Good! I'm Georgie to my friends." She held out her plump, freckled hand toward Leslie.

"Leslie Weldon. I'm staying out at my cousin Wayne Riker's Ranch for a while."

"Glory, yes, I knew your cousin. Wayne came to our church last year for a spell. I heard he wasn't doing too well and then passed away, quite suddenly. Sorry for your loss."

"Thank you. We weren't close, but I liked him when we met."

"Folks who knew him said he was a sweet man, helping those he could—good Christian man." Shoving the wrapped box toward Leslie, she added,

"Now, Leslie, it will take me a little while to gather Robert's painting supplies. I'm going home for lunch in a few minutes. I could bring them back with me after lunch, or hold them here at the shop until you come in another day. Which is more convenient for you?"

Handing Georgia the exact amount for the nativity set, Leslie answered, "I'm in town for a luncheon appointment of my own. There's no reason I can't return after lunch and pick up the supplies when I purchase some of the frosted bulbs." Her excitement was mounting.

Leslie picked up the box of wrapped pieces and started for the door when Georgia stopped her. "When you return, pull your car around back through the alley where there is parking for shop owners. I'll transfer the art supplies directly to your trunk from mine. Have a nice lunch, dear." She waved as Leslie made her way from the shop with the small box.

With her cane hooked over arm, Leslie lowered the box into the back seat of her car before walking the short distance to Roger's office. After all the time in The Christmas Shoppe, it was still only 11:15 a.m. *What possessed me to leave the ranch so early?* The high sun felt hot on her back as she entered the small waiting area.

Roger's secretary, Stephanie, looked up, nodding her awareness of Leslie's arrival. Gone was the perky, bright smile of greeting from Leslie's first visit. Leslie could almost feel a notable chill in the air.

Selecting a chair in front of the window overlooking the sidewalk, she reached for a magazine at the same instant the inner door opened and a large man backed out of Roger's office, still talking as if his conversation had not ended. As the man turned, Leslie recognized the bank president she'd met at the winery restaurant, Hamilton Longworth.

Catching sight of Leslie sitting across the room, his robust manner was quick to acknowledge her with a hearty hail. "How nice to see you again, Miss Weldon. I do hope your injury is mending nicely?" Before Leslie could respond, the huge bulk of the man shifted to regard Roger, who stood behind him in the office doorway.

"It's not wise to keep a beautiful woman like Miss Weldon waiting around, Roger. Consider our meeting concluded." Turning back to Leslie, he remarked warmly, "Your smile is like a summer breeze, my dear. Roger's a lucky man."

"Thank you," she murmured as he exited the building. His open friendliness was inviting, but she couldn't help but wonder about his meeting with Roger. Was this more evidence of his possible close involvement with the young lawyer?

Could be Hamilton Longworth is Roger's secret contact in Dahlonega. If so, what is the reason for keeping a secret? Secrecy made her distrustful. It also made her sad to have such thoughts, bringing more suspicion to the coming lunch date. She would have preferred to cancel the entire affair and simply go home. The anticipated pleasure was gone.

With Roger advancing rapidly toward her, she sat torn with indecision. If she went home on a pretext of one sort or another, she might miss an opportunity to gain information about his mysterious backer. Leslie looked from Roger to the inviting doorway and back.

"Leslie, Mr. Longworth is right. You are much too beautiful to be sitting out here twiddling your thumbs, as an old aunt used to quote. I'm terribly sorry to keep you waiting. I hope Stephanie has made you comfortable?"

With effort, Leslie kept her focus away from Stephanie's desk. A jealous secretary wasn't the issue. "I was quite comfortable, Roger, and I haven't been waiting long. Really, I'm fine. Actually I was early and..."

Roger was absently checking his pockets, as if looking for something important. Pulling a small square of pink paper from his pocket, he seemed relieved, tucking it deep inside the wallet he retrieved from his back pocket. "Excuse me, Leslie, what were you saying?"

"It's not important," she murmured. "I'm ready. Where are we going today?"

With his eyes alight with mischief, he could have passed for twelve years old, grinning as if he held a special surprise. "Today, we're going to get some local flavor. There is a charming buffet in one of our newer buildings, no older than twenty years or so, but the walls are lined with old mining pictures. You'll be getting history with your meal. I'm anxious to share it with you. For dessert, we'll go to a charming bakery and sweet shop on the square, housed in the old Price Building, dating back to 1897."

"Sounds marvelous!" she lied, forcing an enthusiasm she didn't feel. Leslie couldn't let down her guard. Could she really trust Roger's seemingly casual speech and his occasional words of endearment? She hated doubting everything he said or did. *If I could only get past all the shadowy, unexplained connections to the accidents, maybe I could begin to trust him.*

Then thoughts of the locked garage overwhelmed her, reminding her that she could have been killed the day before. As she lowered her gaze to avoid him detecting her conflicted feelings, Leslie mourned her ruined afternoon. On any other occasion, the idea of a mystery afternoon with an attractive man would be exciting. Roger's next words interrupted her sober thoughts.

"Normally I'd recommend we'd walk to our destination on this gorgeous fall day, but with that foot of yours, we'll have to take my car. I'll drive around front and pick you up. Watch for me. I'll be right back."

Glancing at Stephanie on his way through to his office, Roger directed, "Finish up that one letter to Bieteut and Company, and then take your lunch break."

"Yes, Mr. Galbraith," she answered dejectedly.

Roger sailed on by without giving any sign of noticing his melancholy assistant. It tired Leslie just watching the tragic drama played out within the confines of this office. She almost felt sorry for Stephanie. How could Roger not know what was going on with his own secretary? Shaking her head, she shifted so she could watch out the front window for Roger to drive up for her.

*

During the meal, Leslie managed to keep up with most of the conversational discourse until Roger asked her point blank why she hadn't driven Wayne's old Jeep the day before. Her spine stiffened, wary of his intentions. *Is he baiting me to find out what I know? Might it be possible he doesn't know what happened to me yesterday in the garage?*

"Why do you ask?" she asked, slowly and deliberately, trying to keep suspicion from her voice.

His confused reaction made her eye him even more curiously. "Why?" he repeated. "Because I warned you that it might need tuning up, that's why. The last time I saw it, the old relic looked as if it should be towed to the junk heap years ago. I was dubious about you driving it from the beginning. The fact you made alternate plans only confirms those feelings."

"You're right, Roger. I should have listened. In fact, the Jeep is at the mechanic's shop even as we speak." She reached for a buttered roll, but by now her sagging appetite was completely depleted. It no longer mattered that Roger's choice of question had been explained. It neither confirmed nor denied anything.

Her hand rubbed her tender forehead. Leslie felt too weary to play the game of wondering any longer. Leaving a half-eaten plate of food, she pled an oncoming headache as reason to bypass dessert. With woeful eyes, she asked to be returned to her car. The whole meal was a waste of good food and both of their time.

As they drove the short distance back to his office where her car waited, he studied her soberly, with the hint of a pout. "I'm not happy, you know. I'd planned on a much longer time together today. What's going on, Leslie? You haven't been yourself today. I don't think ranch life is agreeing with you. You're under too much stress." He regarded Leslie with dismay.

Her mouth opened, but no ready response came to mind. What could she say?

"Have you thought any more about your future plans? The investors are getting impatient. If you take too long making a decision, I can't promise their offer will stand. Time is of an essence, especially in our sagging economy. I don't understand what the holdup is. What holds you to this rundown ranch that hasn't shown a profit for years? It's not that Masters fella, is it?" he asked sharply.

She shifted in the seat, making direct eye contact. "Family, Roger. I need more time to decide. When I first came, I had no idea of the strong family ties embedded in the history of this ranch. I have to play it out—discover my roots, so to speak. It may very well be that my destiny will lead me back to New York. I wasn't raised to be a country girl, and as you said, there's a lot of work connected with a ranch."

She considered her next words. "This time that I'm spending at the ranch may settle a lot of questions I've had the last few years. Bottom line, Roger, I'm just not ready to leave. So I guess the investors will have to wait. If they're available when my decision is made, I will count myself fortunate."

Roger's hands rested on the wheel of his shiny car. His head lowered as he said solemnly, "I'm truly sorry to hear that."

Leslie felt an involuntary chill at his tone. "Why is that?"

"Because a lot hinges on the sale of your property. These investors can do a great deal for this part of country, Dahlonega in general. And if they change their mind and start looking in another direction, it will be a huge loss for many people—not just yourself. I'm talking jobs for out-of-work cowboys and ranch hands, not to mention a marked influx of people, wealthy buyers and such. Is there anything I can do to speed up your decision-making process?" He glanced up at her with a tender smile.

Leslie smiled in return, her cynical side wondering if he'd already been involved in trying to do just that, with frequent accidents. She shook her head free from the thought. *I'm judging without evidence.* She felt a twinge of guilt, but the doubts wouldn't leave her. *Maybe that's the motive, to make me sell—but why? Is it all so a few investors can breed highbred cattle?* Looking tiredly at Roger, she asked, "Rain check for that dessert?"

Roger's smooth, long fingers reached to lightly touch the side of Leslie's face. "You got it, Beautiful, just as soon as it can be arranged. I'll call."

As soon as Leslie closed Roger's well-polished door with care and stepped backward, he slowly backed out of the parking place, merging into traffic. Leslie wondered if he would park around back. Remembering Georgia McCray's parking instructions, she waited a few minutes before leaving.

Moments later she eased her way through the narrow alley into the limited parking behind the offices and small shops. Seeing a bright red station wagon parked behind the rear entrance of The Christmas Shoppe, Leslie smiled and pulled her car alongside on the right. She made her way to the rear door, her gaze roaming down the row of businesses to Roger's car parked behind his office. If he came out and noticed her car, it might prove awkward after she'd made such a point of pleading a bad headache. She knocked lightly and hurriedly entered the shop.

*

Leslie stacked a couple of bulb boxes on the counter. "I think that's it, Mrs. McCray."

"Georgie, my dear, please. I just feel we're going to be friends. I can't wait to see those finished bulbs. People around here appreciate artistic talents."

Leslie looked at her shyly. "I hope I don't disappoint you or the people who appreciate art. Did you say the supplies are in the back of your car?"

"Oh my, yes! Everything you need should be in there, even hangers to hold the bulbs while you work on them and the final spray when you're finished. Just follow me out to my car and bring your bulbs."

The ample-figured woman moved swiftly; her energy infused Leslie with enthusiasm. By the time Leslie caught up with Georgie, the white-haired vision of Mrs. Claus, in a red shirt and skirt, had the hatch of her van open and waiting with the box of supplies. Together, Leslie and Georgie transferred the box from one car to the other.

Georgie lifted her hands to push back her hair from her face, a trickle of perspiration on her forehead. "These wonderfully warm fall days are a blessing. Too soon it will be cold and gray looking. Then comes the snow. You'll not find me complaining about the heat." Her flushed cheeks matched the color of her blouse.

"I thought Mrs. Santa preferred the snow," Leslie teased the joyful woman.

"This Mrs. Santa wouldn't mind a few palm trees in her backyard. I need to get back inside the shop. Enjoy your painting, Leslie. I wrote your number down by the phone." With a final smile, she disappeared inside the building.

Turning, Leslie was making her way to the driver's side when she heard voices down from The Christmas Shoppe. Lifting her eyes, she squinted to make out who was emerging from the back of Roger's office. Her body tensed.

Something held her silently in place. She was shielded from sight by the parked cars and only able to make out the back of a suited man of medium build. The other man stepping outside the confines of the building was clearly Roger. She saw him hand the first man the pink note from his wallet. Was that a hat or a briefcase clutched in the man's free hand? Leslie couldn't tell. Their conversation was animated, their voices raised to a partly discernible pitch.

The shorter man was doing most of the talking. Leslie caught words like, "Make this happen! Stay on it! Nightly, as always."

The man moved toward a black car next to Roger's. Leslie wanted to watch, hoping to catch a glimpse of his face, but she was afraid she would be seen. Pulling back in the car shadows, she held her breath, waiting until she heard the engine rev up and drive out. By the time she looked to the rear entrance of the law office, Roger was gone. She expelled pent-up air, wondering what it all meant. Likely, it was all harmless conversation between client and lawyer, but what if it wasn't? Leslie felt a massive headache coming on—for real this time.

*

On the way out of town, her thoughts were so clouded by the mounting layers of suspicion against Roger that Leslie realized too late she'd turned on the wrong road. It wound her deep inside a foothills subdivision, a labyrinth filled with mazes of intricate loops. After backing around twice and becoming totally confused, she finally admitted she'd lost her direction and was hopelessly lost.

Parking her car near the end of a long driveway alongside a mailbox, she pawed through all of her maps on the passenger side floor. Leslie pushed her hair back from her face, and sat up to sort through the pile, startled to see the inquisitive face of a strange man peering at her curiously through the window.

Drawing in a frustrated breath, she rolled down her window partway. "I'm lost! Eight miles from home and I'm lost. I can't believe the kind of a day I'm having!"

Cocking his head, the sixty-odd-year-old man smiled reassuringly. "Follow me to the house and bring that pile of maps with you. My wife, Jackie, has a fresh pot of coffee and banana bread on the counter. We'll figure it out. Can't be too hard if you're only eight miles from town, now can it?" He smiled again.

Turning, the man emptied his mailbox and motioned for Leslie to follow him in the car around a short upward curve and then straight down the steepest driveway she'd ever encountered. At the bottom of the drive sat a brown ranch, happily situated beside a creek running with gently flowing water. The landscape was dotted with pine and oak trees splashed with sunlight between the branches. It was a peaceful scene. Leslie had a sudden urge to cry. She was so tired and confused.

At first glance this man appeared friendly and eager to help, yet being a stranger, Leslie observed the need to be cautious and hesitated to climb out of her car. The gentleman seemed not to notice and quietly disappeared inside the middle portion of the house. By squinting, Leslie discerned it was a screened breezeway extension. She scanned the full extent of the long ranch, and waited, uncertain if it might not be better to back her car around and leave.

She was yet undecided when an attractive, dark-haired woman emerged from the breezeway and approached the car with an inviting smile. "Walton told me he left you sitting out here. Come on in and have a cup of coffee with us while you and Walton figure out the best way to get you home. You're new in the area, I gather?" Not waiting for a reply, she opened the breezeway door and waited for Leslie to release herself from the confines of the car and slowly make her way toward the house. "You've injured your foot, I see. I hope it isn't serious."

Shaking her head, Leslie mumbled, "Thank you" and followed her inside. She was soon seated at an ample-sized table in a warm kitchen that smelled of fresh-baked banana bread. Relaxing for the first time since she saw the bank president come out of Roger's office, she extended her hand. "Leslie Weldon. I'm staying out at my cousin's ranch on Dunn Road. It's the old Riker place."

The couple exchanged glances. The man reached for Leslie's hand, shaking it warmly. "Walton Peabody, and this is my wife, Jackie," he said gesturing toward the dark-haired woman. "Would that mean your cousin was Wayne Riker?"

"Yes," Leslie said, brightening. "Did you know Wayne well?"

"Oh yes. He and I visited several times. He loved to go on about the history of the ranch. We'd exchange tidbits of local and past history on many a cold winter day," Walton said, chuckling, as if he were remembering.

"Walton was a history professor for several years," Jackie explained.

"Oh. How interesting," Leslie said. "Do you still teach?"

While Walton reached for a plate, Jackie answered Leslie's question, "Oh, no. You see, later on, Walton made the decision to become an Episcopal priest." Her lips held the hint of a smile.

Leslie swallowed again in surprise. "Remarkable! That is interesting! I bet you and my cousin had a lot to talk about. Tell me, did Wayne ever mention old family journals?"

Leaning back, Walton lazily eyed a piece of warm bread. "Often. We'd meet and pore over those journals together by the hour; trying to see how they connected with the times his relatives lived through. It was fascinating! Wayne became quite a student of history."

Walton's hand rubbed the side of his face. "But, now that you mention the old journals, there is someone other than myself that was even more acquainted with the Riker journals. In fact, his family had connection to Wayne's ancestors in some manner. Once I steered Wayne to contact him. Wayne and I only had occasional reasons to meet. I'd recommend you look for this man. He might have the information you need."

Leslie was stunned. Of all the places she could have stopped for direction. Reaching into her purse, she withdrew her small pad. "Do you remember his name?"

Walton pulled the banana bread nearer, looking up thoughtfully. "Um, Romero, I think. It's been at least ten years ago. Lives in a deep wooded area, I heard. He used to do a lot of hunting when he was young, until some debilitating disease dictated otherwise. I can't recall what it is."

"Romero?" Leslie allowed the name to roam through her memory bank. It sounded strangely familiar, but she couldn't place it. "Do you have a first name or address?" she asked hopefully.

"Miguel Romero. He must be getting up in age. I heard he was forty or more when his family was born. But that's the extent of my knowledge. Now, let's figure a way to get you home."

While Walton drew a pencil map leading her back to the main road, she sipped the rich flavored coffee, her hand moving steadily from her plate to her mouth. Her lack of lunch was gnawing at her stomach.

After he handed her the simple map, she shook her head. "So that's where I made my wrong turn." Raising her eyes to the helpful couple, she smiled. "Maybe it wasn't a wrong turn after all." Thanking them profusely, she left them standing outside waving her off.

Nice people, Jackie and Walton Peabody, she mused as her car steered upward toward the main road and home. *What are the chances of my stopping by their mailbox?*

Once again she had the sense of a guiding Hand. It was coming more often. She had experienced the same sensations years earlier, before she made her disastrous decision to meet Kevin on the Island. Her father had told her he was praying for her heart attitude and life decisions. He had put it to her straight: *"Leslie, ask yourself, 'Will my actions be pleasing to God?' Sin separates people from God."*

Leslie remembered her sharp response, wishing a hundred times over she could have taken it back. It made her wince to remember that shameful time, and she didn't want to think about it. *Is someone praying for me now?* she wondered, thinking of her new friends. The thought was unnerving but not unpleasant.

*

Honking her horn as she drove by the Schiller farm, Leslie arched her neck, attempting to catch a glimpse of anyone outside the farmhouse. She knew that Mona had been scheduled to work at the hospital most of the day, but hoped her friend would not be too tired to talk with her later about the events of her troubling afternoon with Roger. Leslie trusted the petite woman to keep her confidence. Without her friend Diane to sound out ideas, she felt at a loss. Leslie and Diane had been extra close since Bill Weldon's death and she thought often about calling, but there was no point in worrying her.

Leslie chuckled, thinking what Diane's reaction might be to everything that had happened. *She'd tell me to sell the place and get myself back to New York pronto.* Diane wouldn't understand what all was at stake. *Dear friend, I've lived a lifetime since that day we sat together in the restaurant, but we'll speak soon—I promise.*

Turning in beneath the unhinged *Riker Ranch* sign, Leslie's steered her SUV around the curving drive to the ranch. Exiting the car, she carried her purse high on her arm, so she could also heft the box of art supplies. She lugged everything to the back entrance, somehow managing to unlock the door. With the pain in her ankle, she passed through the kitchen searching for a quick place to unload the box.

Releasing her load on top of the dining room table, Leslie stretched her back. Inhaling, she tensed with fear, sensing she was not alone in the room. Her blood went cold. Whirling about, she gasped in terror. Boris faced her, no more than four feet away.

The wolf-dog is inside my house! He'd followed her in, leaving her no avenue of escape.

Leslie tried to say something, but her mouth was void of saliva. Clearing her throat, she made a guttural sound. The dog stepped forward, and Leslie braced herself against the table. Common sense told her she shouldn't show fear, but every instinct screamed at her to run for the nearest room with a door. Her eyes scanned the hallway.

Boris crouched, moving forward. Leslie quit breathing. What did he want—food? He wasn't growling, but then some animals had been known to attack without a sound. Her eyes locked in on his bristly face. His pale, yellowish eyes kept her under surveillance, while she poised for any sign of attack. The dog paced the room in a semi-circle. In a flash movement, the animal leapt up on the worn seat of Wayne's recliner and curled around before plopping his head on his paws.

Leslie's ridged shoulders slumped, her breath coming in short gasps. Even though the forlorn-looking animal continued to watch her, she now felt he meant her no harm. "You're still missing Wayne, aren't you, boy? I'm so sorry," she said gently.

Turning back to the painting supplies, she lifted and carried them down the hall to Wayne's bedroom, placing them on his emptied dresser top. Until she set up a work area, the box could remain there. She needed space with sunlight and decided to look for the right spot tomorrow, when her mind was clearer.

Walking into the living room, Leslie's focus reverted to the old recliner, half expecting Boris to be gone, but the dog was asleep in the chair. She found herself tiptoeing out to close the breezeway door so she wouldn't awaken the grieving dog. Passing back through the kitchen, she paused to draw herself a tall drink of water, wondering what, if anything, she should do about Boris, the wild dog.

I'm not brave enough to ask that dog to leave, she thought wryly. Shrugging, she opted to table the concern and worry about supper. A microwave dinner out of the freezer was an easy choice. She had some thinking to do, and her foot needed a rest.

After her simple meal, Leslie carried an ice pack and hot tea with her back to the inviting couch. With her foot propped up, her focus wandered from the sleeping dog in the chair to the compelling colors out the front windows. The sun was settling across the road on Clive's red roof. It was the quiet time of the day—the time she loved. Suddenly all the unanswered questions about the ranch itself, the so-called accidents and her uncertain future all waned as the softness of the couch and warmth of the soothing tea eased her into the crook of the pillows and peacefulness of sleep.

*

It was dark when hard pounding woke Leslie from a deep sleep. Boris came off the recliner like a rocket. Growling, he pounded through the house toward the breezeway. Startled, Leslie sat straight up in the darkened room, unsure where she was or what was happening. Barking and pounding assaulted her ears.

Pushing up to an unsteady, standing position, she clutched the back of the sofa to stay her swaying. Once steady, she quickly made her way to the breezeway door, surprised to view Clive glaring back at her through the window. Boris was growling alongside her, but it no longer frightened her to be near him.

"Open up!" Clive ordered.

11

A Rash Flight

UNLOCKING THE DOOR, LESLIE OPENED IT and backed away, observing Clive as she would a crazed lunatic. "What in the world is the matter with you?"

Seeing Clive, Boris backed off to the side, accepting, yet watchful.

"What's the matter with me?" he ranted. "We have been calling you for two hours. Ray heard you honk and saw you drive by hours ago, so we knew you were home. Your landline sounded like it was off the hook, and you didn't answer your cell. What were we to think?" Catching sight of Boris, he stared as if noticing him for the first time. He regarded Leslie with question.

Leslie yawned, sleepy-eyed, a lax finger pointed at the dog. "He just came in. It weirded me out at first. I didn't know whether to run or scream."

"I can imagine. Boris can be intimidating." His piercing focus returned to Leslie. "That doesn't explain why you didn't answer your phone. Mona's been imaging all sorts of scenarios—none of them good. Ray had an important meeting in town, so she called me."

"Come on in." She motioned to Clive. Though her head was still fuzzy with the need for sleep, she felt embarrassed for causing Clive and Mona extra worry. Walking through to the kitchen, she paused by the phone on the counter. The receiver was on its side off the hook. "I must have hit it with the box I carried in earlier and never realized," she murmured.

"What about your cell?" Clive persisted.

She looked around for her purse, remembering she'd left it in Wayne's bedroom. "Oh! It's in the back room. I never heard it ring," she admitted sheepishly. "I'm really sorry. I was so exhausted I fell asleep on the couch."

They stared at one another as milliseconds passed. Finally, Leslie indicated the couch. "Sit down, and I'll put on some coffee. I need to wake up, myself." When he hesitated, she added, "Look, I appreciate you coming all the way down here to check on me. The least I can do is offer you a cup of coffee, but maybe you should first call Mona and let her know I'm still alive." She headed for the kitchen and fumbled with a can of coffee in the cupboard.

Clive followed Leslie and simultaneously called Mona.

"Ask her if she'll call me later," Leslie requested. "I need to talk with her."

Clive regarded her curiously. "That might be difficult. She'll be gone most of the night. She was heading out the door to meet Ray."

"Oh," Leslie said, disappointed.

Leslie filled the pot with water and prepared the coffee mixture. Afterward, she leaned against the counter, observing the lean, bronzed cowboy, and wondered about questions that had never come to mind before: *When and why did he decide to raise race horses? And why isn't he married?* By the time Clive closed his cell phone, the coffee pot gurgled softly, filling the kitchen with the enticing aroma of flavored coffee.

Clive inhaled. "Hazelnut! I haven't smelled that since two days before Wayne died when he and I sat at that very table after breakfast." He pointed to the table in front of the window, and a small sigh slipped out.

Evidently the dog wasn't the only one who was mourning her cousin, Leslie thought. Looking around, she said, "I think I have a package of cookies in the pantry if you're interested. Mona and I went shopping the other day."

Clive scanned the spotless sink and counters, then the emptied microwave dinner plate deposited in the trash. "I see you had a simple dinner." His curious gaze probed her. "Not very hungry? I guess your big luncheon with Galbraith filled you up."

Leslie averted her eyes. "Not really. I actually didn't eat much at lunch, and I was too tired to fix anything requiring effort tonight."

Acting completely at home, Clive walked to the cupboard nearest the sink and took out two mugs, passing one to Leslie. "Where'd you eat?"

"Park Place on the square." She carefully lifted the steaming pot and poured a full cup. Handing it to Clive, she exchanged it for the empty mug.

Looking puzzled, he sipped the dark, fragrant brew. "The food at Park Place has always been quite good..." It was a leading question.

"The food was great! I-I just wasn't as hungry as I thought." Staring out the window, Leslie pressed against the sink.

"Did something upset you?" Clive studied the insides of his cup.

Leslie debated the merits of answering his question.

"Leslie?" Clive inched closer, pressing for an answer.

She shrugged. "The whole thing is silly, but while I waited in Roger's entry area, the president of the National Pride Bank came out of his inner office. It looked as if they were having a meeting."

"They probably were. Why did that bother you?" He studied her.

"It was something Mona said when I first met with Roger about the inheritance. She indicated that Roger's rapid success and acceptance in the business community of Dahlonega could have been helped by a secret promoter—an important backer. Even Roger mentioned he's only in town because a 'special friend' invited him. So when I saw Hamilton Longworth at his office, I remembered them talking at the vineyard restaurant and couldn't help but make an assumption. I really like Mr. Longworth," she said soberly.

"Did you ever ask Galbraith who this 'special friend' was?" Clive asked.

"He got all nervous and told me his friend was shy. In other words, his secret friend doesn't want to be known. That sounds pretty iffy to me."

Checking his watch, Clive nudged Leslie. "Sit at the table and get off your foot. I'm going to scramble some eggs with toast. My supper was cut short, and I'm still hungry."

Leslie winced, realizing she was the reason for his shortened meal. "Be my guest. The eggs are fresh—courtesy of Ray and Mona's chickens." She watched him move with confidence, pulling out a bowl and scrounging in the refrigerator. "Look on the third shelf," she directed from the table.

"I know where the eggs are. I'm looking for green pepper, onion, and cheese. I've decided on an omelet."

"Green pepper and onion in the bottom hydrator, cheese in the top. I'm duly impressed. You do cook! How is it that no one has snapped you up?"

He froze briefly behind the refrigerator door before gathering his ingredients. Leslie waited, feeling like she had crossed an invisible line.

He closed the door with his knee, carrying the omelet fixings to the counter. "Because the one lady in question thought becoming a Philadelphia lawyer was more important than being on hand to be my wife, and I wasn't interested in a long-distance marriage. I'm an old-fashioned guy in that respect."

Concentrating on his project, Clive moved quickly to prepare his concoction. He removed a large fry pan from the bottom drawer of the stove. "Think you can handle buttering the toast?" He threw her a challenging look.

Jutting her chin outward, Leslie pushed up from the table and walked across the kitchen to an opposite cupboard to pull out a toaster. She turned to add, "Oh, we're in luck, I bought some new jam. I'll get that out too." Pausing, she noticed Boris watching them from beneath a chair near the far wall. At some point he'd made his way into the kitchen.

"Clive, look!" she said quietly, not wanting to make any rash movements or loud sounds. "What do you think he wants?"

"Do you have any food? Try putting some out in the breezeway and see what happens. That's where Wayne often fed him." He tossed the words over his right shoulder as the omelets sizzled in the hot pan.

Carrying a dish of dry dog food out to the breezeway, Leslie sensed the wary animal following her. She placed the dish down on a worn rug and backed away to observe him, but Boris stood off, staring back at her, his head lowered. "It's for you, Boris. Go ahead." Still the dog remained at bay. Though he eyed the food with obvious interest, the half-wild beast seemed hesitant to move. The two stood at an impasse. Slowly turning her back, Leslie headed for the kitchen, not glancing back until she heard the chomping of hard food behind her. Smiling, she returned to the toaster.

After Clive carried their plates to the table, they sat quietly eating until he revisited their earlier conversation. "So, considering this new information, what are your present feelings about Galbraith? Do you think it's possible he had a part in the *so-called* happening on the ranch?" The very fact he'd emphasized *so-called* was a major concession—seemingly a peace offering.

"So called?" She stared blankly at the jam-coated toast lying on her plate. "I don't know. I could have sworn he knew nothing about the accidents in the barn, but he did know about me planning on driving the Jeep that morning. It messed me up. I guess that's why I freaked when I saw Mr. Longworth coming out of Roger's office. I connected everything to Mona's earlier statement."

Clive's brows knit. "I wouldn't jump to conclusions about Longworth quite yet, but keep your eyes open. About Wayne's Jeep…when I go into town tomorrow, I'll check on its status. The mechanic's findings could tell us something about the garage incident." He hesitated. "Did Galbraith appear to sense anything awry today in your manner?"

"I-I'm not sure. Wait, he did say that he thought the stress of the ranch was affecting me." Leslie stared at him, frowning. "What made you ask?"

He shrugged. "Come on, Leslie. You wear your emotions on your sleeve. You feel things deeply, and it shows. That day we rode out to Rocky Ridge, your eyes danced like a child at the circus."

His appraisal made her uncomfortable, and she focused on her uneaten toast. "It's nice to know I light up like a neon sign for *all the world* to know my innermost feelings," she flung out.

"Look, don't get your back up..." He softened his tone. "Feeling deeply is not a bad thing. Your unexpected joy at the simplest things is a good thing. Like that day in my truck. Your delight makes everything around you light up as well." He averted his eyes, as if he'd revealed too deeply of himself.

Feeling her heart quicken at the tone of his voice, Leslie panicked, thinking how she might tiptoe past this awkward moment. She drew quickly from her afternoon conversation with the Peabodys. "Clive, do you happen to know of a Miguel Romero in these parts?"

Clive gave her a strange look. Nodding slowly, he replied, "I do."

"Wonderful!" Leslie said, relieved. "Next question, do you have any idea where this man lives?"

Again, he nodded slowly, appearing puzzled. "Up west of here. I can draw you an easy map. You'll need one if you want to pay a visit. It's a remote wooded area. Miguel did a lot of hunting when he was young."

"Yes, Walton said the same thing." She couldn't believe her good fortune. This was one clue she didn't have to dig for. "Thanks, Clive. I really appreciate your help." She rose from the table to locate paper for him to draw the map.

When Clive said good-bye later, Leslie stood next to him at the breezeway door. Gesturing toward Boris, she asked, "What should I do about him?"

His cowboy grin twisted into a smirk. "I'd take care not to make him angry. Outside of that, treat him like any other dog." Opening the door, Clive called, "Boris, out."

Leslie was startled as the large, bristly dog slinked out from the kitchen and through the opened door. "You make it seem so easy," she murmured, finding it hard to regard Boris like she would any neighborhood dog.

Clive winked. "I think Boris likes you. In fact, after tonight, I'd go so far as to make the statement that it might be hard to get rid of him. He has adopted you, Leslie Weldon. Boris makes strong alliances and never forgets—remember that. Try calling him back inside the house in fifteen minutes."

Dropping her jaw, Leslie asked, "Why would I do that?" The idea of that wild, unpredictable animal inside while she slept made her breath catch.

"Because you'll never get a better watchdog. Besides, if I knew Boris was inside with you, I might not feel a truck parked in your driveway at night was necessary."

Leslie stared outside at the dense blackness, interrupted in part by reflected light streams from the large yard light. "Really?" She searched Clive's face for confirmation.

His eyes were solemn. "Really!"

"Hmmm," she murmured. "I'll give it a try and let you know. Keep my protection unit at bay until I call, okay?" she said, hopeful.

"Will do." Lifting his worn, cowboy hat from a hook by the door, he tipped his hat like an old Western hero and disappeared into the night. His voice echoed from the darkness, "Don't forget to call!"

She stuck her head outside. "I'll call—quit nagging!"

Hearing the familiar engine rev up, she closed and locked the door, checking her watch. *Fifteen minutes. We'll see, Boris. We will see.*

Stacking the dishwasher, she allowed the pan to soak in the kitchen. Leslie stared out the window, squinting at the visible bushes while she wondered about Boris. With his stomach full, why would an undisciplined dog with no loyalties want to come back inside?

After the suggested time frame, she opened the door feeling rather foolish. *I promised I'd try.* Shuffling outside, she concentrated the thrust of her voice in the direction she'd seen the animal melt into the landscape. "Boris! Boris!" Waiting, she called again. When there was no response, Leslie reluctantly shut the door. She was surprised to realize a part of her had hoped the dog would prove her wrong.

Leslie was at the entrance into the kitchen when she heard scratching at the back door. Whirling, she rushed back to throw it open. The huge animal entered warily, studying her every move. Like a statue she stood, watching Boris make his way through the house to Wayne's chair. One easy leap and the dog settled in. Leslie followed him into the living room, regarding the dog in awe. *Unbelievable!*

"He's here, Clive! You were right! I really didn't think he'd come back inside." She held the phone against her head, leaning against the sofa cushions and chuckling softly. "So you can call off your human watchdogs tonight. Thanks for supper."

"Think nothing of it. Every cowboy knows how to cook eggs," the deep, sleepy-sounding voice came back.

"Good night, Cowboy, and thanks again." Closing down her phone, she rested her head back and mused on her unusual evening with rancher Clive Masters. *You're truly an unpredictable man, Mr. Masters. I don't know how to figure you sometimes.*

*

The long afternoon nap had taken the edge off her need for immediate sleep. Hefting Wayne's journal up on the bed, Leslie flipped pages at random, allowing her eyes to flit over various paragraphs. She had no patience for systemized study at this time of night. She passed by the writings of the early days on the ranch when Wayne was learning how to run the everyday operation. When her eyes rested on a certain portion, she read a highlighted section where Wayne talked about his search for God. Emotion caught in her throat. Suddenly she was afraid to read further—where it might lead.

Instead she flipped a few pages over, to read of his growing friendship with the Schillers and Clive Masters, how the three ranches worked together, helping one another whenever a need came up. It caused her to smile. *They're still helping me, Cousin Wayne. But somehow I think you know that.*

She scanned through more pages, resting on a sentence here and there, until she came to a section entitled *A New Friend.* Wayne talked about meeting a friend in town…a man who sought him out. The man told him he'd heard Wayne enjoyed fishing and was looking for a guide who was acquainted with the best fishing holes. Pausing, Leslie thought on what she'd read.

Clive had told her that anyone who knew about Wayne knew he loved to fish. From the writings, Leslie could tell Wayne's new friendship spiraled overnight to great heights. There were notations about them fishing at one spot and then trying another. After such occasions, Wayne and his friend would return to his ranch, where they'd fried up their catch and play cards.

Reading on, she saw a smaller notation indicating his friend was well known in town, a professional, who preferred Wayne not spread his name around. The friend didn't want people to try and pressure Wayne to impose upon his friendship for greedy reasons. *Interesting choice of words.* Leslie paused again to mull over what she had just read, troubled by its implications. *How could anyone impose upon Wayne's friendship with this man? What position in town was so important that people could manipulate it for greed? Greed suggested money might be involved. Was he a rich man?*

Leslie scanned through additional pages. Never once was this "new friend" mentioned by name. She found this odd, maybe even ominous. *Was Wayne afraid to write the name down?* More than that, the whole scenario sounded surprisingly familiar. Rubbing the back of her neck, she tried to ignore the nagging irritation. It was too late to deal with suppositions and innuendos. She closed the journal.

Tomorrow held the promise of new answers to some of her questions. Speaking of friends, Leslie had hoped to ask Mona to accompany her on a visit to an old friend of Wayne's, Miguel Romero—supposedly someone who could tell her about the old journals. Unfortunately, while sharing the omelet, Clive let it slip that Mona would be working at the hospital again tomorrow. "Looks as if I'll be going it alone."

The day she and Mona had traveled cross-country in Mona's little truck had been a day to remember. A bond had formed between them on that crazy cross-country ride. Mona had courage as well as wisdom, a good combination for a friend. Tomorrow, Leslie would have to pursue her quest for answers on her own.

Talking with Miguel might be an easier route to ferret out important information than sorting through complicated, hard-to-read pages of some of the older journals. If Miguel could condense the information, it would save time and be a great help. Leslie wanted answers, but something warned her that time was important. It had been almost three weeks since the boot had been on her foot. Another three weeks would put her close to the end of her New York apartment lease. Still unready to make a decision about the ranch, she pondered the idea of extending her lease for yet another six months.

Whether she'd be financially able to do that was doubtful, and with no means of support, she'd have to delve into the savings her father had left her. It was her cushion fund for emergency, and she hated to violate it without good cause. Rotating her neck to ease the tightness, Leslie was thankful a few days of grace to decide remained. She turned out her lights, suddenly remembering the wolf dog asleep in her living room. Sighing at the bizarre irregularities of her topsy-turvy life, she rolled over toward the window and blocked out her thoughts.

*

Meg McDonald slipped out of her bed fully clothed. Tonight was the night! She'd overheard Cleary talking with the Vanook brothers before supper. They would be going up into the woods again tonight. Everything she had of value was inside her worn jean backpack.

Her head inched around the trailer door to scan the area for any sight of Cleary or Fred and Zeke. It was cloudy tonight, but Meg knew those clouds would part and even a half moon shining clear could reveal her position. Running a tongue across her dry lips, she wondered at the distance and time it would take to race down the hill, past the Vanook shack, and over to the waiting pickup that was parked in the drive. The tricky part would be passing the house. What if one of them was looking out the window?

Summoning every ounce of courage she had, she made a dash for the first cover of trees. From there, she zigzagged down the hill, praying the cloud cover held. Arriving at the back of the house, Meg inched slowly toward the front corner. She drew in a deep breath. Everything depended on her reaching the pickup truck without being seen.

Both the truck and backhoe had been ready for hours, ever since the call had come in from the boss—whoever the boss might be. Cleary came storming inside the trailer, flush-faced and half-drunk as usual, demanding she lay out his clean overalls and work boots. "I've got important work to do tonight. So don't go sassin' me or messin' around, or you'll cause me to miss somethin' I need to take proper care of. What are you standin' around for? As soon as you're done fixin' supper, hurry and pack me a lunch for later." That was the moment Meg knew for certain she had to make her move.

Hugging the edge of the house, she peered around the corner. Seeing no obstacles, she backed out into the front yard just far enough to observe the edge of the front windows. They were still haphazardly covered with faded sheets highlighted with lights blazing from within. Backing further away, she held her breath, seeing a stark shadow moving about inside. If she were caught outside, Cleary would beat her for sure. But it was the Vanook brothers she feared more than anything.

Standing still as a lawn ornament in the front yard, Meg felt sweat dripping inside her T-shirt until her skin felt clammy all over. The moving shadow sat with his back toward the window, and then the yelling and swearing began. Catching a word here and there, she figured maybe the whole bunch was playing cards. Hoping to make a break, Meg whirled and raced for the pickup, climbing like a frightened squirrel over the tailgate. She scampered underneath the huge tarps covering their mud-covered tools.

Squirming down between the tools far enough to disguise her existence, she hoped she wouldn't be discovered, should they lift the tarp. What she didn't know was how long the wait would be between now and the time the men would drive off.

Feeling the pockets of her thin jean jacket, she fumbled out a cold biscuit. Necessity told her to go easy on what food she was able to carry. There hadn't been much time, but she had her wits about her to fix double the portion of fried fish and biscuits at supper, slipping in the rest of the cheese from lunch. At the last minute, she'd stashed a jar of peanut butter, a handful of bread slices, and a bottle of water.

Remembering the money in Cleary's dresser, she argued with herself about how much to take. In the end, she'd left half of the wad of bills for Cleary, just in case he ever caught up with her. If she'd taken it all…well, there'd be no telling what the man might do in his meanness. Her fingers lightly touched the bruised area around her eye.

Brushing the biscuit crumbs from the front of her shirt, the tired young girl settled back against hard metal objects to wait. No matter how Meg worked to stay awake, as one hour followed another, she gradually dozed off, awakening sometime later to loud voices and the cranking of the truck engine. Over to the side of the truck, the jarring sound of the backhoe erupted, and piercing lights crisscrossed their blinding rays far out into the darkness. Fear stuck her heart. There was no turning back from here on out. She braced herself as the truck rumbled over the rough drive, turning out on the road.

Meg had no idea where they were going. She knew only what she'd learned by listening to Cleary brag while talking with the Vanooks. Whatever they were doing included going up to some woods on a secret job. Suddenly the ride turned unbearably rough. The truck rumbled over the rockiest surface she ever felt. On and on the truck bounced and pitched her into the sharp-edged tools. She was slammed against the side and bottom of the truck. Her shoulders and legs were bruised in so many places, she lost count. There was nothing to do but hold on the best she could and pray for relief.

When the truck started upward, she lost hold of the side panel and slid clear to the back of the tailgate, banging her head. Trying to right herself, her hand went to the pain on the side of her head. "Oooh," she murmured, feeling a warm, sticky substance on her fingertips. "I'm bleeding!" Her words were lost in the vibration of the truck.

She tried to wipe her hand on the tarp but was jarred to the side. *When is this ride from hell going to end?* Meg didn't know how long she could stand being thrown about in the back of this truck. The handle of a shovel skinned her cheek and something pointed stabbed her in the thigh. When the ride ended abruptly, she sat stunned. Suddenly, she was struck with the realization she had to move fast, while the lights on the backhoe shined down on a rocky plateau away from the back of the truck. Now was her chance, before Fred or Zeke climbed out of the truck cab.

Aching in every part of her body, Meg slid her bruised limbs over the left side of the tailgate down in the blackness and limped up over the incline into the nearby woods. *I've got to get as far away from them in this darkness as I can. I'll look for a place to hide out later.* If she didn't hurt so badly, she could move faster. *Push yourself, McDonald, you can't stop!* she told herself.

I can't let them find me!

*

Stirring, Leslie heard a dog whining and sat up in bed to get her bearings. Again she heard the whining. *Boris! The dog wants out. That's what I get for letting him inside for the night.* Sliding to the edge of the bed, she slipped into her surgical boot and hobbled from the bedroom through the long house. Passing the living room, she noticed Wayne's empty chair and followed the whining to the breezeway door. She found Boris up on his hind legs scratching against the window.

"Stop that! Down," she yelled, too sleepy to be intimidated by the half wild animal. Boris stood down and growled at the closed door, his feet prancing in place. Opening the door wide, she waited for Boris to run outside, but he stayed right beside her, whining. She stared down at him, frustrated. *What is it? What does this dog want?*

Leslie was ready to order the animal outside when she heard the haunting cry. It was the same crying she'd heard first at Mona's house, sleeping next to the opened windows. The eerie sound grew louder, and Boris began to whine again. Instinctively her hand went to the back of the dog's head. "Hush, boy. It's okay," she comforted. Closing and locking the door, she hobbled back through the house with Boris on her heels.

Turning into Wayne's bedroom, she located her purse and phone. She speed-dialed Clive's number and listened to it ring repeatedly. "Pick up, Clive. Pick up! Clive!" she cried, when he finally answered the phone. "Open your door and listen. *The crying!* Listen to the *crying!*"

"I hear you. Hang up and stay where you are. I'll check it out."

"Please would be nice," Leslie murmured, closing down her cell. Limping back to the breezeway, she unlocked the door to listen, biting on her lip. Had the crying stopped? She imagined Clive running to the side door, hearing nothing. *I'll look like such a fool!*

Starting to close the door, she heard the sobbing begin. Leaning against the door facing she listened to the eerie sound pierce the night. *No wonder Henri O' thinks the woods are haunted.* The phantom sounds gave her chills. She rubbed her arms and closed the door against whatever spirits were out there—be they human or otherwise.

Turning, she almost tripped over Boris and caught herself in surprise. "I forgot about you. Come on, boy." Stopping at the refrigerator, she threw the dog a piece of meat and reheated herself a cup of coffee. Sitting down at the kitchen table, Leslie raked her hand through her long, ruffled hair and waited.

Raising her head from her propped hand cradle, Leslie regarded the dog with curiosity. "So why didn't you run out outside when I opened the door?" The wiry animal studied her with pale eyes. "Strange." This wild animal had stayed right by her side. Leslie wasn't quite sure what to make of it. Cocking his head, Boris stalked back into the breezeway and lay down by the door, whimpering from time to time. Hearing the dog, Leslie sighed. "I know just how you feel."

*

Meg staggered through the brush, feeling it tear at her clothing and skin. Once she covered a safe distance, she pulled out the penlight she'd stolen from

Cleary's top drawer and flicked it on, pointing the tiny beam ahead of her near the ground. Maybe it would help keep her from tripping over dead logs and jutting rocks. There was no clear trail. She had to make her own way through the undergrowth of trees and tried hard not to think about snakes or anything larger.

She froze in place hearing the sound, not wanting to believe her ears. "Why would a child be crying away out here? The eerie sound was coming from deeper in the woods. Was it possible a small child had wandered away from home and become lost in the woods? Her heart ached at the thought of a lost child. She remembered the night her mother died and left her with Cleary.

Rushing on, she pushed the branches out of her way, holding the miniscule glow barely ahead of her footsteps. Her heart was pounding from exertion, her body aching from the beating she'd suffered riding in the back of the truck, but she plunged through the brush toward the compelling cries.

Meg's lungs were too depleted to call out a word of comfort. The fear of having her position discovered kept her mute. The cries suddenly ceased. After a few minutes of silence, she paused beneath low branches of a towering pine, holding to a huge branch for support. Lifting her head, she held her breath so she might hear even the faintest of whimpers. Aside from the sound of her beating heart, only a gentle breeze rustling leaves of nearby trees filled the night air. Meg had no idea which way to turn. Why had the crying stopped? Had someone come for the child? No one had ever come for her.

Weary, she let go of the branch and lowered her body to the pine-needled covering below. Meg longed for deeper rest, but fear of falling to sleep and being discovered urged her forward. *I need to find a safe place to hole up for the night.* A child's piercing cry caused Meg to leap to her feet. Yanking up her backpack, she headed in the direction of the last the sound.

Deep into the dense foliage, she blindly followed the distant cry. Wherever she was headed, it was high on this wooded ridge. Never once had the cries veered from this height or led her downward onto the rockier slopes. From time to time the disturbing cries would cease, only to begin again moments later. It struck her as odd, but she plunged ahead to shorten the distance.

Following the last sequence of eerie vibrations, their sound mixed with the wind and wafted through the trees branches, creating a terrifying whine. Hating the sound, Meg forged through the brush until she heard something more frightening than the cries—voices of men. Their words were unclear, but their very presence could mean danger.

She switched off her penlight and moved cautiously in their direction, her heart in her throat. Had kinfolk come for the child? If indeed the men were family, this might be her opportunity for freedom. Surely they would take her to a bus stop so she could get away. But why were her feet reluctant to chance the opportunity? Mentally she berated herself for the cowardice.

Spotting a low-lit lantern, Meg quietly slid down between the trees to observe. Two men were stooping in a dark area off to the side with their backs to her. She scanned the visual clearing. Where was the child? The crying had come from this section of forest, Meg was sure of it. She squinted but couldn't see anything to indicate their reason for being there. She strained to listen, not understanding.

A honkin' big dude stood to his feet and addressed a smaller guy squatting near his feet. "Pack everything up, Al. That's enough for tonight. I heard some rumbling over in the west, and I don't plan on staying on this ridge in a thunderstorm. I'll not end up a freakin' lightning rod for nobody, not even the old man."

The little fellow had a floppy hat and she couldn't see his profile, but she heard something distinctive in his high-pitched voice. "What about Zeke and his men?"

"What about them? If they don't have brains enough to pack it in early before the storm hits, it ain't our fault."

"But the old man's pushing for a breakthrough. The rig's been down for too many nights already. It's putting things behind."

"Is that our fault? It's his agenda." The big man swore. "He's so worried someone is gonna get wise before it's legally in his hands." He reached down and picked up a large box in one arm and lifted the lantern with his free hand. "I got this stuff. Can you manage the rest?"

"Yeah! I got it. You lead the way and keep that light away from our faces."

The big guy swung around, the lantern level with Meg's face. She turned her head down and away from him, so the light couldn't reflect off her face. As he passed her bushes, she saw he was wearing cowboy boots with tooled snake designs.

Meg cringed deeper in the brush, not daring to look up as the slight man followed behind. All she saw was the floppy hat disappearing into the woods in the direction she had just come from. Minutes passed and she remained where she was, afraid to move. *What were those guys doing out here in the woods at night? They knew Zeke and Fred Vanook!* It chilled her to the bone. *What if I'd run right into their midst?*

In the distance the hooting of an owl echoed through the trees making her jump and her skin tingle with fear. *It's spooky how the child's cries stopped!* Meg shivered. All she wanted was out of these woods. She clamped her hand over her mouth to keep from screaming. She was so frightened. There was something evil in this place.

Crawling into the small clearing, she found she was able to see more of her surroundings. Lifting her eyes, she noticed the parted clouds. The moon brightly lit up the trees, faintly showing a narrow path a head. As the big man said, thunder was rumbling in the west. Meg knew her space of time was short to find a way out of these woods, away from those creepy men and the pending storm. Standing, she whispered a prayer of thanks for the moonlit path. Lengthening her steps, she pushed her stringy hair away from her face and forced her waning energy to the surface. How long she pressed forward, through the shrubbery, she didn't know. Each time she stumbled, she pushed herself up and tried again. *How big is this woods? I'm so tired. If I could just lay my head down.*

Clouds covered the moon and cloaked the woods in shadows. Only by switching on her penlight was Meg able to follow the path again. Whoever had created this path hadn't walked it for a long time. It was almost grown over. Reaching the edge of the tree line, she almost stumbled over an outcropping of rock. It was a ridge that dropped sharply to a rocky ravine. Two steps further and she might have pitched over the side. Her thin shoulders heaved in relief. *Thank You, Jesus.*

Backing away, Meg picked up the path leading away back into the woods. When the path ended, she held to the side of a huge pine tree and looked out upon a vague outline of a possible refuge. She pressed her lips to keep from bawling.

Wiping her dirty face with her jacket sleeve, she extended her light just far enough to know she'd have to climb down from this ridge. She positioned her backpack and carefully took her first step down. *All I want is a place to sleep...someplace safe from Cleary, Fred, and Zeke.*

12

Miguel Romero

AFTER CLIVE'S LATE CHECK-IN CALL, Leslie turned out the lights and went to bed. Disappointed and confused, she'd left Boris to curl up in Wayne's chair. *Nothing!* Clive had found nothing. He'd driven his truck past the end of her drive and then turned, hoping to pick up the source of the cries by following the farm drive out past the big barn. At that point the crying had faded off and he couldn't get a bearing. She remembered his final remark with irritation.

"Forget the cries, Leslie! It's probably some unusual phenomenal occurrence...the wind in the trees up on the ridge. Evan tells me that people in this part of the country have been talking about a whining in the woods for years. Some of them, like Henri O', have connected the sound with the old stories of ghosts."

Wind noises—ghosts. Leslie wasn't buying any of it. *Somehow I'm going to get to the bottom of those weird sounds.* It was a long time before she could drift off to sleep. Hearing thunder clap over the roof and seeing the lighting flash outside her bedroom window didn't help her state of mind.

*

It was later than usual when she awoke the next morning to Boris's whimpering. Heavy with sleep, she staggered out to the breezeway and opened the door, allowing the eager dog to rush past her. Leslie's eyes lifted to the sky, where a warm peachy glow hovered over the low mountains. Trees and bushes were still wet, heavy from last night's storm. By the time she glanced around, the dog had disappeared. With a shake of her head, Leslie tried to line her thoughts with the coming events of the day.

Gnawing on part of a bagel, she slid into her car and backed around to head out of the drive. On the seat next to her purse, lay the simple map Clive had drawn for her, directions to Miguel Romero's home.

The directions led due west of Dunn and Ryman road in much the same direction she and Mona had driven home the day of their cross-country ride, with the slight variation of a gravel turn off winding up the side of the mountain. Clive had said Miguel's house was remote in the woods. Wondering how anyone was able to scale this drive in the winter, she carefully followed the twisting road.

Following the sweeping curve, Leslie spied the cabin-like home tucked up on a wooden mound. Smoke spiraled up out of a double-stone chimney. There was a series of steep stairs leading up to the expanded wraparound porch. "Interesting," she murmured, noticing the handicapped entrance off to the right side of the porch.

She mounted the stairs, scanning the peaceful surroundings. Late-morning sun created deep shadows throughout the woods and across the porch. Hoping she wasn't calling too early, Leslie knocked gently on the worn, wood-planked door. Hearing an indiscernible verbal response, she took it as an encouragement to enter and hesitantly opened the door.

"Oh, please, come on inside. And forgive my not answering personally."

Leslie's gaze swept over the rustic log interior to a sunlight window where an elderly man sat reading in a wheelchair. "Mr. Romero?"

"That would be me most days, unless you're a bill collector," he said, chuckling. "How may I help you, miss?"

He was a swarthy skinned man with white, thinning hair and looked to be of medium height, though the wheelchair might be deceiving. Deep lines of age and character etched his strong, square-shaped face. Some of the lines were laugh lines, Leslie determined, feeling more comfortable.

"I'm Leslie Weldon, Wayne Riker's cousin. I was told you could tell me about him…as well as the Riker journals." She watched for any hint of disapproval. There was none.

He smiled, acting pleased to have the company, and urged her closer. "Pull up a chair, my dear. I hope you've got a little time to spare. Wayne himself was a complicated subject."

She grinned. "I've got the time." Her eyes gravitated toward his blanket-covered legs and sobered, wondering why he was wheelchair bound.

Miguel lightly patted his knees. "It's too long a story to tell today, especially if you want to talk about Wayne. He mentioned you, you know?"

"Really?" She was stunned. "We only met a couple of times at most. I'm shocked that he even thought of me at all."

"The way Wayne talked, I got the feeling that he and your pa kept in close contact with one another. Wayne must have kept up on you through him."

"Oh." She wondered how much of her life Dad had revealed to Wayne.

Miguel arched his back, gently rolling his shoulders as if they ached. But he made no mention of his pain. Leslie was amazed that he could smile.

"Not being from around this area, Miss Leslie, I don't imagine you know much of our local history. This might not have been the Old West, but we had our shootouts and excitement nevertheless. Why, there was a foiled Wild West bank robbery right on the public square in Dahlonega. It was back in 1913." He leaned forward in his chair as if to emphasize the importance of his story.

Leslie took the bait. "You said *foiled?* How in the world did they prevent the robbery?" she asked, inching closer to catch his low-pitched voice.

Miguel's features came alive with animation. "It happened in the middle of the night, when there wasn't a soul in sight. Those rotten scoundrels came slinking into town, thinking they'd get a jump on a small-town bank, but some light-sleepin' fella in a second-floor apartment heard a suspicious sound next door. He sounded the alarm with one of those newfangled telephones."

Miguel chuckled. "Would you believe, the president of the bank himself, was on the switchboard that particular night? Mr. Bob Meaders. Leaving his wife to phone the sheriff, he took out after those thieves armed with a gun."

Leslie was captivated by the story.

"When the sheriff caught up with the bank president, the two marched side by side down the sidewalk with their guns a-blazing. It was a scene right out of Wyatt Earp at the OK Corral. Those bad guys high-tailed it out of town on the run." Miguel slapped his knee, enjoying the retelling of an old tale.

"Did they ever catch them?" she asked.

"Oh yeah," he said lazily. "Two days later, they found the bright lads sleeping in a ditch outside of town. As it happened, they never did get into the bank safe. Seems it was one they weren't familiar with, and they left the bank without a single dime. It was a black day for them when they rode into Dahlonega." Leaning back, he bobbed his head. "Oh, yes, ma'am, our little town has seen its share of action. We had train robbers in the area in the old days, and the gold rush had its own brand of claim jumpers. I find that no matter what the generation, there is always some form of claim jumper."

The old man's expression was secretive, almost as if he knew something Leslie didn't. It brought her back to the reason she was there. "About Cousin Wayne and the journals...," she prompted.

"You say you heard we were friends?"

She nodded.

"That's the truth and then some! Our families go back a good deal further than Wayne and me. I knew Wayne's brother long before Wayne came to

Dahlonega, and their uncle before that. Why, my great, great, great granddaddy knew the *very first* Riker to own the ranch back in the early 1800s. Jamie Cohen was a recipient of the land lottery set up by the government of Georgia in Lumpkin County in 1830." Miguel smiled, as if he'd mentally stepped back into those exciting bygone days.

"My ancient granddad was pure Spaniard, Don Jose Devasquez. He was a settler in Indian Territory and married a beautiful Cherokee girl, back in 1827, a year before the Cherokee nation was destined to change forever." He shook his head.

"It was the craziest thing you ever heard of...an early settler by the name of Benjamin Parks went hunting one day in 1828 and stubbed his toe on a glittery rock...gold. Gold was discovered and all hell broke loose—literally! Gold seekers flooded the area, and the government took charge of the territory. Somewhere along the line, the mining town of Dahlonega became the county seat. It was a time of pure bedlam!

"The government sent in surveyors to divide the land into lots for distribution to white settlers, but people weren't waiting for that. They smelled gold! Both Don Jose and Jamie got themselves good land parcels. That was before Jamie met his Clara. He wasn't looking for gold—just wanted to be a rancher and raise crops and cattle. Figured he'd make his fortune that way. Down through the years, the family acquired more land."

"What about the Cherokee Indians?" asked Leslie, bristling, "It was their land!"

"The Indians didn't like it none, that was for sure, but the Cherokees were smart, literate people. By this time, they had them a written language and their own newspaper. Their leaders could see the way the wind was blowing. There was no holding back the tide of gold seekers. By 1835, Indian leaders signed a treaty agreeing to exchange their land for equal land out west and five million dollars...but the getting there nearly killed them."

He grinned. "Will you listen to me? I'm getting way ahead of myself. Getting back to Don Jose Devasquez and Jamie Riker. They became friends soon after Jamie's great tragedy. Since that time, the families have been linked together in some manner through every generation down through the years."

Leslie felt a stirring of connection within her and looked at the old man with new interest. "No, Mr. Romero, I didn't know any of that." She couldn't help but wonder about the great tragedy in Jamie Riker's life. Hopefully Miguel would explain.

"You haven't read much of the journals, have you?"

Leslie shrugged. "I have to admit, I have not. I keep falling asleep before I get very far into them. Perhaps you can skim through some of the important things."

"I'll do what I can, but it's essential you get caught up on those journals. Wayne told me if the opportunity arose that I should instruct you to read through to the very end of his journal. It was important."

"Important? When did he tell you that?" she asked curiously.

"The very week he died. He acted a little strange, as if he wanted to say something. Looking back, I'd say the man had a feeling he was going to die."

Leslie felt her heart jump. "He knew?" It was hard for her to believe he had foreknowledge. It frightened her to think of it.

"Something was definitely troubling him, but he hemmed and hawed, acting like he was protecting me by not telling me more. I was confused as all get out—still am, though I've gathered a few ideas along the way. The two weeks before it happened, Wayne seemed obsessed with rereading the very first Riker journal. He muttered something about discovering more than he wanted to know."

Miguel's expression altered. "I saw fear in your uncle's face that day, but he plumb refused to talk about it. When Wayne left, he had this weird smile. Said the puzzle pieces were beginning to fall into place and he needed to talk to an old friend."

Hearing those troubling things about her uncle had increased her heart rate twofold. *What could all of it mean?* Whatever the meaning, it frightened her. "Miguel, do you think my cousin was afraid of *someone* in particular? You sound as if you think there was more to Wayne's death than an accident."

The dark-skinned man stared at her. "You have doubts or you wouldn't be here, Miss Leslie." It was more a statement than a question.

Leslie lowered her head, unable to put into words all the confusing incidents and troubling thoughts.

After long seconds passed without comment, Miguel spoke. "Yes, I think Wayne was afraid of someone, but I don't think he had any proof. Without proof Wayne Riker would never accuse anyone. He would have acted only on solid proof."

The old man pursed his lips. "No. I've had months to think on it, and I believe he suspected something serious but was unable to pinpoint exactly what was wrong. For several weeks, many of his comments were confusing to me. He talked like a man reasoning things through the gridwork of his mind without really coming out and saying something. I wish I could have been of more help." Miguel's gnarled intertwined fingers twisted back and forth in obvious agitation.

"Then you have no idea what part of the first journal was troubling my uncle?"

A curious smile formed at the corners of his mouth. "My speculations would do you no good, my dear. It's better to decipher the meaning yourself. But I will pray." He smiled broadly. "Wayne taught me to do that, you know. He said, 'Miguel, now that you are a believer in the true Lord, you need to talk to him and share your heart. You need to listen to His heart too...they call it prayer—a mystic communion with the God of the universe.' I've since learned that prayer isn't a shopping list you hand the Lord, asking for a new house, a new mate, or brand-new body. His spirit makes all things better, even this." He patted his wheelchair arm.

She sucked in a deep breath, feeling as if the proverbial Hound of Heaven was hot on her heels. She couldn't deal with the God element at this moment. Everywhere she turned someone was praying for her or telling her how great God was. "I suppose I should thank you for the offer of prayer, but honestly, Mr. Romero, God and I haven't been on a talking basis for some time. I hope you'll take no offense."

"Oh, I take no offense, Leslie. God can work whether you cooperate or not. He is God." He smiled, his words relaxed and nonthreatening.

She nodded, not willing to get into the subject further. Hearing the low murmur of a car motoring up the drive, Leslie felt sudden relief. She shifted toward the door. "It sounds as if you are about to have more company, Mr. Romero."

The man raised his arm weakly, squinting at his watch. "That would be my daughter coming to fix my lunch. Please stay. She's a marvelous cook."

Before Leslie could think of a gracious way to decline, the door opened. Her jaw dropped at the sight of Henri O'. Frozen in position, she stared at Mona's cook, unable to utter a word. Leslie remained in a mild state of shock, while the exotic beauty showed no surprise whatsoever.

Henri O's raised eyes calmly took in the situation. "I recognized your car, Miss Leslie. I hope you and Pa are having a good conversation." Henri O' carried in a small pot and set it on the stove. Turning to the crippled man, she nodded. "I'll have this hot for you in no time. There's plenty for you, Miss Leslie. Pa won't like it if you don't stay. He loves company."

"Ah...he's been very helpful." Leslie stared in wonder. She couldn't take her eyes off Henri O' who was, as usual, quite in charge. *How did I miss the connection between Miguel and Henri O'?*

Mona talked of Henri O's invalid father, and just the other day, Henri O' had stated her father knew Wayne better than anyone.

"Where have I been?" Leslie chastised herself for being so dense. If she hadn't been centered on Roger Galbraith and the garage catastrophe...

"You'll stay, then?" Miguel pressed, jarring her focus back to the present.

"I'll be delighted. I have no other plans."

Miguel excused himself, wheeling his chair into another room off the living room. It gave Leslie the opportunity she needed. "What's wrong with your father, Henri O'? He didn't seem to want to talk about himself."

Henri O' gently stirred the dark, enticing mixture inside the cooking pot. "Pa laughs a lot, but I hear him cry out with his pain at night, or at times when he doesn't think I can hear him. He suffers with severe rheumatoid arthritis. It's a family plight. My grandfather had it and my great uncle as well. Osteoporosis set in years back. His bones can snap like dry firewood. Osteoporosis put him in a wheelchair, where he has stayed the last four or more years. It's been hard to watch. Pa loved being outside. We go out at night and look up at the stars. Sometimes he sits and reads books about the galaxies."

Henri O' was more open than Leslie had ever seen her. Intrigued, she wanted to learn more about the Romeros. This family who knew Wayne might hold the key to the mystery surrounding the ranch.

Leslie pressed further. "Mona said you quit school and came back to help your dad out."

"Pa couldn't afford a nurse, and he couldn't manage without help. It was that simple. He used to be one of the best stone masons around. He's put in the best part of the stone fireplaces in this area, did excellent work." She added, "Pa was no slouch of a carpenter, either," indicating the rich pine cabinets mounted in the kitchen.

Leslie looked at the flickering embers in the masterful fireplace. "He did that?"

Henri O' nodded, just as Miguel wheeled his chair back in the room. "You like my fireplace, Miss Leslie?" he asked.

"It's lovely." She noted the exquisite contours of the stones. There was something familiar about the design. "Mr. Romero, did you put in the fireplace in Wayne's ranch? And the Schiller fireplace, is that your work also?"

"Miguel, please, Miss Leslie. Those and the one in the ranch house of that big horse ranch across the road. I think that was the last one I was able to do. If you get a chance, go see it." Miguel's gaze became wistful, as if he were remembering the years when he could step back and admire his work.

"I'll try," Leslie said thoughtfully, suddenly anxious to see Clive's fireplace.

As Henri O' dished up their lunch, Leslie admired other crafted accessories inside the cabin. Knowing Miguel made them created more interest. After the blessing was said, Leslie asked more questions. "Is most of the family line Spanish?"

Miguel laughed heartily. "Goodness, no! More than a few are right out of the Cherokee nation. Our great, great, great grandmother was Cherokee, as I said earlier. She was spared the March of Tears back in 1838 because of Don Jose, her husband."

"The March of Tears? I'm afraid some of my American History is somewhat foggy."

"There was a set deadline. All Indians were to be out of the territory by May 1838. For the Cherokees around Dahlonega, a holding area called 'The Station' was the beginning of their Trail of Tears. It was a long walk from Dahlonega to Oklahoma's Indian Territory with few wagons to accommodate the needy. The last groups suffered the most from the bitter winter—many died." The old man's face grew somber.

Picking up where he left off in the family line, Miguel began, "Henri O's grandfather on her mother's side was also Cherokee. His name was John Beecher, and he married an Irish girl." He held up a crooked finger. "There might be even an Italian or two thrown in there somewhere."

Leslie laughed with him, trying to keep up. "Did you say Henri O's Cherokee grandfather's name was John?"

Henri O' answered her, "Actually, John is a common name in the Cherokee culture."

"When did your name change from your ancestor, Don Jose?" asked Leslie.

"A few generations back our name switched to an only daughter when she married. Following our family tree is like walking a snake's back." Miguel laughed.

"It is rich with family heritage—a family to be proud of." Leslie knew it was almost 2:00 p.m. and time to leave. "Henri O,' lunch was wonderful. Thank you for having me. I hate to eat and run, but I have a project to work on at home."

"Nothing physical, I hope?" Miguel asked, staring at her black boot.

"Only if you count my fingers in that physical equation. Actually, I'm trying my hand at painting some Christmas bulbs for The Christmas Shoppe in town. I haven't picked up a brush in years. The result should be interesting." She shrugged. "It's one of those secret desires in life. Not profitable, except perhaps inside. I use to love to paint."

Miguel nodded, his eyes serious. "I understand. It was like that with my stone and woodwork. It filled a need." He thumped his chest with his finger. "Please tell me, Miss Weldon, you will come back?"

"Of course, I'll be back. We've got more talking to finish up. I'll try to get some journal reading done before our next visit." Leslie started for the door. Without knowing why, she turned on impulse. "You said you were going to pray? Would you pray for direction for me? I've got a lot of thinking to do." She hardly believed her own request.

"Yes. Always. Are you acquainted with Proverbs 3:5-6?"

She narrowed her eyes. "Vaguely. I presume there's a message in them?" she asked with amusement, trying to place the Scripture reference.

His smile was secretive.

She resumed her walk to the door. Leslie was on the porch when she heard the roll of Miguel's wheelchair across the floor. Aware of the door opening behind her, she paused on the second step and turned. Henri O' stood behind him on the threshold of the doorway.

"You be careful, Leslie Weldon," he called. "Henri O' told me about the Jeep malfunction in the garage. There have been far too many accidents happen on Riker Ranch." He wagged his gnarled finger. "Just remember, I personally know a goodly number of good ole boys if you ever have need of help. Just call. Take care now."

A flood of emotions choked her throat at Miguel's sweet offer of help. "Thank you, Miguel. That means a lot."

"I'll add protection to that prayer," he said with a definite nod.

Leslie's features clouded as she descended the stairs. *Miguel is afraid for me too.* Fear was an insidious spider. If she wasn't careful, it could immobilize her. She shook the chilling thoughts away. Climbing inside her SUV made her think of Wayne's Jeep, recalling that Clive was supposed to have checked on the mechanic's report. Why hadn't she heard back? It was one more thing to add to her afternoon list.

13

The Break-In

LOCKING THE CAR DOOR, LESLIE SCANNED THE SHRUBBERY around the garage and tool shed for a sign of Boris but saw none. Disappointed, she made her way to the house. Everything Miguel had said, coupled with his parting warning, had made her jumpy. In effect, she would welcome the sight of the big wolfish mutt right now. Making sure the sliding lock was in place when she closed the breezeway door, she stiffened her resolve. *I'm acting crazy here. It's the middle of the day.*

She walked through to the kitchen in time to catch the receiver on the first ring. "Yes?" she answered, curious who would call at this time of day. Mona was working.

"Bert!" Leslie exclaimed. "It is so good to hear from you. I've missed our girl talks after work. How is New York treating you, or should I say, how are you treating New York?" Leslie laughed, savoring every syllable of Alberta's words. Her life in New York was like a chapter out of a different life. Carrying the phone into the living room, she propped her booted foot on an ottoman.

"Slow down. There was a break-in at the apartment? How many other apartments were broken into? None?" Leslie felt the gulp in her throat. "I'm just glad you didn't walk in on them, Alberta. No. No. Don't worry about not catching them in the act. I have no idea what they were after." She ran her fingers through her hair, totally confused. "I appreciate your calling before the police notify me. I miss you too, dear. How is your close friend on the next block?"

By the time she hung up, Leslie was in a total funk. "Great! My apartment was tossed, and Alberta lost her closest friend to a heart attack. All in all, a very uplifting conversation," she muttered. Her spirits were the lowest she had experienced since her arrival. She felt guilty being so far away she could be of no comfort to the dear woman.

It was a huge effort to rise from the chair and enter the kitchen to warm up a cup of coffee. Leslie stood at the kitchen window slowly drinking her coffee, looking out at the wild brush and distant mountains. There was nothing at the apartment of value, only a few personal papers, and who would be interested in those?

Leslie thought about those papers. *Could there be anything of interest to someone in any of them? Old bills, tax statements, a copy of Dad's will, some of his personal letters from friends.* She wished now she had read some of the letters from Wayne she'd noticed when she'd rifled through the pile. Reading his mail had not seemed fitting at the time of his death, and later, they'd been forgotten. A break-in on the heels of all the unaccountable occurrences at Riker Ranch—a coincidence?

Cousin Wayne, what was the puzzle you were unraveling? If you had only left some viable clues... Was someone afraid of what you found out? What is it that they wanted from you, and now me?

Draining the cup, she closed her eyes. She'd promised Georgia McCray she'd paint her some bulbs and standing here wasn't getting it done.

Leslie set the cup down with finality, walking toward Wayne's bedroom with determination. She gathered some newspapers in the living room, deciding she'd use Wayne's long, pine-topped dresser to lay out her supplies. Setting herself up would take a few minutes, but her excitement was mounting. The bedroom was a large room. Leslie chose the round table by the window with plenty of light for her art table. *Pencils. I need sharpened pencils.*

Forty-five minutes later, she heard footsteps coming down the hall. "Leslie. Leslie, where are you?" Mona's voice carried throughout the rooms.

"I'm here! In Wayne's old bedroom." Leslie appreciated her friend using her key and entering by the front door. It kept Leslie from being interrupted in her project. The light was strong, and she wanted to make the most of it. The call from the New York Police department had used up a good chunk of working time.

Entering the room, Mona stopped and surveyed the art supplies strewn across the dresser. Reaching the round table, her focus centered on the bulb in Leslie's hand. "Well, I'm constantly learning new facets about you." Peering over Leslie's shoulder, she exclaimed, "That's a cardinal! I love the bright red. Nice work!" Her eyes scanned the penciled designs on the unpainted bulbs. "When did all this happen?"

"I'm keeping it simple until I can practice up and collect some reference material. Any chance you have a stash of old Christmas cards? I need some ideas for the bulbs."

"I might be able to round up some old cards. Leslie, what is all this?"

Carefully hooking the wet painted bulb on a waiting brass hanger, she cleaned out her brush and laid it aside. "Take a seat on the edge of the bed, and I'll fill you in—on more than Christmas bulbs." Leslie lifted her eyebrows for accent.

Mona glanced at her watch. "This is a busy day. I don't have long, so it better be good."

Leslie glossed over the Christmas bulbs, so she could fill Mona in on the last two days. When she mentioned seeing Hamilton Longworth come out of Roger's front office, the petite brunette came alert. Holding up a restraining hand, Leslie told her about seeing Roger and an unidentified man outside the back entrance of his office.

"That's odd. You say you overheard the words, 'Make it happen, and nightly, as always?' " Mona sat on the faded bedspread. "I'm interested in what you think."

Leslie shook her head. "I don't know, but it troubled me. There was something so secretive in their manner. And I still don't know what to make of Roger." She sighed, beseeching her friend. "Do you have time for me to tell you about my conversation with Miguel Romero this afternoon? It left me even more unsettled."

Glancing again at her watch, Mona said, "Well, I can't leave wondering, can I? Shoot."

While Leslie walked Mona through the house on her way out, she related Alberta's disturbing news about her apartment break-in in New York. She downplayed her anxiety. "It's certainly been an interesting week."

Mona stopped her by the kitchen. "Leslie, you've got to have some thoughts on the matter. There have been so many occurrences involving areas of your life, surely there has to be a link somewhere."

"The obvious connection is Wayne, the ranch, and me, but I can't for the life of me understand the what or why." Leslie rubbed the side of her head.

Slipping an arm around Leslie's shoulder, Mona gave her a slight squeeze. "This is where prayer would be of comfort to you. To know that someone bigger and all knowing could put those unexplainable areas together." Her voice, though soft and non-threatening, pierced Leslie's armor.

"I don't think God would be interested in working things out for me at this point." Leslie's focus veered off to the side.

Cocking her head, Mona regarded Leslie with a perplexed expression. "From what I've heard from your conversations, you appear to have a fair knowledge of the Scriptures. So, I'm wondering, how can you say that?"

Leslie's gut twisted. "Because somewhere I've lost my faith to believe that He is there—at least for me. I don't know. Maybe I never really did."

"Your faith isn't lost—misplaced maybe. Faith isn't a feeling like a warm and fuzzy experience. It's both a gift and a decision! You knew God was there that day we bumped cross-country looking for answers."

Leslie's head drooped. Part of what Mona said was true. She had experienced a Presence that afternoon, but it seemed so distant today. Clive had also said that faith was a decision. Why couldn't she act on it?

"You don't know the circumstances of my life." The words poured out.

"The circumstances matter only to God, but if you want a listening ear sometime, I'm available. Listen, Les, I've got to run." Pausing by the door, Mona called back, "Eat something nourishing. I mean it!"

"I will. I promise," Leslie called to her friend's retreating back, wondering what in the world it would be.

*

Leslie set her painted bulbs on the dresser to dry and cleaned up her brushes, saving her paints for another day. All the time her thoughts churned. By the time she walked out to the kitchen to think about supper, darkness had settled in. She opened the freezer, realizing she should have taken something out hours ago to thaw.

Spying a small-sized container of lasagna was a life-savor. She withdrew the frosty container and read the instructions. Cooking for one was no fun at all. *Maybe if I had someone else to consider meals for...*

Her thoughts roamed to one man in particular, but she yanked them back with a vengeance. *Fix the lasagna, Leslie Weldon, and don't daydream in that direction. Don't you have trouble enough?*

Perplexed, Leslie stared at the refrigerator shelves. There appeared to be a significant depletion of packaged food. *Strange, I don't remember eating any of the lunchmeat or sliced cheese.* She sighed. *Well, I'll just have to put them on the list.* Closing the door, she concentrated on the container of lasagna. With a flick of the wrist, she preheated the oven before heading for the breezeway.

Leslie filled the dog dish and carried it to the back door, venturing a few feet beyond. The stars were clear again tonight, and she thought of those moments she'd spent with Clive outside Mona and Ray's ranch house. Tonight she felt lonely and so very small beneath those stars. Her hand rattled the food dish. She shivered, repeatedly calling for Boris. Her words were crisp on the night air. Getting no response, Leslie turned to reenter the breezeway. Setting the dish on top of the dryer, Leslie remembered the lasagna and rushed to slide the container inside the oven and set the timer. She wondered why the bristly dog hadn't returned. Meandering back, she opened the door to call again. Boris brushed by her leg and ran straight to the dryer, rearing up on his hind legs to reach his dish.

"Down! I'll get it for you," Leslie said, laughing. "You goofus dog! Where in the world have you been? Don't eat so fast. It's not good for you."

Folding her arms, she observed the massive-sized canine. He didn't seem nearly as fierce as he had before, and she didn't understand why she ever thought the dog ugly. He had a majestic shaped head. It must have been those pale eyes that were so unnerving. "I'm really glad you came back, big boy," she said softly, leaving the dog to finish his dinner.

After her supper dishes were put away, Leslie made a place on the sofa and drew out the oldest journal from Wayne's collection. The worn inside cover read 1800 and something. The exact year was hard to decipher. Wayne had stored the weather-beaten book in a new leather sleeve to preserve what was left. She carefully turned to the first page finding the faded simple scroll. Reaching to the nearest lamp, she readjusted the lighting. So much mystic had been made of this old book, she was hesitant to read it for fear it would cast dark shadows across her ancestor's character.

> I, Jamie Daniel Riker, begin the writing of this story under the guidance of my one and only true friend, Don Jose Devasquez. My heart is so burdened with the grief of this telling, I may not be able to continue at some point. Don Jose, a godly man, tells me I must relieve the heaviness by releasing its contents to pen and paper, and then forever set it aside to live out my life as God dictates. Clara and I, we were so happy when we married and first came to the land...how am I to bear her last parting words before death: "Greed and lust for gold have been your only gods, Jamie Riker—you murderer of children! You killed our baby!"
>
> Clara's words plunged a knife in my chest, twisting night and day until I fear I shall go mad.

"Whew!" Leslie expelled a low whistle. "What an opening!"

Withdrawing her hand from the crinkled page, she reached for her steaming coffee cup. Something told her the next few pages would tell her more than she wanted to know about the infamous Riker tragedy.

Sipping gingerly, she pulled back from the cup and gently blew to cool its contents. Leslie was easing it back to its coaster when her phone rang.

Thankfully, it was within her reach. "Hell-o," she said drearily.

"My, aren't we cheerful this evening." Clive's teasing tone echoed through the receiver. "Have a bad day?"

"Not really. Only a bunch of little things, and I've just started to read one of the old journals. So far it's pretty much a downer. I'm not sure I want to read the rest."

"That must be the one Wayne mentioned, about the family tragedy. How far have you gotten?"

"The *first paragraph!"* she said dryly.

"Oh, that far. I won't keep you from its compelling story. I just wanted to know if Boris came back tonight."

Lifting her head, Leslie saw Boris curled up in Wayne's old recliner. "He sure did," she said with enthusiasm. "I had my doubts for a while, but he ran inside a little after dark. I wonder where he's been going during the day?" She threw out the remark as the thought crossed her mind. "Anyway, there's no need for bodyguards tonight."

"Well then," he hemmed awkwardly, "I guess I'll say good night."

"Clive?"

"Yes." His voice came back strong. "You need something else?"

"I was wondering if you happened to stop by and check with the mechanic about Wayne's Jeep."

"I did check on the Jeep, talked with Bob at the shop about why it wouldn't shut down, but there was nothing conclusive about the tests." Clive spoke slowly.

"What are you saying, Clive? They can't tell, or it was all an accident?"

"It's hard to say. Bob said his tests wouldn't stand up as conclusive evidence in a court of law, but..."

"But what? Clive, you're not making sense. Why don't you just say what you're trying so hard not to say?" She was feeling frustrated with the man.

"I'll try to explain it as Bob related it to me. First of all, remember you're dealing with a thirty-year-old Jeep. It's no spring chicken."

Leslie was nodding at the end of the phone. "Yes, yes, I know."

"The problem area is called an ignition lock switch, or more commonly known as an 'ignition switch.' "

She could hear him take a deep breath.

"This part is attached with two screws to the topside of the steering column down under the dashboard near the brake pedal. It is activated by a od that runs down along the steering column. In the picture of this ignition itch you could see a black plastic slider inside the slot along the bottom of the switch. If that black slider breaks inside this switch, the engine could continue to run regardless of the position of the key. I realize it might be a little hard to picture from where you are sitting, but that is what happened."

A little hard to picture? Leslie sat blank-faced listening to the technical gibberish that had no more meaning to her than any other foreign language. She yawned. "Basically, the bottom line is that it boils down to an accident—right?" she said, not knowing whether to be relieved or disappointed in the wake of recent events.

When there was no reply to her question, she called, "Clive?" and waited, wondering if they had lost their connection.

"I'm here," he said, his voice tense. "Bob implied, from what he'd examined, he thought it was deliberately tampered with. It looked to him as if that black plastic slider had a little help in breaking, but he can't prove it—except in his gut. It didn't appear to him to be wear and tear. The official report reads 'inconclusive.' "

Leslie reached for her coffee and downed half of it. "It was tampered with?"

"Yes, but it can't be proven. Though an interesting item came up. It seems our sergeant came by to talk with Bob even before I stopped by."

She said up straighter on the sofa. "What do you suppose that means? He never called me back or asked any more questions."

"It could be that he's just following up to sign off on his report. Then again, maybe he thinks there has been an above average percentage of accidents at Riker's Ranch in the last year and is digging deeper."

Leslie was mulling his words over. "I hope it's the latter."

"What happened to 'I think this could have been an accident' theory?"

It was then Leslie realized her thinking had altered. When had she began feeling like a target? Was it in the garage when she couldn't open the door, or Roger's unusual meeting outside the back of his office? Or maybe it had been when she talked with Miguel that some of the dots began to line up. "I'm not sure, really," she murmured huskily. She cleared her throat. "Did Bob mention when the Jeep would be fixed?"

Clive responded quickly, "Oh, a few more days or so, I would imagine. Bob will call when it's ready. I'll go with you to pick it up to show you where the distributor is."

"Why would I need to know where the distributor is?" she asked, weary of playing question-and-answer games.

"If the engine doesn't turn off, pulling out the distributor coil is one of two ways to turn it off. If you're going to keep the Jeep, that might be useful."

"And how about the garage door?"

"I plan on putting in windows and a side door for you—one with a key."

"Thanks," she said a little gruffly. "You don't need to take on extra work on my account."

"That's what good neighbors do, Leslie."

"That might be, but there's no way I can repay you."

"Then allow me to be a blessing. That's what Christians do."

Inside she argued against owing him more than she already did. He'd done so much on the ranch while Wayne wasn't well, not to mention his effort since she'd come and completely disrupted everyone's schedule. Silently, she admitted it made her feel warm to know Clive wanted to do it for her, but she distrusted those feelings. They hadn't served her well in the past.

"I might see you tomorrow then, when I'm working on the garage."

"Could be. I don't have any appointments that I know of."

"Roger hasn't called back?" His voice was tight.

"Not yet, but he said he would be busy the next few days."

"Tomorrow, then," Clive said briskly.

Staring at the disengaged phone, Leslie set it down, smiling quizzically. "Boris, I don't think Clive cares much for our Mr. Roger Galbraith," she mused. If only she and Roger could have an unhampered date without added suspicion, perhaps her true feelings could surface.

Roger was attentive, thoughtful, and never quarreled with her, like Clive was prone to do. Leslie thought of their luncheon at the vineyard restaurant and Roger's delight in sharing everything he thought would bring her pleasure. But she also remembered how quickly his personality could change. That troubled her.

Roger had shown an eagerness to please. Moreover, Leslie felt in control when she was with him. Never again did she want her heart to be held captive, only to see her emotions and pride trodden under. It was hard to overlook Roger's good looks or his success as a lawyer, until she remembered Kevin's attractiveness—as well as his fickle heart.

Alberta would say Roger was a good catch. *If I only knew for sure he had nothing to do with the accidents, then perhaps...*

Leslie sought out the old journal to pull her thoughts away from her warring emotions. Jamie had entitled the next section *The Courtship of Clara.* She settled in, hoping to detect something that would help her understand a reason for all the odd occurrences at the ranch.

14

Clues and Reflections

Jamie Riker: 1832
The Courtship of Clara

Clara and I met and fell in love on the long stagecoach ride to Atlanta. My good sense should have taken me straightaway back to the hills at that moment.

I could see Clara was proud of her family's status, caught up in all of the glitter. She was like a happy, yellow butterfly that day, flitting from object to object. My Clara was a social princess. I should have known. But I was drawn to her brightness, like a moth to light and blinded by my love. When I sat in the Landers' parlor, awed by all the fine furnishings, I'd wondered, *Can a girl raised in this finery survive in the Georgia wilds?*

If only I had listened to my good sense, Clara might be alive today. Her daddy owned the largest mercantile in two counties and did a lucrative business. Is love truly enough for marriage? I cannot answer for others—only from our experience. Clara told me she believed love could carry us through every hardship. It was a romantic fantasy. Her eyes were filled with stars for the adventure ahead. Poor Clara!

After the wedding ceremony, we left Atlanta in a buckboard filled with dreams and supplies for our new life on a ranch in the foothills of the Appalachian Mountains. The nearest social contact was the rough mining town of Dahlonega and distant farms.

At some point along the trail, my mind cleared of wedding cake and good wishes. All I could think of as we bumped along each mile, carrying us further from civilization was Clara's dreams. *What is she gonna say when she sees our humble house?*

In reality, it was no more than a two-room shack, but I was looking to our future plans when I'd called it a ranch. It had been enough for me for two years, but after seeing the Landers' home, I began to worry hard. Would it be enough for Clara?

I will never forget my bride's face when we drove up to the

homestead. Her horror-stricken expression will haunt me all the days of my life.

"What have I done?" I asked myself.

LESLIE CLOSED THE BOOK, not emotionally equipped to handle more negative input. She promised herself to continue the next day. In what little she'd read, she felt sorry for Jamie as well as Clara. Their marriage was obviously a calamity bent on destruction. She shook her head as she thought back on her engagement to Kevin.

As painful as their breakup, she could now see it was a good thing. God had done her a favor allowing Kevin to show his true colors before their wedding. *If only he didn't humiliate me in such a manner. After I came so far, and quarreled with Dad, only to be stood up! I sacrificed so much to fly over to meet him, and all he could manage was a note attached to a bouquet of red roses. So little effort to say good-bye and break my heart. "Better before the weekend, than after,"* a little voice whispered.

Not only did the haunting words mock her, but the pain was still there. *Why? Why can't I rid myself of the accusing memories?*

When Boris's head shot upward of his curled position in the recliner, Leslie came alert. Had the dog heard something she hadn't? She cranked her head toward the front windows, following the line of Boris's focus. The blinds were still wide open from the afternoon. *Is that a human form moving outside to the left?* The dog came off the chair barreling toward the windows. Sliding the journal off her lap to the couch, Leslie hobbled along behind the barking animal.

She stayed the dog from leaping up against the glass. Turning from the window, she started back through the kitchen to the breezeway door, pushing the curtains aside, to peer into the lighted area. Whoever had been staring in at her was gone. Leslie debated the merits of sending Boris out into the night to chase the intruder or keeping him inside the house with her. She patted his bristled fur. "You stay with me, big fella."

Her heart was still pounding when she called Clive. Before he could even say hello, Leslie shouted, "Someone was on the property watching me through the front window. When Boris started barking, they ran off. I can't see them anywhere and I heard no car start up."

"Didn't you have your blinds drawn?"

"No, I didn't think..."

He cut her off. "What a darn fool thing to do. You're a sitting duck inside that glass front of your house. I can't believe you wouldn't automatically close those blinds, considering everything that's happened. Common sense would tell you..." He sighed. "What were you thinking, Leslie?"

"Sorry I called!" she retorted. "Obviously, you'd rather berate me than check on the perpetrator." She slammed down the phone. When it rang back, she debated answering. Finally, she grabbed it up and held it to her ear, not saying a word.

"Look, instead of getting in a snit, why don't you close the front blinds and watch for me to knock at the back door? I'm going to leave my truck at the end of the drive, while I'll check out the surrounding area. I want to see if there's any different tire prints in the driveway." Not waiting for her to respond, Clive clicked off.

Her anger kept her too preoccupied for fear to penetrate. Irritated, she yanked the drawstring on the front blinds and considered turning off her light and calling it a night. "Let Clive do what he wants," she muttered. Walking back to the breezeway, she stared out at the driveway and bit her lip, undecided. While turning away from the door, she caught sight of Clive loping down the path leading from the barn.

She opened the door waiting for him to approach, giving Boris ready access to run past her into the night and escort Clive inside. Leslie regarded Clive curtly when he entered. He quietly nodded and followed her through to the kitchen, automatically reaching into the cupboard for a cup. Yawning, he filled it with her leftover coffee.

Leslie leaned against the counter waiting until the coffee heated in the microwave.

When the buzzer went off, Clive removed it, his back toward Leslie. He sipped slowly from the steaming cup before turning to address her stormy face. "Why don't we sit down at the table?" His arm extended toward the bay window.

Her eyes bore into him. "Only if you are finally ready. I wouldn't want to rush you." She turned toward the nearby table.

Chuckling, Clive sipped his coffee and followed. "Did you close the blinds?"

Whirling, Leslie drilled him with a look that could have wilted spinach. Without a word, she directed her halting steps to the nearest chair. Seating herself, she waited for Clive to get settled. She placed her hands together out in front of her and waited, seeming in no hurry to converse with him.

Leslie could have screamed at Clive's mocking grin as he stared down her challenging look. *He's enjoying making me angry.* She determined not to give him the satisfaction. "Well, Sherlock, did you find anything?"

"There are no tire prints that don't belong to your car, my truck, or the Schillers. They didn't drive in, whoever they are. I even checked out on the road where I recognized the mailman's truck.

Already riled, her next words were brisk. "Are you saying I imagined seeing someone run across my front lawn from the window?"

Clive yawned again and lifted his hat from his head, tossing it to an empty chair. "Nope! I don't think so. I found some clear footprints right by the window and tried to follow them. It's difficult at night. I'll try again tomorrow morning when I come over to work on the garage. Ray is planning on joining me later when we cut in the windows and an extra door opening." Clive stared down at his coffee, deep in thought.

Wincing, Leslie remembered all the work Clive was planning on doing on her garage and felt petty for getting angry at him. But the man was so darn maddening! She tried a different approach. "What's wrong? Did you recognize the footprint?"

Clive shook his head. "No. I'm not that good at tracking." He paused, lifting his eyebrows. "But I do know the difference between a tennis shoe and a cowboy boot."

Leslie looked at him with no comprehension. "Excuse me?"

"I expected to find a large cowboy boot, measuring about the same size as the imprint in the barn flooring the day you crashed through."

"You found a tennis shoe print outside the window?" she asked, leaning forward.

His lips came together in a pucker. "Yes. And not a very large one at that. I was able to follow the print upward toward the barn a ways before losing it in darkness."

"Are you thinking this is the work of teenagers out for a lark? Why would they run up the barn lane, to throw you off track?"

"At this point I don't have any ideas, but rowdy teenagers is an unlikely bet. I'll check more tomorrow." Reaching for his hat, Clive stood wearily. "Get some sleep and stay away from windows at night." Without another word, he carried his cup to the sink, rinsed it out and, after placing it in the drainer, he lifted his hat before turning to leave. "Good night, Leslie."

"Good night." She followed him out the breezeway door. "And thanks," she added in a small voice, almost as an afterthought.

She heard him laugh as he walked down the long drive toward the road. In a flash, her irritation was back. "That man!" She gritted her teeth and slammed the door harder than she meant.

Reaching the sofa, she surrendered her body to its comforting arms, barely aware of Boris, who lay at her feet. Pulling Velcro straps aside, she withdrew her injured foot and positioned it on a waiting cushion while drawing the old journal to her lap. Her body had too much adrenalin working through her system to sleep. Leslie tugged her unruly hair away from her face and focused on the next few pages of the journal.

Jamie wrote how Clara rebelled against her parent's wishes for her to marry a rich man in her own town, for the promise of romance and adventure with handsome Jamie Riker. But after her first view of the shack that Jamie had romantically, though misguidedly, described as a ranch house, she grew sullen and disillusioned. In spite of all his loving and apologetic words, Jamie found it hard to console Clara. He attempted to help her catch hold of his vision for their ranch, to see it as it would be—as he saw it.

> I promised we would build bigger and she would have pretty things. I knew Clara was raised to be a lady of leisure, but I had no idea she couldn't cook the simplest of dishes, nor had the first idea of how to keep house or even wash clothing.
>
> Those beginning days of our marriage were a nightmare! Her lack of abilities, anger, and constant frustration caused much strife between us. She would rant and beg for me to return her to her parent's home. I also was frustrated and torn, not knowing what to do. I still loved Clara and hoped she would adapt, that someday she'd learn to love the land I loved. I couldn't leave. Our survival depended on my working the farm.
>
> The crops needed planting, and Atlanta was so far away. We were at an impasse, Clara and I. She was miserable until new neighbors stopped by, and Clara found a friend she could learn from. Though still unhappy, Clara gradually learned to manage farm life on a satisfactory level and appeared able to cope with our sparse life, but there was no sparkle in her eyes. Life went on, and day after day was the same.
>
> Often I'd find her standing on our tiny porch looking off to see the lights of our neighbor's house nearly a mile away. Every week, Clara would polish the silver candlesticks, a wedding gift from her parents. They sat on our bare wood mantle as a reminder of the life she gave up. Every Saturday, she begged to be taken to town to pick up our mail, hoping for letters from family and friends. I'd take her to town, but it wasn't enough.
>
> Clara complained daily about her life and blamed me for her unhappiness. I longed to give her the life she'd had and make her smile. When her one friend moved away, she became stoic and aloof...almost unreachable. I knew I had to do something.

It was obvious to Leslie that Clara was not a woman to live a solitude life with only the love of a tired man for company. She was too fragile—a woman without faith or strength of character to live the harsh life of building a ranch.

What type of woman am I? Leslie questioned. Her ponderings sobered her.

Her heart grew heavy as she read on about their difficult situation. Jamie worked hard and scraped out a living. He tried everything in his power to rekindle the light in his wife's eyes, but Clara punished him daily with her bitter and hateful spirit.

Leslie nodded off and came awake with a start, squinting at the faded scroll. The next heading was titled *The Birth of Our Son.* "Well," she murmured drowsily, "I sense the scene is about to change." Pulling the afghan off the back of the sofa, Leslie snuggled down, content to doze in the brightly lit room.

The jarring ring of her cell phone awakened her sharply. Leslie fumbled to get it to her ear. Boris sat upright, his head cocked. "Yessss?"

The quizzical voice of Roger Galbraith inquiring about her headache two days earlier confused her briefly, until she remembered her excuse for leaving in the middle of lunch. Skillfully avoiding the touchy subject, she encouraged Roger to talk about his schedule while she tried to clear her mind from the cobwebs of sleep. When his invitation for a new lunch date entered the conversation, she stalled, uncertain of the desirability of spending time with this man.

"I have to beg off for a few more days, Roger. I want to be able to thoroughly enjoy both food and company when we go again." Her guilty conscience reminded her that there was nothing wrong with her head or her stomach for that matter. But how could she tell him she didn't trust where he fit into the maze of dangerous happenings directed at her? "Besides, Roger," she went on excitedly, "I've got this new project I need time to work on. I truly want to do a good job. I—"

Roger cut her off. "I hope you realize how disappointed I am, Leslie. I'll keep calling. I'm not known for giving up easily, and I-I want to spend time with you. Is everything going all right at the ranch?"

Leslie wasn't sure how to answer Roger's question. She'd almost lost her life in a closed garage filled with carbon monoxide, and earlier in the night she'd been stalked by a peeping Tom watching her from outside her front window. "Nothing much out of the ordinary." *May God forgive me for all my lies,* Leslie thought.

“There are so many things I’d like to share with you, Leslie—the Country Club, all the best restaurants. We could take a day trip up to Atlanta and take in a play and dinner. I feel we’d be very good together, you and me,” he said with tenderness.

Leslie felt the air leave her lungs. Part of her wondered if Roger could be right. Maybe they would make a good match—a good, safe match. If only the ranch business and the accidents could be explained and put behind them…

She kept her voice light and open. “That is very flattering, but right now I need to concentrate on standing on two good feet and making up my mind about what to do about the ranch.”

“The ranch shouldn’t be a problem. You’ve got a money-making solution right at your fingertips—just say the word. Get it off your hands, Leslie, and then you can take time for what is important,” he urged.

His words sounded so easy. Sell the ranch and she wouldn’t have to worry about any more accidents happening on the property, or wonder who was making the crying sounds in the middle of the night. Suddenly, the thought struck her: *If selling the ranch will eliminate the accidents, maybe that’s why they are happening.* Suspicion now raged. It was hard not to see Roger as the enemy. He and his northern investors were pushing for the sale. *Who are these men?*

It was difficult to keep her tone free of suspicion when she begged off, entreating Roger to try back in a few days.

As she regrouped her thoughts, Roger’s bright voice shot back, “I’ll call the first of the week, so work on getting better.”

His words reminded her of her schedule. “Wait. Clive Masters is taking me to the garage to pick up Wayne’s Jeep either Monday or Tuesday.”

“Oh.” He hesitated. “Well, when you go, ask for Joe Crider. He’ll take good care of you. Just mention my name and tell him we’re friends.”

“Thanks for the tip.”

After they’d said good-bye, Leslie was troubled. Roger Galbraith was such a contradiction, he made her head spin. Returning the old journal to the leather case in the office, she prepared for bed. Boris took up his station in Wayne’s chair.

*

Leslie awoke to pounding outside and the bright sunlight of midmorning. It took a few seconds to recall Clive telling her he’d be working on her garage today. Twisting her neck to relieve a kink, she wondered why she hadn’t heard Boris whining to get out...unless Clive had used his key and opened the back door for the dog. She grabbed her clothes and proceeded to the shower.

Dressed with blow-dried hair, she prepared coffee before making her way to the breezeway. As suspected, the door was open and Boris was gone. Stepping outside, she braced herself against the morning cold and shielded her eyes from the sun to peer across to the old wooden garage. Working hard, Clive had already peeled down to a long-sleeved shirt, jeans, and his worn cowboy hat.

She called, "Coffee's almost ready!" and waved.

"Sounds good," he said, returning to his sawhorses, where he'd spread measured planks of lumber. "Pour one for Ray. He'll be here shortly."

She suddenly wished she had some rolls or coffeecake to offer too. Hearing the rumble of Ray's truck, she headed back toward the house. Ray was already in the kitchen by the time she maneuvered herself there.

"Henri O' sent these over. She thought they might come in handy." He smiled, setting a plate of heavenly smelling cinnamon rolls on the counter.

"Great!" Leslie said brightly. "Call Clive in. He's ready for a break. You can have coffee and a roll before going out."

Ray's tanned face crinkled in amusement. "Only coffee for me, Leslie. I just finished breakfast. I'll get a roll later, but I'll take a second cup of coffee now." He walked out back to get Clive.

It was nice to sit at the table and listen to Clive and Ray converse about the best way to tackle the door and windows. It would have been perfect if Mona had come along. Leslie left the men at the table to finish while she tidied up the counters. Peering out the window, she looked up toward the lane leading to the barn thinking she'd seen movement. Blinking, she convinced herself she was mistaken.

Ray's next words drew her attention. "Oh, Leslie, almost forgot. Henri O' is coming over later to prepare dinner. Mona's going to join us when she gets done with chores." He turned back to take up his conversation with Clive.

She was astonished how everyone took bringing in dinner and fixing garages as a matter of course. It had been a long time since she'd been involved in such an atmosphere of helpful camaraderie. It was like a crackling fire on a cold day.

Between housework and working on her Christmas bulbs, Leslie put together hearty sandwiches and tall glasses of iced tea for the men's lunch, calling them in around 12:30 p.m. As soon as the kitchen was straightened again, she went back to the bulbs, growing more and more confident and sure-handed. Her brush strokes were steady.

Standing back, she got a better perspective of her work. The old Christmas cards Mona brought had given her wonderful ideas for designs. Surprisingly the work was going faster than she expected. She was cleaning her brushes when Henri O' arrived, so Leslie hurried to make herself available to help with the vegetables for a pan of three roasting chickens.

"I can't remember when I've see so much food. Good grief!" Leslie shook her head in amazement.

"No sir, Miss Leslie. Those hungry men will make short work of most of that food. Besides, Miss Mona wanted me to make enough to leave dinner with you for tomorrow." The raven-haired woman swiftly gathered the fixings for an apple pie.

Leslie found a knife and worked with her, finding to her amazement how much she was learning as they worked together.

"Are you going to church tomorrow, Miss Leslie?" Henri O' asked, fluting the edges of the crust.

The question took Leslie off guard. "I'm not sure about this week." She averted her eyes.

"Too bad. I heard Mr. Clive say he hoped you'd decide to come tomorrow."

Leslie stared at her. "Mr. Clive said that?"

"Yes, ma'am, he did. I think this pie is ready to bake."

Leslie was glad the subject had changed. She hurried to clean up the counter. With the pie in the oven, the women walked outside to see what the men had accomplished. The unique smell of fresh sawed wood mingled with the crisp fall air. The new door was visible as they approached. Stepping through the doorway, Leslie's hand ran over the smooth wood facing and smiled. "Nice job, guys!"

"Be careful, you might pick up a splinter. It's not varnished yet," Clive warned.

Ray wiped his face with his handkerchief. "If we hurry, we can get those windows in before supper. Varnishing can wait until the first of the week."

Leslie and Henri O' walked back to the house. With the dinner preparation complete, Henri O' left work for the day. The serving and clean-up were left to Leslie and Mona, and the day ended on a positive note in good fellowship.

As Leslie watched Clive and the Schillers pack up and head for their ranches, she hugged her arms and gazed at the sky, thinking how she couldn't remember when she'd spent such a thoroughly pleasant day with friends. By the time she reached the breezeway, Boris was waiting for her to open the door. Startled by his silent approach, Leslie wondered if she'd ever get used to his wolf-like ways.

Leslie slid the lock in place, wishing she'd accepted Mona's invitation to ride with them to church in the morning. Her heart froze at first, then impulsively overreacted by declining. Clive's somber gaze compounded her discomfort and made her wince. He'd looked away, and she'd been immediately sorry for her rash decision. It was the only low point of the day, and Leslie didn't even know why she'd said no, *Habit, I guess.* She sighed. The dog waited as she filled his dish. He'd settled in to a routine in a remarkably short time. Was Clive right? Had the animal adopted her?

Passing through the dimly lit kitchen, Leslie paused at the phone, still uncertain what she should do about church. Her spirit warred within her.

*

Arriving early, Clive studied his church bulletin, glancing over the events of the weekly schedule as his mind vaguely registered the familiar melody the organist played. This was the quiet time when his heart should be centered on the Lord, but he found it hard to concentrate this morning. He'd gone to bed with troubled thoughts and found they hadn't lifted with the dawn. He didn't understand Leslie Weldon. The woman clearly had spiritual knowledge. What he didn't know was the status of her relationship to Christ. Knowing *about* God and *knowing* God were two different things.

Leslie was obviously treading some pretty heavy waters and deeply troubled. For a while yesterday, he'd thought he'd noticed a softening in her, but her refusal to attend church this morning bothered him. What unsettled Clive even more were his deepening feelings for her. *How can I stop this rampant tide of emotion in her direction?* He knew how futile those growing feelings were if she wasn't a believer. He could be headed for another patch of heartbreak. His bowed head concealed a heavy heart.

Clive continued praying as more people entered the church, milling the aisles around him. He murmured a silent amen and raised his head. Nodding to several friends, he glanced across the aisle where the Schillers generally sat and found himself staring into the dark, moody blue eyes of Leslie Weldon. Willing his jaw to close, he was unable to conceal a small smile inching in place. "Mornin', Miss Weldon. I'm glad you decided to come, and hope you enjoy the service."

A cloud of uncertainly crossed her face. "Good morning, Mr. Masters. I hope I will enjoy the service." As she turned her head frontward, Clive saw her take a deep breath. *She's scared, Lord. Cloak her in Your protective arms.* He couldn't help but wonder what mysterious demons troubled her.

*

The worship service brought such a rush of memories to Leslie's heart, it was all she could do to remain seated. Following the service, she kept her comments bright as she moved in the direction of the exit. Ignoring Clive's probing eyes, she urged Mona and Ray to take her home. Even in the car, Leslie worked to sidestep comments regarding the message—the Prodigal Son, of all topics. She found it very exhausting! She wasn't ready to discuss her impressions or feelings. How could she, as disturbed as she felt now. This course of rediscovery was slow and unsettling.

Reaching her ranch, she'd swiftly exited the back seat of the Schillers' car and thanked them for their kindness. As they drove away, she heaved a sigh of relief, drawing comfort from the brisk mountain air. It was a balm to her battered emotions.

Walking with purpose toward the house, she focused on preparing lunch. With a whole chicken and assorted leftovers from the previous day, she knew it wouldn't prove a problem. Her goal was to keep busy, anything to keep her thoughts from becoming introspective. She'd attended a church service; it was as simple as that. Throwing her coat and purse off to a chair, Leslie's motions were jerky as if she argued with herself.

Staring mindlessly inside the refrigerator, she withdrew the platter with yesterday's chicken and plopped it on top of the counter. Pulling away the foil cover, she cocked her head in disbelief. "What the...?" Where was the other half of that chicken?

Leslie examined the bird. Someone had ruthlessly ripped half of the chicken away. Returning to the refrigerator, she opened container after container, finding part of each portion had been removed. She slowly closed the refrigerator door and walked to the kitchen sink, where she looked outside, thinking back over the last few days.

Several unconnected occurrences paraded through her thoughts, pushing her hunger aside. Stuffing the rest of the bird back in the refrigerator, she hurried to the bedroom to change her clothes, unsure if what she had in mind was wise.

15

Unexpected Guest

USING HER CANE FOR SUPPORT, Leslie trudged up the farm lane toward the massive barn at the top of the hill, her finger on her cell phone dial. She knew the Schillers' number position on the phone by heart. *This is a wild goose chase—not to mention a crazy idea,* she told herself, wincing at the burning ache in her foot.

Pausing midway of the lane, she supported her weight on her good foot and rested, her breathing heavy from excursion. Leslie studied the barn, remembering that vague movement she thought she'd seen a day earlier. *What if it was the one responsible for the garage accident?* She swallowed, reconsidering her rash plan. The first time she'd checked the barn, she'd crashed through the floor, and the time she gone up there with Roger, the hay shoot had released unexpectedly. Turning, she started down the lane.

Leslie stopped. *I need to pull it together.* Squaring her shoulders, she pivoted to retrace her steps upward toward the barn. By the time she reached the huge sliding door, she was desperate for rest, and leaned against a stack of cement blocks. Listening for any unusual noise, she heard nothing but a squirrel scudding up a near tree. His chattering told her he wasn't happy to have his space invaded. Enjoying the respite and this view of Wayne's ranch, Leslie tried to ignore the untimely growling of her stomach. Her hunger made her think back on that missing chicken half.

She lowered her foot to the ground and pushed the latch across the sliding door. Using her body weight, Leslie moved the door open enough for her to slide through the opening. With her back flush against the door, she drew in a ragged breath and scanned the vast interior, listening for any sign of an intruder.

Her heart jumped when she heard a fluttering, relieved to find it was a trapped bird anxious to find an open window. Leslie moved cautiously away from the door, keeping her footfalls as quiet as possible. Unsure what she expected to find, she sought the visual assurance that nothing or no one was inside this barn.

The huge space was silent and vacant, so she relaxed as she walked across the main area, keeping a watchful eye. Coming to the rough wooden ladder leading to the hayloft, she inhaled deeply, knowing she had to climb up to the second level. If she didn't, she would never be sure.

Mounting the ladder took twice as long when she had to take each rung with the same foot and bring up the other alongside, her arms dragging her upward. Her breath was labored by the time she reached the hayloft floor. Had she heard a scuffling, or was it her overwrought imagination? Piled mounds of baled hay were stacked in several places, but Leslie saw nothing out of the ordinary.

She made the effort to walk around the largest groupings of hay before deciding she could dismiss her nagging suspicion. The aroma of hay and dust made her sneeze several times, forcing her to draw out a Kleenex. She might have laughed at the silliness of her situation if she hadn't caught a scent of something very familiar—roast chicken.

Leslie drew her wooden cane tight in her raised hand and stepped quickly around the small stacking tucked under the back eave. She stopped in horror, staring at the huddled figure backed tight against the eaves. Under the dirt and tangled hair, it looked to be a young girl in filthy jeans and shirt. The leavings of roast chicken, bread, and other unidentified food were scattered on the floor with scraps of paper toweling and newspaper. Leslie studied the littered scene. The girl was existing like a rat on paper and stolen food.

"Come out of there," Leslie said softly. "I'm not going to hurt you."

The waif crawled out and stared up at her as if afraid Leslie might hit her.

"What's your name?"

"Meg." The pale blue eyes reminded Leslie of a cornered raccoon complete with the remains of a blackened eye. Instantly, she wondered who'd hit this child and why.

Leslie shivered from the dampness inside the barn. Looking at the nest-like debris, she said, "We need to talk, and it's too cold to stay here. Besides, I'm hungry. You might have already eaten, but I haven't. Come on."

"Are you going to call the po'lice or somethin'?" the girl asked.

"I don't know what I'm going to do yet." She motioned with her hand until the girl stood to her feet.

The rumpled girl reached behind a bale of hay and grabbed a tattered jean backpack before scampering down the ladder. "Look, lady, I'll work off that food I stole. There's no reason to call in the law."

"Well, one thing you're going to do is clean up that mess in the hayloft."

"Yes, ma'am, I'll do that."

Leslie had thought the walk down the lane would be easier than going up, but she was mistaken. By the time she and the girl reached the breezeway door, her teeth were clenched in pain. Opening the door, she asked the timid girl, "Just how long have you been living up in my barn?"

"Two, maybe three days, I forget." The girl's voice was breathy as she followed Leslie through to the kitchen area.

Leslie paused at the sink to fill a glass of water and partially downed it in one gulp. Pausing, as if the idea just occurred to her, she opened the cupboard, withdrew a second glass, and filled it full of cold tap water. Turning, she handed the glass to Meg. "Why don't you take a seat over at that table by the front window?"

Meg emptied the glass and set it on the counter, glancing toward the window. With lowered eyes, the thin girl walked with hesitation over to the table, looking down at the upholstered chair. "Oh no, ma'am, I can't sit on these. I'm way too dirty for that."

Lifting the dishtowel from the hanger, Leslie threw it to the girl. "Sit on this, then. I'm going to make myself a sandwich. Are you still hungry?"

The girl shook her head, obviously uneasy. Her eyes furtively roamed the interior of the large combined room. Over the refrigerator door, Leslie regarded the waif, curious how she could have remained inside the barn with Boris roaming the grounds. *Why hadn't Boris run the girl off? Where is he?* With a cold chicken sandwich and a glass of milk in front of her, Leslie puzzled over the disheveled wisp of a girl sitting across from her. "Why don't you tell me how you came to be living in my barn? Are you a runaway?"

*

Meg's lips were parched from living two days on one bottle of water. She glanced longingly at the empty glass on the counter. "Not really, ma'am. What I mean is, I don't got any real kin anymore. My stepdad, he kept me around to cook and clean for him and beat me whenever he got drunk," she mumbled, rubbing her healing arm.

She looked at the table. "We was driving from state to state lookin' for a job. When I woke up in that last motel, Sam was gone. He'd lit out in the night and left me stranded," she lied, afraid this woman would call the police or worse.

Meg's heart was beating through her rib cage. She was panicked at the thought of this woman driving her back to Cleary and the Vanook brothers. They were too close for comfort. *God forgive me for telling a falsehood.* Her tongue ran over her lips as her brain worked feverishly, hoping this red-haired woman believed her story. Her plan was to get to a bus stop and head for parts unknown—anywhere away from them. With the money she'd taken from Cleary, she could get far enough before having to look for a job.

Raising her eyes, she squirmed under the probing stare of the pretty woman. "I-I really am sorry about the food I ate, but I was real hungry. I left a quarter for the bar of soap I took from the bathroom. Look under the lip of the soap dish."

"You left a quarter for my bar of soap?" the blue-eyed woman asked.

Nodding, Meg replied, "Yes, ma'am. I planned to bathe in that swampy pond out back of the barn. Please don't call the po'lice. I'll work off the food I ate."

The lady waved off her pleading. "My name is Leslie Weldon, and I'm not worried about the food. I'm worried about an under-aged girl living in my barn because she has no place to stay." She chomped on a huge bite of sandwich.

Meg pushed up from the chair. "Can I have another glass of water? I'm fearful thirsty."

Leslie nodded. "Sure. Would you like a glass of milk?"

Meg glanced at Leslie's glass of milk. "That would be nice, ma'am, but I would sure like the water first." Moving over to the counter, she carried her empty glass to the sink to refill, her hand shaking. Would this Leslie call the police? If they traced Meg back to the Vanook place...well, there'd be no telling the amount of trouble. She could picture her stepdad's face.

Dear God, I need a helping hand here. I know I just lied to that lady and I'm real sorry about that, but I can't let them contact Cleary. If he don't kill me, those Vanooks will. Don't let this woman call the po'lice*...please, God!*

*

Pouring a glass of milk for Meg, Leslie lifted her phone and walked in the living room. "Mona, I hope you're not busy because I could really use some expert advice about an unusual situation I've got here. Could you drive over in a few minutes?" Leslie shot the undernourished girl a glance, watching her guzzle the entire milk glass in a matter of seconds. "Yeah, it would be better explained in person."

Leslie cradled the phone, giving the girl a thorough appraisal. "Meg, I'm going to need some time to consider your situation. In the meantime, I think it would be good for you to use some personal time cleaning up. While you take a bath, I'll try to round up some clean clothes to put on."

The pleased surprise on the truant's face was better than a huge thank you.

Returning her smile, Leslie led Meg to the bathroom and indicated the towel shelf. Leaving her to her own resources, she turned with a final request. "Place your dirty clothes in this paper bag by the door, and I'll put fresh clothes next to the bag."

*

Thirty minutes later Leslie and Mona sat across from a squeaky clean, pale teenager who sat dwarfed in an extra-big shirt and too long jeans. As Meg fluffed her damp hair, her eyes shifted from Leslie to Mona as if unsure which one to watch.

Mona gazed at the pathetic child. "To begin with, I'm going home and look for something this girl can wear without tripping over her pant legs. I'm Mona Schiller. I live on the farm next door. Miss Weldon has filled me in. I understand you have no living relations. What is your full name, please?"

Meg inhaled. "Margaret Jean McDonald.

Leslie leaned forward. "You said your stepfather was driving through several states looking for work. Where were you living before—your home state?"

The young girl's eyes darted outside. "We're from West Virginia, ma'am. That's where my mama's buried alongside my baby sister and real daddy."

"And your stepfather's name?" asked Mona.

Meg paled visibly. She scanned the room as if she were thinking. "Norton. His last name is Norton."

"Sam Norton?" Leslie volunteered.

Meg sighed. "No, ma'am. It's Cleary. I called him Sam because I was afraid you'd try to find him and make me go back to him...and I just won't!" she cried in honest anxiety.

The rush of blood to Meg's face made her blackened eye stand out clearer than before. Leslie and Mona exchanged looks even as Leslie moved from her chair to sit next to Meg, encircling her with a protective arm. "Don't get upset, dear. We haven't decided anything yet. We're just trying to understand what you've been through."

Meg nodded. "Just don't send me back to him. He'll hurt me bad. He never liked me when Mama was alive and got pure mean after she died."

Mona indicated to Leslie that the two of them needed to talk, and Leslie pointed to Wayne's office off the hall. "Meg, Mona and I need to talk for a minute. Stay here. If you're still hungry, help yourself to the refrigerator. We won't be long."

Meg nodded again but looked anxious. Her eyes mirrored a lifetime of sadness.

Leslie sent a knowing look Mona's way before telling Meg, "Everything is going to work out, all right?"

Meg's lowered gaze was her only reply.

Stepping inside the cluttered, tiny office, Leslie pushed the door closed behind them. She eased herself up onto the desktop while Mona sat across from her in the worn leather chair. "What do you think? The poor girl needs a place to stay."

Mona frowned at her friend. "She's not a stray cat, Leslie. You can't just take her in. She is a minor. Someone has to be responsible for her. I've got a friend in the sheriff's office. I'll have them check her out and make sure she's not a runaway. And of course we'll have to contact Social Services."

"Can she stay here until you check her out?" Leslie's eyes strayed beyond the French doors. "She has nowhere else to go. You should see that spot up in the barn hayloft. I believe she's half starved."

Mona followed Leslie's gaze to the hall. "I agree. She needs a little stability right now. Besides it's Sunday, and nothing is open." She laughed. "Leslie, I don't think you can go two days without something bizarre happening. Keep the girl for the next day or so. I'll bring over some clothes. She's more my size than yours. Oh, and see if you can get more information out of her. Something tells me she knows more than she's telling."

"I agree. She keeps looking at us as if she is not sure she can trust us."

Walking out to Mona's truck, Leslie thanked her. "You keep coming to my rescue. Sure glad you live close." She leaned on the edge of the truck window.

"Life would be dull without you, Leslie Weldon. I'll be back in a few minutes with the clothes. How are you fixed for food? There are two of you now and, well, culinary arts don't seem to be your strong suit."

Leslie chuckled. "Diplomatically put, but I get the message. I've got lunch meat along with what's left of that chicken and plenty of eggs, cereal, and milk for breakfast. After that I can go to the store. Mona, I used to keep house for my dad. I admit it's been awhile, but it'll all come back. I've just been a little preoccupied lately. Which reminds me, did Ray ever check out those tracks we found?"

"Yeah, he and Clive went over, but it rained again, and they couldn't see much except the dry bushes stuck in the ground, but that was enough. They believe what we saw. Ray's been asking around about the name *Vanook.* People don't seem to know much about them. They keep to themselves." Mona started the truck. "See you shortly."

*

By the time, Mona returned with the clothes, Leslie and Meg had settled on a place for her to sleep. Instead of choosing a guest bedroom on the second floor, Meg begged to stay in Wayne's old bedroom amongst the clutter of Leslie's art supplies.

"I don't mind, ma'am, really and I'd rather be on the ground floor, closer to people. It'd be awful lonely upstairs."

"Well, it's up to you, but I've got a royal mess in here, and there's no way I can move it until I'm finished with my project."

"I don't mind really. The bathroom is real close." Meg sat on the bed edge.

"There are better mattresses in the upstairs bedrooms."

Meg shrugged, looking down. "I've been sleepin' on the floor of your barn."

Leslie nodded. "Okay, then. You can sleep right here. Here's a satchel of jeans and shirts." Staring at the hole-filled tennis shoes the girl was wearing, Leslie shook her head. "I'm afraid shoes will have to wait. Neither of us has anything your size."

Locking up after Mona, she walked away wondering what the days would bring with this frightened teenage girl. When she closed the front blinds, she thought of Clive and smiled. Obviously it was Meg who'd been watching her through the window.

A scratching noise brought her attention back to the breezeway. "Boris!" In all the commotion, she'd completely forgotten the dog. Letting the wiry-haired animal inside, she poured him a bowl of food and watched him woof it down with pleasure. "Where were you today? I thought you were supposed to be my protector."

Leslie stifled a yawn as she made her way toward her bedroom. Hearing Meg moving about Wayne's old room, she paused by the girl's door. There was something familiar about her that nagged at Leslie's memory, and like Mona said, there was more to the teenager's story then what was told today in the living room. Turning away, she continued to her own room. There'd be no journal reading tonight.

Lying in bed, her brain skimmed through the entire day like an old family movie, filled with all the action and confusion of the players acting out their parts. It had begun at church. She visualized Clive looking at her across the aisle, the light of joy springing to his eyes. Her heart tried to ignore the emotions that ran through her at the impact, only to be struck by spiritual arrows during the worship service. Even the Scripture reading had been filled with a directed message, aimed seemingly at her delinquent heart.

In the midst of reeling from the morning, a destitute teenager popped up in the hayloft of her barn—a lost lamb who needed her help. Leslie's head rang with a host of thoughts and questions that tore at her peace. She remembered how Dad used to pray for her when she was troubled and ached for the comfort it had once brought.

Suddenly Leslie felt an unexplainable urge to cry, right here, alone in the dark. Her spirit felt old, tired, and depressed...her soul raw and bleeding. She yearned to take hold of the soothing balm that she knew lay beyond her fingertips. The minister had talked today about the soothing balm of forgiveness. *Why can't I reach it?* Tears slowly cascaded down her face. An uneasy sleep drew her within its folds.

*

Meg stirred, frightened, her face wet with perspiration. Her dream about Cleary looming over her had been so real. She allowed her breathing to slow. The air in the room felt cold against her damp skin. She saw unusual shadow shapes on Leslie's art table in the reflective moonlight from the east window and remembered where she was. In an effort to close the open window she tiptoed from the bed across the room.

Once she reached the open window, her fingers froze in place on the top edge as she paused to listen. She heard the same eerie sound she'd heard that night in the woods, in the dark—a crying child. It chilled her to the bone. Closing the window, she went to sit on the edge of the bed, her fingers clenched in front of her, wondering if Leslie had heard the sound. Meg swallowed hard, scared and confused.

She thought back to the men she'd seen in the same area the crying had stemmed from. Those men in the woods had spoken of Zeke and Fred Vanook in a familiar way. What connection was there between the men, and what connection did the men have to the crying child, if any?

Meg's head sank into her waiting hands, not knowing what she should do. It would be safer if she kept what she knew to herself. Whatever Cleary, the Vanook brothers, and those strange men were connected to, it would not be good—perhaps even illegal. Her goal was to get away from this area as soon as she could manage, but she would have to pick her time…until then, she had to keep a low profile.

Switching on the small table lamp, she reached for an old magazine to calm her.

*

Leslie lay wide-eyed in her bed, her open window carrying the same compelling crying that no one had been able to explain or discover the origin. Discarding wind noises or the ghost of a child roaming the woods at night, she tried to find a reason why someone would want to simulate the sound of a child. *If only my foot was healed, I'd wait up in the woods each night for a week to discover who or what is making the sound.*

She slipped out of bed, strapped on her boot, and shuffled her way from her room down the hall toward the kitchen. Pausing outside Wayne's old room, Leslie saw a light shining beneath the door. She knocked lightly before turning the handle. "Meg?"

Sitting straight up in the bed, the enlarged eyes of the pale girl stared back at her. "Miss Leslie, is something wrong?"

"I couldn't sleep and noticed your light under the doorway. Are you all right?"

"Yes, ma'am, I was just readin'."

Leslie looked at the closed window. "Were you disturbed by the outside noise?"

Meg's eyes darted nervously to the window and back. "Outside noise?"

Puzzled, Leslie watched Meg's agitated response. "Yes. It sounds like a small child crying."

"I-I was cold so I closed the window. I thought I heard somethin' weird, but wasn't sure what it was. Do you know?" The girl wet her lips.

Leslie sighed. "No, I don't, Meg, and it's very troublesome. If you know anything or have any ideas, they would be welcome. It's been a mystery ever since I arrived at the ranch."

"When you came to the ranch?" Meg repeated, leaning forward. "I thought you had been here always."

Laughing, Leslie shook her head. "No. I've actually arrived only about three weeks ago, after my Cousin Wayne died in a ranch accident."

The girl eyed her curiously. "Ranch accident?" she parroted again.

"Yes, apparently, he was found at the bottom of a ravine beside his tractor. No one seems to know exactly what happened."

"I'm sorry," Meg mumbled, glancing down at the wrinkled magazine.

Leslie hesitated. "Yes, well, thank you. I didn't know him well...but strangely I'm missing him more all the time." She thought about the journals. Shaking her thoughts from their reverie, she added, "Try to get some sleep, Meg. You must be tired. We'll worry about the crying sounds tomorrow."

Leslie exited the room and walked through to the breezeway. She wasn't surprised to find Boris lying by the back door whimpering. She parted the curtains but saw only darkness and shadows from the yard light. Frustrated, she turned back to the kitchen, pausing for a glass of water. Feeling a strange sensation against her leg, she glanced down to find Boris standing beside her. Without thinking, she reached down and gently patted the dog's head and neck. "Thanks for the loyalty, Boy. Let's go back to the bedroom."

She was puzzled to find Boris accept Meg's presence so readily. It made her wonder if the two hadn't become friends while Meg hid out in the barn. Perhaps the girl had shared part of her food with the animal to gain his acceptance.

Leslie lay between the sheets listening to the faraway sounds in the woods. Her body was tense as she strained to decipher them. The sudden crack of a rifle ripped through the night, followed by a second and third retort. They shattered what feelings of safety she'd managed to gather since Boris began staying inside the house at night.

Springing from the bed, Leslie started for the hallway, only to wince and turn back for her boot. She rushed to secure it on her foot and half hopped to the door. Meg met her in the hall and together they hurried toward the breezeway. In the kitchen, Leslie stabbed at the phone buttons. Waiting for Mona to answer, she called to Meg, "Don't open that back door. Keep it closed. I'll be right there." Turning back to the phone, she began to tell Mona about the shots, when Mona cut her off.

"I know, Leslie, we heard it too. I can't reach Clive on either his cell phone or landline and I'm starting to worry. Ray is throwing some clothes on now so he can check on those shots. Don't open your doors to anyone but Ray or Clive. Hang up, so I can keep our phone line open. I'll get back to you, promise. Bye."

"Mona," Leslie injected before her friend rang off, "I'll call the police."

Silence. "Good idea. Talk to you later."

After reporting the shooting, Leslie put on a large pot of coffee and joined Meg at the back door, peering up the lane toward to the barn and beyond. She wondered why Mona hadn't been able to reach Clive on the phone. *Is it possible Clive is up in the woods...please Lord, no!*

Meg's nose pressed against the glass, and her fingernails dug deeply into the flesh of her palms.

*

A State Patrol officer knocked on the door to identify himself before heading up into the woods. The women remained at the back window until Leslie's foot drove her to find a more restful place to wait. Minutes ticked slowly as they waited for some kind of word. It was not something Leslie did well. As time passed, Meg followed and curled up on the couch, her head resting on a pillow. Neither found the need to make conversation, yet their silence filled the atmosphere with nervous static.

The back-door bell shattered the quiet like crystal crashing against the hearth. Meg sprinted to the back before Leslie had yet to reach the kitchen. Her eyes were enormous as she threw open the door to the police, the Schillers, and Clive. While Leslie soberly directed everyone to the table, Mona stepped out of the group to give Leslie and Meg a hand with making coffee.

In minutes they were all seated at the table watching the officer write on a clipboard report. He introduced himself as Officer McIntire. "We were asked by the Dahlonega police to investigate the situation. I'll be sending in a report tonight. Now then..." He took down everyone's name and address, pausing to consider Meg when she stumbled nervously over her name.

"She's staying with me for a while to help out with my broken foot," said Leslie quickly, figuring that what she said was the truth in the broadest sense of the form. Ignoring Mona's sharp glance, she smiled back at Meg and the officer in charge.

The patrolman leaned on his elbow. "Though we didn't find shooters on site, with the help of Mr. Masters I was able to retrieve some empty casings where the perpetrators stood to shoot their weapons. Are any of you here able to offer a suggestion as to who these men might be, or for what reason they were up in Miss Weldon's woods tonight?"

Everyone looked from one to another except Meg, whose gaze was locked onto the napkin holder in the middle of the table. The officer regarded Clive. "Okay, tell me again, Mr. Masters, why you went up into the woods tonight."

When Clive finished relating the repetitive pattern of the eerie crying sounds in the woods, everyone around the table reiterated the same story. Meg hung back shyly, as if trying to fade into the upholstery.

The patrolman looked grim and scratched the back of his head. "What is this, more hype to add to Dahlonega's ghost stories?" he asked sharply. "It's too late for ghost stories, people!" Bombarded with defensive denials, he held up his hand. "Okay! I get it; you've all been hearing some kind of noise that resembles a crying child. Fine! The sheriff's office will love this!" He scribbled a few lines.

Clive spoke up. "It's just as I first told you. I was trying to discern the origin of the sounds when I heard men's voices a short distance away. I called out, 'Who's there—identify yourselves! This is private property!' and all of a sudden this volley of shots rang out in my direction."

Nodding, the officer laid down his pencil. "I've got all that, Mr. Masters. Without any other information to go on, I have to assume that the voices you heard were poachers who didn't take too kindly to being intruded upon. I'll file my report, and if the sheriff's office wants to pursue it, he'll get in touch with you."

After escorting the patrolman out, Leslie returned to the table to join the others, who were in the heat of a discussion. Seating herself next to Clive, she nudged him. "So...after telling me the sounds were nothing but night noises, you went out on your own to investigate?" She regarded him with amusement.

Clive turned, his gaze connecting with her. "You didn't expect me to take you along with your bum foot, did you? Besides, one of us getting shot at was plenty."

Mona and Ray exchanged anxious looks. Mona asked, "Do you agree with the officer? Were those guys up on the ridge tonight poachers?"

Ray nodded at Clive. "Why don't you tell them your theory?"

Rotating the cup in his hands, Clive glanced around the table before answering, "When Ray and Mona called me, I was already in the woods. Ray and I bantered around a few ideas, and it is our opinion that the men might be the same people who have been coming on Riker land at night and digging around with equipment." He eyed Leslie. "Remember that camouflaged path across from the gravel road, where dead bushes are stuck in the ground? Could be those are the same men."

"But wasn't the digging further away from the top of the woods, down by Rocky Ridge?" As Leslie waited for Clive's reply, she noticed Meg's furtive glances. The girl was definitely uneasy about something. Maybe it was all the talk about shootings and guns. She looked like a rabbit ready to dash into the brush.

"Meg, are you all right?" Leslie inquired. "You don't have to sit up with us, you know. If you're tired, you're excused to go back to bed."

Pushing away from the table, Meg stood. "Thanks, Miss Leslie. I'm just restless. Could I get anyone more coffee?"

Clive raised his cup, eyeing the girl with curiosity. "I would appreciate another cup, Miss…Meg, is it?"

Meg nodded and hurriedly took his cup to refill. Her hand trembled when she handed the hot mug to him.

"Thanks," Clive murmured, watching her closely.

Swiping at her flyaway blond hair, Meg nodded toward Leslie. "If it's okay, I'd rather just clean up in the kitchen a mite. It'll help me relax."

"Whatever you'd like to do, Meg, would be fine."

"Since you're looking for something to do, young lady, I'd like a second cup of coffee too," Ray said, giving her a huge smile.

Meg smiled back, responding to his warmth. "Right away, sir."

"Ray is my husband, Meg," Mona said. "You can call him Ray."

Hurrying to fulfill her task, Meg replied, "Thanks, Mrs. Schiller."

"That's Mona," Mona called after her. In lower tones, she added, "This girl sure is polite. Someone taught her manners at some point in her life."

"You don't know the half of it," Leslie added. "She didn't want to sit on my chairs this afternoon because she was too dirty. Plus, she admitted to taking a bar of soap to take a bath but she left a quarter to pay for the soap!"

"How much *is* soap these days?" asked Ray out of hand.

Both women stared at him. Huffing, Mona retorted, "Does it matter? The point is, the girl attempted to pay for what she'd taken. That shows character!"

"Right!" added Leslie.

Everyone ceased talking as Meg neared the table with Ray's coffee. They smiled at her as a group. Handing the mug to Ray, Meg eyed everyone strangely. "Is somethin' wrong?"

"Everything's fine, Meg. Thank you. Why don't you turn in for the night now?"

Nodding, the thin teenager moved toward the hall. Leslie watched her slumped shoulders, wondering if her uneasiness was due to the earlier shooting. Obviously the girl carried a heavy load and didn't trust them enough to tell them what it was. Leslie sighed and turned back to the conversation.

"Who's this Meg, and where'd she come from?" questioned Clive, his puzzled eyes lingering in the direction the teenager had gone.

Leslie tensed as she and Mona exchanged knowing looks.

16

Close Call

BY 7:30 A.M. MONDAY MORNING LESLIE WAS DRESSED and sitting alone at the kitchen table by the window. She stared out over the wild shrubbery and unattended weeds in the front acreage, across the road where she could barely see the red of Clive's rooftop. Sipping her coffee, she wondered what Mona would find out about Meg today.

Her friend had promised to conceal the fact the girl was staying with Leslie, at least until they knew for sure whether or not Meg was listed as a runaway. The poor kid had been scared to death last night when the police had showed up. No wonder she had acted so weird at the table. Leslie winced, remembering Clive's reaction when he'd learned she'd discovered Meg living up in the hayloft of the big barn.

He'd stared at her like she'd sprouted a second head. His accusing words still gnawed at her, *"Do things like this always happen to you? Every time I turn around, you're in some 'out of the park' situation—a calamity or near-death experience. What is it with you anyway, Leslie Weldon?"*

Leslie remembered how she'd wanted to crawl under the table. He'd made it sound as if he blamed her for everything that was happening—like she walked under some dark cloud or conjured up some bad mojo.

She thought of Clive's insensitivity, even more irked by his denseness. He was actually confused by her responsive coolness. Was it possible he hadn't realized how much his words stung? "Men!" She reached for the dark toast lying limp on the plate in front of her.

Her thoughts wandered to Miguel Romero. Had he heard the shooting the night before? She and Miguel had not spoken of the night crying at any time during their first visit. As much as she'd like to stop by and question him on the matter, Leslie remembered her appointment with Clive. Today was the day they were scheduled to go pick up Wayne's repaired Jeep.

Excitement rippled through her at the thought of retrieving her Jeep and driving it home under her own steam. With Clive following behind, Leslie couldn't feel safer. Turning at the sound of Meg's footsteps coming from the bedroom, she smiled at the tousled-haired, sleepy-faced teenager. *Meg looks so normal. It's a shame her life has been anything but,* mused Leslie.

*

The sweaty-faced man with the bleak eyes looked scared. "I told you, Zeke, I don't mess with guns or jobs with guns involved."

"Those guns last night weren't none of our doin', Cleary. Those boys shootin' up in the woods, they work for the boss. We got our job; they got theirs. It ain't our fault! We was doin' our job like always. If the truth be told, I'd bet those shots were just to scare off someone from gettin' too close to their operation. Don't sweat it."

"I don't like guns!" said the slovenly dressed man between clenched teeth. "I have half a mind to quit and pack up today. I ain't gettin' paid all that much anyhow. It sure ain't enough to get mixed up in a shootin' and spend the rest of my life doin' time. I don't have enough life left for those shenanigans." Cleary mopped his unshaven face with a dirty handkerchief.

Zeke glared at Cleary. "When you signed on, you signed on until the job was finished. I suggest you stick around, or the boss might send his special boys to talk with you. You'd never make it to the border—believe me!"

Cleary ran his tongue over his puffy lips. "I didn't mean nothin' by it, Zeke. You know I'd never tell nobody a thing, but guns always bring trouble." He rubbed the knuckles of one hand on the other and began to move away.

The tall man behind him called out a question that brought him up short. "Where's that girl of yours been keepin' herself lately? I ain't seen nothin' of her in three days or more. She sick or somethin'?"

Cleary mopped his face again, shifting his body around partway. "Oh, her. She's dumb as a sack of peas. I think that last black eye I gave her scared her good, 'cause she lit out on me. I figure she'll show her skinny face anytime now, starved and crawlin' back, beggin' for me to take her in." He hacked out a short, dry laugh and shrugged as if it were a foregone conclusion.

Zeke swore. "How many days has she been gone? We can't have her roamin' around knowing what she knows! Why didn't I know about her runnin' off?"

Cleary stared at Zeke Vanook's twisted, mean face. "I told you, ain't nothin' to worry about. She'll be back lookin' for food. She's got nowhere else to go and she don't know nobody. Like I said, she's dumb as peas."

Zeke pointed his finger in Cleary's face and swore again. "You! Find her fast! Take the green truck and cover all the back roads in the area, lookin' for any sign of her. Stop at a few places and ask if you have to. Give them a sob story about your kid bein' lost in a strange state. I don't care what you tell them. Find that kid!" He stalked off, mumbling, "The boss won't like this."

Cleary hustled after him, stumbling over his large feet. "Don't tell him yet, Zeke. Give me a chance to find her. I'll find her."

"You better be quick. I ain't takin' the heat." The man walked away.

Cleary had only met the boss one time, but the man's cold eyes scared him good, especially after he heard the Vanook boys laughing one night when they were drunk and running off at the mouth. They'd bragged about how the boss had the old man eliminated so he could have a better shot at the poor slob's ranch. Had the girl heard them that night? Cleary couldn't remember. If she had, then maybe she was a liability Zeke couldn't allow loose.

After he got some food in him, Cleary determined to comb every road in the area until he found the girl. *And when I get her back...* His jaw tightened, thinking about the money she'd stole from him out of his dresser. *Good thing Zeke don't know she took money. If she gets away, they'll have my head!*

Cleary took time to think. Shaking the way he was, he could use a drink even more than food. It was almost 9:00 a.m., and he was sweatin' like a hog. Rubbing his mouth on the back of his dirty plaid sleeve, he surveyed the unkempt yard in front of the Vanooks' shack, frantically seeking a partially filled bottle of liquor.

He was desperate enough to drink his own stuff, and he knew for a fact it would clean rust off a bumper. His head was too fuzzy to remember the exact night the little witch lit out. *I have to concentrate. If I knew when she left...*

*

Leslie was nervous when she climbed into Clive's truck. Shifting in her seat, she surveyed Meg's slim form standing at the breezeway door. She debated her hasty decision to leave the teenager unattended.

Clive frowned at Leslie. "Look, if you want that girl to come along with us, just say the word. I don't mind. If you don't trust her alone in the house, that's understandable. You only know what she's told you."

"It's not that. I trust her. I do...well, sort of. But she's been here such a short time, and we haven't had a chance to get well acquainted. Meg promised me she'd spend her time cleaning up the mess she made in the hayloft."

"Did you leave a lot of money in the house?"

"Clive!" she snapped. "I said I trust her." Turning back, she craned her neck to see if she could still spot the girl's slight form in the doorway. She inwardly sighed. *How good am I really at judging people? I hope I'm not making a stupid mistake.* Her quota for stupid mistakes was way over the mark as it was. Forcing a confident façade, she looked forward.

"Feel better now?" Clive prodded.

She flashed him a look. His mouth was twisted into a wry grin, his eyes twinkling with amusement. She lifted her chin. "I'm not letting you jerk my chain this morning, Clive Masters. It's a perfectly beautiful fall day, and I'm going to pick up my Jeep and drive it home—a banner day!" She suddenly frowned. "Oh dear, I hope I brought enough cash to pay for the repairs. If not, I'll have to use my credit card, and my current balance is iffy. I don't know why I didn't think about this earlier." She chided herself for being such a ditz.

Clive chuckled "I can't imagine why. You lead such a placid life."

Leslie couldn't help but laugh at his remark. "True…almost boring, you might say." She gave him a slow wink.

"Why, Miss Weldon! Are you flirting with me?"

"You wish, Mr. Masters," she shot back.

Clive laughed louder. The morning was full of signs and sounds of fall. Nuts falling to the ground and the squirrels scurrying around to find them. Large gatherings of birds were seen at an increasing rate, but Clive seemed more focused on Leslie than the wonders of his surroundings.

As they entered the outskirts of town, Leslie marveled at the appeal of this north Georgia town. The two-story buildings encircling the town square boasted railings revealing the charm of the 1800s. "Dahlonega is truly a beautiful town!" she exclaimed, enchanted with the layout and design of the buildings and businesses.

"You should see it at Christmas with all the lights and greenery, especially if there's a light dusting of snow," Clive said softly. "It really is something!" He smiled as if picturing the scene.

"I bet." She marveled again at the small groupings of people talking with friends and mentally compared it to New York. No one stopped to converse with anyone there. It also brought unwelcome recall of her sighting of the sharp-featured man in the floppy hat she'd spotted weeks earlier in town.

"Are you going to be here at Christmas, Leslie?" Clive asked in a low tone.

Her smile faded. "I don't know. I really haven't decided yet."

That one question silenced the conversation for the duration of their drive to the garage a few streets over.

"I'll park my truck over to the side and go in with you," offered Clive, steering to the left.

Leslie looked around at the various vehicles lined up across the back of the garage area of the dealership. "Thanks," she said gratefully. "This place is a little out of my element. I feel pretty awkward."

Ambling inside the darkened area where the mechanics worked on multiple vehicles, Leslie watched in amazement as men darted here and there, calling out part numbers and mechanical jargon to each other.

"Roger said to ask for Joe," she whispered behind her hand. "He said Joe would give us a special deal."

Smiling down at her, Clive chuckled. "Let me understand this. Roger said to ask for Joe for a special deal?" he repeated. "Bob Mitchell owns the garage and gives everyone a fair price. Not only is he a crackerjack mechanic, but he's one of the most honest, respected men I know."

Leslie huffed. "Sorry I said anything. I was only trying to help."

Clive gave her arm a surprise squeeze. "Appreciated, but I've got it covered. Look, I'm going to wander around and find Bob. Take that chair and stay here until I come back for you. No point in you being on that foot unnecessarily."

Before Leslie could answer, Clive left her standing, weaving his way into the congested area of the large garage. Backing up, she lowered herself to one of the plastic chairs lined against the dark wall leading into the main office. She scanned the interior, lingering on two familiar forms talking with a mechanic midway in the garage. The larger man was easily recognizable but one she hadn't expected to find here.

When the two men turned to walk her way, Hamilton Longworth boomed out, "Well, look, Johnny, everywhere I go I keep running into this lovely young woman. How are you today, Miss Weldon?"

Leslie stood to greet the president and vice president of the National Pride Bank of Dahlonega. "Mr. Longworth and Mr. Hager, what a surprise to find you here," she said pleasantly, hoping Clive returned quickly.

Longworth chuckled. "I know nothing about cars. As long as they work right, I'm a happy camper. Unfortunately my Cadillac hasn't been working right—something with the brakes, I gather. Johnny came along with me to introduce me to his favorite mechanic. The man's lining me up with a rental right now. I'm a busy man and pretty well stranded without my wheels."

The large man sidled up to his vice president, whose diminutive size and quiet manner caused Leslie to almost overlook his presence. Patting Hager on the shoulder, Longworth extolled his assistant. "Johnny here has his pulse on the heart of this town. He's quite a mover and a shaker in his own quiet way...not to mention a great asset to me. He makes me look good!" He laughed heartily.

Smiling, Leslie gave the smaller man her full attention. "Those are high compliments indeed, Mr. Hager."

The man's heavy glasses partially hid his hazel eyes. He seemed uneasy with the unexpected focus and praise thrust upon him. Leslie wondered if he was humble or just uncomfortable with the attention. Shy people often were. The small, nervous smile on his thin lips never reached his eyes. "Thank you, Miss Weldon."

Shifting, Hager pointed to the back of the garage. "Your ride is here, Ham," he said quietly. "We really shouldn't keep Joe waiting," Hager nodded pleasantly in Leslie's direction before turning to walk swiftly toward the mechanic who stood by a white, expensive-looking car.

Mr. Longworth inclined his head. "Good day, my dear. It seems my presence is required elsewhere. Too bad, but I do have pressing work. Hope to see you soon."

"Good day, Mr. Longworth. It was good to see you." He was such a charming man; it was hard to think ill of him. From the corner of her eye she saw Clive motioning for her to come his way.

Threading her way through the busy throng, she came to a less hectic area where Wayne's old Jeep sat waiting—at least she thought it was Wayne's Jeep. It now boasted a bright, shiny new paint job.

"I threw in a coat of paint, ma'am. It needed it badly, and Wayne was a good friend as well as a customer. He always came by with free produce from his garden for me to take home to my Mrs. And he never had a sour word—a good Christian man. I'm sorry he's gone. We will miss him."

Leslie swallowed the huge lump stuck in her throat. "Wow! Thanks, Mr. Mitchell." She could hardly take her eyes off the old Jeep. "What a face lift!"

"Bob. I'm Bob to everyone in town," he said, laughing. "Now, let me try to explain exactly what we did to fix up the old girl."

Clive moved in to look at the work statement Bob was handing to Leslie. "When we're done going over this statement, you and I are going to give this lady a quick course in Classic Jeep 101. She has to drive her home."

Taking another glance at the shiny Jeep, Leslie chuckled. "She is a handsome old girl, and I'm going to give her an old-fashioned ladylike name, like Ruby."

Clive and Bob raised their eyebrows, exchanging amused glances. Looking down at the paper in his hand, Bob pointed to a column. "Now, as I was saying, Leslie, the parts I had to replace are listed here on the left...."

*

Closing the breezeway door, Meg moved slowly through the silent ranch house trying to collect her thoughts. From the time Miss Weldon found her in the barn, her life had turned into a fantasy existence. Meg's first goal remained to get away from Cleary, but after spending a whole day with these nice people, her thoughts were a little crazy, not quite so clear. She was eating good food and sleeping in a clean bed. Maybe if she stayed for a few days, she could find a way to get to a bus station, and everything would work out. Mama was right. God was watching over her.

Layering the sweatshirt Miss Mona had brought over for her, Meg brushed her clean, blond hair off to the side of her pale face, staring hard at the mirror. The black eye was barely noticeable today. Lifting a lipstick she'd picked out of a bathroom drawer, she dabbed color lightly across her lips and looked back at the mirror. *At least I don't look like a haunt any longer,* she thought.

Placing the lipstick on the dresser top, she turned to accomplish her task. It wouldn't take long to clean up the barn mess, and then her time would be her own. Maybe she would scrounge around and make Miss Leslie a nice lunch. It would show how thankful she was to have a place to stay, and perhaps the lady might think she was worth her keep. Meg hurried from the house with a trash can, broom, and dustpan.

The morning air and sunlight was free and welcome on her face. For the first time since Mama died, she could breathe deeply without the fear Cleary would walk in on her, drunk, and slap her around. Sometimes she never knew the reason. *What would it be like to really live on a ranch like this one? Mama always wanted to live on a ranch.*

Reaching the barn she worked to slide open the heavy door. She'd never been afraid of good hard work. Mother said it made a person feel worthwhile, like they had a purpose. It was a pity she didn't marry a man who felt the same way. Positioning the cleaning supplies, she mounted the ladder to the loft above.

By the time Meg finished her task, the sun was high in the sky. Gathering her supplies, she pushed the hair from her face, closed up the barn, and started down the farm lane toward the ranch house. Her heart felt light enough to sing, and she found herself lifting her airy, soprano voice in an old hymn she'd heard her mother sing when she was a little girl. The song, "What a Friend We Have in Jesus" always comforted Meg's heart—especially during the last year when Jesus had been her only friend.

Singing was something she and Mama often did together. After her mother married Cleary, the singing had stopped. And now with Mama gone, there was no one to protect her from her stepdad. Feeling the joy of sheer abandon, Meg sang with pure, clear tones, allowing them to soar high. Singing was also one of the few things she did well. Mama said it was God's gift.

Meg's humming was cut short by a terrifying sound—the familiar squeal of the Vanooks' truck. Instantly, her limbs were paralyzed with fear. How many times had she hid in the woods when that truck drove in the driveway? She gasped for control, squinting to see the partially visible road from her highpoint on the lane. The front part of the hateful lime green truck was edging into view. Where could she hide?

She raced down the lane, fearful she might have been seen. Riker's Ranch was positioned at the end of a dead-end road. Why was the truck here? Were they searching for her? *Did they somehow figure out I'm here? Did Miss Mona tell the wrong person?* Meg fought her rising panic as the drone of the engine increased. It was turning into Riker's private drive.

The tool shed next to the garage was the closest building. Could she reach it before the truck covered the distance up to the ranch? She knew the curve of the driveway and high shrubbery would block all view for a short space of time...but would it be time enough?

Meg dove for the tall grasses behind the tool shed, her heart rate pounding through the roof just as the truck cleared the curve of the driveway. Seconds passed as she lay on her back panting, afraid to move, but her curiosity drove her to peer between the grasses. The truck rolled to a stop, and a familiar shape exited the driver's side. She settled in to watch, totally unprepared for the thundering body bounding through the tall grasses behind her on the hill. No more than two feet away appeared Boris!

The fierce animal leapt though to the gravel beyond and pounded onward up the drive leading up to the ranch front, just as Cleary mounted the brick steps. Boris reared up on his hind legs again and again, his harsh bark turning to a low growl, backing the terror-filled man flush against the front of the ranch. Meg was torn. As much as she hated Cleary, she couldn't hide in these bushes and watch Boris rip the man apart—if only for her mother's sake.

She positioned herself to rise from the weeds and call to Boris, hoping the dog would listen to her, but Cleary bolted from his position, making tracks for the truck. Meg watched in horror. Would Boris attack before he reached the truck? The dog bounded over shrubs to cut him off, but Cleary was crafty enough to scramble inside the passenger's side of the truck. Unfortunately, before he could yank the door closed, Boris's huge jaw raked at the back of the man's pants. From where Leslie watched, it almost looked like the dog had bit Cleary in the butt. She covered a small gasp with a hand over her mouth.

Cleary crawled over to the driver's position and hurriedly started the engine. She heard the truck grind its gears and watched it roar out of the drive. Meg sat back on her haunches locked in a semi-daze. A tiny smile formed. It was a real sight watching Boris chase Cleary into the truck, not to mention...her fingers covered her smile. Somehow it didn't seem quite right to laugh at Cleary's misfortune, but she couldn't help herself. Just then she realized how close Cleary had come to finding her. Was she really safe at the Riker Ranch, or should she leave as soon as she could figure out a way?

Meg gathered up all the cleaning supplies she'd discarded in her panicked haste to hide herself in the grasses. Clutching them to her chest, she sprinted down the hill to the breezeway door and scurried inside away from the window. Dropping the supplies in the breezeway, she continued to her bedroom and locked the door. She paused briefly to study the frazzled girl in the mirror, wondering what she should do next.

*

Clive followed Leslie with the patience of Job while she fumbled to find and execute the right gears on the Jeep. By the time they were halfway home, she was able to drive with a measure of confidence. Passing the driveway leading to Clive's ranch, Leslie checked the mirror, surprised to discover he was escorting her home.

A cloud of dust roared toward her from the direction of her ranch. She stared at the rusty lime-green truck rumbling by her at an exorbitant pace and focused her attention on the flabby, unshaven man behind the wheel, a man she'd never seen before. *What was he doing at the ranch?* Leslie questioned. The stern-faced driver leveled a glare in her direction, jerked his face away, and gunned his engine.

The dust was so thick, Leslie shut off all outside air vents. *Jerk* was the only word that came to mind until she remembered Meg was at the ranch all alone. Pushing the gas pedal, she peeled off under the swinging *Riker Ranch* sign and sped up the drive, only to skid to a fast stop in front of the breezeway door. Clive roared up behind her.

They exchanged concerned looks as she hobbled quickly through the door and on into the kitchen. "Meg! Meg," Leslie called.

Hearing the girl's bedroom door open, Leslie waited, watching the uncertain face appear in the hallway. An overwhelming relief washed over her. "Oh, good!" she exclaimed. "I passed this wretched green truck coming from the ranch and got worried. Did that horrid-looking man come up to the house?"

Meg's facial muscles relaxed. "Yeah. I mean, I saw him on the front porch, but Boris ran him off. In fact, he might have torn his pants. I-I was just coming from the barn." She smiled oddly at Leslie. "Thanks for being worried about me."

"Of course I'd be worried. You were here all alone. I sure hope Boris didn't bite the man. I don't need a lawsuit."

"He didn't look too injured when he ripped by us on the road." Clive walked up alongside Leslie. "Well, now that we've passed that crisis, I'm going to head home and get to work. Do you think you can get the Jeep started again and put it in the garage?"

Turning her attention back to Clive, Leslie nodded. "I think I've got the hang of how she handles on the drive from town. Thanks for the patience. Most men would have been screaming out orders."

He chuckled. "I can't say it didn't occur to me. But I figured it would get you all worked up if I rode you too hard." Raising his hand in a wave, he walked back through the house. "Glad you're all right, Meg." He threw the comment over his shoulder, enroute through the breezeway.

Regarding the dusty, rumpled teenager in the hooded sweatshirt, Leslie checked her watch. "Meg, how about you get into a clean pair of jeans and tidy up? Then we'll grab a sandwich for lunch and take off for the afternoon. We need to pick up a few groceries, and there's someone I want to visit. And just maybe, if there's time, we might try to find you a new pair of running shoes."

Meg's eyes grew large. "Really? For me."

Nodding, Leslie paused. "Where's Boris?" She wondered about the dog's strange habits. The blank look on Meg's face gave Leslie her answer. "You don't know?"

"No, I don't. I'd dropped my supplies on the hill, and while I was gathering them up, he took off again. Where does he usually go?"

Leslie looked puzzled and shrugged. "What direction did he come from?"

"I remember him barreling past me from somewhere up the hill....he must have come from behind the barn."

"Strange. Well, go get cleaned up, and I'll fix lunch." She observed the girl sprint down the hall toward her room, wondering if they were going to have time to visit Miguel. That feeling of urgency was getting stronger within her, as if the time was short. Leslie sensed Miguel had more to share.

*

Meg's freshly washed face and combed hair gave her an air of feeling good about herself. How long had it been since the girl had felt that way? Noting the light coating of lipstick on Meg's lips, Leslie complimented the effort she had made in her appearance, "Looking good, girl! All you need now is a pair of shoes that fit."

Her beaming smile of appreciation was Leslie's best reward. Exiting the house, she was careful to lock her doors. "I'll park the Jeep in the garage, and we'll take the SUV to town." She wasn't sure, but she thought she caught the slightest hint of disappointment in the girl's expression. "Don't worry. I'll take you for a ride in the Jeep later this week if there's time. And if everything works out so you can stay," she added.

At the mention of being able to stay, a cloud of doubt inched across Meg's face, making Leslie speculate on what her thoughts might be. "What's wrong?"

"Oh, nothing, Miss Leslie." She shrugged.

Typical teenage answer, thought Leslie, wishing Meg might open up with her. *Trust takes time,* she reminded herself, conscious of her own struggle. She pitied the girl's loneliness, understanding it all too well.

The shopping schedule went quickly, and Meg pranced out of the store in her new running shoes like she was wearing glass slippers. Her countenance was alight with wonder, forcing Leslie to halt the girl's repetitive thanks. Their time together brought a measure of well-being, until a red warning flag shot up to squelch those feelings. Leslie noticed Meg casting furtive glances down side streets and groupings of people in town.

The realization struck like a blast of cold air. *She's afraid of being recognized! The girl told us her stepfather left her stranded at the motel. Who is she afraid of?* The possibility this girl was a runaway suddenly looked more probable. Leslie eyed the teenager. *How many more secrets is she hiding?*

For the first time Leslie doubted her wisdom in allowing the girl to stay. *I don't need more trouble than what I've already got.* She headed the car out of town. Glancing at Meg, she asked, "Did you put all the cold stuff in the back cooler with the ice packs as I asked?"

"Yes, ma'am. Are you planning those pork chops for supper?"

Leslie nodded. "I'll warn you up front. I'm not the best of cooks."

"Would you like me to fix the pork chops the way my mama done showed me?" Meg asked eagerly. "I'd love to cook in a fancy kitchen like yours."

"Really? Well, we'll see how it goes when we get home." A small relief eased her building tension.

Their ride was markedly free of conversation. Thinking on Meg's recent actions, and aware of her own lack of experience with kids, Leslie decided to confer with Mona. The situation now posed new questions. Leslie recognized real fear when she saw it, and Meg was afraid of someone.

Leslie drove to Ryman Road, knowing Romero's long private drive was an off-shoot from there. Meg huddled in a slumped position until Leslie made the turn. The girl sat straight up, her head swiveling anxiously from side to side. "This isn't your road?"

"No. Remember I said I wanted to visit someone? It's important, trust me."

Without comment, Meg slumped even lower in the seat, her chin tucked down into her chest.

"Meg, are you all right?"

"I'm fine, Miss Leslie. A little tired, that's all." She didn't look up.

Perplexed and growing more concerned, Leslie turned onto the steep lane leading up the mountain side to Miguel Romero's log home. The higher they went, the more Meg gave evidence of new interest.

Sitting up, she asked, "Who lives up here?"

"An invalid who was a close friend of my cousin Wayne—the one who left me the ranch. He loves company. You'll like him."

Meg eyed her uneasily. "Is that the cousin who died in a tractor accident?"

"Uh huh," Leslie murmured, pulling up in the front yard. Turning off the ignition, she gathered her purse. "Come along, Meg. We won't stay too long."

Meg's apprehension was stark. Leslie reassured her, "It's all right."

Opening her car door, Meg followed Leslie like a pet lamb, hardly a centimeter behind. Once inside, Leslie adjusted her eyes to the diminished light.

"Miguel," she called, "this is Meg McDonald. She's staying with me for a few days. I wanted to come by sooner, but things have been kind of hectic." Leslie smiled over at Meg, receiving a strained attempt in response.

The man's deeply tanned, rugged face showed years of exposure to sun and outdoor elements. "What a joy to have two lovely ladies pay me a visit."

As Miguel rolled his chair about, his focus rested often upon Meg, his pleasant face filled with interest. Unfortunately, this unmasked curiosity only increased Meg's nervousness. Her slender shoulders rolled inward as if she were seeking to hide within her own skin. Instinctively she lowered her eyes.

When Leslie and Meg declined offered refreshments, Miguel centered his attention on Leslie, his manner serious and business-like. Crossing his arms, he asked pensively, "Have you been reading in the old journals?"

Leslie gave a slight nod. “As much as my crazy schedule allows. I’ve reached the place where Clara is depressed with her life and Jamie wishes he’d never brought her out to the ranch.”

“Keep reading. Pay special attention to the sequence of events. Look for anything that could have a bearing on today,” he said soberly.

“Sequence of events?”

“It’s been a few years since Wayne and I discussed the journals, but I believe what takes place in Jamie and Clara’s marriage and his subsequent discovery could have a bearing on your life today. It was after Wayne finished rereading this account last winter that he became depressed and talked about puzzle pieces coming together.”

“Interesting. Wonder what it could mean?” Suddenly, she asked, “Did you hear the shots the other night up in the woods around Rocky Ridge?”

His expression didn’t change. “Yes. They alarmed me a great deal. Whatever is happening is accelerating very quickly. You need to get through those journals.”

“Why won’t you tell me what you think is happening, Miguel?” Leslie was frustrated. “I feel like I’m stumbling around in the dark and running out of time.”

“Because, I, like Wayne, have no proof, and suppositions without proof are only speculation and gossip. I’ve got a gut feeling, but you need more than that. I don’t want to lead you wrong.”

“What about the crying in the woods? What do you think it means?”

“I heard something that resembles a child, but I don’t believe it for a minute.”

“I agree with you, but Henri O’ first thought it was a ghost.” Leslie wrung her hands.

“I think that’s what someone wants everyone to think. There’s a fair amount of ghost lure around this area from years past. Henri O’ still has some process weeding to do, the ousting of old plantings that won’t serve her well in Jesus’ kingdom. Unfortunately she was influenced by others at a very impressionable age…but I’m confident of her complete metamorphous. She’s growing in the Word more all the time.”

Meg’s fingers had tightened on the arm of the chair where she was sitting as she listened to the talk of the crying child and stories of ghosts. Her tension-filled eyes connected briefly with Leslie’s but darted away.

*

Staring out across the room, Meg projected her thoughts back to the night she escaped from Cleary in the back of the Vanooks' truck. That cloudy night of the storm, the crying child, and the two men—the little man with the floppy hat and the big guy with the snake decorated cowboy boots. Casting a sidelong glance in Leslie's direction, she felt like she was part of the conspiracy, keeping all this information to herself, but she was afraid to tell. How did Miss Leslie fit into all of this? Meg's connection to Cleary made her feel suspect. Would they think she was part of something wrong?

Was Miss Leslie's cousin the old man I heard the Vanooks talking about that night they were so drunk? They boasted how the boss had eliminated the old man from the picture. It was so creepy the way they said it, and then laughed, like it was a joke. I wish I'd listened harder, but I was too sleepy to hear what else they said.

Who and what should she believe? Meg determined it was better to keep quiet. She was pulled back into the conversation when Mr. Romero waved his gnarled finger at Miss Leslie. "Be careful who you trust. Did you read any of Wayne's journal?"

"Some," Leslie answered. "There was something that confused me about meeting a new friend, a friend who didn't want his name mentioned. Did he ever tell you who that friend was? It sounded like he was a person of position or power in town."

The old man's wrinkles seem to converge. "Wayne pretty much told me the same thing. He'd promised this friend he'd never speak his name to anyone, and Wayne was a man of his word. I've often wondered if Wayne mentioned his friendship with me to his mysterious friend." His look told her that he hoped he'd not shared such information. Was Miguel afraid of this unknown man?

Miguel's intense glance sent an unspoken message. "You must come back soon, Miss Leslie, very soon. And bring the journals with you. I resist the urge to project my ideas into your thinking, but perhaps together we can make sense of things." Then he turned to regard Meg with continued interest.

Anxious to leave, Meg avoided his probing eyes. As nice a person as Mr. Romero appeared to be, she had the feeling he was able to look clear through her. She was sure he somehow knew she was hiding something, and that feeling made her nervous. Standing, she positioned herself by the door.

*

Leslie and Meg were heading for the SUV when Leslie's cell phone roared to life in her jacket pocket. Grabbing it, she turned in a circle, trying to get the best reception she could on the remote mountain hillside. Her eyes lifted to the tree branches whipping about in the increased wind. "Yes. Who is this? Speak up, please. Roger, is that you? Talk louder, I can't hear you very well." Leslie put her hand over her other ear.

"Where am I?" She decided it was better not to say. "Outside at present, which is why I'm having a hard time hearing you." She squinted, as if narrowing her eyes would help her hear better. "Did you say one of the investors is in town and would be willing to meet with me? That's great! Where? When?"

Smiling with satisfaction, Leslie clicked off her cell phone and hurried to join Meg, waiting inside the SUV. While heading down the snake-like drive toward the main road, Leslie thought back on her conversation with Roger. *Why now? After two weeks of adamantly refusing any personal contact with the investors, how is it that one of them is suddenly willing to meet with me?*

Whatever! It would work for her, and she was determined to utilize the situation to her advantage. She wanted to get a better feel for what the investors had in mind in regard to Wayne's ranch. An important factor would be how the sale and development would affect the other ranches around her. Now that she knew Ray, Mona, and Clive personally, there was no way she would do something that would work against them.

Leslie cast a glance in Meg's direction. "We need to do a little house cleaning before tomorrow, Meg. It seems we are going to have a visitor."

17

The Investor

WHILE MEG ACQUAINTED HERSELF WITH LESLIE'S KITCHEN, Leslie pulled out the two journals in question and made her way to the living room. Hesitating for a moment at Meg's bedroom doorway, she looked wistfully at the partially painted Christmas bulbs and promised herself an opportunity to finish them. Everything in her life was cramming together in a limited space. Drawing a weary breath she established herself on the living room couch.

Leslie plumped up the pillows and pulled over an ottoman for her foot before switching on the table lamp. The next portion of Jamie's journal was headlined *Joyful Event.* She murmured, "Sounds more promising than the last section."

"Miss Leslie, would you like mashed 'tators and gravy with our pork chops?"

Raising her head, Leslie regarded Meg with new admiration. The girl seemed more at home standing in her kitchen than at any time to date. "You don't have to call me *Miss* Leslie, and yes, that sounds wonderful. You know how to make gravy?"

"Yes, ma'am. My mama taught me lots about cookin'. Didn't yours?"

"Not really," Leslie said in an offhand manner. "She died before we really had the opportunity. Dad did most of our cooking when I was in high school." Leslie looked back at the journal, ignoring Meg's expression of sympathy. She needed to concentrate, not dredge up old wounds.

> After a year of struggling with the land and coping with Clara's troubling moodiness, a deeper challenge assaulted our fragile home. Clara began having alternating periods of silence and spontaneous weeping—her stability was worsening. I was at my wit's end, near total despair until one clear afternoon when Clara ran out to the pasture, waving at me with both arms.
>
> "A baby! Jamie, we're going to have a child!" We rejoiced together, dancing like children under the hot sun. Clara's eyes were overly bright. She was bubbly and brimming with plans for the baby.

Then, abruptly, like a sudden dark cloud, Clara's mood changed black as the inside of a mule's throat. Her joy vanished, instantly replaced with an insane-like fear. She began screaming, refusing to bring her child into nothing but poverty and filth. She pounded me with her fists and ran back to the house. I was afraid for Clara—afraid for our child.

It was then I decided on a course I knew would ultimately bring disaster; gold always did. I began my search in earnest. Claims had been filed all around the area; my chances of finding even a small amount of gold were good. But I had to try for Clara's sake.

Picking an area, I dug with shovel, pick axe, and sledge hammer every night after chores were completed. Weeks passed before I found even the beginning of color.

One night, exhausted and weary of Clara's unhappy ranting, I slammed my sledge hammer into the gigantic boulder on the side of the south hill and stomped into the house, discouraged and angry. It was late afternoon of the next day before I revisited the site and discovered the heavy vein in the split boulder.

How long I stood staring at the startling sight I do not know. I knew enough to know this was a good, solid vein of gold, perhaps one of the strongest in the area. I knew something else. I had to play it down to Clara and everyone else. A certain amount of gold wouldn't cause eyebrows to rise. There were hundreds of mediocre claims. It was my goal to keep the quality of the find underplayed and not to bring unwanted notice to our claim.

The land was ours, but I registered the claim and began to slowly pull out the gold. We saw few people, and I convinced Clara it was to be our secret for our child's sake. I took out small amounts to trade and hid the rest. Gradually, Clara's outlook improved as I bought her pretty things, and we planned to build a bigger and better house, but I made her realize it would be a slow process and take time. She knitted and sewed like any other expectant mother. Together we talked of a wonderful life for us and the baby. I built a cradle and, for a long while, our life was good.

Meg broke into her reading by announcing dinner was ready. Leslie left everything open and walked to the table.

As she methodically forked her food, her thoughts remained locked in the journal, wondering what would turn Jamie and Clara's now wonderful life into a tragedy. Knowing a tragedy was in the making, she wished she could turn back the clock and undo the coming sadness in the lives of her early relatives.

"When will Miss Mona let us know what she found out today?" Meg asked anxiously, bringing Leslie's thoughts back to the present.

Leslie's hand went to her head. "Sorry, I'd almost forgotten about that." She looked at the clock on the kitchen wall. "Probably not until after supper sometime. The fact she hasn't already called is good news. Relax. Finish your supper. I'll help you clean up. That was a fabulous meal you cooked. You shouldn't have to do dishes too."

"Oh no, ma'am. That Mr. Romero told you it was important for you to read the journals...whatever they are. Besides, what else do I have to do to earn my keep?" A tiny smile curved up the ends of Meg's mouth.

"I appreciate that, Meg. Trust me...you earned your keep tonight."

*

It was 8:00 p.m. when the phone rang. Meg was sequestered in her room and Leslie was entrenched once again in Wayne's journal, trying to keep a balance between the first and the last. She'd reached the portion where Wayne had seen a need to reread the original record about when Jamie and Clara first came to Dahlonega. Someone had offered to purchase Wayne's ranch lock, stock and barrel, and for some reason he looked for answers in Jamie and Clara's first journal.

"Leslie," the voice responded. It was Mona, and she sounded tired.

"Hard day?" she asked, centering her interest on her friend.

"Incomplete. I've got a friend checking on the list of runaways. It'll be a couple of days before we know anything. I can't see any point in contacting Social Services until we have an answer on that. Have Meg keep a low profile. Speaking of such, how are things working out? Does she need anything? Ray and I will cover extra expenses. Try and find out when she last attended school. There's nothing we can do about that now, of course, but still..."

"Mona, school can wait. With everything up in the air..."

"I know. It's just that a young girl needs to keep up with her education. She seems fairly intelligent, but her grammar needs work."

Leslie chuckled quietly. "You're sounding like a parent."

"Don't go there, Leslie. Anything new?"

"Meg has a new pair of running shoes and, wonder of all wonders, one of the 'mysterious investors' reportedly interested in purchasing the ranch is willing to meet with me. And hopefully he will answer a few questions."

"Really? When?"

"Tomorrow afternoon, right here. It should be interesting."

"Curious. Strange that they should want to meet now. They're getting anxious, Leslie. Tired of waiting. Be careful. They're shrewd, and I don't think they're used to being told no. Get ready for some high pressure."

A cold feeling ran through Leslie. "I'll be careful."

"Talk to you tomorrow. Good night."

Leslie lowered the phone, thinking on tomorrow's visitor. She reminded herself to line up a list of questions to have on hand. Hearing scratching at the back door, she asked Meg to let Boris inside and feed him. Returning to Wayne's journal, she thought how much her situation was similar to Wayne's at the time of his writings.

It surprised her to read that, for a short time in the beginning, Wayne had actually toyed with the idea of selling. He wrote about having only one relative to pass the land down to, adding there were some doubts in that area. Leslie paused, realizing that relative was her. It troubled her to think Wayne had such poor reserves to choose from. If Dad had lived, he would have been a worthy recipient. She sighed. *I'm trying, Cousin Wayne. You left me much more than a ranch.* Her hand raked her hair. "Yes, there's a lot more going on than just the question of selling the ranch," she murmured.

Ambling slowly into the family room from the kitchen, Meg flopped in the overstuffed chair, fingering an apple in her right hand. She looked at Leslie. "You look troubled, Miss Leslie…sorry, Leslie," she corrected, smiling sheepishly.

"I've got a lot on my mind. A lot of decisions, unanswered questions—problems! We've had a rash of bad accidents that can't be explained."

"My mama would ask you if you'd prayed and asked for Jesus' help."

Leslie's head shot up, staring at the slip of a girl with pale wispy hair. "I haven't been able to actually pray in a long time," she admitted. "I don't think God is listening anymore—at least to me. In fact, I question at times what I really believe." She looked at the page in front of her, the printing now strangely blurry.

Meg cocked her head. "Did you once believe Jesus was God's own Son who died for your sins?"

The question took Leslie aback. Clearing her throat, she measured her answer. "Yes, Meg, I did."

Meg pressed, "And did you believe He rose from the dead three days later?"

"Yes, and at one time, when I was younger than you, I even asked Jesus to be my Savior," she said, agitated. "I remember it was a special meeting at our church. But time passes, and that was a long, long time ago."

Meg regarded her with a wizened appraisal. "Mama would say, 'You got blockage.' " She nodded matter-of-factly, chomping on her apple.

"Blockage?" Leslie was startled.

"You know, like plumbing, only with your heart. Maybe you've got something you're mad at God about...or maybe you feel guilty, like God's mad at you?" Looking down, she shrugged. "That's the usual blockage."

Leslie stared at the childlike face, wondering at the wisdom in the words. Everything Meg had mentioned struck a nerve. Leslie had been mad at God for allowing Kevin to break her heart, but most of all she blamed God for taking her father before she could make things right. Then there was the blanket of guilt that never left her. Her hand worked with a strand of hair. "And what suggestion would your mother have for situations like you mentioned—like blockage?" she asked with a cynical, sad smile.

Meg's blue eyes met hers. "Being you're already His child, you just say I'm sorry to God. You have to mean it, of course." Her eyebrows rose. "Mama said true repentance means you stop going one way, because it's wrong, and start going in the other direction. The good thing is, Jesus promised to forgive, and He never breaks promises." She chomped more apple.

"So—ooo simple," she mumbled. "Thank you, Meg," she added hurriedly, her eyes seeking the clock. She was suddenly weary of secondhand advice. "Look, it's getting late. I think it's time we both got some rest." She fumbled nervously, placing bookmarks in both journals before hefting them into her arms. She stood and stretched, nodding soberly in Meg's direction.

Boris followed Leslie to the office, where she returned the journals to their empty slots on the shelves. Remaining in her crouched position, she patted the wiry head of the panting dog. "Out of the mouth of babes, Boris," she whispered. "Out of the mouth of babes." Withdrawing her hand from Boris's coat, she brushed off a thin film of dirt. "What have you been up to, old boy?" she mused out loud.

Her heart felt heavier than her leaded boot as she made her way to her bedroom. When she saw Meg's light beneath the door, she knocked lightly. "Good night, Meg. I'll see you at breakfast."

"Good night, Miss...I mean, Leslie." The voice fell off, sounding very alone.

Leslie's fingertips rested on Meg's door as seconds passed. There was nothing she could say to the child to ease that lonely feeling. She hadn't found the secret to her own loneliness.

Lying in the darkness, she thrashed back and forth in her bed. *"Say I'm sorry to God...so simple."* Leslie had lists of Bible verses memorized in her head from years of family devotions with her father. One flashed to mind: *"If we confess our sins, He is faithful and just to forgive us our sins and to cleanse us from all unrighteousness."* The answer had been inside her all the while.

Slipping from her bed to her knees, Leslie swiped at the tears in her eyes, going over all the questions Meg had asked her. Yes, she'd believed Jesus rose from the grave. Easter had been a big deal in her house for deeper reasons than the Easter bunny.

When exactly had she pushed that faith into a cupboard of doubt and guilt? The reason had never been more stark and blatant: the instant she pushed God away to do her own thing. Then, later, it became more subtle—to believe in God meant she had to face her sin. Tears streamed down her face.

The words that had been stuck so long flowed from her heart upward to the God of her childhood. She laid out her stubborn rebellion against His commandments, admitting she'd thrown aside God's command to remain pure the minute she bought the plane ticket to the Island. Recognizing she'd justified her actions when Kevin left her stranded, Leslie finally gave up her anger and accepted the blame for the results of her actions and the weights of her heart fell away.

A huge sigh escaped as she lay her head on the edge of her bed. "I'm back, Daddy," she whispered. "I wish you were here. I wish you could know..."

Swiping her tears with the edge of her sheet, she whispered her first request to her heavenly Father in many years. "Dear Lord, I know You've been here all along, protecting me from danger, even when I denied You—and I believe You know what's going on. But I need guidance and eyes to see the truth. Help me!"

Back in bed, she stared out at the blackness of night through the partly open blinds and allowed the new peacefulness to replace all her tension. Soon her eyes closed, and her breathing deepened.

*

Leslie and Meg were up early the next day, straightening the house for the important visitor. Leslie paused at the window to admire the rising sun on the subtly changing foliage. All of her world looked brighter this morning, and her outlook was stronger. She was firmly aware of the power surrounding her, and it gave her peace.

Lifting the ringing phone on her way into the kitchen, Leslie laughed lightly, assuring Roger that she would be at home when the northern investor arrived. "I got it, Roger. He'll be here about 1:00 p.m. Don't worry. I'll be home, and I'll listen to his proposal. Relax." She stood listening as Roger made a preparatory sales pitch. "I've heard all this before, Roger, and no I can't give you a guarantee I'll accept his offer. Good-bye." She finished on a high note but couldn't shake a lingering uneasiness. Roger's anxious tone troubled her. *How deep is Roger's interest in this sale?*

Replacing the phone, she finished up the cleaning. As soon as saw Boris's food dish, she realized the potential danger. What if Boris showed up when the investor arrived? Hurriedly, she poured his dish part full of food and ventured outside. She called repeatedly, shaking his dish to entice the animal.

Leslie spotted the dog coming from behind the big barn. As soon as Boris was closer, within coaxing range, she lured him inside the garage with his food and closed the door. Brushing off her hands, she headed back to the house. Everything was ready.

The sleek, dark rental car moved smoothly into the drive and parked. Leslie parted the kitchen curtains. "He's here, Meg. I think it would be better if you stayed out of sight. The fewer people who know you're here, the better."

Meg started for her bedroom. "I'm here if you need me," she called back.

Leslie smiled. "He's a businessman, Meg, not a henchman!"

She watched a large man in a dark striped suit unfold his long legs from behind the wheel of the car and stand beside the closed door. His imposing head and squared face was obscured partially by dark sunglasses. Above his collar, slicked-back hair lay neatly trimmed. The curtain fluttered back into position as Leslie went to open the door.

Leslie wasn't a small woman, but standing in front of this mountain of a man made her feel that way. He introduced himself as William Gaetzi in a monotone voice and smiled little. "My time is short, Miss Weldon, and I know you have been amply comprised of the basics of our proposal. Is there somewhere I can lay out my folder?" He looked around, shifting his briefcase to his left hand.

Leading the man to the front table where there was plenty of light, Leslie indicated a chair for him to sit and withdrew a piece of paper from her pants pocket before taking the adjacent chair. "I have a few questions of my own, Mr. Gaetzi," she stated, matching his professional tone.

With his glasses intact, he turned his head ever so slightly. "Of course." His tone was hard, causing Leslie to be taken aback, sensing this was a man to be reckoned with. Her anxiety rose while examining the papers laid out on the table. The figures of the proposal were impressive, but none of the particulars of their plans for the ranch were stated in specifics. The more Leslie pressed for answers, the more vague Mr. Gaetzi became. His unresponsive attitude increased Leslie's fears tenfold.

More so, she found it unnerving that the man deemed it necessary to wear his sunglasses inside her house. It was hard to read a man whose eyes you couldn't see. Her gaze roamed the expanse of the long hall, where Meg peeked out from behind the setback midway of the hallway. Whether the girl was protective or merely inquisitive, it was hard to tell.

Leslie hid a smile and refocused on the matter at hand. After he skillfully avoided a host of questions, their conversation ended in uncomfortable silence. Following several extra-long seconds, Mr. Gaetzi collected his many papers into a pile. It was obvious they had hit an impasse.

"Miss Weldon, I'm leaving the basics of our proposal for your further consideration. There is a specific section of land that my fellow investors have noted. They asked me to come back with a firsthand appraisal. Is it possible for us to take a drive out to a section known as Rocky Ridge at this time?"

Leslie's eyes flew open in surprise. This was a twist she hadn't expected. "I-I don't know of any reason why that couldn't be arranged." She quickly organized her thoughts. Chuckling, she said, "I hope you weren't planning on that rental car handling the rough roads out to Rocky Ridge."

His expression remained stoic. "Actually, I was told you have a Jeep at your disposal and assumed we'd ride out to the site in it."

His assumption ruffled Leslie's feathers, but she kept her feelings to herself. If this man wanted to see Rocky Ridge, it was fine with her. It didn't mean they were any closer in coming to an agreement. She forced a smile and stood, anxious to get the whole ordeal over. She didn't like this man, and the sooner he left the better.

As Mr. Gaetzi opened his briefcase to stuff in his remaining papers, several fluttered to the floor. She watched him kneel in frustration beside the chair. As his huge hand stretched to snatch them quickly, his expression twisted with open irritation. Leslie tensed. Mr. Gaetzi was not a pleasant man.

*

Meg frowned from her hidden position in the hallway alcove. There was something familiar about this man—his motion and raw energy. It wasn't that she recognized his face, but there was a definite feeling, they'd met before. *Good. He's gathering his papers to leave.* As loose papers flitted to the rug below and the massive man kneeled, his pant leg lifted, revealing his boots...boots with snake designs tooled into fine leather. This was the man from the woods that night of the storm, when she escaped Cleary's grasp. This was a bad man. Meg knew it instinctively.

Clenching her fists, she remembered back. Whatever he was doing that stormy night was secretive and wrong. Somehow this supposed businessman was connected with the sounds of the crying child—he and the small man with the big hat.

Leslie was standing. If only Leslie would walk down the hallway where she could warn her.

Turning from the table, Leslie started for the breezeway. "I'll get my keys for the Jeep and back it out of the garage. Mr. Gaetzi, you'd better wait for me to tie up my dog. He's not very friendly with strangers." She paused in the doorway.

Meg's heart pounded inside her chest. How could she stop Leslie from going somewhere with this dangerous man?

*

Grabbing the keys from the breezeway board, Leslie pushed open the back door. This was not how she'd envisioned her afternoon. She didn't want to waste a drive out to Rocky Ridge with this stone-faced businessman, especially when it was becoming quite clear to her that selling was not what she was supposed to do. Exhaling, she tried to alter her increasingly bad attitude.

The way that he simply assumed we'd take my Jeep out to Rocky Ridge...

She was fuming by the time she reached the drive.

A swirling cloud of dust mounted toward her from the curved drive. Out of the center of this foggy mass appeared Mona's sturdy little truck. The vehicle braked sharply in front of her, and Mona emerged with a widespread grin. "I got off early and decided to come over and hang out for a while. Is that okay?"

"It's great! In fact, you've arrived just in time to take a ride with me and Mr. Gaetzi up to Rocky Ridge."

Mona's long dark hair blew over her shoulder. She raised her sunglasses. "Rocky Ridge?"

A noise brought their focus to the back door, where the massive figure of Mr. Gaetzi pushed through to the outside, his head down and dark sunglasses in place. With hardly a glance in their direction, the bulky-framed man moved rapidly toward his car. "I received an urgent call, Miss Weldon, and won't be able to take that ride with you today. If there's time, I'll call and set up another appointment. Thank you. Good-bye."

Without waiting for a reply, he slid inside the rental car and backed around. His wheels spun out from the drive in record time. Both women stood speechless, studying the settling dust with puzzled expressions. "That was Mr. Gaetzi, Mona. He apparently had a prior commitment." Leslie arched her neck to peer after him.

"Apparently!" Mona watched the departing car. "I thought I'd offer my support for the meeting. I knew you were somewhat apprehensive."

Leslie nodded. "I was. But there were no hopeful surprises in his proposal. Mr. Gaetzi wasn't nearly as open as Roger. After the first few minutes, I began to wonder why he'd even made the effort to meet with me. He sat there like a stone Buddha, wearing those huge sunglasses. It was all very strange."

"That guy was supposed to be one of the investors interested in buying this ranch?" Mona questioned, clearly perplexed.

"That's what Roger said. And just as our meeting was ending today, he practically demanded to be taken in my Jeep out to Rocky Ridge to do an appraisal." Leslie shook her head in confusion. "Why don't we go inside?" She led the way.

Meg, ghostly pale, waited for them in the kitchen. "Is he gone?"

"If you mean the mysterious Mr. Gaetzi, he left in a whirlwind," said Mona.

Leslie frowned. "Meg, do you remember Mr. Gaetzi answering a phone call while I was outside?"

Meg's lips thinned. "His phone never rang. He watched you from the kitchen window. When Miss Mona drove up, he grabbed his briefcase and rushed out the door like the devil hisself was after him."

"What do you think that means?" Leslie looked from Mona to Meg.

Mona rubbed her bare arms. "I have no clue, but it gives me the willies."

Meg looked away, her bottom lip trembling. "I-I'll make some coffee," she offered, stammering.

As Mona and Leslie walked to the table by the window, Meg's hands shook while she put a pot of coffee on to perk.

*

After Mona left, Meg and Leslie put together a makeshift supper of leftovers. Meg offered to release Boris from the garage for his supper while Leslie tried in vain to call Roger, her mind filled with troublesome questions about Mr.

Gaetzi, the investor. Somewhere she had a card with Roger's private cell phone written on it but found she was unable to locate it.

After Meg returned to the house with Boris, she kept mainly to herself. Taking a novel off one of Wayne's bookshelves, she curled up in the family room, leaving Leslie time to work awhile on the Christmas bulbs.

About 7:00 p.m. Leslie wandered out to the kitchen for a drink. Passing Meg's chair, she paused. "You're unusually quiet tonight. Did that man upset you?"

Closing the book, Meg nodded. "Yeah, I guess he did." Her eyes veered away.

Leslie didn't press. "If you want to talk later, I'm available." She left the invitation out there for Meg's consideration and returned to her work. When it was time to quit, she cleaned up her brushes and made Meg's bedroom presentable for her to reenter. "I'm sorry to monopolize your room."

"Oh, don't be, Leslie. Do you s'pose you could you teach me how to do them?"

It was the first light of interest Leslie had seen in the girl's eyes all afternoon. "I'm still feeling my way around, but I might let you try drawing something on a piece of paper and see where that leads us."

Waiting for the girl to settle in for the night, Leslie carried out the two journals to the couch. After today's strange meeting with the investor, the urgency was stronger than ever to understand what was going on.

Jamie Cohen entitled the next portion of his journal *Little Gus.*

> Clara's birthing pains were so sharp, I was afraid I might lose them both. She screamed for hours, cursing me for putting her in that position. There was no one to help. Our closest neighbors had sold out and returned to Ohio, and I couldn't leave Clara and ride to town. In the end it was just her and me. I was scared out of my wits. Little Gus was born at 1:00 a.m.—wrinkled, red, and not breathing. I remembered something I'd heard from a miner's wife and smacked him hard on the backside.
>
> His angry scream was the sweetest sound I'd ever heard. My son was alive! Clara and I spent the rest of the night staring at this tiny person who had entered our life. Little Gus consumed Clara's every waking moment from that point on. She threw all her energy into the child. I didn't mind because Clara's moods leveled to a place where our home was relatively peaceful. She was the happiest she'd ever been since her arrival.

Gus was bright. By the age of four, Clara began teaching him to read with big plans for his future. The little fella loved to follow me out to feed the livestock and into the mine, but Clara was always anxious about him. I created a special area for Gus to dig at the mine entrance where he would be safe. I continued to work night after night.

After what seemed an endless wait, a United States mint was opened in Dahlonega in 1838, before Gus's fifth birthday. It was what I'd been waiting for. Though I'd never tapped into the mother lode, I quietly took small portions of the gold I'd salted away the last few years and had it minted into coins. Clara gave me a glass jar to keep the half-eagle five-dollar coins. Before long we had several jars filled with the coins.

Funny thing was, I knew I hadn't even tapped into the mother lode, and I didn't care. The gold was for Clara's comfort and peace of mind. Clara couldn't stand poverty. We had years ahead of us to dream. It would be our security. And, more importantly, Clara's sanity—and mine.

Leslie flipped the page to continue reading, only to find it blank, along with the page after that and the next. On the fourth page, the heading was printed in a neat scroll-like flow: *Gus's Memorial.*

Rubbing her eyes, she closed the journal. The section title indicated the next portion was loaded with sensitive material. Leslie checked her watch. It was too late to start anything that might affect her sleep.

18

A Trail of Crumbs

After a light breakfast the following morning, Leslie kept trying to reach Roger with no results. She rustled through the papers by the phone looking for a paper scrap or card with his home phone or cell phone.

"What are you looking for?" asked Meg, inserting dishes in the dishwasher.

Leslie sighed. "A phone number of my lawyer...actually, he was Cousin Wayne's lawyer. Oh, well. I left a message on his office phone, and he'll get back with me, eventually. The thing is, I can't remember him saying he was going out of town."

Hearing the sound of a car in the drive, both Leslie and Meg went to the back door. Pushing the door open, Leslie smiled and waved as the tall form of Henri O' climbed out of Mona's truck carrying a plastic-covered bowl. Henri O' wore jeans, a long-sleeved shirt, and leather vest with the ease of a woman born to a saddle.

With a tilt of her chin, she extended the bowl. "Miss Mona sent over some leftover mac-'n'-cheese for your lunch today, and I'm supposed to inform you all she's expecting both of you for supper tonight."

Accepting the bowl, Leslie passed it over to Meg, who hung back by the door, awed by the exotic, dark-haired woman. Seeing her, Henri O' took measure of the thin, insecure teenager and gave a small nod of greeting before raising her eyes to Leslie. "Shall I tell Miss Mona you accept?"

Chuckling, Leslie said, "I didn't get the feeling I was given a choice. We'll be there, Henri O'."

Henri O's mouth turned up in amusement. "Yes'm, I'll tell her. That will be 6:00 p.m. tonight." Sobering, the woman's dark eyes locked on Leslie's face. "My pa sent you a message. He had a dream last night that made him scared for you. Pa said, 'You are to hurry with the journals...and you are to pray.' "

Leslie swallowed. "Tell him thanks, Henri O'. I'm trying."

After the tailgate of the truck rounded the curve of the drive, Leslie turned to face Meg, who stood, mouth open, clutching the covered bowl.

"That lady, Meg McDonald, is not a woman to underestimate on any level. She always leaves you wondering what she's thinking." Leslie added, "But I have a gut feeling, if she ever made up her mind to trust you, you'd have a friend forever." Having said that, she directed Meg inside.

Jamie Cohen's journal was waiting for her.

*

Zeke Vanook crouched in the bed of the lime-green pickup truck, next to a grouping of tools, and fingered a coarse substance between his fingers. His eyes grew hard and marble-like, narrowing in thought as his mouth twisted in anger. Standing, he took hold of the truck side and swung his long legs over the edge to the ground below. His fist closed on the coarse crumbs before cramming his hand into his dirty, corduroy pocket.

He stalked up the steep hill to the trailer eye-sore visible in the tree line. Zeke was looking for answers. There was too much at stake. Throwing open the broken door, he climbed inside, scanning the filthy contents with disgust.

Cleary was passed out cold across the couch, his hairy stomach half exposed beneath his dirty undershirt, with his unshaven jaw dropped open in a throat-rattling snore. As he grabbed the pudgy old man by the lapels of his unbuttoned shirt, the blood vessels on Zeke's arms bulged with the fury that raged inside him.

"Wake up, you old sot!" he screamed. Swearing, Zeke slapped both sides of the old man's cheeks. "Wake up, I said." He yanked the deadlike bulk up to a sitting position and slapped him again.

Cleary's small, round eyes blinked unseeing at Zeke's chest, his hands attempting to push Zeke away from him. "Le—Leave me alone, you…" He swore a blue line.

Zeke slapped him again as the old man's eyes opened to a thin slit. Noticing a cup of cold coffee on the cluttered counter, Zeke grabbed it and pushed the cup to Cleary's mouth. "Drink this. I want you awake."

Fifteen minutes later, Cleary glared at Zeke with snake eyes. "What are you doing here?" he demanded in a surly slur.

"Focus, old man. We gotta find that girl. Did you show her picture around?"

"Don't have a picture, but I asked good and plenty at every house on our road and the roads that tag into ours. Nobody seen her. I even gave out my cell number and offered a reward." He shrugged. "There's nothing else to be done, Zeke. I can't dredge her up outa smoke!"

Zeke put his hand in his corduroy pocket and withdrew the white, crumbly substance. "Do you know what this is, Cleary? Look real good."

Tilting his head within inches of Zeke's calloused hands, Cleary blinked. His shaky fingers picked up a few of the particles, lifting them first to his nose and then to his mouth. He stared up at Zeke. "Biscuits?"

"Biscuits, Cleary. I found these crumbs under the tarp in the truckbed. Didn't you say she took the rest of your food from supper, includin' the biscuits?"'

Cleary's free hand rubbed his jaw as he stared down at the crumbs, looking as if he was thinking hard. "Yeah, she took the biscuits when she lit out all right."

"This means that kid rode all the way up to the ridge with us that night and got an eyeful at what we were doin'. It also means wherever she went, she started out up on that ridge. The boss isn't goin' to like a witness on the loose. Secrecy is very important to him. No tellin' what she heard while she was here. She's got to be silenced, Cleary."

Cleary's jaw went slack as he contemplated the full meaning of Zeke's words. "She's just a dumb kid, Zeke. We find her and sit on her good…then everything will be all right. I guarantee it'll be all right. She won't tell nobody. She's just a kid."

Zeke's eyes were hard. "Find her, Cleary. Get her back. You're right, she won't tell a soul. You figure out where she might have gone when she climbed out of the truck on that ridge. She probably hid out in the woods. Follow the woods. Find her!"

Cleary dropped his head. "After I run a load of booze to a pickup, I'll follow the woods," he mumbled.

Zeke nodded. "Call me when you got her."

*

Closing the door behind her, Leslie picked up Jamie's journal from her dresser and carried it over to her bed. She stretched out, pulling the tattered journal on top of her.

Her fingers tapped the cover, thinking on Henri O's warning: *"Pa had a dream. You are to hurry with the journals, and you are to pray."*

Leslie closed her eyes briefly, *Lord, what does it mean? I need to understand.* She leafed through the journal to the page she'd left off at the night before…not that she was looking forward to this portion.

It was almost 4:00 a.m. when I threw the last shovel of dirt on top of Clara's body. I had laid her next to Little Gus, following hours of dragging timbers from his broken frame. Blood and mud dripped from my fingertips. Having no idea how long the rain had been drizzling down on me, I now looked at my soaked clothing, feeling nothing, neither wetness nor cold. Only a total, all-encompassing numbness.

It would be light in a few hours, a new day. I had a lot of work ahead of me. Trudging back to the ranch, I emptied some fruit jars and wiped them clean. When my eyes rested on Clara's large, bread-rising bowl, I took it too. It would take time to pick up all of the half eagle coins lying in the broken glass. Clara had raised them over her head, screaming hysterically, "What good is your gold now, Jamie Cohen? Digging every night, filling jars—for what? Our gold is cursed with our baby's blood!"

"For you, Clara, and Gus. I was trying to make you happy and give you the things you wanted. It was for you."

I knew as I talked that Clara was past reasoning. Her face twisted with grief and rage, and something beyond—madness!

"Gus! There is no Gus, Jamie. Your gold mine took my Gus and killed him. You killed him. You murdered my baby!"

"It was an accident. It was no one's fault! I was cleaning tools in the shed when Gus walked inside the mine. I never saw him, Clara. I thought he was with you."

The tears poured down my cheeks as thunder rumbled overhead, even as the rumbling in the mine behind me settled to dust. The side timbers had loosened and given way. There was a simple flaw in my structuring that I could have fixed, had Gus not wandered inside and become trapped.

Normally Gus was at Clara's side this time of day, but the pending storm had sent Clara into a frenzy to collect her drying clothes from the line. Straying unnoticed from the yard, Little Gus had gone in search of his pa. Clara couldn't accept that.

"It was an accident, Clara," I cried out again.

Heaving the coin-filled jars down to the mouth of the mine and granite boulders that circled her dead son, she screamed, "It was your lust for gold, Jamie Cohen. He would be alive if it wasn't for this mine—and you! You're a murderer of children, and I hate you." Her eyes were wild and glassy looking.

I dodged the shards of breaking glass. Seeing Clara turn and run wildly up the hill and into the woods beyond, I scrambled up the side of the crumbling hillside, chasing her into the woods.

Lighting flashed ahead of me, striking a tall pine, but I paid no mind as I followed Clara's crashing trail through the woods. I heard her shrill laughter and turned toward the edge of the woods and a dangerously steep cliff.

Seeing the wind whip her yellow calico skirt and toss her light brown hair, I gentled my voice. "Clara, wait for me...Clara—don't!"

She smiled at me in a strange, sad way before turning back to the rim.

By the time I reached the edge, she lay at the bottom of the water-riddled gorge, her head turned awkwardly to the side and partly covered by her mass of hair. Grabbing hold of the ledge, I slid down the muddy, graveled side of the cliff until I reached the place where she lay motionless at my feet. How long I sat there beside her, I don't know. I was amazed how peaceful my Clara looked, more so than at any time of our marriage.

At some point the rain started, continuing as I struggled to carry her up to the top of the cliff and back to the mouth of the mine where I tenderly laid her alongside Little Gus. It took an hour to layer large stones around them, separating their memorial alcove from the rest of the tunnel bed. At some moment I lost track of time and reality.

I buried them all—Gus, Clara, the gold—and then I looked to the partially crushed mine entrance and made the decision to finish the job. As time passed, I planted two oak trees at the top, fifteen feet apart—one for Clara, one for Gus. Each day I laid wildflowers at their base. Later I would come to pray. I hope to be buried there someday.

A blank page separated this unhappy family reading from the continuation of. Jamie's life story, but right now Leslie didn't have the heart to read any further. She couldn't dismiss such tragedy and simply read on.

Jamie Cohen's story was such a sad start for this beautiful land that had been passed down from generations. The Cherokees called the northern part of Georgia "The Enchanted Land." After all his work, nothing was left but Jamie, himself, and the land he'd toiled for. The gold had been cut off, his profits buried—his beloved wife and son tragically dead. *How could he possibly go on? Where was God when it all happened?*

It was then she thought about the coins Jamie had traded his gold for. What had Jamie called them? Half eagles? Leslie closed the book, rubbing the side of her head. Miguel had told her to look for a sequence, or something that would transfer to profit today, but everything had altered from that period.

Wherever Jamie's gold mine was buried, it would now be nearly impossible to locate. One hundred years of soil erosion and dense foliage changed the whole face of a land. Not to mention, the uncountable large oak trees dotting the entire ridge line with the pine. It was common knowledge that abandoned gold mines were a dime a dozen around Dahlonega. *What was there to glean from dead ends?* She exhaled deeply. The room seemed to be closing in on her.

The stale smell of the old journal, mixed with the heat of the afternoon sun, began suffocating her with their stuffiness. Her brain was too tired to work on any more puzzles. Dream or no dream, the rest would have to wait.

A light knock on the door brought Leslie's attention back to the day at hand. "It's lunch time, Leslie. Can you come out?" Meg's timid voice inquired.

"Coming, Meg." Thankful for the excuse, she laid the journal back on the dresser before leaving the room. *The answer is probably right in front of my eyes.* She shook her head free of agitating loose information she couldn't piece together and looked forward to working with her hands on something she could see and have control over. It was a good afternoon for the Christmas bulbs.

Working with Meg in the kitchen, Leslie marveled at the transformation in the girl's spirit whenever she was involved with food preparation. Turning Meg to face her, Leslie smiled. "After you graduate from high school, you might consider becoming a chef someday."

Meg's gaze dropped. "I'm behind in school. Cleary didn't want to bother carrying me back and forth to any school when we came here."

"Don't worry about school. When we get the okay from Mona's friend, school will be a possibility again. In no time at all you'll catch up. You'll see."

The sober look Meg returned was indiscernible, troubling Leslie. She wished she knew what the girl was hiding...what she was afraid of. Leslie gave her an impulsive hug. "Mona and I will do everything we can to help you. Trust me." Leslie thought back on the earlier phone call she'd taken from Mona, hoping Meg would comply. For a girl in her situation, there were few options.

Meg looked past Leslie out the kitchen window, her brow furrowed. "I appreciate what you've done for me, but I don't want to be any trouble." She paused, seeming as if she wanted to say more, but the words wouldn't come. Suddenly, the girl's eyes widened. "Miss Leslie, look!"

Whirling about, Leslie stared in Meg's line of vision. "That's Boris going back behind the big barn."

“He came from that direction the day that lime-green truck pulled into the drive—right over that hill and barreled past me to the ranch.”

Throwing her dishrag down, Leslie turned. “Let’s follow him. Get your coat. You run on ahead, and I’ll keep up the best I can. It’s time we knew what that animal has been up to.”

“Yes, ma’am, I’m on it.” Meg tore from the room.

By the time Leslie reached the top of the hill by the barn, she was panting like she’d run a marathon and her foot throbbed. “Boy, am I out of practice. When I get this boot off, I gotta get back in shape,” she mumbled.

Leslie could see a portion of the back of Meg’s jacket at the bottom of the incline far off to the right. Beyond that was a small curve at the base of a boulder and a sharp rise leading almost straight up into the woods on the high ridge. Her gaze followed the top of the ridge line, knowing it ended about a mile and a half to the left at Rocky Ridge—a lot of area to consider. Leslie remembered that day with Clive when she’d gazed back to the barn and ranch. A smile formed, thinking of Clive carrying her down the ridge.

She blinked away memories as arms waved below. Meg had turned back and was motioning her down the incline. Inhaling deeply, Leslie started out on her good foot, careful to keep her balance. She envisioned herself tripping and rolling all the way to the bottom. Meg met her as the incline grew steeper, extending a supporting hand. Soon they both were at the bottom.

“Did you find him?” Leslie was short of breath.

*

Cleary moistened his cracked lips while staring out through the truck window across the valley over to Rocky Ridge. If he took Ryman Road up to the curve and around, he could get an idea where the kid might have decided to hole up. The Riker Ranch was the most logical place to start, but he hated the idea of driving up there again. The scab on his backside from the dog was still healing.

Cleary cringed, remembering the nasty look in Zeke’s eye when he talked about Meg. It was a bad day when he hooked up with the Vanooks and their dark boss man. *I didn’t sign on for this kind of stuff. I told them up front.* Trouble was, Zeke didn’t see it that way. There was no getting out of the contract alive until the job was done.

He gripped the steering wheel. He hated this assignment. The kid was a nuisance, but she didn’t deserve killing. He thought briefly of Meg’s mother, a good woman—too good for him. He’d lied to get her to marry him. If he’d realized how religious she really was, he’d of thought twice, pension or no pension money. From time to time, he thought about all her talk about heaven and hell. Not that he believed any of that mumbo-jumbo religious stuff, but he wasn't having anything to do with hurting that girl. No sirree.

Cleary rubbed his mouth across his sleeve as he drove Ryman Road. *If I find the kid, maybe I can grab her quick and the two of us run off with the truck and head back for West Virginia. Slapping the kid around was one thing, but killing her was another.*

Cleary felt for his wallet in his back pocket. He'd brought his money just in case he found her. He knew it was a risky plan, especially because Zeke knew where he'd come from in West Virginia. And Zeke also knew some pretty heavyweight people in the area. No, Zeke would never leave it alone. He'd come after them and hunt them down. He and the kid would be looking over their shoulders anyplace they went. And Cleary had no illusions about what Zeke would do when he caught up with them. That put everything in a different light.

Sweat formed on Cleary's forehead. He'd always been afraid of Zeke, who gave little quarter, especially if it concerned a job, but Fred was more than just a liar and a cheat. He took real pleasure in hurting and tormenting people. Maybe it would be better just to take the girl back to Zeke before Fred got involved.

After all, it was all her own doing. Why should Cleary care? She wasn't his kid. *Man, I could sure use a drink right now.* Gritting his teeth, he followed the road that would lead him around to Dunn Road and Riker Ranch. If that dog got in his way today, he'd take care of him for good. That's why he'd put the knife in the glove compartment. He just wished his head wasn't pounding with a hangover.

*

"I found out where he's been going, but I'll have to show you," said Meg, pulling on Leslie's arm. Together they walked the lengthy expanse of the ravine as it curved around a sharp jutting boulder. Behind the ledge was an area that had seemingly been washed away over the years by water draining off the ridge above.

There was no sign of Boris, and Leslie raised her eyes in puzzlement. "I don't understand."

"Look deeper behind that boulder." Meg pointed at a darkened area. "There's a hole. Boris has to be inside. I saw him disappear behind the boulder." She knelt on the gravel and crawled to the edge of the hole, glancing back up at Leslie. "It will be a tight fit, but I think I can get my head inside at least."

"Try calling him first. I don't want you getting bit in the face."

"He knows me." Meg dipped her head lower.

"Meg, remember he was a wild dog not so long ago."

They took turns calling out to Boris. "Come on, Boy, come out," wooed Leslie gently. They exchanged looks and waited.

The wolfish head appeared at the mouth of the hole, cocking his head quizzically. "Come on, Boy. Come on," Meg called. Boris wiggled his way fully out and bounded happily up in Leslie's face. "Well, he's glad to see you, any way," said Meg.

"He just knows me better. He takes time making friends."

While Leslie gave the dog ample attention, Meg rolled her shoulders inward and pushed her slim upper body into the hole.

"What's in there?" Leslie called over Boris's head. All she could see was the back half of Meg's torso protruding from the small exposure.

Slowly the girl backed out and stood, brushing her clothes off. She grinned. "Boris has a lady friend inside, and unless I'm wrong, she's gonna be a mama real soon."

Leslie stared at her. "Really!" Staring at the dog sitting at her feet, she shook her head. "Is it another wild dog?"

Meg lifted her arms. "Couldn't tell. I was careful not to get too close."

"Did she growl at you?"

Meg looked thoughtful. "No, she didn't, come to think of it."

"Good sign." Leslie fished in her pockets for leavings of cookies from the last picnic with Mona and withdrew a baggie. "They're a little stale, but I don't think she'll mind." After throwing Boris a portion, she turned to Meg. "Lay this just inside the entrance. She'll smell your scent. Maybe next time we can make contact."

Reaching down, she patted the large dog's head, feeling the grit of the dirt on his fur. Rubbing her hands on her jeans, Leslie paused, squinting at the fine silt remaining on her fingers.

Meg's question brought back her attention. "Want a peek before we go?"

*

Cleary's eyes darted from side to side climbing out of the cab of the lime-green truck. There were no cars in the drive, and so far, he could see no sign of that killer dog. He relaxed his hand on the knife handle at the back of his pants.

Exhaling, he marched up to the front door and knocked boldly. Waiting briefly, he knocked again.

When no one came, Cleary stepped lightly over to the windows, pressing his pock-marked nose against the glass. No one was moving around inside. He rubbed his unshaven jaw. Thinking briefly of breaking in, he pushed the notion aside. If by chance he got caught, Zeke would kill him for sure. The man was paranoid about anything drawing interest toward them or their operation.

Peering through the window one last time, he vowed to come back after dark. Somehow this place had some connection to his stepdaughter, he'd bet anything. If she wasn't here, then she must have passed through to somewhere else. Cleary stalked toward the truck, making plans to stop at the other two ranches on the road on his way out. Zeke wouldn't like him coming back without the girl. Maybe he could sneak up to the trailer for a nap without the brothers knowing.

*

"She looked like she maybe has Husky and Border Collie in her. I also think that, unlike Boris, she was somebody's pet at some point. I noticed that she didn't seem all that afraid when I stuck my head in their cave," said Leslie.

"She sure liked that cookie." Meg helped Leslie up the incline to the big barn.

"Maybe, but the closer she comes to having pups, she could get testy. Be on your guard, Meg." Glancing back, Leslie watched Boris try to make up his mind whether to follow them home or stay with his lady dog. By the time they crested the hill, Leslie saw the whirling dust in the drive. Someone had been at the house. Squinting at the parting dirt cloud, she recognized the tailgate of the lime-green truck.

"That's the same truck Clive and I passed on the road the other day. It was coming from the ranch that day too." Leslie pictured the rough-faced man who'd raced past them. Her jaw clenched. "I wonder what he wants. He's been here twice now."

Meg's fists tightened into a ball. "He'll be back." Her voice was little more than a whisper.

Leslie started down the lane toward the house. "Probably," she replied. "He obviously wants to make a connection."

"Count on it," murmured Meg under her breath.

By the time, the women reached the breezeway door, Boris caught up with them. "He's making sure he doesn't miss supper." Leslie laughed, unlocking the door.

"I think that dog really likes you, Leslie. He left his lady and followed us home." Meg hung her jacket up and picked up Boris's dish to fill with food. "I keep giving him dinner, but it's your door he sleeps outside at night."

Leslie turned back and looked down at the dog. "Really? He's been sleeping outside my door? By the time I get up, he's outside already."

"That's because I'm up before you and let him out." Meg set the dish down, allowing the hungry dog to tear into his food. "If you keep giving his lady friend cookies, you'll have two dogs." She grinned at Leslie.

Leslie chuckled. "More than two, if she has puppies like you said she would."

"You're talking like you plan on staying put on the ranch," said Meg.

Leslie drew in a deep breath. "Yes, I am, aren't I? Technically, I haven't really decided. There's still a lot to consider. And right now I'm going to put those thoughts on hold and get some work done. Round up your dirty clothes." She glanced at Boris before turning and heading back through the house.

What will happen to that dog if I sell the ranch and go back to New York? It had been a long time since anyone or anything had depended on her for its welfare. It felt odd, but strangely she found herself unwilling to let him down.

*

It was almost dark when Meg looked out the passenger window on the short drive over to Mona's. Her eyes darted furtively up the road and down, looking like a hounded fox.

Leslie gave her a sidelong glance. "What's got you so spooked?"

Snapping her head back, Meg mumbled, "Nothing. I-I haven't been out much. Cabin fever, I guess."

Frowning at the girl's nervous actions, Leslie turned into the Schillers' drive. Against her will, she found herself wondering if Clive would be present at dinner. Parking the car, they walked toward the door. The night air was still, without a hint of breeze, as if waiting for something to happen.

Clive was standing by the Schillers' fireplace when Leslie walked into the room. Inhaling, she found the wood smoke intoxicating as their eyes connected. His expression made her wonder what everyone had been discussing before they arrived.

Breaking eye contact with Clive, Leslie glanced around the room. She shot Mona a quizzical look. "Henri O' is working late tonight, isn't she?"

Mona shrugged. "I was so tired I didn't have the energy to handle dinner on my own, and Henri O' offered to stay. It was a deal I couldn't refuse. I've been swamped with ranch work lately. Our inventory has increased so much, I've been thinking of hiring part-time help with the chickens."

Meg's timid head rose, her eyes bright. "Chickens? My mama and I raised chickens. I loved working with the little ones especially."

Mona looked from Meg to Leslie with a growing smile. "I find that very interesting. I also have good news for you. My friend on the force called to confirm there were no runaway notices listed on you. After that, I stopped by Social Services to check in with them on your behalf. The woman in charge knows Ray and me well."

Meg's body tensed.

Everyone in the room watched Mona. She looked over at Ray as if to confirm something before continuing. "I convinced them it would be better for everyone involved if Meg stayed with us for the present, rather than be placed in an overcrowded foster home." She shifted her concentration to Meg. "Of course, the ultimate decision is up to you." Her look was hopeful and expectant.

The girl's jaw dropped. "Those people said I can stay with you?" She sounded slightly breathless.

Mona studied the teenager's face. "It's temporary. Remember that. You could get registered for school and settled in for a month or two to see if you like it. In the meantime we could start the paperwork to qualify for foster care." Mona's pretty face looked vulnerable in the firelight and flushed with excitement.

Conflicting emotions crossed Meg's delicate features. "You really mean I could stay with you?" She surveyed the comfortable, appealing room.

Mona glanced at Leslie and then back at Meg. "Miss Leslie isn't in a secure place to offer you anything more than a few days right now, especially with her ranch tentatively on the market."

Leslie nodded. "Mona is right, Meg. I'm not married, and I'm unsure of my plans at present. Staying with Mona and Ray would be a great deal, at least for a little while."

"If you're not happy here, you don't have to stay," Mona added quickly.

Meg's eyes misted with tears. "I'll stay. If you're sure you want me?"

Mona smiled tenderly. "We want you. I'll come over tomorrow morning and pick you up. You can visit with Leslie anytime you want," she added.

When Henri O' stood between the kitchen and dining area and rang her tiny bell, everyone migrated in the direction of the table. Meg walked as if locked in a trance, following in line and sitting where it was indicated. Her thin chest moved up and down as if her thoughts were in turmoil.

Leslie watched her with concern, hoping the child didn't think she didn't want her. If only Meg would open up with someone...

Clive caught Leslie's eye, sending a tender look, as if he understood what troubled her. Table talk varied from ranch problems to curiosity and speculation involving the gun shots that took place on Rocky Ridge. Without new information everything remained speculation. Leslie's eyes strayed often to Clive, yet whenever their gazes locked, she was the first to look away, her emotions unstable.

Mona tried to draw the moody teenager into the conversation. "Boy, am I glad you like baby chickens, because we have more than I can deal with by myself. When you get settled in tomorrow, I'll take you out to the brooding pen. You might have a part-time job if you're interested."

Meg's eyes widened. "I would get paid for working with baby chicks? Truly?" She looked at Mona as if she'd turned into her guardian angel, her expression still dazed. Pushing at the food on her plate, she took hardly a nibble.

Leslie and Mona traded glances, each sensing the young woman was conflicted about something in conjunction with Mona's offer. Leslie sighed, adding this question to all the others in relation to young Meg McDonald.

Following dessert, everyone gravitated to the family room, where several conversations converged simultaneously. While Mona and Ray began making plans for Meg's coming stay, Clive and Leslie moved apart, making idle talk.

Leslie noted the contours of the well-crafted natural stone fireplace. "Miguel Romero was telling me that your fireplace was the last one he was able to put in before his health failed. Judging from Wayne's and Ray and Mona's, I'd say yours is lovely as well." She studied his tanned expression.

"I think we should arrange for you to come see for yourself. My cook isn't as impressive as Henri O', but Jimmy does a fair job at homestyle cooking. How about joining me for dinner one night next week?"

"I-I'd like that. Homestyle cooking is better than my fare any day, especially when it looks like I'm going to be losing my best kitchen help. Truth is, I'm going to miss Meg. I could get used to help like that." She gazed fondly at the gangly girl studying the pictures on the far wall. The thin, young woman had nice features but no self-confidence—not unusual with the kind of abuse she'd lived under.

He nodded. "Meg's looking good for her few days with you. She even appears to have gained a little weight."

"Regular eating does that."

"Not to change the subject, but Mona was telling me about your curious visit with the investor," Clive said.

Leslie frowned. "It was a less informative presentation than expected." She tried to laugh, but the uneasiness she'd felt in Mr. Gaetzi's presence was all too clear. "I can't seem to get hold of Roger to talk about it."

Clive set his coffee cup on the mantle of the fireplace, refraining from comment. He turned and steered her over to the couch. "How's Boris working out?"

Leslie grinned. "Let me tell you what Meg and I found out today. I may need your help a few weeks down the line."

Clive cocked his head with interest.

*

Slowing his speed, Cleary turned under the *Riker Ranch* sign and drove with caution up the drive. His plan was to park this side of the curve and walk in as far undetected as possible. If the little witch was hiding out in this house, he wanted to catch her before she had warning of his arrival and hid herself.

If I can only get to the porch before they know I'm here. Zeke wouldn't accept many more excuses for not finding the girl. She was his responsibility. He'd brought her to their camp and let her get away. Cleary slowed to a stop.

With all those cars back at the last ranch, no one would hear or notice what was going on down the road. Creeping quietly along the drive, he kept his hand on his knife handle. The yard light shone brightly in a large radius. There was no way to get to the front porch and avoid the range of the light. He'd better move fast.

The blinds were open at the front of the house, and a light shone from somewhere in the room. Cleary pressed his face against the window, his eyes scanning as far as the light allowed. Where was everybody? Three times he'd been here, and not once had he seen even one person. It was his understanding that the old man's cousin was staying at the house. So where was she? He pounded on the door, racing back to peer inside.

Somehow he'd missed seeing that big dog sleeping in the old recliner. When the dog threw the full weight of his body against the front windows, Cleary backed away, stumbling over a flower pot, his heart pounding the sides of his rib cage. The dog came back against the window a second time, his mouth open in a snarling, barking fit. Cleary's head whipped around, searching for any sign of someone hearing the ruckus. Accessing his position, he scrambled to his feet and lit out for his truck.

Cleary could still hear that dog howling his head off after he closed and locked his truck door. He was so nervous saliva dripped from the corner of his mouth. *I gotta think. I gotta think. What should I do now? It might be worth waiting to see if someone comes home.* He started the truck and pulled deep into the tall, thick weeds between the driveway and the ranch. Shutting off the engine, he slumped in the seat to wait. Now it was merely a matter of time. He could see anyone who came or went up that drive.

*

Turning from the wall pictures, Meg drew her arms behind her back, feeling increasingly out of place. Leslie was talking with the handsome horse rancher, and Miss Mona was laughing at something her blond husband had just said. They were all friends, yet both Leslie and Miss Mona kept smiling in her direction. Why was everyone being so nice to her...offering her a home and all?

She looked away. Suddenly Meg began feeling terribly bad inside. None of them knew the real truth. What would they do when they learned she'd lied to them about Cleary? Instead of leaving her in a motel, he was out searching the countryside for her. Twice she'd barely missed running into him. She pushed hair away from her flushed face.

Lifting her jacket from the back of a chair, Meg felt the sudden need of cool, fresh air. She looked through the large kitchen area, past the tall, dark-haired cook. Seeing a back door, she moved rapidly toward it, weaving her way through until her hand rested on the door handle. She yanked it open and hurried outside where she stood, breathing deeply. Her emotions were suffocating her. The door closed quietly behind her as she moved through the bricked patio area out to the back fence.

Meg leaned on the fence, hugging her thin jean jacket about her arms. Sucking in the cool air, she wanted to cry, but no tears would come. *Mama, why did you die and leave me in such a mess with Cleary?* She dropped her head in her hands.

Suddenly she felt the weight of an actual hand on her shoulder. Meg's head jerked up, turning to face the Schillers' cook, the mysterious-looking woman who'd stared at her with x-ray eyes. Meg's feet moved backward against the fence railing.

"We need to talk, Meg McDonald." The authoritative low voice compelled her.

Meg swallowed hard. "We do?" she whispered weakly.

Under the glow of the yard lights, Henri O' leaned forward on the wooden fence. "A surly man, calling himself Cleary, stopped by the ranch this afternoon. He asked about his young daughter who'd apparently run away a few days ago...claimed to be worried sick about her. He said her name was Meg, and she had pale blond hair."

Meg's knees buckled, and she clutched the fence to keep from collapsing. She stared at Henri O' with huge, fear-filled eyes. "What did you tell him?"

The hooded eyes of the older woman looked into the darkness. "I had no cause to tell him anything. He was not a likeable man, nor did I trust him. Part of the reason I agreed to stay tonight was to talk with you, Miss. Now would be a good time." She turned to face Meg. "You need to talk plainly with those good people inside that house. They are your friends. Whatever is happening in your life, they will listen and understand."

Meg wet her dry lips. "Maybe I ought to leave before I cause them grief. Cleary is a bad man, and so are those men he's hooked up with. I need to get back to the house and pick up my things. Would you take me to Leslie's, please?"

Henri O's eyes grew stern. "You would leave without telling them why? Do you think that's fair?"

"You don't understand. If they take me back to Cleary, I'm afraid of what he'll do."

"Why don't you give those people a chance to help? God doesn't want you running all over the country on your own. I'll leave you to work it out in your mind, but don't take too long. I don't intend to keep this from my friends."

Meg's head felt like it was swimming as Henri O' walked back inside the house. Her thoughts panicked, racing ahead of her. If she ran home on her own and grabbed her gear, she could start out for town, and with luck make her way to the bus stop. If she stayed, it was only a matter of time before Cleary caught up with her. The last few days she'd been living a fairy tale, lured into a false sense of security. *Cleary will keep coming back until he nabs me! I have to get out of here.*

Her feet pounded with the beat of her heart as she raced around to the front and out to the gravel road. The moon was bright enough to see her way. *I can't let Cleary get his hands on me again.* Henri O' could be telling everyone right now. Her heart raced with the speed of a wild horse.

Meg groped for a workable plan, first to locate the spare key to the ranch under the front rocks. It wouldn't take long to pack. Not feeling right about taking the new things Miss Leslie had bought for her, she'd leave them on the bed with a note. After all, what was there to say? *I'm so sorry I can't stay. I wish I could.* Tears spilled from her eyes. No one had ever treated her so kind since Mama.

Just a short distance further and she would be at the drive to Riker Ranch. The moon was still with her; she could see the ranch sign. With any luck she could be away from the ranch before someone came looking for her. Her steps slowed and then stopped. She sensed something. It was odd, and she couldn't explain the heavy feeling.

Suddenly Henri O's words whirled into her brain: "*God doesn't want you on your own. They are your friends.*" Panting, breathing hard, she bowed her head. *Lord, what should I do?* Again Henri O's words played back: *"You need to talk plainly with those good people inside that house. They can help you."*

Her hand wiped her tears, pushing the moist hair away from her face. Slowly, with hesitant steps, Meg turned and began walking back to the Schillers' ranch. *I need You, Lord. This is so hard.* She was scared. How could she face the disappointment in her new friends' eyes? Would they still care about her after they knew she'd lied?

The front door opened when she stepped up on the porch. Clive Masters stood tall and imposing, holding the door for her to enter. She gave him a wide birth and scurried past. Everyone waited inside, as if they knew she would come back.

Meg searched their curious faces and slipped into a chair by the fireplace, her eyes downcast. Holding her hands to the warming flames, she tried to quiet her uncertain heart.

Mona walked over and kneeled before her. "Henri O' informed us you are in trouble and have something to tell us."

Meg felt something give way inside—a longing to be released of her burden.

Easing up beside the girl's chair, Leslie smiled at Meg. "I've been waiting for you to trust us. Let us help you, Meg."

Ray caught the eye of the dark, quiet woman standing just inside the kitchen. "Henri O'..."

"I know, Mr. Ray. I'll put on a new pot of coffee."

He smiled and walked over to sit next to Clive Maters on a dining room chair. They looked as puzzled as the women and waited restlessly with the others for the teenager to explain.

Squeezing her eyes shut, Meg began her story back when she and Cleary arrived from West Virginia to work for the Vanook brothers.

Leslie brightened. "It was you I saw up on the hill beside that little trailer. I remember now."

Meg told what her life was like and how afraid she was of Zeke and Fred Vanook. "I knew they were doing something wrong loading up equipment late at night. So I planned my getaway, hid in the back of the truck, and saw where they went at night."

Mona and Leslie exchanged knowing glances. "Rocky Ridge," they said in unison.

Meg spoke of running through the woods and hearing a child crying a short distance from coming across two men. "I don't know what they were doing, and I didn't see their faces, but I did see the big man's boots when they passed me." She looked up into Leslie's face. "His boots had snake designs on them. The man who came to the house yesterday had snake designs on his boots. I was so afraid you were going to go somewhere with him."

The room fell so deadly still, Meg heard her own heart beating. Then, one by one, questions were asked. By the time coffee was served, everyone was aware that something bigger than first imagined was happening around them. Pulling out his wallet, Clive asked for the phone. "I think it's time we talked with our Sergeant Ford."

Mona looked up at her cook. "Henri O', why don't you go on home? This night is growing longer all the time. Your father will be concerned about you, I'm afraid."

"I'll call my pa and make sure he's all right first, but I think I'll stay and listen—if that's all right with you, Miss Mona? Whatever's going on at Mr. Wayne's ranch means a lot to my pa. He'll want to know." She backed silently into the kitchen area.

Meg rose from her chair and followed Henri O' into the kitchen. Standing quietly by her side, she said softly, "Thank you, ma'am." She wanted to say more, but right now she couldn't. Maybe someday she'd find the words to tell this lady exactly what her words had meant tonight. Turning, she walked back to sit between Miss Mona and Leslie and wait for the sergeant. Would he think she was a criminal too?

*

It was 1:00 a.m. when Sergeant Ford closed his notebook and picked up his hat. "I'll start making some quiet inquiries. I may pull the Vanook boys and this Cleary in for questioning. If what the girl says is true, there is someone higher in Dahlonega who is behind everything. Just maybe I can scare and threaten the Vanook brothers into giving up a few names. If I find they've got a record, the charge of trespassing as well as property damage will go harder. She said they were digging for something specific?"

"Yes, she did, but she wasn't sure what," Leslie clarified.

Ford glanced into the living room, where Meg had fallen asleep on the couch. "The girl stays here. And I want as few people knowing that as possible. She's not a witness we can afford to lose. You say she had bruises and a black eye when you found her hiding in the barn?"

Both Leslie and Mona nodded. "That's right, Sergeant. She said her stepdad beat her often when he was drunk," added Leslie.

Sergeant Ford's eyes narrowed. "About that investor who paid you a visit, the one with the snake designs on his boots. I don't think Meg's identification of boots is enough to bring any charges against this guy, though I'd love to get my hands on him for questioning. The chances of him using his right name are slim, of course. Could be he had some connection to that shooting up in the woods the other night, but..." He shrugged. "The big question remains, what's the motive for the accidents? You've told me you've been pressured to sell. So what do they want your land for? What are they digging for, Miss Weldon?"

"I'm working on that answer, Sergeant," said Leslie, too tired to even think.

"Keep in touch, Miss Weldon, and be careful. You seem to be a target now that your cousin is gone. We've always had a few questions about his death, but nothing to go on."

Leslie prepared to leave right after the policeman left. Mona walked her to the door. "Meg will stay in the guest room where you stayed. I've got an extra T-shirt and shorts she can sleep in tonight, and I'll come by in the morning. It looks like school will have to wait until this mess is cleared up. Are you going to be all right at the ranch?"

"I'll keep an eye on her, Mona," said Clive, joining them at the door.

"Don't tell me you're going to sit out in my drive all night again?" Leslie put her hands on her hips.

"No. I think you'll be safe with Boris if you keep him close. But I do plan on following you home tonight, so let's get a move on. I've got to get up by 5:00 a.m." He shoved his Stetson back on his head, eyeing her beneath the bill.

Leslie tossed her head, keeping her smile hidden. She was getting used to Clive's bossy ways when it came to taking care of people. "Just make sure you keep up with me."

Clive's counter look made heat rush to her face. She said a quick goodbye to Mona and Ray and rushed out to her SUV, still feeling the warmth of his gaze.

*

When the SUV rolled past in the drive, Cleary sat up in a flash and shook his head to clear it. He was about to climb out of his cab when a large pickup rolled in behind her. Cleary froze, afraid the high truck headlights might have picked up movements in the weeds. When both were safely parked in the drive, he sneaked through the thick weeds, situating himself for a good view of the entrances.

The long-haired woman stood talking with the cowboy for extended minutes before opening her house door. She flicked on extra outside lights and Cleary backed further into the weeds so he couldn't be seen. The cowboy waited until the woman closed the back doors and a string of lights appeared throughout the house. Cleary gritted his teeth. He'd found out what he wanted to know. The girl wasn't staying here.

Cleary didn't understand it. The bus station had no recollection of anyone of Meg's description buying a ticket out of town in the last week. Where was she? Waiting until the cowboy in the pickup backed up and drove out, he returned to his truck. The rusty, lime-green truck rumbled slowly down the graveled road to the highway. He was in no hurry to face Zeke. With the girl loose somewhere, it was going to make working on the ridge riskier, and Zeke said the boss was pushing for results.

Personally, Cleary thought the boss man was nutso. The chances of them finding what he wanted were no more likely than finding the pot of gold at the end of the rainbow. Zeke kept saying that the boss had inside knowledge. Cleary wondered if it had anything to do with that young, fancy-dressed lawyer who handed the money envelope to Zeke that last time when he rode into town with the brothers.

19

Night Search

SUNDAY MORNING AROUND 8:00 A.M. Leslie pushed herself out of bed. She'd heard Boris whining to be let out for the past half hour but couldn't manage to crawl from under the sheets. Meg had been letting the dog out when she rose early, and now the dog was use to the routine—but Meg wasn't here. Leslie stared bleary-eyed at the door.

She pulled her boot on, slipped into her peach flowered robe, and staggered out into the hall. The anxious animal followed her to the breezeway door. Standing by the open door, she watched the huge beast race up the hill toward the barn. She ruffled her sleep-mussed hair. "It's too early to go calling on a lady, Boris," she called after him.

Sighing, she pushed the door shut and locked it. It suddenly dawned on her that she'd promised she'd come over and stay at the house with Meg while Ray and Mona went to church. Maybe a shower would help wake her up.

Getting as far as the kitchen, she turned aside to set up the coffee pot while covering a yawn. Her steps were aimed down the hall, when pounding on the breezeway door made her do an about-face. Holding to the door facing for support, Leslie stared through eye slits at Clive Masters' stern face.

"To what do I owe this pleasure? If it's breakfast, I confess, I'm not very good with omelets."

"Leslie, come outside with me." He motioned with his hand.

"Clive, I'm not dressed. I'm wearing my boot and a bedroom slipper."

"It's not far. Leslie, I need to show you something."

With a supporting hand under her arm, Clive led her out across the graveled drive and around the curve. He pointed off to the right where the weeds were trod down almost to the center of the whole front section.

Startled, Leslie turned with a puzzled look. "What happened here? Did one of your horses get loose?"

"Not hardly," he said grimly. "After I left you and pulled into my drive, I heard a truck coming from down this way. I was in time to see a pickup rumble by. That truck must have been parked in your weeds when we drove back from the Schillers, waiting until I drove off before he pulled out."

The thought of someone sitting out in her weeds watching was chilling. "No one tried to get in to my place after you left. Why do you suppose they were here? What could they want?"

"I don't know unless it was someone looking for Meg."

Leslie blinked. "Of course. I must not be awake yet. Did you see the truck color?"

"It was some kind of light color. I don't know."

"Could it have been a lime-green shade?"

Clive narrowed his eyes. "It could have been. It was an old truck by the sound of the engine and tires."

"Cleary! He was looking for Meg. I wonder if he'll come back?"

"That depends on how fast they plan on bringing in Cleary and those brothers for questioning. How about I stay with you and Meg over at Ray's? I don't want either of you alone right now. I'll meet you there about 11:00 a.m." He surveyed the trodden weeds. "Well, last night's late visitor started the process of cleaning out this area, making our job easier."

"That's the good news?" Leslie lifted a brow. "It's time for my breakfast, Mr. Masters."

"Let me help you back to the house, Miss Weldon. And if you're really interested in an omelet, I can whip one up while you're getting dressed."

"If that's an offer, I'll accept." She winced as a sharp stone penetrated her thin slipper. "Ow! Remind me to have this drive paved someday."

Clive had breakfast waiting by the time she dressed and made it back through the living room. Frowning, she walked to the front window, running her finger over a crack in one window pane. Looking out on the porch she saw an overturned flower pot. *He was here!*

Leslie spun and hurried back to sit down across from Clive. She bowed her head as if waiting for the blessing and tried to collect her thoughts.

Blinking in mild surprise, Clive lowered his head as well and said grace. He picked up his fork, eying her. "Something wrong outside?"

"Enough to tell me that someone was on my front porch last night. The flower pot is turned over, and there's a crack in one of my windows."

"Did he try to break in, you think?"

"Not sure, but Boris was here. So if someone came to the door, he'd make them think twice about staying. It could have been the dog. It's about the right height."

Leslie savored the taste of the flavorful omelet. "This is good, thanks. You're going to be sorry I learned you can cook awesome omelets." She covered a huge yawn. "As tired as I was, I thought I'd sleep like a rock last night, but it didn't work like that. I guess my brain wouldn't turn off. I laid there and prayed off and on for almost an hour," she murmured drowsily.

Clive's head turned sharply, his mouth slightly ajar. "*You prayed* for almost a *whole* hour?"

Leslie shrugged and took another bite. "I had a lot of catching up to do."

Studying her curiously, Clive looked as if he was about to speak, but the phone rang.

"Excuse me," said Leslie. Standing, she made her way to the kitchen phone. "Sergeant Ford, I'm surprised to hear from you. Is something wrong?"

Clive turned in his chair, his body alert.

Leslie listened. "Yes, I'll relate your message to the Schillers. I think Meg's stepfather was here last night, waiting until I got home. Mr. Masters saw his truck leave after he went home. Cleary was looking for Meg. It was good she didn't come home with me." She nodded. "All right. Good-bye, Sergeant." She heaved a heavy sigh.

Clive's brow narrowed. "What's up?"

"The police aren't picking up Cleary or the Vanooks, at least not right now. They want to wait until they catch them involved in the digging process with their machinery on my property. They're also hoping the man who paid me a visit, the one with snake designs on his boots, will show up in the woods again. They think the eerie child sounds could be a cover for the machinery."

"Henri O's ghost. There's been a lot of ghost stories and superstition from the old days of Dahlonega's history. Not many people are going to call the police and tell them they are hearing crying sounds from miles away in a woods."

"That's all fine and good, but what about Meg's safety? We're supposed to keep her hidden until everything breaks."

"I think Meg will be fine at Mona and Ray's. Henri O' steered Cleary away when he stopped by a few days ago, and after last night he knows she's not staying with you. That should buy us some time."

Picking up her dish, she reached for Clive's. "Well, I need to clean up the kitchen and get over to the Schillers."

Clive stood and pushed in his chair. "I'd stay and help you, but I've got a few items to attend to before I join you there. I'll catch up with you about 10:15 a.m."

"Thanks again. I'll have to cook dinner for you sometime." She smiled.

"That should be *interesting,*" he said wryly. "Gotta go, bye." He grabbed his hat and headed for the back door.

"Interesting?" She set the dishes hard on the counter. "I'm better than you think," she yelled after him.

Leslie saw him give her a high-wave on his way to his truck. *Interesting! I'll show him.*

*

By early afternoon, Leslie returned from the Schillers, stopping to check her phone messages, hopeful for a call from Roger. Clicking the machine, she paused, wondering what was up with the young lawyer. There'd been no word for days. With all that was happening, it only clouded him with more doubt, which saddened Leslie. There was something intriguing about Roger. She found him attractive and likeable. It was Sunday. Surely by tomorrow, she'd hear from him. Now she had other things to do.

It had been a good morning. From all appearances Meg seemed to be settling in fine with Mona and Ray, but she was jumpy as a fire ant. The girl had run to the window half a dozen times to check for Cleary's truck while the Schillers were at church. When she'd heard about Cleary waiting at Leslie's the night before, her face blanched. She'd lowered her voice to a whisper. "I-I could have run right into him!"

"But you didn't," Leslie encouraged.

Meg cocked her head. "Words kept playing in my head, reminding me I could trust you. That's why I turned around. It was God. I know it was God!"

Leslie sobered. "You could be right, Meg."

As Leslie thought back on the morning, she remembered how Clive had purposely distracted Meg from worrying by walking with her outside where the chickens were housed. For the rugged type, he definitely had his softer moments.

She scanned the interior of the ranch, marveling at the quietness. Leslie had to decide between a nap and working on the bulbs. Two hours tops and they'd be ready to take back to Georgia McCray. Heaving her shoulders, she reached for her art supplies.

*

The next two days went by slowly. Everyone was tense, waiting for something to happen—even the nights had been silent, no crying or signs of activity on Rocky Ridge. Sergeant Ford kept telling them to be patient, but Leslie didn't feel patient.

Not only hadn't Roger returned her call, but when Leslie tried the office, a computer recording informed her that the office was closed for a few days due to personal reasons. *Personal reasons...what does that mean?*

A troubling new development arose. A number of flyers with an old picture of Meg were showing up at various places around town; a highlighted reward was promised in big lettering. Cleary was covering his bases. Meg wouldn't be able to show her face anywhere in town. Sergeant Ford had personally contacted Meg's social worker and sworn her records to secrecy. All their lives were on hold.

Wednesday morning came up with a glorious sunrise. Temperature readings were scheduled to climb, and Indian summer was arrayed in all her glory. Tired of pacing and patient waiting, Leslie picked up both Jamie and Wayne's journals and climbed in her SUV. Miguel's quiet reasoning was just what she needed.

*

It was cool inside Miguel's mountain cabin. As Leslie laid out the journals on his coffee table, Miguel rolled his chair from the kitchen, handing her a tall glass of iced tea. "Henri O' made it fresh early this morning before she left."

Leslie sipped the refreshing liquid. "Thanks, Miguel. This tastes fabulous."

"Henri O' has been keeping me abreast of the situation. That young girl hasn't had a very easy life."

"No she hasn't. She wants to do right, but life has been hard. Her mother taught her to believe in Jesus."

Miguel nodded. "Good! She's in good hands," he said with a finality that booked no doubts or arguments.

Leslie fingered the old journal.

He rolled his chair beside her. "It's been awhile since I've seen that old book—about five years or more. How far did you get?"

"I read to the point where Jamie buried his family and coins in the mine."

He closed his eyes and smiled. "You've done well! At a later date, past the pain and anger, when he and my great ancestor became friends, Jamie found the peace to finish his life. When you have time, you should read it."

She sighed. "Maybe...perhaps by that time I'll be ready. There was just so much sadness." Her sober eyes connected with Miguel's.

"Life is filled with mountains of joy and valleys of tears. Jesus is the bridge through those dark valleys back to the mountains—if we choose to believe in Him."

"And Jamie found that bridge?" she asked.

"He did. The rest of his life had substance and meaning. Did you know he married again?"

"What?" She stared incredulously at him.

Miguel smiled.

"And he never reopened the mine?" she asked thoughtfully.

"No." Miguel studied her face. "Why would you ask that?"

She tensed, then groped for insight. "Well, because Jamie buried a mine that never reached its full potential. He wrote that he hadn't even hit the mother lode, as he called it, and then there were all those gold coins. Of course, each of the coins was only a five-dollar gold piece. I think they called them half eagles."

Miguel's finger waved in front of her. "You might have hit on the reason this group wants you to sell. I've had my suspicions ever since Wayne was approached to sell the ranch. He never said who wanted to buy it, but that's about the time his mood changed, and he became so troubled. And like you mentioned, the gold in Wayne's mine has barely been tapped. It's easy gold!"

"Easy gold? What are you talking about? I've heard that many of the mines in this area still contain gold, but it is far too expensive and problematic to continue mining." Leslie was thoroughly confused.

Miguel's brow wrinkled. "It's true. Expense is part of the problem, along with environmental issues." He hesitated. "Leslie, I've heard rumors about possible chemical breakthroughs that could change things considerably. They're experimental; but if enough power and money were behind such a project..." Shrugging, he added, "Gold is an all-time high. It's a pretty far stretch, but it could be a possible motive."

She stared at him as the old man's words filtered through her reasoning. "Miguel, that's pretty bizarre! This is reading like some Wild West novel. "

The silver eyebrows rose. "Maybe—maybe not. It would explain a lot."

She didn't know what to think.

"Wouldn't it explain the late-night digging on Rocky Ridge? They could be looking for ore samples, trying to find Jamie Cohen's buried mine. What about the push to make you sell? The extra-generous bids for your land, the dangerous accidents? Had they proved fatal, your land would go on the market with no interference. Think on it."

A vague remembrance formed in her memory, an occurrence from days earlier. "I'll take your thoughts under consideration, Miguel. But if what you say is true, how in the world did anyone put all of this together? It's taken me days of journal reading and, frankly, I didn't put it together. If you hadn't suggested the possibility, I don't know if I ever would have made the connection of Jamie's mine."

Trouble clouded Miguel's dark eyes. "The knowledge of Jamie's mine would have to be obtained secondhand, through someone who knew."

"You mean Cousin Wayne, or his brother before him, somehow passed along enough information about the journals to raise flags of interest? As least sufficient for them, whoever they are, to start digging around in the past?"

"It's a consideration. Wayne's brother was intelligent, but he never had the thirst for family history that Wayne exhibited. Wayne had a passion to talk to anyone who had stories about the history of Riker Ranch. That's how we met, if you remember."

"Yes," she said slowly, "I remember. I also remember Wayne frequently mentioning a new friend who liked to go fishing—a powerful, unofficial, secret friend." She stared at Miguel with a kind of terrifying understanding.

"You think this secret friend is behind all that has been taking place on the ranch?" Miguel leaned forward.

"I don't know, but it's a possibility. Wayne said he was a man of position in the community who was overly concerned that his privacy be respected." Remembered comments swarmed her memory. Did they have any connection to what she and Miguel were discussing? She didn't want to think they did. Looking down at the remaining iced tea, she reached for her glass, her thoughts very troubled.

Miguel rolled his chair over to a well-crafted bookcase. His gaze followed his finger across the multi-shelved unit. Coming to a taller black book, he withdrew it, laid it on his lap, and wheeled back to Leslie. "This scrapbook holds a lot of memories for me over the years. Wayne is in some of these journal notes, articles, and photos. I'd all but forgotten this scrapbook existed."

The old man winced as if he'd experienced a stab of pain. "I missed my nap today. Old people get like cranky children," he said, clutching the thick scrapbook. "I think it might be good for me to review these memories and see if I can find anything that might shed light on the situation."

Closing the old journal, she stacked the two journals together. "I should be getting home so you can get that nap." She smiled. "I, like you, also need to do a lot of reviewing. Thanks for your input, Miguel, mind-boggling as it is. Now I need some crash time to think through everything. You're a very, insightful man, Mr. Romero."

"It is the Lord who gives sight in any form, Miss Leslie. But I do have a couple of other thoughts if you're interested. You mentioned buried coins. Did you say they were five-dollar, golden, half-eagle coins?"

"Yeah, I think that's what I read. Why?"

"You might want to check up on what those coins might be worth today."

"All right," she replied, wary. "I'll do some research. Anything else?"

Miguel rolled his chair to face her as she backed toward the door. "Don't forget to read the last few entries in Wayne's journal when you get the chance."

"I sense another message in your suggestion, Miguel. Please call me if you remember anything that could be helpful."

"I will certainly do that, Miss Leslie. Some days I fear I've forgotten more than I'm able to remember." His smile was tired. He looked older today. "Be careful."

"Everyone keeps telling me that," she said dryly.

"Because they care for you. I believe God will watch over you."

"He has so far. I hope…I believe He will too, Miguel." Her answer resounded in her heart with a confidence she hadn't felt in years, and it seemed to please Miguel.

Rolling his chair to the door, the old man watched her descend the wide pine stairs leading down from the extended porch. Leslie turned and waved.

*

In sheer exhaustion, Leslie fell into a troubled sleep. After the heat of the fall day, the night coolness caused her to seek an extra blanket for her bed. She wouldn't close the window for fear of not hearing the eerie cries from the woods, should they occur tonight. Leslie was torn with a desire for it to be over and an uncertain dread.

She knew up and down the road, windows were open and ears were tuned to pick up on any sound out of the ordinary. Even Miguel and Henri O' in their secured mountain cabin listened for the sounds. As the crow flies from Rocky Ridge, Miguel said, the sounds carried clearly from the Ridge over to his cabin.

Leslie thrashed her head against the pillow and shivered. Suddenly cold, she sat up on the edge of her bed. The wind had picked up, blowing her bedroom curtains straight out into her room, and the air carried a sharp sting. She moved to close the window halfway. On the edge of the bed, she stopped in place.

The sobbing of a young child wafted on the wind through her window—blood-chilling as ever.

Turning back, she grabbed for her phone and clicked on the table light, her finger stabbing the ready dial for Clive. He answered immediately. "I hear it, Leslie. You call Mona and Ray. I'm alerting Sergeant Ford. Get dressed; we'll all wait at your place."

Leslie's hand was shaking as she pushed the button for Mona and Ray. It was going to be a long night.

*

When the knock came at the breezeway door two hours later, every chair around Leslie's table screeched as multiple pairs of feet pushed to a standing position. "I'll go," Leslie called nervously. Every eye followed her steps. The tension in the room was electric, as if one spark could set off an explosion.

A very tired sergeant shuffled through to stand before the small anxious group.

"Would you like to have a cup of coffee, Sergeant?" inquired Leslie.

His gazed traveled longingly toward the pot on the counter. "Ah, no, I guess not. I should be getting back. Look, the long and the short of it is we caught the Vanook boys and the girl's stepdad on the ridge." He rubbed the back of his neck and yawned.

"They're on their way to be questioned now. Curiously, we didn't find them digging as we expected, though there's evidence of previous digging. These boys were up-ending boulders across the ridge. Darnedest thing, I ever saw. They acted dumb. Said they weren't trespassing. Claimed they had been hired to clear the top of ridge—by your cousin, Wayne Riker."

Leslie's head shot up. "What?"

"Yep! Zeke Vanook said he was hired and prepaid by Wayne to clear Rocky Ridge. Supposedly, your cousin had a dream of building a rustic cabin where he could enjoy the valley view." He scratched the side of his nose.

"They're lying! You don't believe them?' Leslie yelled, her patience short.

Clive placed a restraining hand on her arm. "Let him finish, Leslie."

Ford grimaced. "No. We don't believe them. They're stalling until they can get 'lawyered-up' and make bail. Corporal Bailey and I are working together on this. I've been keeping him copied, and we'll be working in tandem from now on. They will be taken into custody tonight and kept for interrogation as long as possible, but it will be hard to get the name of the person who hired them, especially when they figure they'll be out on bail soon. Oh, we'll try to push for property damage, but it'll depend on what the judge decides."

Leslie sighed. "Did you find that man with the snake-designed boots, William Gaetzi?"

"No, but we found where someone with boots trampled through the brush. They must have been running fast and furious. We found some dropped electrical cords. It will take time to identify them. Who knows? Maybe we'll get lucky and find a set of prints to work from. We're taking samples of footprints, but that, too, will take time."

Everyone stared at him, waiting for more.

Shrugging, Sergeant Ford examined each face. "That's pretty much it until we unravel things further. Any additional information you come across that might shed light on a possible reason for all the woods activity would be appreciated."

Leslie instantly thought of her conversation with Miguel Romero. But until she had more to hang his speculations on, she thought it better to hold that knowledge in reserve. She found Clive's puzzled look leveled at her. He knew she was hiding something.

Ford glanced over at Meg's drawn, timid face. "You're going to have to stay hidden, young lady. This isn't over. It's like spotting a Manatee in Florida waters. You know the biggest part is hidden. Unfortunately, it'll come out that there's another witness who can place them digging on Rocky Ridge, and it won't take a great leap for them to figure it was you. So keep out of public places and keep a low profile for a while."

Meg's shoulders sagged.

Mona placed a protective arm around her shoulders. "Sergeant, I don't understand why you'd think she'd still be in danger. These men have already been caught in the act of trespassing."

"Because there's much more to this case than we know. We'll be looking for evidence that might connect them to the accidents on this ranch. Miss McDonald can verify they were on that ridge more than once and that they were actually digging. For what, I wish I knew," Ford added wistfully.

Leslie shot him a furtive glance, her fingers tapping the edge of the table.

Sergeant Ford rubbed his face. "I'll keep in touch, but this will be an ongoing investigation, and we don't have much to go on. The man who's calling the shots has a good enough reason to arrange serious accidents—accidents that could end in death. Wayne Riker is a good exhibit. You've been lucky, Miss Weldon. The only way to stop him is to come up with a reason that makes this land valuable enough to kill for. What is it, ladies and gentlemen? We have to find that reason, and find it fast! Good night." He moved quickly toward the outside door.

Leslie wondered if she was doing the right thing. Should she have spoken up, voicing Miguel's insightful suggestions? The thought of all of these happenings motivated by a greedy desire to reopen a gold mine sounded ludicrous. *In this day and age of technology, could there be that much gold in Riker's buried mine to warrant such radical actions?* Her sleep-deprived mind couldn't deal with this weighty issue.

Leslie watched the rest of her guests gather their belongings to leave. Everyone acted like walking zombies. The closure they'd looked forward to experiencing had eluded them. The evil mastermind was still out there waiting to strike again.

Clive was the last to file out of the door. Turning, he asked sharply, "Where is Boris?"

"I...don't know." She scanned the lighted area beyond the doorway. "I haven't seen him for hours."

Cupping his hands to his mouth, Clive directed his call in the direction of the lane leading up to the barn. Shifting back, he stiffened his jaw. "I'm staying in your driveway until that dog comes back. I'm not leaving you by yourself. So deal with it!"

Leslie looked past him, unable to stay off a siege of giggles. Holding her stomach, she bent to stop a tide of overtired hysterics.

"What's so funny?" Clive demanded. "I meant what I said. I'm not leaving!"

She was sucking in a breath to stop her laughter when hiccups attacked. "Oh my!" she squeaked out. "Uuuph! Look! Uuup! Behind you, silly!"

Whirling about, Clive glared into the pale yellow stare of the wild-haired beast. He swallowed hard. "It's uncanny the way that spooky dog sneaks up."

"Uuuph!" Leslie hiccupped again, startled. She grabbed her nose and held her breath, counting to ten. When she breathed again, the hiccups were gone. "Good!" She squeaked again, drawing in deep breaths. She added softly, "Clive, think about it. Boris was probably waiting out in the weeds until everyone left. I simply forgot to call him in."

"Well, don't forget anymore!" He swiveled sharply and headed for his truck.

"Thanks for caring!" she called after him, a ripple of her laughter floating in the wind.

"Lock your doors, Leslie Weldon." Clive slammed the truck door.

"Come on, Boris." Grinning, she trudged tiredly toward the door, squinting down at her watch. Three hours and it would be daylight. A short night.

With Boris lying outside her door on a hall rug, Leslie left her door ajar and closed her bedroom window. Her toes felt near frozen. Even as she pulled the covers up to her chin, she tried not to think. If she did, she'd never get any sleep.

As warmth seeped into her body, Leslie sifted deeper into her mattress. Then a nagging thought penetrated her logy brain. A thought so huge she sat straight up in bed, her heart doing the fifty-yard dash. Throwing her covers aside, Leslie switched on the table light while slipping into her boot. Then she made her way to the clothes hamper. She had to know.

Pulling out the grubby jeans she'd worn earlier, Leslie reflected on the morning when she and Meg had followed Boris to his private hideout behind the boulder. She carried the pants over to the window light, staring down at the dirty silt on the pant legs where she'd rubbed her hands. "Oh my," she whispered. *Is it possible?*

It was as if she was being led to long-buried answers. Silence in the darkened bedroom seemed to hold the aura of personalities from generations past. Were they depending on her? *I don't understand what's going on, Lord.*

Returning the jeans to the hamper, she retraced her steps to bed, where she prayed her way to a deep sleep. The effects of what she'd learned had larger ramifications than her mind wanted to deal with.

20

Cards on the Table

STIRRING HER MORNING COFFEE AT THE TABLE, Leslie had to shift to keep the sunlight from blinding her as she tried not to dwell on Sergeant Ford's warning. The accidents at Riker Ranch hadn't stopped with Cousin Wayne's death. The bad guys wanted something, and she was in the way. Unbidden tears threatened to surface. If only she wasn't so tired, she could better ward off the increasing fear.

Her hope that Boris might sleep longer dwindled with the first rays of sunlight. His canine body clock woke her up. She determined that busyness would help keep her mind off things she had no control over. But a blank list sat next to her cereal bowl, and thus far she had more doodling on the paper than an actual work list.

A bag of new shelf paper waited in the closet for her to redo the kitchen shelves. Meg promised to help her this afternoon after morning chores were finished and the chickens fed. Leslie drew a smiley face with her pen, thinking of how much Meg was enjoying staying with the Schillers and helping out with those brainless birds. Mona, for her part, was ecstatic with the help. It was a win-win situation. If only Meg could stay on with the Schillers...

Leslie recalled Mona's heart desire for children.

The jarring ring of the telephone brought her daydreaming to an end. She grabbed up the phone on the fourth ring. "Roger!" She'd been waiting so long for him to return her calls that hearing his voice now was startling.

Before she had a chance to ask where he'd been for almost a week, the young lawyer dove headlong into an involved explanation of his father's illness and his family responsibility. "Sorry, I didn't call before I left, but I caught an early plane and there was no time."

Leslie tried to clear her tired mind. "Roger, I want to come in and see you as soon as possible. There's so much that needs to be cleared up. It's become too dangerous not to fully understand each other's position. How about tomorrow morning?"

"Too dangerous! Wha—what are you talking about? Sure, we can get together tomorrow morning. We could meet today if you wish. You have me concerned, Leslie."

"I'm sorry about that, Roger. Hopefully, tomorrow we will clear all that up. I'm glad your father is doing better. I really am. I wish I'd had opportunity to be of more help to my father before he died. About tomorrow, I'll be there about 11:00 a.m."

She hurriedly said good-bye, then laid the phone receiver down. Moving away from the kitchen counter, she gathered her hair into a ponytail and clamped a hair barrette over it.

Suddenly she was in a mood to do physical work, separate laundry, redo the shelves—anything to keep busy. She wasn't looking forward to her meeting with Roger the next day, hating confrontation the way she did. But it was time to lay all her cards on the table. She would watch his reactions to determine for herself if he was guilty.

Roger had been pushing her to sell. He had sent out the so-called investor to her house. She had defended him for weeks; now it was time to make him show his true colors. The way she figured it, the safest way to confront him would be at his office.

Leslie rushed her breakfast dishes over to the dishwasher, lining up her day. She would take her finished Christmas bulbs to Georgie in the morning before her appointment with Roger. Dozens of other unfinished chores sprang to mind. It gradually dawned on her that this sudden urge for busyness was more than just occupying her thoughts. *Am I that afraid?* She searched her feelings. Bowing her head, Leslie mumbled an apology to the Lord. "My ability to trust is somewhat rusty, Father, Help me not be afraid, but also help me make good decisions."

Leslie found hard work gave her less time to worry, and she pushed her lethargic body through the rest of the morning. After lunch she made arrangements to pick up Meg to tackle the shelves, a two-hour job. Working side by side, they laughed easily about Boris and silly things. Being with Meg brought Leslie back to her teen years. She marveled how quickly this young woman was becoming a real personality.

The girl's attitude was lighter and more open since the night she shared her connection to Cleary and the Vanooks. But, sadly, her fear of Cleary drove her often to the windows to check for any sign of the lime-green truck.

Studying the girl with compassion, Leslie stood alongside her, her hand resting on Meg's slender arm as they looked out on the dusty drive. "You're going to be safe from now on, Meg. Mona and Ray, Clive and me, we're all your friends. We care about you."

Meg's hand covered Leslie's. "Thanks, Miss Leslie, but until I know for sure Cleary and the Vanooks are locked up for good, a little bit of me is always gonna be scared. I heard that policeman say they would make bail real soon. If they make bail, they're gonna come lookin' for me again. I gotta be watchful."

Leslie couldn't think of one thing to counter Meg's logical thinking. *What can I say to this girl?* At last, Leslie said tenderly, "I'm remembering the young woman who reminded me that no matter where my thoughts or feelings were, God wouldn't leave me. He won't leave you either, Meg."

"You're right, Miss Leslie. I just forgot for a minute." She looked up at Leslie, her lips pressed in a hard line. "I won't forget again."

"Good girl. Neither will I." Leslie surveyed their work. "I can handle the rest. Why don't I take you back to the Schillers, where you're less likely to be found?"

Meg nodded. "I'd like that. No offense, Miss Leslie."

"None taken." She pushed back flyaway hair wisps. "Besides, while I'm at Mona's I want to borrow some of her history books."

Meg sent her a quizzical look.

*

A short time later, Leslie sat in Mona's kitchen sipping tea while she shared her need for information. Without questioning her reason, Mona rounded up more books and pamphlets than she'd ever use. Armed with a stack of paraphernalia on the seat beside her, Leslie was pulling out of Schillers' drive when Clive's fast-wheeling truck forced her into a diverting swerve—a near-miss collision. He came instantly to a screeching halt across from her car window and shoved up his hat with emphasis.

"Well, the charming Miss Weldon. Any more hiccups?"

She sucked in a breath and grinned. "No! But had I any left, they would have been scared clear out of me." She thought back to the night before. "You—standing there, waving your arms, calling wildly for the dog—and Boris, standing right behind you all the while was a sight to behold. Like I said..." She giggled.

He interrupted. "I'm glad you were so entertained at my expense. Have you heard anything from Galbraith yet?"

Her chin tilted upward. "As a matter of fact, I have. I'm seeing him at his office tomorrow. I plan on laying everything out. All the 'accidents' and the rest of the shenanigans happening around Rocky Ridge, including that so-called investor, Mr. Gaetzi. I want to see Roger's face when he answers."

Clive leaned further out his window. "What time are you going to be there?"

"Eleven a.m. tomorrow. I'm going early to take my Christmas bulbs in."

"Christmas bulbs?"

"Yeah. I'll tell you about them some time."

He nodded. "Keep your cell phone handy. I never did trust that guy."

"I'll keep my phone handy. Bye." His curious look kept her foot paused on the brake. "What?"

"I was just thinking you should wear your hair in a ponytail more often. It's cute."

She flushed, her hand moving self-consciously to her wavy ponytail and flyaway wisps and instantly remembered her father's liking for ponytails. "Thanks," she murmured. Easing her foot down on the gas pedal, she slowly pulled her SUV away from his truck. Like a drawstring was attached to her head, Leslie turned for one last glimpse of the tanned cowboy in the pickup truck.

He caught her look and winked back.

Snapping her head forward, she exhaled, reminding herself that she needed to think about more pressing matters. She fingered the nearby pamphlets and thought about the coin-minting website listed on one pamphlet. Hopefully, they'd have the information she needed. It would be worth her time to check.

*

The next morning, as she pulled into the parking spot next to Georgie's red station wagon, she gazed down the line of parking slots looking for Roger's midnight blue Porsche. It was there. He'd be waiting for her in his office. The brightness of the day reassured her that she would be perfectly safe entering the lawyer's office. It wouldn't be a pleasant meeting. She centered her thoughts on her first task. Lifting the box with as much care as possible, Leslie opened the back door of The Christmas Shoppe and eased her way through the stock area into the main shop.

Seeing her, the white-haired woman stepped back, startled. "My goodness. My heart's in my throat."

"I'm sorry, Georgie, I should have called ahead, but my morning was a little rushed. I wanted to get these bulbs in to you before my appointment with my lawyer down the street." Leslie titled her head in the direction of Roger's office.

"Mr. Galbraith is your lawyer? He seems very nice." She looked around. "Give me a minute, and I'll make a place for that box." Hurriedly, she cleaned off an area. The short woman rose up on her tiptoes trying to see over the rim of the cardboard box like an anxious child. "I almost called you last week to see how you were doing. I can hardly wait to see them. My Robert would have been so pleased."

Once the box was settled safely, Leslie lifted a bulb out. It was still on its metal hanger and swung lightly on the hook. She glanced at the shopkeeper's face, anxious to see her reaction to her first efforts. "I hope you're not disappointed," she said wistfully.

The older woman's hands lifted to her face. "Oh my! How lovely!" She walked over to peer down into the box, looking over four other bulbs. Turning back, she gazed fondly at Leslie. "My dear, these are wonderful—really! I love the barn scenes in the snow and the two landscapes. Where did you get the ideas?"

"To be honest, Georgie, I borrowed some ideas from old Christmas cards."

Georgie stared back down at the bulbs, her expression puzzled. "I thought you bought six bulbs. I only count five."

Leslie nodded. "I'm keeping one of my cousin's large barn and pines on the hill. I still have indefinite plans and wanted a keepsake—just in case."

Georgie's face brightened. "You'll just have to paint more bulbs to make up for it, my dear. I believe these will be big sellers." She wrote down a price for each bulb and lifted it for Leslie to see. "I will get half again as much."

Leslie's jaw dropped at the amount. "That's very generous of you."

Georgie smiled. "I'll get a check ready and mail it to you at the ranch. Will you take more bulbs with you to work on?"

Leslie hesitated. "I do appreciate the opportunity to try something I've always had a desire to do. But my future is very uncertain right now...."

Georgie remained quiet, her expression silently thoughtful.

"I'll stop back in after I know more."

Georgie nodded. "I know what my prayers will be in the next few days. You would be good for Dahlonega, my dear. I hope you decide to stay with us." Her round face creased with her deep smile.

Allowing the shop door to close behind her, Leslie reflected on Georgie's exhortation to stay in Dahlonega. Not for the first time Leslie questioned where she really belonged. *Where is my home?*

She walked in the direction of Roger's office, dreading the coming encounter, yet desperately wanting answers. Lifting her hand to open the glass door, she drew in a deep breath and prayed, *Help, Lord!*

Roger's secretary raised her fine-chiseled face. Leslie swallowed an exclamation suitable for Stephanie's phenomenal look. Her blond hair was lifted high and drawn back into a sophisticated style, accentuating her very sleek black dress. Leslie couldn't help but wonder if the colossus effort was for Roger's homecoming.

The woman closed the ledger in front of her and regarded Leslie without expression. "I'll alert Mr. Galbraith of your arrival, Miss Weldon. Please take a seat."

Leslie was amazed. Stephanie's whole narration had been spoken without a tone change. Restraining an oncoming smile, she said, "Thank you, Stephanie. You look very nice today." She knew *nice* was an understatement. This woman was pulling out all the stops. If Roger didn't notice, he should be labeled clinically dead.

Leslie walked toward the window, praying for intervention in her coming meeting with Roger. The street outside quietly stirred to life. It was an ordinary day until Leslie heard Roger's inner office door open.

*

Sitting across the desk from Roger in the air-conditioned, low-lit office, Leslie felt her fingers turn to ice. Roger's stone-like face set the mood for their meeting. What confused Leslie was the vulnerable, wounded look in his eyes.

"What exactly is this about, Leslie? I didn't get much sleep after your call. I must say I would have expected more consideration from you."

Leslie stiffened. "You might reconsider your feelings after I'm finished relating what has been occurring out at Riker Ranch. For various reasons I've kept most of these incidents quiet."

His head tilted in puzzlement.

"It's better if I begin back on the first day I arrived in Dahlonega. Do you remember our first meeting when I walked into your office using a cane?"

"You mean when you fractured your foot on the motel stairs?"

Leveling a probing look, Leslie stated the incident as it actually happened. When Roger would have interrupted, she held up a restraining hand. "Please, let me finish before questions." She laid out one accident after another—the floorboards in the barn, the hay-loft door dropping open when he was directly beneath the chute. Her descriptions were vividly compelling.

When she explained the suspicious closing of the garage door, and the tampered with Jeep ignition switch, Roger's eyes enlarged. "You don't think...?" he spurted.

"You were the only one I told that I was planning to take the Jeep for a drive in the morning. Please, I'm not finished. The police have verified that unauthorized digging has been going on regularly on top of Rocky Ridge. They have arrested three men they caught in the act two nights ago. Two men by the name of Vanook and another named Cleary something."

The surprise Leslie first saw in Roger's face quickly cloaked over. He diverted his glance, looking wary.

Leslie narrowed her eyes. Though none of his reactions were quite what she expected, his emotional cover-up was very troubling. He remained silent as if he knew she wasn't finished.

"There's one more thing, Roger. That investor you lined up to come to my house..." She described the large, cold-natured man and his unhelpful attitude. "He practically demanded I drive him to Rocky Ridge—supposedly for an appraisal."

Roger stood. "You didn't go with him alone, did you?" His concern seemed real. Leslie read his eyes, and it puzzled her even more.

"No," she said hoarsely. "As soon as Mona drove up in the drive, he took off like a rocket. It was really strange. You can imagine how I felt when I learned that the police have a witness who claims this man, Gaetzi, was up in the woods around Rocky Ridge at night when the digging occurred."

Roger walked dazed-like around his desk and leaned against the edge. The man was impossible to read. "You say there's a witness?"

Nodding, Leslie allowed seconds to pass before adding quietly, "You sent that man to my house, Roger, and you've been pressuring me to sell the ranch. I'm totally confused about your involvement in all this. So I'm asking point blank: What are these so-called mystery investors really after?"

Roger met her gaze, his features tight. "I'll require some time to investigate these claims. Believe me, I'll get to the bottom of this. Do I understand this correctly—the Rocky Ridge area seems to be the focus of all the excitement?"

She nodded.

Appearing agitated, he hurriedly escorted her out of his office. "I'll call you. I promise," he said even while turning away. When Stephanie tried to hand him a list of messages, he waved her aside without a glance and retreated back inside his office.

Leslie reached in her purse for her sunglasses, anxious to leave the law office. Her conclusions about Roger were still undefined. She wanted to believe he had no part in any of the accidents, but that belief required a huge leap of faith.

Hearing the sound of a truck engine, she glanced up. Directly across the street Clive Masters stared back at her from the cab of his dusty truck, his hat pulled low over his eyes. *How long has he been waiting outside to make sure I'm all right?*

Checking for traffic, she slowly crossed the street and approached his open window. "Nothing to do at this time of day, Mr. Masters?" She lifted her chin, a wry smile playing on her lips.

"Just covering all bases, ma'am, like my daddy taught me." He glanced at his watch. "How about a burger at this little place I know? It's crowded and loud, but the burgers can't be beat."

Leslie laughed. "How can I say no to such a tempting offer?"

"Jump inside my truck, lady. Your chariot awaits."

"A dusty chariot! Don't you ever wash this thing?" Walking around to the passenger's side, she eyed the big step up inside the truck cab and wished for her cane.

Clive exited the truck and came around to give her a boost up with one smooth motion. "Service with a smile, in spite of the cutting remarks about my truck."

Neither spoke on the short drive to Clive's favorite diner. Leslie was thankful for the quiet respite to collect her thoughts. It wasn't until the waitress brought their order and Clive offered a quiet blessing for their food that he spoke of her appointment.

Leslie emotions were flat-lined, her voice, a monotone. "Actually, it was quite simple. I described each accident in detail, and Roger said he needed time to investigate my statements. He promised to get to the bottom of everything." She stared up at Clive.

"That's it? Did you ask him to explain how he was the only person who knew where you would be the morning of your garage attack?" Clive's tone rose in anger.

Leslie peered around the small diner with tables in close proximity to one another. "Ssshhh! Roger was honestly shocked. I mean it, Clive. He's not that good of an actor."

"Most lawyers are great actors. They take drama their second semester, right after Lying 101," he said with animosity. "Galbraith has been pushing you to sell before you even arrived in town, and you know it!" He waved a French fry.

Leslie stared at her juicy hamburger. "That's true. That's partly why I'm interested in hearing what he comes up with. We don't have any proof that he is involved…at least not at this point." Lifting her sandwich almost to her mouth, she leveled a stern look at Clive. "Now let me eat my lunch in peace. I don't want indigestion."

"Fine! But watch your step with this guy. I think he's got some kind of investment in you selling the ranch. Money's a great motive. "

Savoring her first bite, Leslie quietly conceded that Clive's thinking was a probable possibility. Why else would Roger pressure so hard?" She nodded. "You're right; this is the best burger I've ever eaten."

Clive's hand snaked across the table and nimbly picked out a long French fry from her plate and dropped it into his waiting mouth while Leslie watched in amazement. When his hand returned for more, she rapped it soundly. "Eat your own fries, Mooch!"

He chuckled. "I was planning to, right after I eat yours. Everyone knows that pretty women never eat their fries. They're too afraid of getting fat."

"Well, this one does," Leslie flashed back. "Invite me for lunch and then steal my French fries...hmmmph!"

Clive's brows narrowed. "Shoot! I should have ordered a double batch."

"At your age," she taunted, "I'd think you'd start to consider your heart. All this fried food..."

Clive laid his burger down on his plate, wiped his fingers, and leaned forward. The intensity of his gaze compelled her to focus on him. She stopped eating.

"Actually, I have been considering my heart of late. Do you want to know what I've been considering, Miss Weldon?"

The air left Leslie's lungs. Emotion welled up as a rush of heat rose from her neck upward. It had been so long since she'd allowed herself to trust her feelings—or anyone else's. A bad experience was hard to let go of.

As she opened her mouth to speak, their waitress rushed over with the bill, extending a different menu. "How about it, folks...anyone for dessert?"

Lowering her head, Leslie chuckled at the irony of the situation. Clive shook his head, a wry grin spreading across his face.

The waitress glanced curiously from one to the other. "Seriously, folks, we got a special on pumpkin pie today."

For whatever reason, Clive chose not to resume his previous conversation on the drive back to her car. The mood of the diner had flown.

Following minutes of strained silence, he cleared his throat. "How about coming to the ranch for dinner tomorrow night? You did say you wanted to see my fireplace," he added, a bit too rushed.

Leslie, pulse quickening, centered her focus out the truck window. "I'd love to, Clive. I've been looking forward to seeing your whole ranch. I caught a glimpse of some of your horses the other day when I pulled up in your drive to turn around. They're beautiful!"

"Great, but we'll save the ranch tour for an afternoon and plan a picnic."

Leslie wondered if the picnic might end up back by the private waterfall Mona spoke of. "Sounds terrific!" She smiled, noticing that strange warmth she'd experienced in the diner had returned.

Clive waited until she was safely inside her car and on her way before he revved up his own engine.

Driving home alone gave her time to unwind. Leslie could hardly wait to pull up into her drive. She gazed in several directions. How quickly this place had become home to her, a sanctuary. She was tired, emotionally and physically. Reaching her back door, she sensed Boris's presence even before turning to see the dog come up alongside.

"I feel flattered, Boris. It's the middle of the day, and you've chosen to spend it with me. Come on, I'll find you a treat." At the sound of treat, Boris barked, panting in anticipation. The dog was loyal and intelligent, staying right on her heels.

*

Sometime later, Leslie's eyes fluttered open. She hadn't meant to fall asleep on the couch. The last she knew she'd been reading Wayne's journal. Unfortunately she'd been so tired she couldn't remember a word she'd read. Boris eyed her from Wayne's recliner. Having the dog near had become a comfort.

Walking to the windows, Leslie drew the blinds, noticing the last of the sun disappear over Clive's ranch roof. The outside darkness was dense and foreboding, holding the secrets of potential danger. Trouble was, Leslie didn't know the direction her danger was coming from.

She shivered—whether from her dark thoughts or the dropping temperature, she wasn't sure. As every child could testify, night time was much scarier than daylight. Sighing, she hoped this night would pass quickly. After feeding Boris, she turned him out, praying he would return soon. Boris still pretty much did as he pleased. She made a salad with cheese and crackers suffice for supper.

Placing her empty salad bowl in the dishwasher, she went to check if Boris had returned. Not seeing the animal, she turned nervously and paced between the kitchen and breezeway, praying for a release from her fears. She remembered how strong Cousin Wayne had sounded in his journal. He suspected the evil around him, yet he seemingly wasn't afraid. Then again, Wayne was an ex-cop.

The thought caught her attention and directed her steps down the hallway into Wayne's office area, where she stood gazing across at the gun case. She remembered seeing the key in the large desk drawer and quickly retrieved it. With shaking hands, Leslie knelt at the base of the gun case and turned the key in each drawer.

She slowly slid down to sit fully on the floor to examine the contents of the drawers. Lifting a semi-automatic pistol into the palm of her hand, she saw a loaded clip lying separate in the drawer. Wayne had called it a Glock. This pistol frightened her. She'd only shot the weapon once under the tutelage of her father and Cousin Wayne. Its rapid fire had been hard for her to control.

Laying it down, Leslie picked up the revolver. It was unloaded, and "clean as a whistle," according to Wayne. The .38 Smith & Wesson Revolver felt solid in her hand. Her aim at the target had been steadier with this gun, if she remembered correctly. She laid it back in the drawer next to two boxes of ammunition and a holster. Closing and relocking each drawer securely, she sat considering the weapons for several minutes.

Would I ever be able to use one of these if the need should arise? It was a question she couldn't answer, but she did know from Wayne's journals that his faith had stayed his fear more than his expertise with a gun. Suddenly she stood, leaving the cluttered room for the warmth and brightness of the living area.

Pulling an afghan around her shoulders, she curled up on the couch and picked up the journal. Her questions continued to distract her. She wondered when the Vanook brothers and Cleary had been released from jail—and where they were now. She understood Meg's apprehension. Leslie wished she'd thought to call the sergeant earlier. Setting the journal aside, she went to the back door to call Boris, scanning the darkness for unusual movement.

Why am I so jumpy tonight? Was it not knowing Cleary's whereabouts, or because Roger was now aware of her suspicion? It bothered her that he had not voiced a denial. Had she told him more than she should?

Fear was her worse enemy. She went to get her Bible, choosing verses of God's protection, His promise of watchful angels. Leslie prayed for an awareness of those angels. Slowly her fear ebbed away, and peace settled in its place. Finally she was able to focus on Wayne's journal.

He'd set aside two pages to record his memory of a special celebration—a birthday celebration for Miguel Romero. It was held at an historic inn with a large dining area. Its gracious ambiance was enhanced with round tables covered with white cloths and candle-like centerpieces. The Inn was a favorite place for small dinner parties.

It took a great deal of work to ensure Miguel's safe travel from his home to the restaurant. A man with his arthritic deterioration could not be heavily jarred. Henri O' reserved an extra large table with decorations and a birthday cake. Several of Miguel's friends arrived, and Wayne was thrilled to capture the evening's memories on Miguel's camera. A separate note was inserted at this point.

> We hadn't been there long when I noticed my "unofficial friend" several tables over with a grouping of his peers. I didn't expect he would acknowledge me in public after taking such care that no one knew anything about his private life. It amused me to see him grow edgy when he saw me in attendance with the Romero party. Was he afraid I would acknowledge him? I couldn't help but wonder. Ever since his generous proposal to purchase the ranch was refused, our relationship has been strained. I sense he is not a man to be denied and question his true reason for becoming "a friend."
>
> Believing I'm close to completing the puzzle, it saddens me to accept the ugly truth. I had hoped the outcome would be different. It distresses me even more to know it is my responsibility to confront what I believe is wrong, to misdirect and expose the darkness. There have been too many "near" accidents lately. It is far too dangerous to share what I know with Miguel. What I don't know is whether I should give "my friend" a chance to do the right thing before I talk to anyone.

Leslie pondered the wording of the special insert. She judged that the mentioning of his "unofficial friend" and his offer of purchase for the ranch was not a random insert. The hint of danger was strong, if not identified. But the mentioning of memory photos at the party in Wayne's earlier journal notation…did they have a significant meaning also? She searched the folder pockets of the journal, finding no prints. Leslie heaved a disappointed sigh. Wayne's vague notes only served to perplex her more.

It was comforting to hear Boris scratching at the breezeway door. Leslie hurried to let him in, exhaustion creeping down to her toes. All she wanted was sleep and lots of it. Something told her she was going to need it in the near future. Boris stayed on her heels through the house. She smiled as he lay down right outside her bedroom door.

21

Dangerous Picnic

LESLIE LAID THE PHONE DOWN. Mona was working at the hospital. She'd asked Leslie to connect with Meg from time to time throughout the day. Ray would be working in the far section of Wayne's ranch today, and Mona was concerned that, with both of them gone, Meg might feel alone, having only the remote company of Henri O'.

Reading the unspoken words, Leslie knew everyone was edgy with Meg's stepdad roaming the territory searching for the girl. Swiveling, she was forced to step around Boris's prostrate form. For some reason, he was shadowing her. From the time she woke up, the dog was everywhere she turned. Five minutes after she'd let him outside in the morning, he was back scratching on the door.

"What is wrong with you today?" She frowned at him, wondering if his canine sensory signals were working overtime. Animals had an uncanny way of knowing things. Whatever it meant, it was making her nervous.

Leslie headed for the back bedrooms to do some much-needed cleaning. Armed with a dust rag and a bottle of lemon oil, she purposed to keep herself busy. Her injured foot ached less all the time, until she walked too far or over-did her standing time. She couldn't wait to get the cumbersome black boot off.

Hearing the phone ring, Boris's head shot upward, the hair on the back of his head raised. "Easy boy, it's just the phone. You've heard a phone before."

Lifting the receiver to her ear, Leslie tensed at Roger's voice. As she listened, doubt stressed her thoughts to the limit. "Wait a minute, Roger! You're saying Mr. Gaetzi was unauthorized to pay me a visit? He was working on his own? I don't understand."

Roger sounded tired. "I've been on the phone half the night. My contact phoned New York and talked with those in charge. It seems they have been concerned for a while that he had his own agenda on the side. No one has been able to reach him since he arrived in Dahlonega. Frankly they are as confused as I am about why he was so interested in the Rocky Ridge area. It has no value for grazing purposes. The way they figure it, Gaetzi was probably responsible for the digging up on Rocky Ridge as well."

Leslie heard him sigh. Hearing his explanation, everything made a crazy kind of sense…if she could believe him. "I don't know what to think, Roger. I really don't. Do they think Gaetzi has been behind the serious accidents that have occurred on the ranch? Do you know that the police have unanswered questions about how Wayne died?"

"Wayne?" Roger's voice cracked. "They now doubt Wayne's death was an accident?"

"That's the key word, Roger. An *accident* that never made sense to those who knew Wayne well. Think about it. Did you know someone offered to buy Wayne's ranch shortly before he died? He wrote about it. He also mentioned that, after he refused, a rash of accidents began happening. Does that sound familiar?"

The silence on the phone lasted for several seconds. "I'd like to see his writings."

Immediately Leslie was sorry she'd mentioned what Wayne wrote in his journal. She sent up a prayer for wisdom before she replied, "I'm sorry. Wayne's journal won't be at the ranch. It will be in the hands of Sergeant Ford with the sheriff's office." Everything she'd said, she intended to make happen.

"We still need to meet," he inserted quickly. "I feel there's a big misunderstanding between us that I'd like to make go away. How about having a picnic?"

"A picnic—today?" She tried to keep any fear out of her voice.

"It's a beautiful fall day, and I'm bringing a pre-packed basket. If you can supply a nice large blanket and a couple of pillows, I can be there about 11:30 a.m. Give me a chance to explain in person. Believe me, I'm not the bad guy here." His voice trembled.

"Do you have a place for this picnic?" Leslie wavered, not wanting to be unfair. It was possible Gaetzi had acted on his own.

"I have a spot in mind that will serve two purposes—Rocky Ridge. The investors have asked me to personally look around Rocky Ridge to get a better understanding of what has been taking place. You say there has been illegal digging on the ridge?"

"Ye—s," Leslie answered slowly, still trying to wrap her head around the fact he wanted to picnic at Rocky Ridge.

"Besides, didn't you tell me how beautiful it was to look out across the valley?" Roger pressed home his point.

"It is quite lovely, and there's always a breeze. But, I-I don't know…"

"I don't understand…are you afraid of me?" His voice was filled with hurt.

Leslie could picture his expression and felt terrible. "It's not that. It just seems this area is the center of so much…skullduggery." She groped for a word, not intending the one that came out.

"Skullduggery?" He chuckled.

"It's the best I can do. Let's plan on leaving at 11:30 a.m." After they hung up, Leslie rationalized, *It's the middle of the day out in the open spaces, so what could go wrong?* She stared at Boris. "What am I going to do with you today?"

The dog sat up.

*

Leslie felt guilty walking away from the tool shed where she'd tied Boris at the back. His barking told her he wasn't happy, but she knew Roger would be even more unhappy if he and Boris came face to face. Hearing Roger's Porsche enter the drive, she reminded herself not to forget to collect the blanket and pillows for the picnic.

Henri O' had not minced words when Leslie had called moments earlier. The force of the woman's response to Leslie's lunch plans ate at her confidence. "You're going to Rocky Ridge with the lawyer?" Henri O' might as well have screamed, "You're crazy!" In truth, "You're putting herself at unnecessary risk, Miss Leslie," were her actual words, but the message was the same.

"I have my reasons, Henri O', but I wanted you to know where I'll be."

"Keep your phone handy, ma'am. When do you expect to be back? If you're not home on time, I'll alert Mr. Clive. Maybe I should call Mr. Clive anyway..."

"Henri O'! Hold up on alerting Mr. Clive." Leslie had an alarming vision of Clive charging Rocky Ridge on horseback. "I just thought it was smart for someone to know where I'd be. I'll call in every hour."

"Fine! Just keep your head about you and watch him like a hawk."

That last discourse with Henri O' left her with little resolve as Roger's car pulled to a slow stop. She saw him exit and stare with disdain at the settling dust on his hood.

Leslie squared her shoulders and stepped forward. "You're not planning on driving that to Rocky Ridge?" she asked, incredulous at the thought.

Roger looked horrified. "Naturally not! I assumed we'd take your Jeep."

Leslie forced a smile. "Naturally. Well, transfer your picnic basket. I'll go grab the keys, blanket, and pillows, and meet you in front of the garage."

As they neared the garage, their voices sent Boris into a barking tirade. Roger's face blanched, his eyes searching for the source of the threatening danger. Leslie laid a quieting hand on his jacket sleeve. "Just keep walking. He can't reach you. He's tied up, but you might want to keep your voice down," she encouraged.

Roger shot her a doubtful glance as they pulled the garage door wide. Pausing, Leslie experienced a flashback to that near fatal morning in the garage. She fought off a wave of fear.

"This is the garage where you were locked inside with the Jeep engine racing?" Roger asked.

She nodded, expelling a breath. "Since then Clive and Ray put in new windows and a new side door so that situation can't happen again." She urged, "Come on, we really should hurry. I can't be away from the ranch too long. I told my neighbor I'd be with you on the ridge. She's planning on coming over later."

She was warning Roger that others were aware she was with him—just in case. Perhaps her approach was a tad obvious, but she wasn't too concerned at the moment. As it turned out, her comments went totally unnoticed. Roger's focus was locked on the direction of Boris's snarling growl.

"You're sure that dog is tied up? He sounds terribly large!"

Leslie began loading the back seat of the Jeep. "He's tied, trust me."

Roger plopped the picnic basket on the Jeep floor and rushed around to slide in behind the wheel. While he threaded Leslie's key onto his elaborate key chain, Leslie did her best to acquaint him with the old knobs and levers. "Are you sure you can drive this Jeep?" she asked, observing his troubled expression.

"I'm sure! It's been a few years, but the principles are basically all the same." He straightened his position behind the wheel and turned the ignition.

Leslie was anxious to leave the confines of the structure. She directed Roger up the lane leading past the big barn. As they passed colorful foliage, her stomach tightened into a knot. Had she been foolish to accept Roger's invitation? Yet how else was she to learn the truth?

*

Leslie couldn't help but compare this stressful trip with her first exciting ride with Clive to Rocky Ridge. It was the day they discovered the digging. Roger's slower, more calculated driving gave her more time to think, like wishing she'd bypassed her pride and allowed Clive to know where she was going.

Something told her he wouldn't be pleased she was here. She sent Roger covert glances as the Jeep rounded the curves, threading through the Riker acreage into the valley leading up to Rocky Ridge.

Arriving on the lower plateau of the ridge, Leslie directed Roger to park the Jeep. "From this point, we'll have to carry our picnic over to the base of the ridge near those low boulders, but the view is lovely, and it's a good starting point to hike up to the top."

Roger exited the Jeep. He lifted out the heavy, decorated basket and stood back to view the sun-drenched ridge. After Leslie grabbed the blanket, she turned to face the ridge. Lifting her head, she allowed the ever-present breeze to toss her hair about her shoulders and face. This place never failed to stir her emotions. Curiously, she felt a ripple of cold apprehension and reached back for her coat.

Roger shifted to look out across the valley expanse. "It is quite nice here, though higher than I expected."

"That's part of its charm," said Leslie, walking in the direction of the base of the ridge. Eyeing the elegant basket on Roger's arm, she laughed. "If our lunch inside is as tasty as its designer basket, I'm looking forward to a feast!"

Staring at the basket in his hand, Roger said, "I hope so. This catering shop was recommended to me. It's reported to have rave reviews."

The irregular terrain forced Leslie to walk slower. As she considered his words, she asked, "Who recommended the catering shop? Was it anyone I've met recently?" *Did Roger tell someone they were coming here?*

Keeping his eyes forward, Roger frowned. "I—ah, don't remember."

His evasive answer told her more than his words. She caught up and walked ahead, throwing the large quilted blanket on as level a spot as she could find and pointed off to the side. "Place the basket down on this corner. It will help hold the blanket in place."

Leslie arranged the contents of the basket across the blanket and allowed herself a reprieve from all the tension. Instantly, she found herself caught up in the joy of a picnic on a beautiful day. But a tiny part of her remained on constant guard, fending off nagging questions.

Turning her head, Leslie stared at Roger's tense features. He stood focused upward on the towering boulders above them. Suddenly, the stark realization of their total aloneness on Rocky Ridge struck her with a rush of sickening fear. Her breath came faster as she fought for emotional control. *Get a grip,* she told herself.

Swallowing hard, she asked, "Would you like to eat before venturing to the top of the ridge?"

Glancing briefly at the basket, Roger seemed distracted, his focus centering once more on the ridge above them. "Actually, I think I'd rather get my assignment out of the way before lunch so I can concentrate on us, Leslie. We have much to talk about," he said soberly. Shifting, he studied her with a definite cold remoteness.

Leslie couldn't dispute that an invisible wall of suspicion existed between them. Forcing a bravo she didn't feel, she said, "Hopefully you won't be offended if I nibble while you scale the ridge? I'm starved!" She lifted a delectable looking chicken leg from a white box.

Her honest statement seemed to lighten Roger's mood. He chuckled and extended his arm in a gallant gesture. "Please, be my guest." Moving closer toward the ridge, he murmured, "Maybe when I return I'll have more of an appetite." He frowned, as if in conflict with himself.

Leslie's arms prickled. Roger's strangeness was scaring her.

Removing his outer jacket, he laid it across the blanket and started up the semi-worn path weaving between the rocks and boulders upward of the hill. Watching him, Leslie remembered the forgotten pillows in the Jeep. Pushing up to a standing position, she called to Roger, "I'm going to get the pillows from the Jeep. Where are my keys?"

Roger shifted where he stood, holding to a nearby rock. "Check my jacket pockets." Resuming his direction, he climbed upward.

With the dangling keys in her hand, Leslie moved as quickly as possible in the direction of the Jeep. Within a car's length of the vehicle, she heard an explosion and whirled about to stare at the top of the ridge, where a haze of smoke filled the area. Two huge boulders blasted off the top of the ridge gathering boulders, gravel, and smaller rocks as they plunged in an avalanche down the face of the cliff-like formation.

Unable to find her voice, Leslie watched, horrified, as Roger stood as a statue, gaping upward at the onslaught of the avalanche. Another two explosions erupted, and two more boulders roared like rocket balls from the ridge top, collecting speed. Leslie screamed seconds before she saw Roger dodge a boulder, only to be struck with an airborne missile rock. He was propelled off to the side and tumbled downward on the grassy slope to the bottom, where he thumped to a stop atop fallen gravel.

Leslie's first instinct was to rush to his side until she saw a boulder plummet beyond the ridge base onward toward her and the Jeep. Backing away, she hobbled swiftly to the other side of the Jeep, where she took cover, bracing herself against the Jeep. She held her breath, preparing for the impact of flying rocks.

Waiting until the deep rumbling passed and the pelting of gravel and debris subsided, she peered over the side of the Jeep. Weirdly, Leslie found herself dismissing a passing regret about the lovely new paint job on her Jeep. She shook her thoughts free. *Roger is the important one. Is he still alive?*

Covering her mouth and nose against the dust saturating the air, Leslie cautiously picked her way through the smog and fallen rocks in the direction of the ridge base. She passed the closest boulder, realizing once again she'd been kept safe from impending danger—or death. *Thank You, Lord,* she breathed. But what about Roger?

"Roger!" she tried yelling but convulsed into coughing. "Ro-ger!"

There was no answer. Leslie kept going in the last direction she had seen him roll down the ridge. Her foot found Roger's unmoving body before her eyes spotted his prostrate form. Falling to the ground beside him, she stared at the blood on the rocks beside his head and felt sick to her stomach.

He lay still and ghostly white under a layer of gravel silt. Coughing, Leslie called his name over and over, gently shaking his shoulder. She was afraid to move him, even if she thought it was possible to lift him.

Standing, she shook from shock. *Phone! I need to phone someone quick.* Clive's name shot to her mind. After pulling her cell phone from her jacket pocket, all she reached was voice mail. Henri O' answered at the Schillers on the second ring, but Leslie's panicked explanation was incoherent.

After several tries, she was able to make Henri O' understand what had happened. "I can't move him! He has a head injury, perhaps neck injuries too. I don't know what all..." She broke down, sobbing.

"Is he conscious?" Henri O' asked anxiously.

"No!" Leslie said, crying harder.

"Okay—okay, let me think," said Henri O', sounding rattled for the first time Leslie could remember. "I'll call the police and have them get a helicopter out there pronto. Then I'll get a hold of Mr. Ray. He's not far from you with the cattle in the eastern pasture. Keep the lawyer warm, Miss Leslie! Keep him warm!"

In the lifting haze, Leslie strained to focus on the picnic blanket now buried beneath good-sized rock fragments. And somewhere beneath all that was Roger's jacket. Pulling off her own jacket, she kneeled and tucked it in around his upper body. She bent lower to listen for his breathing. Not able to tell, she gently reached for his wrist and prayed, "Please Lord, let him live!"

How long she sat next to him, she didn't know. She heard a heavy engine mounting the plateau and twisted to watch the road. It was Ray's big truck. She sighed, a single sob slipping out.

Ray's large frame lumbered in her direction, carrying something over his arm. Towering over her, he quickly knelt and removed Leslie's coat from Roger. "Here, put this back on. All I had in the truck was a horse blanket, but I think Mr. Galbraith is past caring for the moment." He covered Roger with the blanket before checking his pulse.

She licked her chalky lips. "Is he still alive?"

"He's alive, at least for now. A chopper's on the way. I'll drive you to the hospital in my truck after they lift Galbraith out and the police arrive."

"I'm not hurt. I went to get some pillows from the Jeep before the explosions went off. Roger was about a third of the way up the incline."

"They'll still want to check you out." He craned his neck to look her over. "Are you sure you weren't hit by any rocks or debris?"

"No. I hid behind the Jeep until the landslide was over. What could have caused those explosions on the ridge?"

"The police will go over the ridge with a fine tooth comb until they know. Where's your purse? In the Jeep?"

Her head turned toward the picnic blanket. "Somewhere on that blanket, along with our lunch. Roger was going to talk with me when he came back down from the ridge." She wondered what he might have said.

The next forty-five minutes moved in a haze. The helicopter arrived and efficiently airlifted Roger to the hospital. After a brief exam by one of the attendants, Leslie was released. Now all they had to wait for was the police.

Ray sat beside Leslie, his quiet nature a wonderful sounding-board for her guilt. "Can you believe I came here today half afraid of Roger, considering he was the dangerous one? Now he's the one who is seriously hurt."

Ray drew a couple of bottles of water out of his deep jacket pocket and silently passed one to her. "It seems to me this *accident* was set up to include both of you. If your boy is involved, as you obviously considered he might be, someone is not happy with him—or maybe afraid of him."

Startled, Leslie gaped at Ray's stern, sun-darkened profile. "You think they meant to injure him as well as me?"

"That's the way it looks. Those explosions were prearranged. Someone had to set them off at just the right moment." His pensive expression cemented his comments.

Leslie gawked at him as the wind stung her face. The temperature was dropping. "That means someone was on the ridge waiting to set the fuse. But I—"

Ray injected, "You went to the Jeep for pillows! That couldn't have been factored into the equation. Someone expected you to be with him." He swigged down water from his bottle, leaving her mind to wander in a sea of turbulent thoughts.

Clive arrived in his truck about the same time as the police, but Leslie didn't have a chance to speak with him. Sergeant Ford led her off to a side to question her at length. Twisting, she watched Clive stand alongside Ray. While the two talked, Clive raised his head, his gaze connecting with Leslie.

"Miss Weldon," Sergeant Ford's voice cut the air sharply, "there are many unanswered questions I need the answers to."

She jerked her focus back to face his stern features. "As do I, Sergeant," she said stiffly.

*

When Sergeant Ford was satisfied Leslie had told everything, she was allowed to leave, but the police crew was just getting started. Lights were brought in and set up to continue working after dark. Leslie felt numb all over, whether from the day's events or the cold there was no way to know.

Backing away from the scene, she felt a pair of strong arms encircle her with a large blanket that smelled of Clive's aftershave. Making a small attempt at humor, she asked, "Is this a horse blanket like Ray covered Roger with?"

"No," Clive whispered in her ear, "this is the blanket I keep on my family room couch. I grabbed it up before leaving the house." Lifting his head, he nodded to Ray who came up alongside him. "I'll take her home in my truck and send Evan up with one of the boys to drive back the Jeep."

Addressing Leslie, Clive asked, "Where's the Jeep key?"

Her mind went blank. "I-I'm not sure." Pulling her dirty purse apart, section by section, she searched frantically. "Wait a minute! I remember."

Pushing her purse at Clive, Leslie plunged her hand deep in her lined leather jacket and pulled out Roger's cluttered keychain with her Jeep key attached. Within seconds she handed Clive the right key and pocketed the rest. "I've got to go to the hospital." Her anxious eyes sought his. "That could have been me in that copter right along with him."

Clive's face twisted in emotion. "You think I don't know that could be you? But for the grace of God, you would be dead!" Then his voice turned angry. "What were you doing up here with him by yourself anyway?"

Ray stepped closer, looking from one to another. "Ah, I'm going to head on back now...that is, if you two are okay?" Hearing no answer, he added, "Great. I'll catch up with you later, Clive."

"That's fine, Ray, thanks," murmured Clive, his eyes drilling Leslie.

She heard Ray's fading footsteps, her eyes unable to veer from Clive's penetrating stare. "It's a long story, Clive. I wanted information; he wanted to see the top of the ridge where everything has been happening. Plus, I accused him of being involved, and he wanted to talk—explain—whatever."

Clive's strong hand took hold of her elbow, steering her toward his truck. "You can tell me all about it on the way to the hospital. I just can't believe you accused a guy of doing something illegal and then promptly drive out to some secluded spot with him!" He rolled his eyes. "Not the smartest move!"

She opened her mouth to retort but decided to wait until they were in the truck. At least he was willing to drive her to the hospital to check on Roger. Hearing the situation reviewed from Clive's point of view, she secretly admitted her actions had been impulsive—rash even. But Roger had sounded so earnest. She couldn't explain why she'd trusted him; she just had.

She thought of everything Roger had said and done before he began to climb up the ridge. He was different—cold and mysterious. It had frightened her then. Now she wondered if he'd wanted to tell her something but was torn in his decision. *Why didn't I press him to sit and talk first?*

Clive's voice cut through her thoughts. "So, start from the beginning. Tell me everything you can remember. I want to understand why you bypassed protection to drive out here with a man who looks guilty as Bluebeard himself."

By the time they arrived at the hospital and Leslie explained the best she could, Clive's manner began to soften. His rough concern for her welfare gave way to a measure of understanding, though he maintained his mistrust of Galbraith. Once they were parked at the hospital, Leslie ran ahead, determined to find out about Roger's condition.

*

Two hours later included supper from a vending machine. Leslie sat on the edge of the vinyl-padded chair, searching the face of each hospital staff member as he or she came out of Roger's intensive care area. But there was no word. Finally a woman doctor, Edith Proctor, stood before the small group: Clive, Leslie, and a weary officer from the sheriff's office. The doctor described Roger's condition in layman's terms before leaving them to speculate.

"It was obvious he had a head injury!" Leslie exclaimed. "She didn't tell us a thing except Roger's in a critical state, and they don't even know how long he'll be in a coma." Her fingers raked her mussed hair as she and Clive walked toward his truck in the lighted lot.

A Dahlonega police car stopped them in their tracks, and the driver's window lowered. Sergeant Ford's head emerged through the opening, his expression sober. "There've been further developments. Climb in the back seat and we'll talk."

Exchanging perplexed glances, Leslie and Clive entered the vehicle, and her eyes locked on Ford's face, waiting for an explanation. Had Cleary found Meg? She tried not to speculate worst-possible scenarios.

Sergeant Ford was half turned in the front seat of his patrol car. His eyes had new circles under them. "What do you think the odds are of Galbraith's law office being practically gutted in a fire this afternoon?"

Leslie's hands flew to her face. "Was anyone hurt?" She briefly thought of Stephanie before her mind leapfrogged to Georgie's Christmas Shoppe. "Did the fire spread through the other shops on the street?"

The policeman's thick lips protruded outward. "Nope! The fire was apparently centered in his office only. Proprietors of connecting shops reported hearing a small explosion...kinda like a truck backfire. The fire captain will get me a report as soon as the arson crew is finished with their investigation." His head drooped wearily.

"The arson crew?" Leslie repeated.

"That's the way it's adding up at the onset. We'll know more later."

"But why would anyone want to burn out Roger's office?" Leslie looked at Clive and back at the Sergeant.

"Files could be the only reason," Clive murmured.

Sergeant Ford stuck an old toothpick in his mouth. "That's right. All the file drawers were open."

"What about his computer?" asked Leslie. "Wouldn't his files be mostly on his computer?"

Removing the toothpick, the sergeant nodded. "All the power lines and accessories are scorched and melted. Even the monitor is scorched and peeling. And just in case that wasn't good enough, all his computer folders have been affected with a killer virus. They were very thorough."

"Did anyone in the area see anything?" asked Clive.

"No. Seems there was a traffic accident across the street and everyone in two blocks was outside watching that for at least a half hour or more in the early afternoon."

Leslie widened her eyes. "Coincidence?"

"A well-planned diversion," replied Sergeant Ford. "An unknown person was seen fleeing the accident scene. I've got a man checking out Roger's house, but I don't expect to find any evidence."

"What was worth all that?" Leslie shook her head in disbelief that something could be so arranged for the purposed of malicious destruction.

"Clients and their business affairs for one," the sergeant injected.

"But I thought lawyers had that client confidentiality clause. Why would anyone bother if that clause was in effect?"

"It had to be a very thorough client who wanted to be sure. Someone who doesn't trust anybody or like to leave loose ends," added Sergeant Ford. "It's my guess that Galbraith could probably give us the name of that client."

Clive leaned forward. "Except he's in a coma, and they aren't sure when he'll wake up. If he does, the possibility is high he'll have memory problems."

Nodding, Ford stifled a yawn. "I know, my officer on duty phoned me. Tough break, but we'll wait and keep a watch on him."

"Do you think the Vanook brothers and Cleary Norton set those explosions on the ridge?" Leslie pressed. "Are you going to arrest them again?"

"If it were only that easy," Ford replied. "The Vanook crew moved the boulders in place, but my guess is, that's all they were told to do. None of them has any experience in explosives, and my officers can verify there were no explosives on the ridge that night we arrested them. Besides, it's not their style. Norton's a moonshiner from the hills and not the brightest firefly I've ever met. The Vanooks are more dangerous but not skilled for a job like this. No. They were only the rock movers. A couple of patrolmen are bringing them in for questioning, but we've got nothing that will stick."

Ford seemed to consider his next words. "Miss Weldon, I'm not sure what to do about you at this point. I don't think anyone will try anything again so soon, but you are an apparent obstruction in someone's plans. My other problem is our limited manpower is stretched to the limit at present. Corporal Bailey is now busy on another case, and frankly, I can't afford to assign you any full-time protection."

"She'll stay at my ranch," Clive interjected without asking Leslie.

"No! *She* won't! I can't, Clive. There's no way I can leave Boris to fend for himself."

"Don't be silly. That dog has been fending for himself most of his life. You'll stay at the ranch! Either that, or I'll park in your drive, and no one will get any sleep." He glared at her as if she were the most unreasonable woman he'd ever met.

Squaring her shoulders, Leslie glared back. "Clive, you know Boris is just beginning to trust me. I can't let that fragile trust be broken. He might never come back if I leave. So, if you have to stay, then stay! You can have Wayne's old room. Just don't get in my way," she said angrily.

Sergeant Ford expelled a long blast. "Well, I'm so glad we've come to an understanding. Now I can go home and have supper with my wife. Good night, you two." He stared at them when neither moved to open the door. "Good night!"

Leslie and Clive exchanged self-conscious glances. "Good night, Sergeant. Keep us updated," said Clive, opening the car door quickly.

Nodding curtly, the policeman shifted into drive and pulled out of the hospital lot. As Clive and Leslie walked to his truck, neither was willing to rehash the depressing developments. Everything had already been said. Leslie wasn't in a rush to share her ranch home with Clive—even for protection. The idea of having him in such close proximity increased her anxiety, and she had no plans to explore the depths of that reasoning.

When they turned onto Dunn Road, she said, "I'm sure Ray and Mona are waiting to hear from us."

Clive shot her a sidelong glance. "Afraid to be alone with me?"

"Oh, grow up! It's simply being neighborly not to keep them in suspense. You know how Mona frets. It's only right, but if you're too tired..." Her chin went up.

Turning into the Schiller drive, Clive mumbled, "I can see our time together is going to be pleasant."

Leslie instantly felt guilty. "Sorry," she whispered, "I haven't been very congenial." Suddenly she was fighting an onset of tears.

Clive pulled up and stopped. "You're running on empty, and your nerves are stretched taut. Having escaped death one more time by the grace of God must be humbling, among other emotions." A low chuckle rumbled in his throat. "Your guardian angel is probably asking for hazard pay right now."

She managed a tiny smile.

Watching her wipe her eyes, Clive asked, "Ready to go in?"

Leslie summoned her remaining energy. After hearing the gentleness in Clive's voice, she couldn't afford to look at him or she'd lose the fragile guard holding back more tears. "Let's go," she murmured, looking at the lighted opening, where Mona waited for them.

The Schillers had anticipated their visit.

22

An Old Enemy

BY THE TIME LESLIE WOKE UP, DRESSED, and made her way to the kitchen, Clive had breakfasted and left for his ranch duties. Having been read a list of dos and don'ts the night before, she'd been left on her own—prison was more like it. Boris was allowed outside only three times a day and immediately called back in. She rolled her eyes. *Like Boris is going to mind me and come to me when I call.* The last mandate demanded that she was allowed only to venture into town or elsewhere if she was accompanied by Mona or Clive.

Boris was an unpredictable wild dog. Leslie never knew if, why, or when the dog would come, though lately Boris followed her everywhere, and even now lay at her feet. The poor dog had been tied up the day before until Leslie and Clive arrived home from the Schillers. Leslie had apologized profusely, giving the animal an extra serving of food. Now she stood, coffee in hand, scanning the landscape. It was a cold, rainy day. "Perfect!" she murmured.

She looked up at the clock. At 9:00 a.m. she planned to call the hospital and check on Roger's condition. Would he be able to tell them anything when he woke up—if he woke up? She sighed.

Not feeling hungry, Leslie reached for a bagel anyway. She'd have to hurry to be ready when Mona came by to pick her up. If they hurried with their purchases, just maybe Leslie could stop by the hospital. Still fighting the guilt of escaping injury while Roger lay fighting for his life, she gulped her coffee and pushed the toaster lever down.

She knelt, petting the wiry-headed dog with the vise-like jaw. "If we're real sneaky, maybe you can run up and visit your lady while I'm gone…but don't tell Clive when he returns." She laughed softly.

*

Seeing Mona pull up in her little truck, Leslie went out the door, allowing Boris to come out with her. "Take off, Boy, go ahead." She shooed him away, but Boris ran only a few feet and turned, coming back to stand by her.

Leslie shrugged at Mona. "What's with him lately?"

"His senses are telling him to stick with you," Mona said thoughtfully. "Let's take him, Leslie; he's car trained. Wayne took Boris with him in the Jeep all the time. Of course he was the only one who could get near the dog."

Looking from Boris to Mona, Leslie considered the option, unsure it was wise. "Oh, all right," she finally said. "I'll get a leash." She opened the back door of Mona's truck. "Come Boris, ride!"

Like a shot the large dog was up in the truck, his tongue lolling happily out of the side of his mouth. Leslie dropped her jaw in surprise. "This dog is amazing! But he confuses the daylights out of me." Slamming the door, she climbed up in the front seat.

Mona threw Leslie an amused glance. "Boris isn't so confusing. He's a wild dog meant to be a pet—a loyal, fierce, watchdog pet."

"That's what I'm afraid of. Boris is attaching himself to me. It worries me how he will react if I choose to return to New York." She stared solemnly out the window.

"Is that what you've decided?" Mona said quietly.

Leslie pressed her lips. "It's no longer what I might or might not decide. My decision may be made by sheer necessity. I have a ranch and little else—no job or any knowledge of how to run a ranch. I'm practically broke, Mona, with no money to pay taxes, or even to buy bread for much longer. Oh, I have a small bank account left to me from my father, but after that is gone..."

Mona backed out of the drive, then steered the car onto the main road leading into town. "It sounds as if God has to work out something pretty quick. Have you been praying?"

Leslie stared at her. "I've prayed more lately than the last ten years total."

Mona laughed. "With everything that's been happening, I'd say God has been in your corner, so maybe we'd better trust Him for the rest. Have you found out any more?"

Leslie looked down at her hands lying listlessly in her lap. "I've read some interesting facts in Jamie's journal that may have some bearing on what's happening—but no proof." Chuckling, she glanced up at Mona's profile. "And just this morning I learned the value of half-eagle coins. I talked with a man on his car phone."

Mona frowned. "Half-eagle coins? I don't understand."

"I'll tell you when we've more time. It goes back to Jamie's journal."

Mona couldn't find a parking place even after circling the square a couple times. "We'll park down this side street and walk back. It's not far from the specialty market I want to visit." She selected a wide spot near the corner under a shade tree. Rolling down the windows halfway, the women left Boris lying comfortably on the back seat and directed their steps toward the square. The rain had ceased, but the gray cloud cover remained.

Talking as they exited the market, Leslie and Mona turned almost point blank into Jonathon Hager and Hamilton Longworth, along with two men Leslie had never met.

"Well, well, Miss Weldon, what a delightful surprise to run into you and...Mrs. Schiller, isn't it?" Ham Longworth's large voice had a way of making their unexpected encounter nothing short of a holiday. He turned to the other three men. "I believe you've already met Jonathon Hager. The gentleman on his right is Chuck Mayer, our leading real-estate guru, and this handsome devil next to me is Jack Criswell, a hotshot lawyer from New York."

Looking with admiration at the women, he continued, "Gentlemen, may I introduce Miss Leslie Weldon, a newcomer to Dahlonega and Mrs. Mona Schiller, one of the best ER nurses this town can boast." He stepped to the side, smiling proudly.

Mona stepped forward. "Everyone in town knows Mr. Hager, at least by sight, and Chuck Mayer sold Ray and me our chicken ranch...but a new lawyer in town is always news, so welcome, Mr. Criswell."

Mona's natural charm was a lesson in itself, but Leslie wondered which of these men was Roger's secret friend.

"Thank you, Mrs. Schiller." Mr. Criswell's warm eyes moved smoothly over both women.

Leslie inched closer to Mona, nodding pleasantly to each of the men.

Ham Longworth responded to Mona's comment. "This new lawyer was called in on a fast jet all the way from New York City to hightail it out here and help us out." His face sobered. "With our Roger clinging to life..." He paused, seemingly at a loss for words.

Jonathon Hager cleared his throat, his tone subdued. "Mr. Galbraith handled most of the bank's affairs, and naturally we needed someone to step in for him until we know the outcome of his injuries."

Leslie stiffened, gathering from Mr. Hager's tone that he wasn't putting much stock in Roger pulling through.

As she stepped forward to speak on Roger's behalf, Mona's gentle hand restrained her. "Yes. It is sad. We are all praying for him." Turning to Leslie, she added, "I think we better be on our way if we plan to accomplish our other errands." She smiled back and nudged Leslie to move past them.

Leslie could almost feel their eyes on them as they walked toward the bakery. Inside the door, she whirled to peer up the street, her mind racing with plans. Mona had reached the counter with her purchase when Leslie pulled her away. "Forget the bread. We'll come back. Come on!"

"Wha—where?" Mona stared at her friend.

Pulling her aside, Leslie hurried to explain, "I think now would be a great time to go for lunch, but we need to hurry so we can get a booth or table close by. Hurry!"

Mona glanced longingly at the loaves of fresh bread before following Leslie out the door and down the street to the bar and grille. Barely able to keep up, she listened close as Leslie's plan tumbled out like a box of Cracker Jacks, with no real pattern.

Her mouth gaped in stunned silence. "But why? What do you expect to learn by stalking the four of them at lunch?"

"You never know. Trust me. We need to get fairly close, yet take care not to be noticed." Leslie talked excitedly, planning as she went.

"And how do we manage that?" whispered Mona. "It's not all that large inside the restaurant."

Mona's words caused Leslie to doubt her quest for the first time, but she pressed ahead. "We'll just have to figure it out as we go."

Mona eyed her with disbelief.

The interior of the restaurant was decorated in dark tones with low lighting, separated in part by a line of high-backed booths. Leslie sighed with relief. She had one thing in her favor—perhaps more would fall into place. As soon as her eyes grew accustomed to dim lighting, she spotted the four men sitting at a round table in the bar section, menus in hand. They were too busy talking amidst themselves to notice Leslie and Mona's entrance. "Thanks, Lord," she murmured. *One more hurdle accomplished.*

A friendly hostess approached, directing the girls to a far booth to the left, but Leslie pointed at the furthest booth to the right near the bar section. On the opposite side of that booth sat the round table with the four men. "We'll take that booth, if that is all right?" she asked sweetly.

The hostess nodded, leading them to the booth. She left the women with menus. Mona's gaze followed the hostess's departure. She whispered, "I hadn't planned on eating out, Leslie. I've got work to do. Besides, we can't even see their table. What good will it do to stay here?" She was clearly agitated.

Lifting her huge leather bag to the table, Leslie rummaged in its deep pockets, extracting her New York friend's listening device. When Mona frowned and stared up at her, Leslie winked. Inserting the apparatus in her left ear, she moved close to the side panel of the booth, knowing the four men sat just beyond the panel.

"What are you doing?" Mona demanded, looking around self-consciously. "Is that what I think it is?" Her eyes registered alarm.

Leslie leaned close. "It is. The trouble will be deciphering who is who. I can't always discern which person is talking without seeing them. But actual spoken words come through loud and clear!" She moved closer to the paneling, pressing the slide controller in her hand to up the volume. In seconds, she exclaimed, "My!" softly, leaning further in.

Mona hefted her menu higher, partially covering Leslie's actions. She covertly watched the area while sipping her water. Setting the glass down, she murmured, "Hurry! The waitress will be back soon."

"Ssshhh," replied Leslie. "They're discussing who is ordering the buffet and who plans to order from the menu."

Mona rolled her eyes.

Leslie heard feet shuffling as if one or more were rising to go to the buffet tables. She winced as a woman laughed too loudly at a nearby table. More shuffling was heard, and then everything grew fairly quiet. She was about to pull out the apparatus when she heard a man's ominous words. "This thing at the hospital needs to be finished. Get word back and make it clear I want no more slips-ups. The ridge was sloppy timing—sloppy! I want it finished!"

The air in Leslie's lungs felt suddenly cut off. *Are they talking about Roger?* Whoever the first man was talking to responded in low tones. She pressed harder against the booth partition, barely catching his words.

"Quit worrying. The way it looks now, the problem might take care of itself. If not, we will finish it. Do you still want the other item taken care of?"

Leslie heard no answer, only a sinister chuckle. Yanking the listening apparatus out of her ear, her mind fought to process the obvious threat. She bit her bottom lip. "Let's get out of here. I've got to see who's sitting at that table," she hissed at Mona. Standing, they waited impatiently for talking people to pass before exiting their booth to rush around to the other side.

But they were too late.

Leslie furtively scanned the empty table, trying to determine which of the four men had just left. Mona's hand jerked her back where they could observe without being seen. Squinting through the darkened room, Leslie spotted each of the men milling around the buffet tables.

Which two were talking at the table minutes ago? Which two are murderers? Bile rose in her throat. Feeling a tug on her sleeve, Leslie responded to Mona's urging to leave.

"I left a couple of dollars to cover the cost of the water—now hurry!" Mona pushed her friend past booths and tables to the door furthest from the men's line of view. As soon as they reached the outside, Mona yanked her along the sidewalk. "Come on, Leslie. Let's get back to the bakery and finish our errands. Your face is white as a sheet, and you need time to calm down. Whatever you heard you can tell me all about it on the way home...though I'm not sure I really want to know. You're freaking me out, girl!"

Leslie allowed herself to be pulled along. Her confused thoughts dulled her motor skills as they threaded through foot traffic to the front of the bakery. Yanking her arm back, Leslie spoke quietly, "Listen, Mona, it's urgent that I get ahold of Sergeant Ford. Go on in and get your bread, while I phone his number." She searched for his card.

Mona glanced nervously back to the restaurant they'd just left before walking through the bakery door.

*

On the side street where Mona's truck sat parked under a shade tree, Boris had at some point slipped from the seat to sleep on the floor behind the driver's seat, contented and snoring softly. A young mother pushed a happy toddler in a stroller down the sidewalk while balancing a satchel. Passing the little truck, she paused to listen to birdsong and smiled as if her world lay in perfect order.

Across the street, two elderly women sat quietly side by side in wicker chairs on the wide covered porch of an old, two-story house. Over their knees lay warm lap blankets. They settled in to watch cars go by and people move up and down their street, speaking little and watching much.

Upon this scene, a medium-tall man with sharp features ambled casually around the corner off the town square, his hands in his pockets. A floppy, leather hat covered a good portion of his face and his oversized leather coat concealed most of his slim physique as he walked the sidewalk scanning both sides for anyone within viewing range. He smiled, confident of his ability and content in the solitude of the quiet street. He'd been only a short distance away when the boss had called him in on short notice.

Morey Santana wasn't a man for impromptu actions and, up until lately, neither was the boss. But the boss man's calm, calculated methods had given way to desperate actions in the past two weeks. Had his agenda pressed him beyond good reason? In Morey's opinion it wouldn't serve any of them well in the end. He felt increased nervousness. Was it time to get out? *Imagine pulling a job like this is broad daylight....*

Pausing under the shade tree adjacent to Mona's small truck, he waited, again checking the sidewalks on both sides of the street. He was a careful man by nature, unlike his partner whose bull physique and brutal quick mannerisms were often hazardous to discovery. He knew it was a mistake to try working together again. This, added to the change he'd noticed in the boss, was causing Morey to think of moving on. He couldn't afford a third conviction. After his hospital job was concluded, he'd pick his time and disappear. It seemed as if the whole scenario had been jinxed from the start.

The quiet scene of the street gave him a weird feeling of suspended time. It was the right moment to make his move and move quickly. Satisfied that all was well, the lithe man sprinted with bird-like speed to the driver's side of the truck. He stuck his head inside the open window, interested only in the dials on the front dash.

His eyes darted from one dial to another, uncertain which was his best course of action. He hated impromptu action that opened him up to mistakes. Suddenly, his lips thinned in thought. Drawing his head back, he dropped to the side of the truck, his hand on the running board as he peered underneath the truck's chassis. In seconds he located the brake line. After a final look around, he withdrew a small tool from his leather coat pocket and lowered himself to the blacktop beneath him.

Morey Santana would have scooted under the chassis, had Boris not awakened at that instant. When the brute dog hit the front seat of the truck, thrusting his upper body through the open window, Morey came close to losing control of his bodily faculties.

He watched the drool of the slobbering dog drip down on his jacket and stared into the piercing yellow eyes of hatred. The beast's sharp barking shattered the neighborhood quietness like crystal against stone. In two houses down the street a door cracked; windows were opening. In seconds, people would be on the street. Morey panicked. *I've gotta get out of here fast!*

The two elderly women stood, exchanging alarmed glances. They'd watched the entire transaction in puzzlement and were now shocked to see the slight man right himself from the blacktop by the truck and run with great speed toward the town square.

*

Mona and Leslie hurried from the shopping area down the street toward their truck, dismayed to find an agitated Boris in the driver's seat. Slobber covered the seats, window, and door. "What happened here?" asked Mona, her voice terse.

Leslie shook her head. "It looks like Boris tried to protect your truck. I fear some poor person walked too near the vehicle. The dog probably came unglued and gave them a heart attack. Maybe we should have rolled the window up higher."

"Well, he certainly made a mess of my truck. Put him in the back seat so we can get out of here."

While Leslie was settling Boris in the back, Mona worked to clean off her truck with a container of wipes. She turned at the sound of a human voice to find an old woman laboring across the street, frantically beckoning to her. Closing her door, Mona hurried to meet the woman, who waved off any offer of help.

Leslie watched with curiosity as Mona stood in the middle of the street listening in earnest to the white-haired, thin-faced lady. With her hand on Boris's collar, Leslie calmed the dog and waited. When Mona reached the truck, Leslie wondered at her alarmed expression. *Now what?* Every direction, she met with calamity.

Mona opened the truck door, her breathing heavy. "We need to have this truck checked out before driving it home." She reached for her purse on the front seat. Leslie watched in stunned silence as Mona pulled out her cell phone and dialed her husband.

"Ray, listen, we've got a situation that needs serious attention. A neighbor woman on the side street where we parked informed me a man was seen coming out from underneath the truck. Apparently Boris frightened him off almost immediately, so I don't know what he would have had time to accomplish—still?"

Her mouth agape, Leslie watched Mona nervously twist the ends of her dark hair. Absorbing every word, she heard her say, "Okay, honey, we'll wait here."

Shutting down her phone, Mona turned to Leslie. "Ray is driving in to pick us up. He's going to call Bob at the dealership and have him send someone to check out the truck. Why don't we wait for him with those two ladies on the porch? Just keep Boris on his leash."

Leslie's head dropped in defeat. She nodded. "I better call Sergeant Ford back and update him."

"What next, Leslie…what next?" Mona's voice rose in frustration.

*

Ray's panel truck rumbled over the roads, rattling chicken cages stacked in the back. Mona sat in the bucket seat while Leslie held tight to Boris's leash behind the front seats. Ray made few comments after listening to their account of what happened.

When Mona described the man who'd been seen standing by their truck, Leslie stopped her in mid-speech. "Mona! He fits the description of the man I told you about earlier. The sharp-featured man I recognized in town—the one from New York!"

Mona's jaw went slack. "You're kidding! What connection do you think he has to the rest of the accidents?" The two women exchanged shocked glances.

Ray's jaw tightened. "Look! I have no idea what either of you are talking about," he exclaimed crossly, "but someone obviously tried to kill you today, or at the very least cause you bodily harm. This situation has got to stop!"

Leslie and Mona stared at the normally calm, easy-going man.

"I'm all right, honey," Mona encouraged him softly. "God was our protector!"

Leslie cleared her throat, unsure if it was the best time to interject. "Sergeant Ford will meet us at my ranch. He wants to know everything: what I heard through my hearing gadget and what happened with the truck. Now that I know who was at the truck today..." She buried herself in the communal silence the rest of the way home.

*

Leslie remained at the table long after the Schillers and Sergeant Ford left. Her head was propped in her hands. She racked her brain for a connection between the sharp-featured man and the situation on Rocky Point. *He has to somehow be a part of what is happening!*

When Boris leaped from the chair darting for the breezeway, her head snapped around. Hearing the click of the door unlocking, she sucked in a breath.

"Leslie?"

"In here, Clive," she answered, relaxing.

The instant she saw his face she knew he'd heard about the episode in town. Good, maybe she wouldn't have to regurgitate everything that transpired. When her stomach growled, she looked at the clock. It was suppertime, and she'd given no thought to fixing anything. There'd been no time.

But food appeared to have no interest to Clive. His long strides took him directly to a chair across the table from her. "Tell me about the sharp-featured man, Leslie. Mona said you saw him first in a New York restaurant, and then something about a listening device…"

Leslie stared at him in silence. Sitting up, she nodded. "Yeah, I eavesdropped, never realizing that the woman he was planning to eliminate was me." She pushed her hair away from her heated face. "Crying can wreck havoc with a woman's complexion."

Clive gently lifted her chin and turned it toward him. "You look just fine to me."

She knew if he said one more tender word, she'd melt. Stiffening her resolve, she turned away. "Clive Masters, if you're going to say something to the effect that I'm some kind of catalyst for calamity, I'm not in the mood to hear it!" She rose from the table, went to the cupboard, and pulled out a box of crackers. Ripping open the box, she withdrew a handful and filled her mouth, unwilling to meet his eyes. Still, she could feel his watchful gaze.

"I understand Galbraith is still in a coma," he said.

Bringing the crackers to the table, Leslie stood by his shoulder. "I know. His life is in danger too, Clive. And I don't understand any of it." She clenched her fists.

"Ray was telling me there were four men today having lunch together in town and that you suspect Hamilton Longworth, and either Chuck Mayer, or some new dude from New York of plotting against Galbraith and yourself."

She winced. Hearing Clive's version made the whole episode sound far-fetched—if she didn't know better. "I don't know for sure which man I heard, but there were only four at that table…and two of them are guilty. And it's true; my thoughts have been leaning toward Mr. Longworth. He fits the bill in so many ways."

Leslie's gaze held Clive's. "Sergeant Ford told me he has an APB out on Cleary and the Vanooks to bring them in for questioning about the fiasco on Rocky Ridge yesterday, but they've gone to ground. Cleary's trailer was gone from the woods behind the Vanook house and there was no sign of either of the brothers. Even the 'moonshine still' in the woods was broken to pieces. They must have figured they'd get blamed for the explosions on the hill and lit out. Road blocks are set up and down the state line."

Having pushed another cracker into her mouth, Leslie found it nearly impossible to comment. Raising her hand for patience, she hurriedly cleared her mouth enough to speak. "Why is he bringing them in if he doesn't think they lit the explosives? Why all the rousting?"

Clive cocked his head. "I think he figures they can give evidence of some nature." Suddenly pushing up from the table, he removed the box of crackers from Leslie's hand and set them down on the table. "Where's your coat? In the breezeway?"

Her response was dull and slow. "What did you have in mind?"

"Dinner at my place," replied Clive. "It has to be better than a box of crackers." He nudged her toward the kitchen and beyond where her coat waited on a wall hook. "We'll leave Boris inside to guard the house so we don't return to any surprises."

"I'm not fit company tonight for anyone, Clive. Why don't you leave me here with my crackers?" She couldn't help feeling sorry for herself.

"Let me be a judge of the company. Besides, didn't you say you were anxious to see the fireplace Miguel built before he retired?" His dark eyes were compassionate and caring, moving Leslie to an emotional brink.

She could feel her resolve fading. Lowering her eyes from his scrutiny, she felt two teardrops slide quietly down her cheeks. She wanted to speak but the words wouldn't form in her mouth. *If he would just leave me alone...*

His fingers brushed her hair back from her face and tilted her chin upward until their eyes connected. In one fluid motion, Clive leaned down, tenderly kissing her on the lips. It was a soft, lingering kiss.

In that instant the rest of Leslie's fortitude was blown away. She began to sob and hiccup loudly, sucking in air.

Startled, Clive drew back at her outburst.

"I'm sorry," she sobbed out between hiccups, "but it's all your fault."

Clive looked slightly wounded. "My fault? Why?"

She sobbed deeper. "Be-cause." She hiccupped before finishing. "Be-cause you're being so sweet..."

Smiling, he drew her into his arms and let her cry until her tears were spent. When she'd calmed, he went to the kitchen for a wet cloth, came back, and sponged off her face and partially swollen eyes. Tossing the cloth to the counter, he kissed her lightly again and pulled her jacket up around her with a gentle tug. "Come on. You can finish crying at my place. I'm starved!"

His typical male attitude jolted Leslie to the point she was able to regain control. Drawing up her shoulders, she swiped at her moist cheeks and tossed her hair. "As am I," she stated brusquely, brushing off crumbs. "Those crackers were stale and tasteless. You've got a key. Lock up, Clive." Pulling the jacket closer, she sailed through the back door toward Clive's truck.

Shaking his head at her, Clive hurriedly followed, careful to leave many lights burning. He clearly intended for the place to look occupied.

23

A Dangerous Memory

ZEKE'S TRUCK WAS WELL HIDDEN in the brush at the end of the dead-end road. He'd come before dawn, remaining all day with provisions to last up to two days—whatever it took to accomplish the job. What did he have to lose? With Fred tucked safely away in a sleazily motel near Atlanta, he only had himself to worry about. Cleary should be halfway back to West Virginia if he'd made it across the state line.

When the Weldon woman had driven away in that little truck with the neighbor woman late morning, he'd carefully made his way through the brush behind the garage area. His plan was to nab her after she came back home and was finally alone. His thoughts were on their payoff money deposited in a post office box.

It was a new method of money transfer. Zeke wondered why the boss had quit sending their money through that slick, dandy-looking lawyer. Just as well. He'd acted as if he were too good to hand them an envelope of money. *The dude said it was payment for construction work—overtime pay.* Construction work? It made Zeke laugh to remember. *Was that jerk really that dense, or was it a cover-up?*

After those explosions on Rocky Ridge, further work plans were suspended, taking with them his chance for some heavy-duty cash. *This is my last opportunity for a big payoff.* Zeke was never one to get too introspective. There had been a printed letter included in his envelope. The words were vague, but the meaning clear enough—a "hit" had been put out on the Weldon dame, but it had to look like an accident. At the bottom of the page a bonus was offered should Cleary's stepdaughter, Meg, be found and eliminated. The boss wasn't taking any chances. He was a stickler for loose ends.

Zeke wiped his dusty lips on his sleeve and pulled out a bottle of booze, Cleary's private stock. Zeke chuckled. Pure gut rot was what it was, but it took the edge off of waiting and swatting at gnats and late barn flies. An accident was all laid out for him in a separate print out. The boss was thorough. Zeke wondered if someone else had tried to execute the plan and muffed it up before him. Zeke had always been patient.

While he waited, he felt around for his knife. The last thing Cleary had said before leaving was, "If you go near that house with that vicious dog, you'll need a knife." Cleary had wanted no part of that job or the girl either.

When the panel truck drove slowly up into the drive early afternoon, Zeke hurriedly snaked his way back to his truck to wait, knowing the dog would be let out. He wanted no attention coming his way. Once inside his truck, he rolled down the window and carefully parted the tall weeds to wait and watch. His heart went to his throat when he saw the police car roar down the dusty road and up into Riker Ranch.

For the first time Zeke toyed with the idea of leaving and dropping the whole idea, but then he thought about all that money and settled back down in the truck. *After the police leave, I'll make my move.*

*

Meg had worked outside with the chickens for hours and afterward paced the house. After the excited phone call had come in from Mona and Mr. Ray had hurried to help her and Miss Leslie, she couldn't settle down. Henri O's refusal to discuss any possibilities left Meg to the darkness of her own imagination. She was tired of being scared. How often had she told the Lord her woes? Wasn't He listening?

That familiar tension remained after Mr. Ray and Mona come home—the fear of the unknown. Everyone was waiting to see what might happen next. Miss Mona had told her everything the police sergeant had told them.

It was the worst possible news ever, and it put Meg on constant guard. Now no one knew where Cleary and the Vanook brothers were; not even the police could find them. She was confined to the ranch. The bad guys were doing anything they wanted. She tried not to be grumpy, but sometimes it was easier to go to her room. Maybe she would take a long walk outside after dark. Surely there would be no danger there.

*

Her heart swelled just looking at it. Hugging her arms, Leslie admired the stone fireplace. The shapes of the rocks, the colors so carefully chosen and arranged—all was a tribute to the artist's life and faith. *It's a masterpiece!* "Great job, Miguel."

"I'll second that comment," said Clive, coming up alongside her. "It's too bad this area is now deprived of his art. I feel blessed to have this last trophy."

Leslie nodded. "I understand. You have a lovely ranch, Clive," she said so matter-of-factly it almost didn't come off as a compliment. She scanned the rustic wood and stone design with earth-toned leather furniture and accessories. "It has a very warm, masculine feel. It's definitely a man's home."

Leslie continued to walk around and familiarize herself with the wall hangings and exquisite sculptures with Clive close at her heels. He seemed unusually quiet, but something in her was suddenly hesitant to turn and look at him. Her heart quickened when his strong, work-calloused hands steered her toward the dining room.

"That comment about this being a man's home, is true, Leslie," he said hoarsely. "This room—the whole house—is missing something. I suspect a woman's influence would soften the look a great deal." He turned her toward him and searched her eyes. "I'm working on that situation, but I have trouble putting things into words."

Her heart sped up to double time. She didn't trust herself to speak, so she held her tongue as they entered the simple, cozy-styled dining room. The rugged pine furniture had a Southwestern feel. A double swinging door opened from the kitchen, and a medium-sized man in a long tie-around apron ushered in a huge platter of BBQ chicken halves, along with a large bowl filled with roasted, herbed potatoes, placing them on the table. The smell alone was enough to make her stomach growl, embarrassing Leslie.

When Clive grinned at her, she looked quickly away. "That's what happens when you totally miss lunch."

The double swinging door opened again and through it sailed Henri O', balancing a heaping salad and a steaming bowl of baked squash. The two women exchanged awkward glances as Henri O' set the food on the table.

Leslie didn't know what to think. Had Clive brought her home only to keep an eye on her? Leslie looked to Clive with question, but he was too busy pulling out her chair.

Multiple questions ran through her mind seeing Schillers' housekeeper at Clive's ranch. Her head turned as Clive's foreman stalked into the dining room from a long hall leading from the back of the ranch house. He flashed a warm smile meant exclusively for Henri O' and hurried over to pull out her chair. Grabbing a chair next to hers, the blond-headed man sat down, nodding a cursory glance toward Leslie.

Clive stood quietly behind the chair to Leslie's left at the end of the table. "Evan, I don't believe you've ever met Leslie Weldon, Leslie, this is my ranch foreman, Evan Robinson." Glancing at Henri O', he chuckled, pointing a finger at her. "When you're invited for dinner, Henri O', we don't expect you to help out in the kitchen. You're Evan's guest."

Henri O's calm expression remained unmoved. "Jimmy was a little rushed tonight. He wasn't expecting so many people." She smiled, looking Leslie's direction.

"Look, if my being here is a problem…," Leslie began, feeling increasingly awkward.

Evan leaned forward. "No, ma'am, it's not you. Henri O' and I are the unexpected guests. Clive only asked us this afternoon. He thought it might be nice for the four of us to dine together."

Leslie felt the color rise from her neck upward. She managed a gracious smile, unable to find adequate words. Clive winked at her and bowed his head. "Let's thank God for our dinner, shall we?"

*

After dinner, Meg paced the length of the house and back, until Mona cornered her in the kitchen with yet another attempt to draw her out of her moodiness. It put her in a bind. She knew Mrs. Schiller was only trying to help, but it had been so long since Meg was able to share her feelings that now they lay bottled up inside like hardened cement. Squirming uncomfortably, she murmured, "It's nothing really, ma'am. I'm just restless, I guess. I think I'll go to my room and read."

She felt Mona's hand on her arm. "Someday I hope you will learn to trust me, Meg. I want to be your friend."

After closing her door, Meg's taut emotions tore at her insides. She'd been afraid she might start screaming at the top of her lungs or break into tears. Long weeks of tension had brought her to the ragged edge. Maybe a cool walk would help.

Grabbing a long-sleeved sweatshirt, she lifted the window sash high. Once she found the screen release, it was simple. Meg swung her long legs through the opening and dropped lightly to the ground below, combing the darkness for a course of direction. The crisp air was just what Meg needed. She enjoyed the tingling sensation on her warm cheeks and couldn't wait for a brisk walk to clear her thoughts. When she'd been forced to move to Georgia with Cleary, her only moments of solitude had been her long walks after dark in the moonlight. One quick glance to the high window she'd exited told her she would have to be creative when returning later.

Rounding the side of the Schiller ranch, Meg plotted a course she knew well. Once she made her way to the road, she would walk down to Leslie's drive and take the farm lane up to the barn. Back when she'd first hidden out in the hayloft, she'd discovered a secluded place behind the big barn where she'd sit and pray.

She would revisit that special spot tonight. When her feet hit the gravel road, she stayed to the far edge, where she'd have a better chance to take cover if the need arose. The moon gave little light on the road, and Meg wished she'd thought to bring a flashlight. It was so dark in the distance where it dead-ended in tall weeds. A shiver raced through her body, but she didn't feel cold. Once again Meg experienced a sudden reluctance to continue. Her mind fogged, remembering the time before when it was discovered that Cleary had been hiding in the weeds.

Brushing her nervousness aside, she reminded herself that she could always run to Leslie's ranch for help if need be. She tried to whistle a hymn, but her mouth was too dry. She walked slower, with caution.

*

The conversation at dinner had been sparse, as if everyone was trying to avoid talking about the elephant in the room—namely the fact there was a killer roaming around, a killer hiding behind a cloak of respectability, bent on accomplishing his goal.

Following the rather quiet meal, Clive rose from his chair. "Evan, if you and Henri O' would be so kind to drive Leslie home, I'd appreciate it. I've got some paperwork that won't wait until tomorrow." His expression was sober. "Sorry Leslie. I'll be up at the ranch as soon as possible. Until then, keep Boris inside, the locks in place, and your cell phone handy."

She smiled at his definite orders. "I'll be fine, Clive. Get your work done and don't worry."

Evan stood quickly, almost knocking over his chair, his sandy-colored hair drooping slightly over his forehead. "Listen, Boss, Henri O' and I can stay with Miss Weldon until you can get there." He shot a quick glance at Henri O' as if to confirm he'd not stepped out of line. Her silent nod assured everyone she was willing.

Leslie pushed up from the table. "Don't be silly, people! We're only talking an hour or so, right? Evan and Henri O' do not need to babysit me, understood?"

Clive's lips pursed. It was evident to Leslie that he would have liked her to accept Evan's offer graciously, without an argument. He nodded. "Fine! Just drive her home, Evan. But watch her closely all the way inside the house."

The corners of Leslie's mouth turned up. Finally, someone was listening to her. She was tired of being a constant burden. She laid down her napkin. "Clive, please tell Jimmy how much I enjoyed his dinner. I'll get my jacket and wait by the door for Evan and Henri O'." Leslie turned away from the table.

*

Zeke was getting antsy, tired of waiting. This Weldon woman was seldom home, and she had more visitors than he'd planned on working around. The police car had thrown him a shocking curve earlier, but he'd stuck it out. The boredom was worse than anything. He'd already downed a half flask of moonshine and the night was young.

He shifted uncomfortably and rolled down his window to part the weeds. He'd driven deep into the grasses so the truck was not noticeable. Now Zeke worried that he wouldn't be able to drive out in a hurry if he had to. He'd make his plan work somehow.

Lifting the flask to his mouth, his hand froze mid-air. He parted more of the grasses. *Am I stoned, or is that Cleary's girl walking down the road—straight to me?* Zeke rubbed his blurry eyes. It was her all right, her straw-colored hair reflected in the moonlight, slight as it was. "Come on, sweetie, come to Uncle Zeke."

His hand slipped behind his back and pulled out the long, skinny knife from his belt. He cracked the door of his truck, slipping unnoticed into the grasses. Crouching down, he waited. *This is going to be easier than I figured. Just maybe I'll take my time first.* The Weldon woman was the major hit, but Cleary's girl was second best, and Zeke wasn't going to pass up an opportunity for a little fun with no one around.

As her footsteps paused briefly, he held his breath until she continued walking forward. Zeke was curious where she'd come from. It was like she'd just appeared. He pinched himself to make sure he wasn't in a drunken stupor or dreaming. It wouldn't be long before the weeds would hide her body well. Just long enough for him to wait for the Weldon woman and bag them both.

Cleary's stepdaughter was only a few feet from the ranch driveway. It was time for him to make his move. He'd grab her in the drive and pull her into the weeds. Glancing down at his dingy-white T-shirt, he regretted his poor choice of colors. White was the easiest color to see at night. Too bad. It was too late to change.

Zeke leaped from the tall grasses into the center of the road, his knife clenched tightly in the palm of his hand. His long legs made lengthy strides to cut the girl off at the drive. Clearly, she hadn't spotted him yet. That would work for him. He chuckled softly.

*

Meg's thoughts were deep, working their way through the last year of painful memories, trying to put some order to her life. It had been a nightmare after mother's death, each year worse with Cleary. She desperately clung to the belief that God's hand was working all things out according to His purpose. Yet her faith felt so small and this night so very dark, she could almost feel an evil presence around her.

Perhaps the walk had not been a good idea. Her imagination was running wild. It took everything inside her to keep moving, but she determined not to give in to her fear. Raising her head, she focused on the driveway ahead. In that same instant she saw him—her worst fear! She'd know Zeke's ugly face and dark shaggy beard anywhere.

Meg scanned the weeds at the side of the road. *Should I try to lose him in the weeds? Oh why did I sneak out without telling anyone? I was so stupid. Is this where I die?* Her legs felt like lead weights locked in place. Fear blocked her thinking.

A truck engine roared to life behind her on the road, and a glaring light engulfed her body, wrapping her in a milky-like cocoon. Zeke's white shirt glowed like a neon sign, his beard making him appear like Satan himself. In the space of a breath, her instincts took over and she whirled, racing back in the direction of the blinding headlights.

*

"Look!" Evan's finger pointed down the length of the gravel road. His foot floored the gas pedal.

Sitting on the window side, Leslie leaned forward and squinted through the highlight glare to the figures on the road. "That's Meg closest to the truck."

"Who's that man in the white shirt?" asked Henri O', pointing beyond Meg to the tall, unkempt figure racing after the girl.

Leslie's gasped. "Zeke Vanook! Hurry, Evan!" Her finger grasped her cell phone. She hit the key for Clive's number. Before he had finished saying hello, she spit out the scene before them. "Help us, Clive!" She hung up.

Evan put on the brakes, skidding sideways to a stop. Shifting to park, he jumped out of the truck and took out running after the white-shirted man who'd turned about and was now tearing back to the end of the road.

Leslie piled out of the truck, heading straight for Meg, who raced into her arms vibrating like a blender on high speed. They clung to each other fiercely, Meg buried her face in Leslie's shoulder. Henri O' had telephoned Mona and Ray and was hastily filling them in. She walked up alongside Meg and Leslie.

Evan jumped into the deep weeds several yards behind Zeke but couldn't catch up before the fleeing man reached his truck door. Just as Zeke's hand yanked open the door, a tall man in total black attire stepped out from the back of the truck bed, leveling a revolver on Zeke's chest.

"Halt! Police! Show both hands out in front of you, palms up." When Zeke ignored the orders and yanked open the truck door, the officer put a well-placed shot mere inches above the handle. "Halt and turn around to face me with your hands showing. Move now before I shoot!"

When Zeke turned palms up, his knife was starkly visible, dropping to the ground. Evan was panting as he stood alongside the police officer. "Need any help?"

The patrolman lifted a handheld radio from his belt and hit a button. "I got me a skunk at the end of the road. Send backup." Glancing at Evan, he nodded. "Thanks, I'm good. Get that girl off the road."

*

The women were waiting by Evan's truck when Clive and the Schillers arrived simultaneously. Together they watched in silence as Evan appeared through a mound of grasses walking to meet them.

*

Sergeant Ford poured himself a mug of strong coffee and turned to face the assembled group around Leslie's front table. He blew on the steaming brew, sipping it gingerly. "When this case is finished, I will miss our little get-togethers," he said dryly. "Lately, I'm seeing more of you than I am my three kids!"

Clive was the only one who attempted a smile; the rest remained sober and tense. Sipping a large gulp, the sergeant set his mug on the counter with apparent reluctance. He ruffled his hair, drew in a breath, and glanced around the ring of faces before speaking.

"Zeke Vanook will be out of public life for some time. He was caught trespassing with a knife in his hand while pursing Miss McDonald, here. Attempted murder is just the beginning." Ford's eyes once again surveyed the rapt faces before him.

"Unfortunately Zeke was the only one we found, and he's not inclined to be chatty about the whereabouts of the others. Oh, we'll do a little threatening and try to tie him to the explosions, but I honestly don't think he's ever met the man in charge."

"Do you think Cleary is still around the area, Sergeant Ford?" Meg asked meekly, her eyes still wide with the night's trauma.

"We don't know for sure, Meg. The APB is still out on him, but only for questioning, I'm afraid," he said gently. "We're doing all we can." His focus moved to Leslie. "I had a man staked out here tonight, which in hindsight proved to be a prudent move. I'll keep him on duty at night as long as possible, but you have to understand, Miss Weldon, at some point I will have to pull him." Ford seemed apologetic.

She shook her head, dismissing his words. "I'm more concerned about Roger Galbraith at present. I haven't had a chance to check in with the hospital today. Is he still in a coma? Do you have someone protecting him?" Leslie asked, anxiously.

"Mr. Galbraith remains in a coma, but the doctors maintain it's still too early to tell. Yes, we do have a man guarding his room. About the fire in his office, we're waiting on a final report. The chief thinks the fire began with a small explosive attached to the electrical unit." Ford raked his hand through his hair and picked up his mug.

"What about the break-in at Roger's apartment?" Leslie pressed.

Finishing his coffee, he looked at the empty cup with a hint of sadness. "Nothing! No fingerprints. The apartment was tossed, but the housekeeper can't list anything taken. The key to this series of crimes is connected somehow to this ranch and the land. I would be most appreciative if anyone can shed light on this matter.

Leslie debated whether or not she should share what she and Miguel had talked about. What if they were totally wrong? She stood to address the small assembly. "Bear in mind, I don't have anything concrete—just speculations gleaned from early ranch journals. One in particular was written by the original owner, Jamie Cohen; another was Wayne's own writings."

Every eye focused on her face.

Leslie voiced her thoughts. "Gold. I believe the desire for gold is the reason behind everything. This ranch is a unique situation. It was not shut down because the bulk of accessible gold was played out. Tragedy closed the Cohen mine. Today the mine remains buried as it stood, with most of its gold intact—if we can believe the journal." Drawing in a deep breath, Leslie looked at Henri O'. "I—we—believe someone of power, with the means and backing to purse the reopening of the mine, has been patiently plotting to gain total control of the ranch."

"How would that be profitable in this day with miles of red tape and environmental pressures using restrictions like a power vise?" asked Sergeant Ford.

Everyone at the table leaned forward as if they wondered the same thing.

"This is where it gets sticky. I'm quoting secondhand information here. But according to rumors there might be a new chemical break-through that could possibly eliminate a good part of the problem. The price of gold is high, as everyone knows. Perhaps it is high enough to make the risk acceptable. All of this is speculation," she said.

"Even so, that might explain a lot, especially the digging up on Rocky Ridge. They've been looking for the closed mine," mused Ford, more to himself than anyone in particular. He looked at everyone. "It's not over yet. If Miss Weldon is correct, the man pulling the strings can't afford to pull out now. There's too much at stake. It's my guess that he's arrogant enough to think he can still pull his irons out of the fire, so to speak. Stay close and watch out for each other. I'll leave a man on guard tonight. Call my office if you think of anything. Stay alert," he urged, reaching for his hat.

"And pray," added Leslie softly.

When Clive reached for her hand, she didn't pull it away.

*

Clive untied Boris and led him inside the ranch house for the night. Everyone left with mixed emotions and somber thoughts. Under Clive's guidance, the group had prayed together after Sergeant Ford took his leave.

Mona lingered to encourage Leslie. "Don't lose faith."

"Sometimes I'm afraid it will disappear completely...and that scares me."

"Hold tight to Jesus. He will never let go of you. He promises to never leave or forsake us," Mona added.

Together they walked as sisters to the back door. Mona took hold of Leslie's hand. "You need to pray for Meg tonight. She was forced to look her worst nightmare in the face, and that's scary! It might be a rough night for her."

Leslie nodded. "I have the feeling it won't be long before this thing comes to a head. I sense it." The women turned as Clive returned with the big hairy dog, who strained at his collar to rush to Leslie's side.

"Well, well, I'd say this dog has attached his loyalties to the fair Miss Weldon. Like it or not, Leslie, you have a dog! Treat him right, and he'll be your friend forever."

Leslie glanced at Mona, who knew her concern about being forced to leave the ranch and Boris.

While Clive fed Boris his dinner, Leslie went to clean up the kitchen and wash the coffee cups. She was close to the phone when it rang and answered with apprehension. Miguel's low voice took her by surprise. She wondered if he'd already heard about the happenings on Dunn Road.

"I've found the picture, Leslie. I couldn't wait to tell you. It's the picture Wayne took the night of my birthday party months before he died. This picture may hold the answer to our mystery. Wayne's photo includes several people in the background. Either by accident or design is for you to determine. Come when you can, but don't linger. If news of this picture leaks out, it could be dangerous for all of us."

"Who all is included in the background, Miguel?" Apprehension rose.

"Come soon, Miss Leslie. Good night."

"Miguel?" Leslie called as he hung up.

"What is it?" asked Clive, coming through from the breezeway.

"I'm not sure what all it means." She stared out the window over the sink into darkness, wondering if it was possible the identity of Wayne's secret friend could have been caught in the birthday photo. It lined up with the journal entry. Had Wayne hid his evidence in a memory photo for all to see? Was her cousin that clever?

But if Wayne's killer knew about the photo, that would explain why Wayne's file cabinet was searched and her dad's personal papers rifled through in her New York apartment. If Miguel was right, it wouldn't be wise to wait too long to check out.

Shifting from the sink, she saw Clive making his way toward Wayne's old bedroom and a well-deserved rest. "Clive, wake me in the morning. I'll fix you breakfast before you leave for the ranch. You're in luck; Mona gave me two dozen fresh eggs. I may not be a gourmet, but I'm able to scramble eggs," she added brightly.

"It might be worth it just to watch you try," replied Clive, chuckling as he turned the knob to the room. "Good night."

She switched off the kitchen light and looked down at the bristly dog lying at her feet. Leslie had seen Clive's questioning gaze after Miguel's call, yet he hadn't pressured her for information. The fact he trusted her to tell him in good time encouraged her to reciprocate that trust. Did he realize how difficult it was for her?

"Come on, Boris, it's time we turned in." The day had been one of the longest she'd remember in years. Leslie ruffled the fur on the top of his head.

Walking the long hall, she promised herself she'd rise early and call her New York friend Diane, but it wouldn't be the easy call she'd looked forward to. How could she catch her perceptive friend up on all that had happened and yet not worry her? *Diane has always been able to read me, even over the phone.*

24

The Coma

LESLIE CLUNG TO THE SIDE OF THE VEHICLE as Clive wheeled the truck off Dunn Road and headed toward town. With her free hand her fingers combed through strands of her wild hair, wondering if she'd taken time to brush her teeth before leaving. The early morning call from Sergeant Ford had stamped *rush* on their routine. "He's awake! Galbraith is out of the coma. That's all I know, so don't ask any questions."

"Honestly, Clive, you didn't need to drive me in to the hospital. What about your work? Your ranch can't run itself. I could have driven myself in easily. It's daylight, for goodness' sake!"

"It's too early to argue, Leslie, and I'm far too hungry. Don't worry about my work; Mona is planning on meeting us in an hour and a half to drive you home. About that daylight protection...how did that work out for you and Mona yesterday in town? You have a short memory, Miss Weldon."

Leslie had tried to block yesterday from her mind. "Sorry about breakfast, Clive. I *was* planning on something nice. I even took bacon out to thaw."

He glanced away long enough to grin. "We'll find something at the hospital...a vending machine if all else fails. I hope Galbraith can shed some light on this whole nasty business. If he'll reveal the names of the investors who offered to purchase the ranch, it might be the big break the police are looking for."

Leslie frowned. "It's bigger than that, Clive. One of the so-called investors requested for Roger to go out to Rocky Ridge, supposedly to get a better understanding about the strange occurrences and illegal digging. That someone he spoke with was actually ordering him to his death—along with me, of course. Roger knows the name of that someone. I'm concerned that his life is in grave danger."

"Do you care about Galbraith so very much?"

"Well, don't you? How can you not care that a person's life is being threatened—even Roger? I know you don't like him, but..." Leslie probed for a clue to understand.

"That's not what I meant, Leslie. I'm questioning how deep your feelings go for this man. You've been making excuses for him from the start. Do you love Galbraith?"

Leslie wasn't sure why it irritated her to be pressed about her feelings, but it did. "Now isn't the time for this, Clive. We have answers to find, and life and death issues to consider."

They arrived at the hospital in static silence, but Leslie didn't know how to rectify the situation. When Clive dropped her off at the door, she almost felt relief as she hurried through the large glass doors to the information desk.

Clive caught up with Leslie in the Intensive Care Unit. She was waiting in one of three chairs sitting along the hall and looked up when he took the chair next to her. "Which room is he in?" he asked.

Leslie pointed to the furthest room at the end of the hall. "An officer is stationed outside his room," she whispered.

Clive leaned in. "Will they allow you to go in and see him?"

"Hopefully. I was told they are busy changing the bed and giving him a bath. The nurse said his vitals were good this morning. Apparently, he awoke sometime after midnight. They called Sergeant Ford right away. "

Looking down at his watch, Clive nudged her. "I was told the cafeteria is still serving breakfast but only for a short time. Why don't we eat something while they are working with him?"

She was so eager to find clues at first she was hesitant to leave. Then good sense reigned. "Why not? Maybe by the time we get back, he'll be ready for company. His father's too ill to travel, and he doesn't have any close family nearby. I'm hopeful they'll let me in to see him."

Clive rose. "Let's hurry before they close the doors. I could smell the coffee when I passed the hall."

Leslie chuckled. "I'm with you. It'll beat machine coffee any day."

Walking beside Clive felt easy and good again. She assumed he was anxious to set aside the awkwardness between them—as was she. Sneaking a glance his way caused her to wonder if Clive could be jealous. *Is that why he asked how I feel about Roger? Am I that dense?* The thought increased her pulse rate.

*

Twenty minutes later Leslie and Clive approached Roger's hospital room, only to have the officer at the door ask their names. Leslie noted the patrolman's clipboard with a printed list, hoping their names were among them.

"You're been cleared by Sergeant Ford to see Mr. Galbraith, Miss Weldon, and so has Mr. Masters, but the IC unit has a short visiting period you'll have to abide by," said the officer. His name tag read *Frank Wilson.*

Tiptoeing into the dimly lit hospital room, Leslie first saw Roger's pale face, badly scraped along the entire left portion. A light head bandage extended over the whole right side of his head. His forehead was bandaged also. She felt for his pain. It was a miracle he was still alive. It was a miracle she had missed his fate.

Roger's near-white complexion and closed eyes gave her a start, until she reminded herself he was very much alive. Walking to the right side of his bed, she gently called, "Roger? It's Leslie." She glanced back at Clive, who waited by the door.

Turning back, she stared into Roger's puzzled gaze. He blinked as if he were trying to clear his vision. "Le—Li-ly?"

Leslie couldn't hide her alarm. Just how badly hurt was he? "Yes, Roger, it's Leslie. Remember me?"

Dr. Proctor walked briskly into the room and came up on his left. "I see you are rejoining the world, Roger. Can you tell me your name this morning?"

Roger's cracked lips parted slightly, but nothing came out. "'ame?" he finally managed.

"Your name is...," the doctor prompted.

Roger's eyes narrowed as if he were considering the question.

"Don't worry. Let everything come back slowly," the doctor encouraged. Looking at Leslie, she indicated for her to follow her out of the room. Leslie complied.

The doctor regarded Clive as he walked up alongside Leslie and nodded. "Are you family of Mr. Galbraith?"

"Friends," Clive responded before Leslie could say anything.

"What's wrong with him, Doctor? Will he be all right?" asked Leslie.

Glancing down at papers in her file, she paused. "Head trauma cases are difficult to pinpoint, but the next few days will tell us a lot. Roger has Post Traumatic Amnesia."

Leslie and Roger exchanged glances. Clive inquired, "What all does that entail?"

Dr. Proctor opened her folder and pointed to a picture of a human brain. "Roger's injury is in these areas, the Frontal Lobe and the left Temporal Lobe. These control selective attention, personality, problem solving, as well as his enunciation or ability to speak and remember people, names, etc. From his actions I believe he is also having some difficulty with his vision."

"How long will this last?" Leslie exclaimed. "I mean, he will recover?"

"We are extremely hopeful he will recover in all these areas." Her smile was reassuring. "A few days of therapy should help a great deal. We'll know more then. Good news is, I believe we'll be able to start him on a soft diet beginning with his lunch this noon. If he appears to do all right with that, it will be a good sign."

"Thank you, Doctor." Clive steered Leslie off to the side as the doctor quickly made her way to the nurses' station.

"What do you think about leaving? There's really no reason for you to remain, Leslie. He doesn't even know who you are right now. You can do more good at home. I can call Mona and tell her you'll be riding back with me."

Leslie felt conflicted. Her eyes lifted to Roger's room as she debated Clive's logical suggestion. As appealing as it seemed, something tugged at her, a reluctance to leave quite yet. "I appreciate the offer, Clive, but I'll stick here awhile longer. Thanks." She touched his arm, feeling the strength of his muscles through his shirt.

Clive leaned close to her ear. "Remember Ford's warning. Please stay where there are lots of witnesses." He kissed her cheek so lightly, she doubted his lips had actually touched her.

As she lifted her hand to her cheek, Clive disappeared into the flowing crowd heading for the elevator. She watched the numbers as the elevator descended, knowing he'd soon leave the building. Almost instantly, she experienced a sense of loneliness and was forced to admit his very presence provided her with a cloak of caring protection that was easy to bask in.

Dismissing the thought, she whirled about and headed back to the chairs in the hallway. There was a perfectly good waiting room around the corner, but Leslie wanted to be within viewing distance of Roger's room. Why, she wasn't exactly sure.

Procuring a magazine from the waiting room, she resumed her seat. Her watch told her Mona wouldn't be there for at least half an hour. Leaning back against the chair, she barely glanced at the magazine, choosing instead to watch the flow of hospital traffic.

Minutes passed like small lifetimes. Then something vaguely familiar caught her attention. The hospital hall was the normal bustling scene it had been all morning. Aides and nurses in scrubs were everywhere with an occasional doctor lingering at the nurses' station. But Leslie had seen a familiar profile for just an instant. It frightened her. She squinted, unable to bring the person in question into her visual scope. Her heart raced.

Her eyes frantically searched the hallway in small increments until she spotted that sharp profile. She sucked in air, realizing it was the man from the restaurant in New York. His medium height allowed him to blend in with the general mass in green scrubs wearing surgical head coverings. Watching in disbelief, she saw the scene as if in slow motion. Her breath stayed frozen somewhere between her lungs and her throat.

The sharp-featured man strode with confidence down the corridor in the direction of Roger's hospital room. Carrying an innocuous-looking food tray, he flowed in and around medical personal without drawing a second look. It was too early for lunch, but no one seemed to notice. He was almost to the threshold of Roger's room. Something was grossly wrong. There was no officer stationed at the door, no one to stop this dangerous man.

I've got to stop him, her brain screamed, as the daze-like veil fell from the real scene taking place in front of her. Dropping the magazine, Leslie bolted a few feet and stopped, debating what to do first. From the corner of her eye, she spotted Officer Frank Wilson coming from the far right. He was straightening his clothes and slowly making his way back to his post.

She tore toward him. In seconds Leslie had related enough to make the man snap to attention with new purpose. He called in for backup and unsnapped his gun holster. "Wait down the hall, and keep everyone out of that room!" he ordered quietly. Turning, the grim-faced officer entered Roger's room with his gun drawn.

Leslie waited with the nurses. In seconds the bustling hall became hushed and statuesque in suspense. Only an occasional odd sound could be heard emitting from distant rooms down the hall. The silence from Roger's room was the most distracting.

What is happening? Every muscle in Leslie's body strained to remain still. She lost track of how long she'd been holding her breath, her nails digging into the flesh of her palms. Not a single person ventured near the room.

All heads snapped around when the elevator door opened. All elevators had been put on hold for police use with exceptions for medical emergencies. Four policemen charged from the opened elevator door and rushed down the hall toward Roger's room. Leslie backed away and stood with the staff.

Minutes later the sharp-featured man was led out of the room in handcuffs. Passing Leslie, he gaped at her as if she'd appeared in a nightmare. She stared back at the man who had dogged her footsteps all the way from New York. She didn't know what to make of his strange expression—a mix of confusion and surprise. *Didn't he know I could identify him? He must not have noticed I was in the hall. Was it only by chance he was in the booth behind Diane and me that day in New York?* Leslie didn't believe in chance; neither did she have an answer to her many questions.

By the time the all-clear signal was given and hospital routine resumed its normal schedule, Mona had arrived, finding Leslie more than ready to leave.

"Not yet," said Sergeant Ford, striding toward Leslie. After hospital staff confirmed the sharp-featured man was not an employee, Leslie was escorted into a small office by the nurses' station where she was asked question after question. At length she was released. "I'd appreciate you coming by the station later to sign a statement," he added.

Leslie nodded, sending Mona an apologetic look. She'd started for the door when Ford lifted a restraining hand. "We'll be testing the food the suspect was carrying into Galbraith's room. Since he was not found with any weapon on his person, the food becomes suspect. We'll know more after test results come back."

"We're just glad he's going to be locked up, Sergeant," said Mona, standing alongside Leslie.

By the time the women reached the parking lot, Leslie was anxious to collapse in the front seat next to Mona and allow her mind to go numb.

Mona had heard the whole story sitting in on Leslie's questioning session. "I'm glad he's finally off the street, Leslie. It's safer for everyone. Maybe they can find out from him who's behind everything."

Her pixie-like face grew thoughtful. "Especially since Roger is not able to be very helpful at this point. Hopefully his memory will come back quickly. I'd say someone else was afraid what Roger might start to remember as well. I can't help but wonder what that horrid man had planned to do to him."

Mona's comment about the man behind everything brought back the memory of Miguel's late night phone call. Leslie turned in her seat to stare at her friend, adrenaline surging through her. "Mona, we've got to go over to Miguel Romero's!"

"Now?" Mona exclaimed, startled.

*

It was almost 2:00 p.m. when Mona turned into the snake-like drive of Miguel Romero's log cabin. Leslie was collecting their fast-food debris into one bag. Mona pulled her little truck close to the wide steps leading up the cabin. "Leslie, are you going to tell me what all this is about? I've got a heap of chores to attend to at home."

"I'm sorry, Mona, I'll try to make this stop as short as possible. Miguel thinks he might have a photo that can shed light on who might be the person calling the shots."

Leslie rapped twice on the door, but there was no answer. She and Mona looked anxiously from one to another.

"Where could he have gone?" asked Mona.

Leslie tried not to think the worse, but the events of recent days made her fearful. "I don't know, Mona. It's not easy for Miguel to go anywhere." She pounded, greatly relieved to see the door open slowly. His narrowed eyes peered out at her suspiciously. "Miguel? What's wrong?"

"I had a visitor a couple of hours ago—a big man with a face shaped like a box of cereal and just as big. Come on in." Miguel turned his wheelchair around and wheeled himself into the center of the rustic living area.

When both women sat across from him, Miguel nodded at Mona. "Glad to have you visit, Miss Mona. Henri O' tells me you've all been having quite a time of it."

"Thank you, Miguel. Every day brings some new terrifying occurrence. It's like a horrid dream," she said wearily.

"Something else happen today?" Miguel's black eyes flashed in concern.

Leslie leaned forward. "We'll fill you in before we go. Finish telling us what happened with the big guy. Was he wearing cowboy boots with snake designs?" she asked, remembering the so-called investor who had tried to pressure her into selling.

Miguel's bronzed wrinkles plowed like furrows. "I heard his car engine, then watched this mammoth climb my porch stairs. Something told me he was up to no good, so I purposely didn't answer his pounding on my door. I hoped he'd give up and go away, but when I heard him messing with my door lock, it was time for action."

"What happened?" Mona injected.

"I waited while he picked my lock. The first thing he saw when he opened my door was my twelve-gauge shotgun leveled at him through the screen. I cocked that gun as loudly as possible and told him he had thirty seconds to get his sorry self off my porch and off my land."

"And...?" Leslie prodded.

"And he left. Anyone like a cup of coffee? I just perked a new pot. Henri O' isn't the only one who can make good-tasting coffee."

"I'd love a cup of coffee, Miguel, but first I'd like to see that photo you found. I find it interesting that twelve hours after you phoned me about that photo, your box-faced friend showed up." Leslie stared at the landline phone sitting on the kitchen counter. "Has anyone been around working on your phone lately?"

Miguel regarded her with admiration, an awareness clouding his countenance. "There was a man from the phone company. He came around shortly after Wayne died. Henri O' and I lead a quiet life, neither having need of the house phone except for doctor appointments and such. Henri O' calls me on her cell most of the time." Miguel pulled his own cell phone from his sweater pocket to show them.

"Do you by any chance remember what that telephone man looked like?" questioned Leslie.

"He was a strange little man. Kept his face tucked down under his wide hat, but I noticed he was built slight and had a pointed nose. I remember specifically because he was one of the few people I've never been able to engage in conversation." Miguel flashed a sly smile. "It gets lonely way out here, and I take advantage of visitors, be they phone installers or TV repairmen." He laughed, sobering quickly when he noticed their strained faces. "Why? Do you know him?"

Exchanging a knowing glance with Leslie, Mona nodded. "I feel like I'm living *Mission Impossible.*" She rose from the mission oak chair and went to the phone on the counter. Lifting the receiver, Mona unscrewed the plastic cover and examined inside. She motioned Leslie over and pointed to a funny looking device. Leslie raised her eyebrows and whispered, "You think?"

Mona nodded. "Could be?" She carefully extracted the device, raising it high for Miguel to see.

"Throw it in the garbage," he called curtly, rolling his chair over to the bookcase.

Pulling out a worn copy of the Bible, he rolled back and called the girls over to their chairs. Mona smiled, dropping the device in a half glass of water before following Leslie. "Let that sit for a spell, Miguel. You should call Sergeant Ford about your visit from the box-faced man and the man with a pointed nose. "

Leslie held the photo up to get the maximum light and smiled softly. Miguel and Henri O' were in party mode, dressed in their finest, situated beside a table lined with slightly blurred balloons. You could tell it was a joyful occasion by their happy smiles, but the composition was dreadfully off kilter.

The picture had been so centered that Miguel and Henri O' took up only half of the picture. The other half absorbed the dark background of the restaurant, including a separate party of individuals.

The look of surprise on the featured men in the background told Leslie that they knew they'd been caught on camera. The man with a deer-in-the-headlights expression was none other than Jonathon Hager, vice president of the bank, and just beside him was the stark, shocked profile of the bank president himself, Hamilton Longworth.

Rotating her hand so she could see the writing on the back, Leslie read "Special and unofficial friends." She was frustrated. "Which one of them is it—or is it both?"

Miguel shook his head slowly. "No, I think it is only one."

"Which one?" she murmured. Leslie didn't want it to be Hamilton Longworth, but he was the one she'd seen exiting Roger's office on more than one occasion. Closing her eyes, she briefly shut out the image.

She counted to ten and reopened them to see the photo with a fresh approach. Jonathon Hager was the one whose face was center focused. Still, it was possible Hamilton tried to turn away just prior to the camera flashing to avoid being caught on film. Disappointment mounted. Leslie had hoped for more solid evidence.

Remembering her previous encounters with the bank officials, Jonathon Hager appeared to be an unimposing little man, someone she knew little about. She'd heard he was a good worker who didn't like the spotlight, unlike Hamilton Longworth, who obviously enjoyed being front and center, interacting with people. She wondered what he did behind the scenes. Did the man lead a double life? It wouldn't be the first time.

She recalled the luncheon in Dahlonega. The man she'd heard at the table spoke with such vicious authority, her head spun to think it could be either one of the two men. It was hard to connect such a forceful sounding personality with Hager, but Longworth was another matter entirely. Yet the entire idea sickened her. She pointed to the two men in the background. "One of those two men is a killer."

Mona looked shocked. "Leslie, all of this is a little hard to believe. I've known Hamilton Longworth for years. He's a fine man, and Jonathon Hager is always the first in the community to volunteer for a good cause and never seeks credit. I'm more inclined to believe there's been a mix-up where those two are concerned."

"You can't have it both ways, Mona. Somebody ordered a hit on Roger at that restaurant table yesterday. There were two men left at the table discussing the details. If you dismiss Longworth or Hager from the equation, that only leaves the realtor and the New York lawyer, Jack somebody, and that doesn't fit."

"Criswell, Jack Criswell," Mona injected, frowning. "All right, I'll keep an open mind, but it seems improbable. Remember, you're going on voices only, no visual confirmation. What exactly does this writing mean on the back of the photo: *unofficial friends?"* She pointed to the scrawled words.

"It's a quote from Wayne's journal—a quote with great significance," replied Leslie soberly. Glancing at the glass on the counter, she walked over and fished out the electronic device with two fingers. Turning, she asked, "Mind if I take this with me?"

The women left Miguel Romero with a twelve-gauge across his lap. "Tread lightly, ladies," he warned. "Things have heated up, and this man is desperate! When a methodical man is desperate, he makes mistakes. My prayers go with you."

*

"Do you want me to take you to the police station? You have to sign that statement," Mona reminded her brooding friend sitting in the seat next to her.

Leslie pushed herself up from her slumped position. "I appreciate your offer, but I've kept you from your work most of the day. No! Before I go see Sergeant Ford, I need to collect a few items—not to mention my thoughts," she said wearily.

Mona nodded. "Okay, but after you collect your items, call. Someone will go with you. It's not safe to go anywhere alone."

"Who is going to attack me at the police department?" Leslie raised her eyebrows.

"You're extremely vulnerable going and coming," Mona said, exasperated.

Leslie rotated her neck to relieve tension. "I hear you. I just don't see it."

*

Leslie's adrenaline raced from the time she hit the breezeway door. She lingered long enough to watch Boris sprint for the lane leading up to the big barn as soon as she let him outside. He was magnificent to watch with his powerful legs. *Enjoy, Boy. You're going to be inside all night again.* Heading for Wayne's old office, she gathered everything she could think of, then reached for her jacket.

Remembering Mona's words of warning, she called Clive's ranch. Jimmy, his cook, answered with noticeable irritation. It was obvious Leslie had caught him at a busy moment. Discovering that Clive was outside working with his horses, she apologized for interrupting. A direct call to Clive's cell reached voicemail. *I tried, Mona, but everyone is too busy!*

An underlying nervousness caused her to check her rearview mirror repeatedly on the drive in to the sheriff's office. Sergeant Ford was on the phone when Leslie was told to go on inside. Deep lines of fatigue and stress were etched across his face. After he lowered the phone, he crossed his arms, leaning back in his worn leather chair.

"I've got a rundown on your little man at the hospital, Morey Santana." Ford flipped open a file. "Morey has done time twice before and had his finger in about everything imaginable. He was picked up once on suspicion of murder, but they couldn't make it stick. His file indicates he likes to work with a partner and has had several in the course of his history. Morey likes to pick the big, brawny kind to make up for his lack of prowess—someone to do the intimidation, if necessary."

"Someone like William Gaetzi, my so-called 'investor'?" Leslie asked.

"Could be. We won't know for sure until we pick up Mr. Gaetzi and compare notes. Morey isn't doing any talking yet, but we might get more out of him later. Some of them wait until we offer them a deal. We let him make his one phone call, but so far his lawyer hasn't arrived."

"Is that who he called, his lawyer?" asked Leslie.

"We have no way of knowing. We sent the hospital food tray down to forensic for tests. Those results will come in later."

Leslie looked curious. "What was on the tray?"

"Standard stuff: Mashed potatoes, red Jello, and some apple juice thickened with nectar. Apparently they use that junk in liquids for patients they are afraid might choke."

So why had Santana carried the tray in? Was it simply a prop to get inside the room and then make his move against Roger, or was the food poisoned? Looking down at the folder on her lap, she walked to the edge of Ford's desk, dropping the folder in front of him. "I've brought you some reading material."

Sergeant Ford securitized Leslie, eyeing the folder with suspicion. "What's this?"

Leslie walked around to his side of the desk and placed the party photo in front of him. "Wayne took this shortly before he died. He and Miguel Romero were close friends for years. I believe this photo is the connecting dot to Wayne's coded references in his journal to his 'unofficial friend.' "

"Unofficial friend?" Ford breathed a weary sigh.

"It's all in Wayne's journal. His friend was powerful but didn't want anyone to know who he was. It's all pretty freaky!" Leslie flipped through the journal to the beginning section dealing with the secret friend. She pointed again to the photo and explained the when and where. "Notice what's written on the back.

While Ford was studying the picture and the writing on the back, Leslie told him all that had transpired at Miguel Romero's before they arrived earlier in the day. She pointed to the more obscure portion of the photo. "It's obvious that both Jonathon Hager and Hamilton Longworth are aware their picture is being taken. And this is what we found in Miguel's phone. While I was driving in, I remembered Miguel called me about the photo late the night before."

Ford picked up the device with a pair of tweezers and dropped it into a plastic bag. "I'll have it checked out." He seemed distracted.

Leslie hesitated before speaking, "I thought Miguel's description of his aggressive visitor most interesting, especially when it lined up with my investor, Mr. Gaetzi."

Ford's gaze lingered on the photo. "Um, which one is the 'unofficial friend'?" When Leslie didn't answer, Ford looked up at her. "You don't know. This photo is interesting, and I'll read the journal sections, but as evidence...? It's not concrete."

Leslie nodded, suddenly depressed.

Rocking back and forth in his desk chair, Sergeant Ford rubbed his lips. "But it's intriguing to note someone thought it was important enough to try to get it back. Continue to keep your eyes open for anything else and keep this information to yourself for the moment." He looked around. "Who came with you?"

Leslie's eyes dropped. "Ah, no one. Everyone was busy and I thought...I checked my mirrors often, and no one followed me."

"Go home, Miss Weldon, and call me when you get there to let me know. Keep someone with you in the future. After that little episode at the hospital, I decided to pull the man off detail at your place and put him with Frank Wilson at the hospital guarding Galbraith. Be extra careful. I'll read this section of the journal and send it back with a patrolman later today."

25

The Painful Act of Recall

SATURDAY MORNING WAS QUIET. Leslie slept in and took her leisure time with breakfast and household chores. Boris stayed where she stayed and moved where she moved. Clive rose early as usual and let the dog out when he left, but the faithful animal was at the door when Leslie ventured out of her room.

The weather was too beautiful to stay home, so Leslie piled Boris in the SUV and drove down the road to Mona's. Her foot was so much better she found the distance outside to the chicken pens an easy stretch. Pausing at a distance, Leslie observed Meg in action with her sleeves rolled up and her jeans dusty from hard work with the chickens. The transformation was remarkable. Gone was the pinched look. Her cheeks were filling out, becoming tanned and rosy from hours in the sun. A new prettiness was replacing Meg's once tight features.

Seeing Leslie, Mona leaned her rake against a fence and ambled over to sit on a crate. Reaching inside a cooler filled with ice and cold drinks, Mona pulled out a frosty bottle of water. "Have you heard anything more from the sergeant since yesterday?"

"No. He told me it would take time for test results to come back. That little man who tried to mess with your truck is named Morey Santana. He has a prison record. The sergeant indicated they planned on questioning him at length today." Leslie wondered if Mona knew she'd driven into town on her own. The woman had an invisible antenna.

Meg turned to wave at Leslie. She returned the effort, marveling at the girl's exuberance. "She seems to enjoy working with your chickens."

Swigging down half of the bottle, Mona wiped her mouth on her shirt sleeve. "She does! At first I thought she was only trying to impress me, or to pay for her room and board, but now I actually believe she enjoys the work itself—hard worker, too."

As Leslie leaned down to pick out a bottle of cola, her cell phone rang in her right jacket pocket. Abandoning the cola, she lifted her cell. "Yes?" She paled as she listened. "Thanks for calling me, Sergeant. Yes, I'm trying to stay around people, and I'll keep my cell phone with me at all times." Shutting down her phone, her mouth hung open. "Morey Santana died last night. They think it might have been a heart attack. The sergeant tried to shake him awake this morning and found he wasn't breathing."

"A heart attack? That's pretty weird—the same night he was arrested. Are they sure?"

"Sergeant Ford sounded funny-like. He said there'd been a big mix-up at the jail last night. An officer on loan from Atlanta was working at the jail. It seems one of the regular night officers was out sick yesterday, and they called around for a substitute. After midnight a rowdy drunk was brought in and supposedly wrongly stashed in Santana's cell." Leslie paused. "When the mistake was discovered hours later, they pulled him out of the cell and, by early morning, he'd already made bail and was gone. Everyone thought Santana was sleeping hard...until breakfast, when his death was discovered."

"You think this Santana was killed purposely—in the jail? That's pretty gutsy! If it's true, I'd say that, whoever the boss is, he's able to make things happen fast. He's not too keen on witnesses, either."

Leslie shivered, realizing afresh how many times she'd come close to the same fate. If only Roger would wake up and share what he knew about his secret friend... The news from the hospital reported Roger was undergoing therapy. His alertness had increased, but his speech remained garbled.

"Would you be willing to go with me to visit Roger later today?" she asked Mona. "If he sees people he knows, hopefully it will stimulate his mind to remember. He's got to remember! He knows who sent him to Rocky Ridge."

Mona studied her friend's somber expression. "Perhaps! But remember that Roger's office was burned, along with all his files."

"That makes it all the more important for Roger to regain his memory. The only evidence may be locked in his mind."

Mona glanced at her watch. "How about 3:00 p.m. today?"

"I'll drive back and pick you up," said Leslie, gaining momentum. She pushed herself off the crate and started to walk away.

"Could I interest you in staying for supper when we return?" Mona smiled.

Leslie sighed. "I think the general feeling around here is I'd starve without regular handouts."

Mona tilted her head. "Do you wanna stay for supper or not?"

"I'll stay. And thanks." Leslie grinned and headed toward her vehicle.

Pausing at the end of the Schillers' driveway, Leslie turned into Clive's ranch on a whim. His circular winding drive led past the ranch house and out past the barns teaming with activity. She spotted the extended, fenced, pastured land to the left of two long horse barns and parked close to the fence. Climbing out of her SUV, she strolled toward the white fence, mesmerized by the sleek animals grazing in the field. Leaning against the fence, she peered between the boards to observe the playfulness of the newest foals.

"They're beautiful, aren't they?"

Leslie didn't have to turn her head to know who stood beside her. "Yes. They're fine animals. It's like poetry to watch them run or jump...like ballet dancers on stage."

Clive settled against the fence alongside her. "That's a first! I've never heard them compared to ballet dancers before. The big stallion over there might take offense."

She grinned. "Then don't tell him." For some reason she wanted to be happy today—to be around people, to squeeze every bit of life from each moment. It suddenly seemed a sin to her to take for granted the gift of simply breathing in and out. Life was fragile and lost in a heartbeat.

"To what do I attribute the honor of your visit this fair day?" She peered at him as he shoved his hat forward, his face glistening with preparation.

"I was on my way home from Mona's," she explained, "and found myself turning toward your ranch."

"A normal reaction," he said, smirking. "Anyway, I'm glad you did. How about a short drive around my ranch?"

"As long as I'm back by 2:30 p.m. Mona and I are going to the hospital." Leslie sobered, recalling the reality of imminent danger. "Let's go for a ride, Cowboy. I don't want to waste any part of this day."

He scrutinized her. "Did something else happen, Leslie? Tell me!"

Her lips trembled. "That skinny man they caught at the hospital yesterday, Morey Santana—he's dead! He died last night in jail. Can you believe it? " She tried to laugh, but nothing came out.

"An accident?" he asked.

"Oh, I wish! It looked like an accident. A drunk was accidentally placed in his cell for a short time and then whisked away to who knows where. The drunk amazingly made bail before morning and disappeared. They're doing an autopsy on Morey Santana, probably as we speak."

Clive whistled. "Sounds suspicious. Someone could have staged a plant. Let's go for that ride." He led the way back to his truck.

In a short time they'd driven by extended pastures filled with thoroughbreds. Leslie had rolled down the window allowing the wind to blow free through her untied hair. It was liberating and reminiscent of their ride to

Rocky Point. Rounding a sweeping curve, Clive steered the truck off the ranch road onto a one-lane weed-filled path through dense shrubbery.

Overgrown shoots stretched out as if to entrap their truck. Driving slow over ruts and rough ground, they emerged into a cleared opening that resembled Tarzan's jungle paradise, waterfall and all. A rustic picnic table blended into the natural feel of the rugged beauty. Drawing in a deep breath, Leslie held it in as her eyes drank in the secluded hideaway. As she gradually exhaled, her worries drifted away to some mystical place. "How lovely!" she exclaimed, slightly breathless.

"Climb out and come sit by the pond. I had fish stocked here a couple of years ago, in case I want to stay and fish. I can't afford the time to fly away on vacation, so I invested in a vacation spot closer to home. When the pressure gets to me, I run away from home and..."

"You run away to be here," Leslie finished his thought. "What a perfect spot. It almost feels as if nothing can touch us here." Walking to a large rock by the water edge, Leslie lowered her body, resting in its unspoiled beauty. "It's like an island set apart from the outside world," she said wistfully.

Clive sat on a rock across from her. "I always wanted someone special I could bring here who would appreciate it as much as I do."

Leslie savored his words and their eyes locked, saying things not ready to be spoken aloud, as meaningful seconds passed between them. "Thank you, Clive," she murmured, much too aware of the yearning in her heart.

Their time was short, and before long Clive was pushing the accelerator pedal to the floor, making sure she was back in time to connect with Mona. Leslie hugged the window side of the truck, clinging to the moments they'd spent at the waterfall, wishing they had been longer.

*

Roger's condition basically remained the same the next two days, though his ability to focus grew stronger. If he took his time, he was able to form clear words, but his ability to remember names and faces was slower to return. Leslie helped him feed himself one day at noon, and he smiled at her. "I know you, don't I?"

"Leslie, Leslie Weldon. I met you a few weeks ago when I came to Dahlonega to settle my cousin's will. I'm now staying at his ranch, Riker Ranch."

Roger stared with a puzzled expression, as if trying to process her words and what they should mean to him.

*

Saturday and Sunday went by without incident. Leslie sat next to Clive at church, allowing the music and words of encouragement to refresh her soul. Mona and Ray brought Meg for the first time. They arrived just as the music began and sat in the back. While the final hymn was still playing, they were already in their car heading back to the ranch. The normalcy of the day helped everyone put their world into perspective. Yet always they kept a watchful eye for each other's safety, wondering when the next strike might come.

By Monday the test results came back on the tray Morey Santana carried in to Roger at the hospital. Leslie listened to Sergeant Ford run through the findings on the phone. "There was no poison in anything? I don't understand. Was the tray just a ploy to get into his room?"

"Let me finish the findings," Ford interjected. "They also found that the apple juice thickened with nectar contained peanut oil."

Leslie tried to understand the reasoning behind peanut oil. "Why?"

"When you take into consideration Galbraith is highly allergic to nuts, it's self-explanatory. The hospital had a note attached to his file from a previous hospital visit last winter, or it might have slipped by unnoticed. Someone was trying to send our boy into serious anaphylactic shock. If you add that to Galbraith's weakened condition, well..."

Her hand went to her mouth. *It could have killed him!*

"Who would know about his allergy to nuts?" she questioned out loud, her thoughts bouncing back to the luncheon in Dahlonega, when he refused nuts from a complimentary table bowl.

"Someone who knew him well. It's not a pleasant thought," voiced Sergeant Ford.

"Maybe it was his 'secret friend'?" mumbled Leslie.

"His what?" Ford came back.

Leslie heaved a sigh. "I'm just remembering how Roger said his special, important friend urged him to come to Dahlonega, practically promising him success as a lawyer. Mona kept saying she wondered how Roger had climbed to Dahlonega's privileged inner circle so quickly."

"Are you thinking your cousin's 'unofficial friend' is the same person as Galbraith's secret connection in Dahlonega?"

"There's a strong parallel between the two. It makes sense."

"It doesn't matter. I have to be honest with you. As interesting a read as

Wayne's journal is, there is no way to prove any of these speculations...even if I agree with you. The photo and your cousin's journal would only work as supportive information. We need more!"

"I understand, Sergeant."

"I have news concerning Cleary Norton," Ford said. "He was picked up at a bus station near the state line and will be transported to Dahlonega for questioning. There's no further news on the second Vanook brother to date. To my thinking, I'd bet my next day's pay that he's headed for safer ground. He wasn't the stronger of the two or the brightest." There was a pause and a sound like paper rustling through the receiver. "And...so far there's been nothing new on the big, block-faced man you called *Gaetzi.* Knowing he made a break-in attempt as late as a few days ago at Miguel Romero's tells us he's still around. We'll catch him, Miss Weldon."

Leslie was still thinking on what the policeman had said about Cleary Norton. "Sergeant, could you hold Cleary over for at least a couple of days for questioning? I've got an idea that might benefit Meg, but I have to talk with Mona Schiller first."

"A couple of days is stretching it. Whatever you have in mind needs to be put into action soon," he answered.

Leslie countered, "What about Santana's autopsy? Do they know yet if his death was an accident?" Leslie found herself wishing it was an accident and nothing more, as if it would somehow make things not so frightening.

If not, we're dealing with an out-of-control psycho. She shivered. *An unbalanced person trying to eliminate everyone who has knowledge of his identity.* After the explosion on Rocky Ridge, Leslie wondered if she was as much in danger as those who had firsthand knowledge of the elusive man in charge. Then she recalled that, even before she'd left New York, her elimination had been high on the list. Her feelings were almost numb. Where was the evidence to stop this madman?

"I'll let you know when the autopsy results come back," Ford promised.

*

The next two days were packed with business pressures, leaving no time to visit the hospital. Leslie secluded herself in Wayne's office, going through all of the ranch documents. It was a chore she'd put off since her arrival, but the time slot had narrowed, and decision time was eminent. With her bank funds low and her apartment lease requiring a decision, she needed to know what assets she had at her disposal.

Gathering a stack of outdated papers, she placed them back in a folder and shrugged. Now that Roger lay in a hospital fighting to regain his memory and the lucrative offer from the so-called investors was highly suspect, Leslie had no offers on the table to choose from. Of course she could seek out a realtor in town…

Immediately Leslie remembered meeting Chuck Mayer in the presence of Ham Longworth and Jonathon Hager a few days earlier. Could she trust such a man, or was he somehow involved in the behind-the-scenes treachery that was seriously trying to entrench itself in this charming picturesque town? Leslie rubbed her temples to release the building tension. Until the threat of danger was eliminated, Leslie was afraid to trust anyone but her close friends.

She could only pray her money would hold out long enough for that to happen. Sitting on the floor in the midst of stacks of papers, she bowed her head and asked God to work out a solution that now seemed way beyond her capabilities. She prayed earnestly for Roger's recovery, then blocked all worrisome thoughts. She allowed the Lord to comfort and quiet her troubled spirit. The empty years of fleeing from God had slipped away, and the warm, familiar sensation of His presence had returned in all its fullness. *I've been so foolish!*

The clamor of the kitchen phone jarred her. Unfolding her long legs, Leslie stood, hopping over the paper piles, and sprinted for the distant ring.

Still panting from her wild dash, she listened raptly to the excited voice of the young nurse at the hospital she had befriended only a few days earlier. When Leslie lowered the phone to its cradle, she was stunned. Roger wanted to talk to her. How amazing was that? *Roger actually asked for me!* Was his memory back completely? There was no time to lose.

*

After a quick shower, Leslie dressed in record time. She was frantic to get to the hospital and find out for herself what progress Roger had made. Judging from the excitement exhibited by the nurse, Leslie felt an urgency to respond. This could be the breakthrough they'd been waiting for. Even as she dialed Clive's cell, she remembered his schedule. Clive was in town involved in a full day of meetings with fellow ranchers. There was no way he could accompany her to the hospital. She cancelled the call.

With Mona on duty at the hospital, Leslie was in a bind. She'd promised she wouldn't drive anywhere alone, but there was no choice left to her. If Roger had made the breakthrough she believed he had, Leslie intended to be there. There was too much at stake. Leaving a message on Mona's cell phone, she grabbed her keys off the breezeway board and raced for her SUV, leaving Boris to guard the house.

About ten minutes into her drive toward town, Leslie thought to check her rearview mirror. *That's the same old red truck I saw five miles back.* She noticed it pull in behind her right after she turned off their road onto the main highway. *It's a public highway and one of the direct routes leading into Dahlonega,* she reminded herself. It was one thing to be careful, but must she also guard against paranoia settling in? Still, it wouldn't hurt to register the make and color of the truck.

She rechecked the mirror closer to town, relieved to find a different vehicle trailing her. Parking at the hospital, she hurried inside and drew an easier breath. *So far so good.* She would visit a short time with Roger and hurry home while the sun was still up. With a little luck Clive would be none the wiser. *If I can trust Mona to keep my trip into town between us, I just might escape a scathing lecture.*

Reaching Roger's floor, she learned he had been moved from Intensive Care to a private room. Carol, the helpful, blond nurse, hurried to intercept her. "Sorry, Leslie, I should have told you when I phoned, but I was so anxious to share Mr. Galbraith's progress. His friends have been delighted to hear the good news."

Leslie's brain registered alarm. "His friends? How many friends have you been updating, Carol?"

"Just a few—the sheriff, of course, and Mr. Galbraith's secretary. She has been phoning twice a day since Mr. Galbraith was brought in. Such an awful business when that nasty little man tried to hurt Mr. Galbraith, and him such a handsome man," Carol commented, looking distressed.

"Yes, it was." Leslie's reserved smile seemingly went unnoticed by the enthusiastic nurse. Thanking her, Leslie headed for the elevator, wondering how extended Carol's list of people in the know had grown, hoping one of them wasn't the wrong person. There was no way to know the small-town grapevine.

Roger's room was located on the trauma floor, still guarded by Frank Wilson and an extra officer the sheriff's office assigned. Leslie approached the room feeling suddenly nervous. *Will he remember who sent him to Rocky Ridge?*

Frank Wilson nodded in recognition and waved her by. Knocking lightly on the partially closed door, Leslie advanced into the room. Her eyes first rested on Roger's single visitor, who sat on a chair near his bed. Beautiful

Stephanie looked very vulnerable but hurried to stand as soon as she saw Leslie. "I'll wait outside, Mr. Galbraith," she said, moving toward the door.

Roger's curious gaze followed the young blond toward the door. As Leslie walked closer, his focus shifted to her. *Is that a spark of recognition?* wondered Leslie, nodding to Stephanie in passing. "I won't be here long, Stephanie. I'll let you know when I leave, if you'd like to come back in and sit with him awhile longer?"

Stephanie shot her a look of surprise. "Thank you; I would. I'll be in the waiting room."

Leslie smiled, her concentration refocusing on Roger. She forced herself to breathe, walking to the head of the bed where he could see her face clearly. It was hard to tell if his vision had improved. "Roger?" she said softly.

"'ello, Les-lie," he said slowly with marked difficulty. "'ow a-re yoo?"

Leslie moved closer yet. "Better than you, Roger. Do you remember the explosion?"

His head inclined in a half nod.

"Yes, it was bad. It's a miracle you are alive. God must have something for you to do." She smiled tenderly.

His forehead wrinkled as if confused by her words. Leslie pressed. "Did Sergeant Ford tell you anything about your office?"

Roger stared at the white sheets so long she wondered if he comprehended her words. "'es. All 'urned." His solemn tone misted her eyes as she realized how much this proud young lawyer had lost in one day.

"The insurance will help you rebuild. You'll be back to normal in no time," she said, trying to encourage him. "You're alive, Roger. Be thankful!"

Leslie could tell he worked at processing her words. Still, the question burned within her. "Roger, do you remember your secret friend, the one who helped you get established in Dahlonega?"

When he stared at her, she knew he understood but was unwilling to answer. "Roger, I think it's possible your friend is the same person Wayne referred to in his journal as his 'unofficial friend'—someone who really wasn't a friend at all. Wayne thought he was behind the accidents that began occurring after he refused to sell his ranch."

Roger ran his tongue over his bottom lip and looked as if he was trying to form a word. "'orry...I-I-can't. Pri-v-iliged," he sounded out, breathing hard.

Leslie suddenly felt bad she was pressuring him for answers, but the need was so great. "It is *very* important. Someone tried to kill both of us! Who is he? Others have died, and we're still in danger." She sought his eyes, trying to convey the urgency of answering that one important question.

His gaze refused to meet hers. The droop of his head was her only reply. Leslie raked her hair in frustration. "Look, I'm really glad you're going to be all right. I'll come back soon, but I have to go now. Again, I'm sorry your office was burned." She took hold of his hand.

Lifting his head, Roger's stare was so piercing she could almost feel his emotions screaming through his silence. "I-I-'eed to re-member 'ome-thing," he struggled to say.

"You will, Roger, you will!" she said forcefully. "I'll pray for you."

His fingers gently tightened on her hand. His look was pleading, but she wasn't sure what it meant. She patted his hand. "I'll be back."

Leslie's heart was heavy. She knew Roger was struggling to put all the pieces together and that he'd understood her question about his secret friend. The disjointed word *privileged* meant he wasn't legally able to say anything, and she knew enough about the law to understand that he'd been trying to tell her that his secret friend was also a client. Legally he was bound to keep his confidence. *Why then did this client feel it was necessary to burn Roger's records? Was this man that paranoid about witnesses?* The question still remained: How involved was Roger?

Stopping by the waiting room, Leslie stuck her head inside to tell Stephanie she was leaving. The secretary was on her feet in a flash. Clearly, she couldn't wait to go back to Roger's side. "Thanks," she murmured, barely loud enough to be heard.

"My pleasure." Leslie walked toward the elevator.

"Leslie, wait!" Hearing a familiar voice, she stopped midstride.

Whirling about, Leslie encountered Mona rushing toward her, looking extremely young in scrubs and her hair pulled into a ponytail. "I was afraid I wouldn't catch you before you left. How's Roger?"

"Better, but he still has ground to cover. His office burning is hitting him hard."

"Can he tell you anything?" Mona inquired.

"Oh, I think he can tell us plenty, but I don't think he will." Leslie was discouraged. "Some legal mumbo-jumbo about privileged information."

"That's not mumbo-jumbo, Leslie. Roger could lose his license if someone decided to get nasty and accuse him of leaking privileged information."

"I hear you, but I don't have to like it," she said, her frustration renewed.

Mona walked her to the elevator. "I don't like you going home by yourself." Glancing down at her watch, she sighed. "I've got at least two more hours on duty, and I need to get back. Drive carefully, Leslie, and call me as soon as you get in. I mean it. I won't rest easy until I hear from you."

26

Loose Ends

THE ECHO OF MONA'S WARNING rang in her mind as she rushed to the hospital parking structure. Reaching her SUV, she scanned the long rows of parked cars. Nothing seemed out of the ordinary, yet Leslie felt uneasy. Backing out, she turned on the main road to weave her way to the outskirts of town.

Once she was out on the country roads, she allowed herself to breathe easier. In fifteen minutes she'd be home, trying to plan what she wanted to fix for tonight's supper. Thinking on such mundane subjects calmed her nerves.

Leslie arched her neck and relaxed, easing up on her speed. It was a nice afternoon, and she saw no reason not to enjoy the drive home. Traffic was beginning to catch up with her, and the snake-like road made it hard to pass. Leslie pulled far to the right to allow the cars to go around her. Two cars passed before she spotted the old red truck. It hung back, dropping its speed, as if whoever was driving knew they'd been seen.

Leslie's foot pressed down on the accelerator, every instinct screaming danger. *If I can just make it home…* Her right hand fumbled inside her purse on the adjoining seat, found the phone, and clicked it on. After scrolling to the Schillers' number, she hit *Call.* Henri O' answered, listening as Leslie told her where she was. Leslie described the red truck that was rapidly eating up the space separating them.

The truck was gaining. Leslie was afraid to go any faster as she neared the upcoming curve. With both hands on the wheel she steadied the car. The dark shadow on the left side caught her attention too late as the truck pulled up alongside. Leslie sped up, but the truck matched her mileage. *He's driving on the wrong side of the road!* She panicked, realizing her speedometer was topping 80 mph. *This is insane!*

Her pulse raced as her foot shifted to the brake, keeping her focus glued to the truck. The huge figure behind the wheel swerved the vehicle to the right, crowding her car to the gravel edge.

Leslie felt the collision, hearing the scraping of metal as her tires lost traction in the gravel. In defense, she jerked her wheel to the far left even as she lost control. The back right wheel was over the road edge, sliding downward, as her left front fender struck the red truck, knocking it further to the left side of the road.

Clinging to her steering wheel, she screamed as her car slid slowly downward into the wide, sloping ditch. Suddenly a logging truck rounded the curve, barreling toward the red truck. There was nowhere for either truck to take refuge. She heard the screeching impact and cringed.

When her SUV rolled to its side like a beached whale, Leslie's world blacked out.

*

Leslie shook her dazed head, trying to recall the last thing she remembered. Her body felt uncomfortably scrunched between the center console and the airbag, which held her prisoner. Slowly she was able to push and inch her body away from the restraint.

Once she was free, she gazed through sections of windows to the road above, where fallen logs were strewn across the entire area. The logging truck had managed to stop further down the road. From her position there was no sign of the red truck.

Unhooking her safety belt, Leslie fell sideways, grappling to right herself again. With her mind working through a dream-like state, she felt for the door lock. Pressing hard against the door forced it to give way, allowing her to free-fall to the ground below and painfully crawl away up to the road edge. Her entire world felt like it was wrapped in a warped fog. She blinked, looking from left to right.

The hefty logger spotted her and rushed to help her to her feet. "Hey, lady, you all right?"

Ruffled and slightly confused, Leslie peered at him, her hand raising to feel the side of her pounding head. "I'm not sure. I think so. What about the driver of the red truck?" she asked, blinking again to clear her vision.

The brawny driver in a gray T-shirt and grungy ball cap placed his hands on his wide hips. He was visibly shaken and swore loudly. "I never saw the like. By the time I climbed down to the wreckage, the driver was gone!" His hands lifted to his wild-looking hair. "I don't know if he was thrown out or what? The cops are on their way." He shook his head. "What was that jerk doing on the wrong side of the road anyway?"

Leslie felt a little woozy. The driver grabbed hold of her. "Hey, steady there."

The patrol car and ambulance rolled up at the same time, and a whole series of questions and blood pressure tests ensued. Ray Schiller pulled up behind the group and walked through the line to stand over Leslie. Sitting on the back end of the ambulance with an ice pack to her head, she lifted her gaze. "I'm okay, Ray. They can't find the driver of the truck. Can you believe it?" she said, exasperated.

*

An hour later Ray pulled into his drive and went around to help Leslie step out of the truck. "Mona wants you to stay here for a few hours until she's sure you're all right. You should probably have gone to the hospital like the attendant suggested."

Ray's admonition rolled right by her. "I'm fine, Ray. I'm just mad! My SUV is a mess, my head hurts, and heaven knows how much damage he did to that poor logger's load. Yet somehow he was able to get away!" She limped toward the front door. Every muscle in her body cried out for a hot bath. "Did you get a load of that truck? How could he walk away from that?"

Ray opened the door for her. "He was either thrown free from the crash at the point of impact, or he jumped before the moment of impact. I heard the cop at the scene say the truck was stolen."

Leslie's head whipped to the side. "Stolen? I didn't know that. No doubt we'll be hearing from Sergeant Ford about all this." Leslie moaned, as much from frustration as the pain in her head.

Henri O' and Meg rushed toward her as they entered the house. Ray relinquished her into their care and hurriedly excused himself. "I'll be outside. Call if you need anything."

Leslie called after him, "Ray, all I want to do is go home and take a nice, long, hot bath."

"Take one here," he called back. "Mona will cuff me good if I let you go home now. Help her, Henri O'. I've some work to finish up."

"I can help myself," Leslie said tersely. "What about Boris? I left him in the house when I drove into town."

"You go get a bath, and I'll let Boris out," offered Henri O'.

"Would you feed him a little first? There's no telling when Mona will let me go home."

Henri O' shot Leslie a censured look. ""You've made that dog into a regular house pet. How's he supposed to fend for himself, if you trot back up to New York City?"

Henri's retort caused Leslie to wince, silently wondering the same thing. "He can still catch rabbits. I saw him with one in his mouth the other day," Leslie said defensively.

"What good will that do if the poor animal mourns himself to death?" Henri O' threw her parting comment over her shoulder as the door shut behind her.

Leslie sighed. Henri O's words struck deeper than she'd ever know.

"Can I help you up, Miss Leslie?" asked Meg, her face earnest.

"I can get up by myself, Meg, but you could go get my bath started. And if you know where the Epsom salts are, throw a hefty dash in the bathwater."

"I know where Miss Mona keeps them." The teenager dashed down the hall, seemingly eager to be of help.

Just as Leslie pushed her aching body up from the couch, her cell phone went off. Ford's name appeared on the screen. *Here we go....* "Hello, Sergeant. News travels fast, I see."

"The report says you were by yourself at the time of the accident. Is that right?"

With her headache pounding, she wasn't in any mood for a dressing down. "It wouldn't have mattered if I'd had five people in the car. That guy in the truck had one goal—to crash my SUV!"

"Did you get a look at the driver?"

She tried to think back. "He was big—really big, but I couldn't see his features. The windows were tinted."

"The limited description could apply to your Mr. Gaetzi, but without a definite description, it's hard to tell."

"Great!" Leslie murmured.

"I'm having the truck dusted for fingerprints. We could get lucky. I'll let you know what we find. It's also possible the man was injured and will have to seek medical attention." Ford's voice sounded tired.

Leslie was immediately sorry for her testiness. "Thanks, Sergeant."

"Congratulations Miss Weldon."

"Congratulations? For what?'

"On remaining alive. If your vehicle had gone off the road further on the curve, the ditch drops off to a rocky ravine. And the chances of that logging truck coming around the curve at that exact time...well, it was nothing short of great luck!"

Leslie thought on his comment. In all the excitement, she hadn't noticed what might have been. "It was a God thing, Sergeant. It has been all along. For some reason God's protective hand has been on me."

Silence encompassed the space following. Finally the Sergeant said, "It does seem as if a supernatural force has been very gracious to you."

"The one God of the universe—Jesus Christ. He's the beginning and the end. I believe you'll find that in Revelation, the first chapter, Sergeant."

"I might look that up, Miss Weldon. Stay safe."

*

They were finishing supper when Clive knocked, entering by the back door. His gaze went immediately to Leslie, who sat next to Meg at the table. Dressed in a turtleneck sweater and a pair of gray slacks Henri O' had brought back from the ranch, Leslie could feel him examine the various scratches on her face.

"You're just in time for dessert, Clive." Mona jumped up from the table to get him a plate.

"No thanks, Mona. I ate earlier in town. I heard about the accident when I got home. Evan had talked to Henri O'." Pulling up a chair, Clive focused on Leslie. "Are you staying the night here, or do you need a ride home?"

"I'd like a ride home," said Leslie. "I've more papers to go through in Wayne's office." She ignored the frown Mona sent her way. "I'll be as safe there as I am here. That is, if you're still planning to stay in Wayne's old room at night?"

Clive nodded. "I'll stay. Let me know when you're ready to go home."

Leslie looked from Mona to Ray. "Once again you've come to my rescue. There is no way I can repay all your goodness. Not to mention the way you keep feeding me..." She forced a small laugh, emotion clogging her throat.

Mona nodded. "No problem. I'm just glad Ray was around to go get you today. I'm home tomorrow if you feel the need to go back to the hospital."

Clive probed Leslie with a sharp stare, and she squirmed. "Roger is remembering now. I think he knows who is behind all of this. Trouble is, he's bound by that client-privilege thing." She leaned on the table. "But just as I was leaving today, he mentioned he needed to remember something. I could tell it was important to him the way he was struggling. I'd like to be there when he remembers."

"Okay. We'll drive in right after lunch," Mona said. "I don't think your truck friend will try the same thing tomorrow."

Clive stood. "If you're ready…"

Mona and Leslie exchanged curious looks. "I'll get my things and meet you out in the truck, Clive."

Mona accompanied Leslie to collect her clothes and purse. "Do you feel awkward with Clive in the house? I've never known him to be anything but a gentleman, but if you'd feel better having Meg stay in the house too, I'm sure she—"

Leslie interrupted. "That's not necessary. I hardly see him. As soon as we are inside the ranch, Clive high-tails it to Wayne's old bedroom, and he's gone before I'm even up in the morning. In fact, I kinda wish he'd spend more time with me before secluding himself away in the bedroom."

"I think he's afraid to be alone with you, Leslie. Clive has strong feelings for you. Surely you know that. And I also think he's afraid you're going to go back to New York and will break his heart. Be careful with him. He's fragile. Clive's been hurt before. He loved a gal who wanted a career more than she wanted him."

Leslie's own feelings were caught up with similar conflicts. "I'll talk to you in the morning, Mona." She cocked her head toward Meg. "And see what you can do about that other situation I talked with you about...you know, about Cleary." She waved and said good night.

*

Leslie was still in bed when the phone rang in the early morning. Groping to clear her mind, she reached for the phone on the night table. "Yes?"

"Leslie, it's Mona. I'm calling from the hospital. They're shorthanded today and called me in. Sorry. Can we take a raincheck until tomorrow? Please, Leslie, don't come in on your own."

Still trying to organize her thoughts, Leslie rolled over on her back, still experiencing a dull headache. "I won't come in on my own, but I might give Clive a call at the ranch this morning and see what his schedule is today." She yawned.

"I'll save you a phone call. Clive got ahold of Ray right after I left. Someone broke down some of the key fence areas, and a good number of his best horses got out. Ray is over with him now trying to round them up. It could take hours."

Leslie sat up in bed and groaned. "What a headache for Clive! Who would do something like that? Do they think it could have been teenagers?"

"They haven't had time to stop and think about it yet. Leslie, listen close. After I left the emergency room yesterday, some big guy came in for medical assistance. He was pretty skinned up on one side with a couple of broken ribs and a dislocated shoulder. He gave the name of Ralph Colburn and paid cash.

No one thought to make the connection to the police flyer until after he'd left."

"But they did notify the police?" asked Leslie, now wide awake.

"Yes. But I don't know any more about it. I gotta go. It's getting busy here. Promise me, Les, that you won't go anywhere on your own today."

"I promise. I'll stick at the ranch." She squinted at the clock. "I'll get ahold of Sergeant Ford after nine and find out what they know about that guy who came in emergency last night."

By the time Leslie had her shower and breakfast it was late enough to call Ford. Finding his line busy, she tried back later, only to hear he was unavailable. She left a message to call her at home and started working on the paperwork in Wayne's old office.

It was nearly 10:00 a.m. when Sergeant Ford called her back. He wasn't in the best of spirits. "You called?" he growled.

"Yes, but it sounds as if I'm interrupting. I just talked with Mona at the hospital and she said a big guy came in last night pretty banged up."

"Yeah, he told them he'd fallen off a ladder at home. He paid cash and gave a phony name and address. We checked it out late last night."

No wonder he's in such a sour mood. Leslie sighed. "So he's loose again?"

"Yes, and I'd advise you to stay at home today. I don't have time to be worrying about where and what's happening to you."

Leslie heard him talking to someone else in his office and the background noise was hard to hear over. "Sergeant Ford, you're busy. I'll just hang up now, all right?"

"No, hang on," he yelled. Everything was muffled after that, as if he'd put his hand over the receiver.

Leaning against the kitchen counter, Leslie yawned. Lately she was always tired, and no wonder! Her mind was so filled with crazy questions and worries about where the next attack would be. It had taken her forever to fall asleep. A soothing CD finally did the job. Leslie wished Clive had sat up and talked with her, but she was hesitant to knock on his door after her conversation with Mona. It was better to keep a safe distance.

"Are you there?" barked the sergeant.

"I'm here, but you don't have to yell."

"Sorry. I just got the report back on that guy who died in my jail, Morey Santana. They think someone gave him an overdose of some form of nitroglycerin pills, but it's hard to detect. They're trying to pin it down."

"Isn't that what heart patients take?" she asked.

"Yes. That so-called drunk who was placed in the same cell must have overpowered him somehow. We checked his fingerprints but so far haven't come up with a match, so we're connecting on the nationwide site. Everything is just out of our reach to grab hold of."

"What about the steering wheel of that truck?"

"I'm waiting on the results of that test now. Watch your step and keep your phone charged."

Leslie hung up, praying that somehow the sergeant could catch a break. She was carrying a basket of laundry when the phone rang again. Dropping the basket, she raced to grab it in time. Hearing no response, she was about to hang up when she heard a weak voice speak her name. "Leslie?"

"Yes. This is Leslie. Who is this?"

"Rog—er. The nurse...dialed for me."

"Roger, what a surprise! You're talking better today. Listen, I really wanted to come in today, but I don't have a ride. Hopefully by tomorrow—"

"Les-lie," he interrupted. "Lis-ten! Keys, Les-lie, keys. Care-ful!"

She could hear him laboring to talk. "What about the keys, Roger?"

Roger's nurse spoke into the phone, reporting Mr. Galbraith was too exhausted to talk further at this time. "But don't worry! He's doing markedly well. You might try calling him later. Good-bye." The cheerful voice hung up.

Still holding the phone, Leslie wracked her brain. *Keys? What keys is he talking about?* Boris's barking caught her attention. The dog was going crazy. Forgetting the laundry, she went to the breezeway door and scanned the drive and farm lane.

"There's nothing out there, Boy. What do you think you hear?" Her nervousness heightened. She trusted the dog's senses. Animals heard sounds humans missed. If Ray and Clive weren't frantically rounding up loose horses, she would call them, but she hated to interrupt unless it was an emergency. She'd caused so much trouble already.

She hurried to find her cell phone and slipped into her farm jacket, securing the phone deep in the front pocket. "Quiet, Boris." Placing her hand on Boris's collar, she opened the breezeway door and stepped outside. She shushed him again. The barking ceased, but the dog's body continued to vibrate. She talked softly to the agitated animal as they ventured outside. By the time Leslie reached the garage, she heard the familiar eerie sound. With her hand stroking Boris's head, she walked upward a short distance of the farm lane to listen further.

Boris would have leaped from her grasp had she not tightened her hold. His barking erupted in full force. While she grappled with the dog for control, she heard muffled sobbing. By now there was no question in her mind what it was. The sound emitting from the barn on the hill was the crying voice from the woods. *What's going on? What do they hope to accomplish with this?* Her heart chilled as she turned back.

Leslie pulled the dog in the breezeway and locked the door. Fumbling to pull out her phone, she hurriedly dialed the Schillers' number, thinking it wise to alert Henri O' what was happening at the ranch. Her face fell in disappointment when the ringing phone trailed into voicemail. Leaving a brief message, she hung up and dialed Sergeant Ford. She sucked in a frustrated breath and left a second message. Closing her phone, she prayed, undecided what she should do. What was the safest way to proceed?

Should she remain in the house, would she be safe, or would the men behind those sounds come down to the ranch after her? There was no one around to help her. *How is it that I'm unable to reach anyone, and Mona, Ray, and Clive are all busy elsewhere? Perhaps it's a weird coincidence, but...*

The glaring thought plagued Leslie that it was a setup—a trap. Yet there was no guarantee she was safe where she was. If she took refuge at the Schillers, she'd surely lead them straight to Meg. Those men were here for a reason.

As real as all the forethoughts, a driving force raged within Leslie herself. She was tired of not knowing who was behind all the terror tactics and death. She had been walking around with an invisible target stamped on her back ever since she arrived. "It has to stop!" she voiced angrily to an empty room. *God help me, it will end today!*

Perspiration formed on her forehead. Suddenly she wished her father and Wayne were still alive. Thinking of Wayne, she directed her feet down the hall into the office, where she extracted the gun case key from the antique desk and knelt to reach the bottom drawer. Flexing her fingers, she made a fist before opening the drawer.

*

Leslie was aware of the cold feel of the gun barrel inserted in the back belt of her jeans as she walked through to the breezeway where Boris's scratch marks on the door facing were evidence of his acute anxiety. "I know, Boy, I know. I don't like what's up there either."

Half dragging the reluctant dog to the attached, worn rope behind the tool shed, Leslie tied him in place. His wild eyes and low growl told her danger was very near. She'd thought about taking Boris with her, but the fact he was a half-wild, untrained dog might work against her in this situation. Not to mention his constant barking would be an immediate tipoff to her whereabouts. "Sorry, fella, not this time." Still, as she dropped to her knees to obscure her approach to the barn, the thought of his comforting presence almost turned her back to release him.

Crouching in the tall grasses, Leslie weaved her way through the weeds in a snake-like pattern. The closer she came to the top of the hill and the big barn, the more she was sure the sound was coming from inside the barn itself. She shooed away an annoying bee buzzing her head. The raging fear inside her cautioned her to reconsider her actions. Leslie knew it was a volatile situation. Her hand wiped the cold sweat off her forehead. Pausing in the tall grass, Leslie withdrew her cell phone and tried the sergeant's number once again. Hearing it go into voicemail, she gritted her teeth in fearful frustration.

Where is everyone? Surely, Ford will check his messages soon and send help. She couldn't help but wonder what was so urgent to have taken Ford from the office. Hadn't he told her he would be at his desk all morning? She wished she could remember the name of that corporal he named a few days ago, but there was no time.

Even as her heart yearned for Clive's protection, her heart spoke in prayer. *It's You and me, Lord.* The crying pierced the air, and Leslie felt real terror. Suddenly her sense of direction was unclear. *If I could just get a glimpse of who is in that barn...* She prayed for courage to stay the course.

Leslie rushed across the lane to tall weeds on the right and made her way to the far right corner of the barn. She had no intention of going through the large barn doors and being a ready target. Staying low, she rounded the corner, dashing down the side of the huge building to the single side entrance. As far as she could tell, there was no vehicle visible to the eye. Her mind raced with questions. The only way anyone could have gotten access to this building without coming through the drive was from the Rocky Ridge area, and that was not a comforting thought. More important, why were they here? An ominous head-voice whispered, *"To finish the job!"*

Having no illusions of the sound being that of a real child, Leslie knew the person behind the sound effects had all the answers. And that was the one she wanted to see. Once she knew the identity of her enemy, she planned to retreat to a good hiding place until help arrived. She ignored her natural sense of preservation nudging her to retreat immediately. A new plan was forming. But it would require courage she wasn't sure she possessed. *If only I had ready back-up.* Perspiration ran down her back.

Backing a few steps from the barn, she dialed Ford's number one last time, this time leaving an urgent message. "Sergeant! Bring help to Riker's barn—pronto. We have company! I'll try to find out who it is, but hurry, please!"

Leslie closed the phone and stared at the side door, an urging telling her to move now. Boris's fierce barking was distanced from her, but she pictured him straining the end of the rope. Now she wished the dog were here beside her. Had she made the wrong decision in tying him up? Doubt assailed her as she took hold of the side door knob and slowly turned it.

Leslie cringed at the creaking of the weathered lumber beneath her feet as she stepped into the vast interior of the building and ducked behind the railing of a stall. Her breathing was rapid, her heart pounding in her ears.

27

The Wizard

SHE PAUSED, ALLOWING HER VISION to adjust to the diminished lighting. The crying wafted from somewhere inside, yet the barn appeared empty. Closing her eyes she listened, trying to determine exactly where the sounds stemmed from. Cocking her head upward, Leslie opened her eyes. The hayloft—somewhere in the hayloft.

"Come in, Miss Weldon. Come closer so I might see you. I thought it was about time we talked." The vaguely familiar voice floated downward. *The wizard is issuing a command performance,* she mused. It made the hairs stand on the back of her neck.

Leslie's heart pounded against her ribcage. She bit back a retort that would reveal her exact position. He'd lured her here, but she didn't want to show her hand yet. Nervously she felt the back edge of her jean belt for the gun. Were others scattered about the barn, or were they alone?

Remembering Wayne's instruction when he'd showed her how to position her weapon, she hesitated. His warning echoed fresh and stayed her hand. *"A novice with a gun is a dangerous thing. They've been known to cause their own injury. Take your time and be sure of what you're aiming at. And when you fire—fire with conviction!"*

Slowly, Leslie withdrew her hand, deciding to use the revolver only as a last resort. Making sure it was concealed under her jacket she tiptoed around the back of one stall into another where she crouched down to wait and listen.

"Come, come, Miss Weldon, don't be afraid to answer me. I know you're in here. Consider my position. If anyone should be distressed, it is me. Surely you can see that. You have pointedly destroyed all my well-thought-out plans. That wasn't wise. If you had just sold the ranch. I worked every detail out, but you insisted on wrecking everything!" He sounded as if he were talking to himself, reasoning out a failed formula. "Now you've left me no choice but to take matters into my own hands," he said bitterly.

Leslie scanned the loft. *Could he be behind that stack of bales?* Making the determination he was alone, she edged toward the ladder. *If I could once reach the ladder and climb up, I might get one chance to see his face.*

"Stand still!" he screamed. "I can hear you. I have a gun." His voice trembled. "I'll shoot! Stay where you are until I tell you to move!"

He sounds panicky. He heard me; does that mean he can't see me? Suddenly she had new insight. *He's not comfortable in this role. Will he have the moxie to kill me himself if I move in?*

She scanned the dark corners of the barn. If she guessed wrong, it could go really bad in a hurry. Her fingers itched, wondering about the weapon in her jeans, but a gun wouldn't give her the answers she needed.

Backing a few steps into deeper shadow, Leslie raised her chin to be heard. "Are you going to shoot me, then? Is that why you lured me up here? What have I ever done to you, Mr.—?" Where were his hired thugs? Not knowing could prove disastrous.

She fingered her phone in her front pocket, having no idea if it could pick up any signal. She felt around for the familiar dial, wishing she could see.

He screamed, "You don't need to know who I am—not yet. Haven't you been listening? I had plans! Tell me how you were able to thwart every attempt. You're not smart enough on your own. Someone on the inside was working against me, right? Tell me the truth! Who is it? Did Roger tell you about my connection with the investors? I saw trouble that first time you were together—the way he looked at you."

She moistened her lips. *This man was paranoid—maybe worse!* "Why is it so important to know?" She could hear his ragged breathing. *Why is he hiding? Could someone be with him? Will he jump out and shoot if I move closer?* These were unknowns Leslie had to consider. She had to make a decision. Was now her best opportunity to make her move? She took a timid step, her foot grazing a bucket with animal feed, and repeated her question. "Why do you want to know?"

"That's my business!" he barked back. "I had a perfect plan before you arrived. Tell me, Miss Weldon! Who betrayed me? Who is it who's been working against me?" The voice rose in irritation, sounding irrational.

Her head pounding had started again. *Why doesn't he turn off that stupid crying? It's enough to drive anyone wacko!* She took another step away from the bucket.

"Do you believe in God?" she asked quietly, inching even further. She lifted the phone up to the edge of the pocket and clicked again on Clive's number. Hearing it go into voicemail, she clicked off, gritting her teeth.

"What? Do I believe in God? What gibberish are you talking?"

"Well, you asked if I had someone on the inside working against you.

And I do, spiritually speaking. For some reason I may never know, God has been protecting me. He knows what you planned even before you planned it." Her mind groped for a something—anything, "Your plans are nothing to God. He has His own plans."

"Are you crazy? God? You're saying God is responsible for all the flub-ups? Who do you think you're talking to? I'm not an idiot!"

"They weren't flub-ups! God does everything for a reason. Consider the time when you will stand before God and answer for all your wickedness." She directed her voice toward the ceiling of the barn, her steps to the ladder.

Fingering the phone again, she raised it far enough to click on Sergeant Ford's number, then hurried to lower it inside the pocket to muffle the ring. The droning of the whining child cloaked any residual sound and kept Leslie's teeth on edge.

His voice cut through the noise and haze of farm dust. "Stop walking! I'll shoot you right where you stand...and quit preaching. You're wasting your time."

Hearing the click of the gun, Leslie froze and swallowed hard, releasing her cell phone to the bottom of the pocket. She felt lightheaded. *This man is dangerous!* Her chest began to heave. She tried to calm her fear, remembering the words she'd spoken only seconds ago. *God is protecting me. Whatever happens, He is in charge.*

Slowly her breathing leveled, and an unexpected calm settled her panic. This could be the moment of truth. In all readiness her right hand rested on the back of her jeans belt, just in case. "I-I don't think you *really* want to shoot me." She kept her voice as steady as she could manage. "You're a smart, meticulous man who plans ahead. Everything that's happened has been made to look like an accident. You know a gunshot will set off alarms. Think about it?" She took light steps. The ladder was within her arm's reach.

His chortle was filled with irony. "Don't play me, Miss Weldon. My assistant won't care whether it looks like an accident or not. He's short on patience these days, having lately experienced a great deal of pain—a direct result of his recent encounter with you. It's not likely that you're his favorite person at present."

Leslie's thoughts went to the collision on the road and the big man who visited the hospital emergency room. "Where is this assistant now?" Her hand took hold of the ladder to rush the stairs.

Now she guessed he was stalling until Gaetzi showed up. She hadn't much time. One last glance toward the wide door opening before making her attack.

His sharp rebuke took her aback. "He'll be here, don't worry! He's finishing his last assignment. An attempt on Roger's life is expected. Every police officer in a fifty-mile radius should be rolling into the hospital parking lot about now. As for your other friends, why do you suppose they aren't here with you?" The attic voice exhibited a bold, excited, new confidence. He was pleased with his cleverness.

Leslie's head snapped in the direction of the bales of hay. He'd thought of everything. "You're responsible for Clive's horses being loose?" she yelled at him, feeling sick with remorse and fear for Clive's horses. There was no way to know whether the threat against Roger was real, or merely a ploy to separate her from all help.

Laughter was his only response. "I know a lot of people in town who owe me favors, Miss Weldon. Money can accomplish almost anything!"

"So that's what this is all about—money? You've done all these terrible things on a gamble that some new chemical process can make you rich with the hidden gold on Riker Ranch?"

"Wha—what do you know about the chemical process, and how did you find out about the gold? Roger knew nothing about all that! Who told you?"

"Wayne. He left a trail of clues in his journal if someone was interested enough to follow them through. You're Wayne's unofficial friend—the one in the photo!" Leslie was feverishly trying to offset some of the man's new confidence. Just maybe she could discern the voice in the loft. *Which one of the men in the background at Miguel's birthday party is up in that loft threatening me?*

"So you have the photo? Where would that photo be now, Miss Weldon?"

"In Sergeant Ford's police file with other evidence." Leslie's foot eased up on the next two ladder rungs waiting for a response.

The impact of her statement brought stark silence. Leslie took advantage of this distraction to race the rest of the way to the top.

"Steady, Miss Weldon, back down that ladder, one rung at a time," a shattering voice echoed across the expanse of the barn. "Don't make me shoot you. I have a better plan in mind, but I will shoot if you force my hand." His voice was cold with no give.

Leslie's fear surged. She'd waited too long, yet she resisted the temptation to look across the barn to the new source of danger—that could keep. She had to know who was in the loft. With steely determination, she lifted her eyes upward to the smirking face of Jonathon Hager. "All this to gamble on gold, Mr. Hager?" she asked in disgust.

"Not just gold. Power, Miss Weldon—power! I like being able to make things happen, and money is just a tool to secure that happening. After I deal with you and Roger, the way will be clear. Oh, there may be a few questions, but without proof, they will fade away. It's that simple." He paused. "All of this could have been avoided if Wayne simply would have sold me the ranch. He was too old to run it anyway. But the old fool wouldn't budge. You had your chance too. Too bad you didn't go back to New York. I really don't like messiness. Now I suggest you do as my assistant asks and descend the ladder."

Leslie eyed the main door, where Gaetzi's silhouette encompassed a large portion of space. Seeing him was no great surprise. One arm was in a sling and his face looked as if he'd collided with asphalt, a fact which gave her a small portion of satisfaction, considering the destruction and trouble he'd caused.

Gaetzi swore at her. "You've made things hard for the last time, woman. Now move!" he fairly snarled.

Seeing a bulge under his jacket, she assumed he carried a gun. His free hand was now empty, so he'd have to reach around and draw it to shoot. And while Gaetzi's immense size was enough to frighten anyone, she judged it would take a good thirty seconds or more for him to cross the room.

Seeing an elongated shadow appear on the flooring below, she glanced up. Hager now stood at the edge of the loft glaring at Gaetz. Leslie noted the small automatic weapon dangling idly in Hager's right hand. It was evident he no longer considered her a threat now that Gaetzi was here to bully her.

Hager's distaste of Gaetzi was obvious. "Did you come in the back way from the Rocky Ridge entrance like I told you? I don't want any tell-tale vehicles sitting around in the drive, nor will I tolerate any more sloppy mistakes. There's to be no attention brought to this area." His new arrogance knew no limit.

For the first time, Leslie recognized Hager for what he truly was. His was the voice at the restaurant in Dahlonega. But instead of the humble, unimposing figure he portrayed, Jonathon Hager was only a diminutive man with a powerful alter-ego. In actuality, he enjoyed ordering people larger than himself around—it oozed in his manner.

Gaetzi limped a few steps inside the barn, his mouth twisting in anger. "If you don't want to bring attention, then I suggest you turn off that soundtrack." He swore. "It's giving me a headache!" Glaring back at Hager, the injured man reeked hostility. He blatantly didn't appreciate this nasty little man criticizing his work.

Leslie's eyes shifted between the two. It was like watching a bad homemade video.

Hager's chest puffed up like a barnyard rooster. He jutted his chin. "I calculated the pitch of the soundtrack myself. It's loud enough to fan out to the ranch, no further, and don't you forget who is paying your salary, Smart Mouth!" Hager bit back, his head jerking in a nervous tick.

She watched Hager turn back to the sound system and twist the off knob. As he moved toward the ladder, Leslie drew out her revolver. Blocking its view with her body, she inhaled slowly. *Be sure of your aim,* she reminded herself. Raising the gun, she aimed and squeezed the trigger in an awkward motion. The next instant, she descended the ladder two rungs at a time with the sound of Hager's angry scream ringing in her ears. By the time he let loose with a string of obscenities, she'd reached the barn floor, still clutching the revolver.

"Gaetzi! Where are you? Grab hold of her!" he shrieked.

Leslie swung around to face her oncoming attacker with a raised gun, but Gaetzi was upon her too fast. His brute force slammed her against the ladder, knocking the gun from her hand. He clutched her throat. She gasped for air and pushed against him.

"Don't choke her, idiot. I want it to look like an accident!"

Releasing his stranglehold, Gaetzi yanked her arm, pulling her around to make way for Hager's slow descent down the ladder. Hager turned to face her, his right sleeve dripping with blood, his features contorted in more hatred than Leslie had ever seen in her entire life. In a raging flash, his left hand rose, slapping her sharply across the face.

As she recoiled against Gaetzi's chest, Hager's fist shook in her face, his flushed face purple in barely controlled cold fury. "If you make one more wrong move..."

Leslie feared for her life in that instant, watching the little man struggle for control. He was close to the edge of insanity. In erratic gestures, Hager shifted his entire body to confront Gaetzi. "I'm shot! Can't you see that? Help me! Tie something around my arm. Stop the bleeding. Move! Do I have to do everything?"

"Why don't you make her do something? She shot you," Gaetzi threw back.

"I don't want her anywhere near me." Hager gritted his teeth. "You do it."

Even as her cheekbone burned with the force of Hager's attack, Leslie rubbed her smarting lip. She groped frantically for a new plan, a way out of her doomed situation. She fought for stability, her body shaking from the trauma of seeing blood pour from Hager's arm. She'd never before shot anyone. Her dazed silent prayers rose in intensity. Would God protect her again, or would this time be different?

Her heart accepted the truth that God was under no obligation to help her, yet Leslie held fast to her slim thread of faith. How strange that she should wonder how Clive was doing with the roundup of his prized horses. She blinked to clear her erratic, foggy thoughts. Staring at Hager's arm, it occurred to her that her aim had been way off. Tearing a rag he'd grabbed from a barn box, Gaetzi began binding up Hager's injured arm with one-handed awkwardness. He pulled the knot tight with his teeth, spit it out, and swore about the bungled situation.

Hager savagely swore back at Gaetzi's clumsiness, blaming him in part for his injury. "If you'd controlled the woman...," he seethed, citing his partner's repeated incompetence where Leslie was concerned.

Gaetzi countered with a sharp rebuttal, their words flying like poison darts.

Hager's good hand suddenly shot outward, leveling a gun first at Gaetzi. Then he swung it directly at her chest. She shuddered. His unsteady gaze told her the man was within a hair's-breadth of pulling the trigger. In a weird way, Hager's nonrelenting bitter bantering with Gaetzi broke his concentration and lent a measured stabilizing element...something for which Leslie was singly grateful for.

Feeling their shared hatred, Leslie wondered how these two men ever worked together. Had it always been this way, or had something changed their relationship dynamics? Whatever...it distracted their focus and gave her time. Leslie stared past the bickering duo to the outside, beyond the barn sliding door. Her reality—facing certain imminent death—was stark, unless...

Like a gentle breeze stirring in the trees, Leslie's awareness of sound heightened. Boris's barking almost seemed as if he were somewhere close, but her fear could be blocking sound reasoning. It was essential she think clearly to plan. She kept repeating Jesus' name over and over in her mind, staring wistfully in the direction of the opening and the freedom it offered. Was there a chance she could make the distance?

Shifting to rub her aching head, she took note of the color draining from Hager's face. The blood loss from his wound was making him weak. More important to Leslie's needs, the gun he held was, if possible, even less steady. A thin hope rose inside her. She might have one brief moment to catch him off guard and make a break for the door.

Gaetzi finished Hager's makeshift bandage. She spotted his hand gun laying loose in his sling and his awkwardly positioned holster beneath his jacket. Leslie braced herself to move fast. Regardless of their guns and the outcome, it might be her last chance at life; she had nothing to lose. Hager didn't plan for her to live.

Leslie glanced at the beckoning opening and blinked away perspiration. For an instant she thought she'd seen the brief outline of a familiar profile, but it disappeared so quickly, she doubted her own sanity and her jaw went slack in disbelief. Leslie darted a sidelong glance back at Gaetzi and Hager. Their bitter conversation had heated up to a high pitch, their voices so loud they were oblivious to everything around them. Leslie caught the familiar name of Santana in one angry retort. *Wasn't that the man with the sharp features who was killed in his own jail cell?*

Her instincts screamed, *Now's the time to run! Go!*

The abrupt rap on the side of the barn facing brought everyone's attention sharply around. Leslie, Gaetzi, and Hager all stared in shock at the exotic backlit lovely form of Henri O' in the barn opening. Leslie's mind grappled with the reality of the cook's presence. *How? More importantly, why?* her mind screamed. The scene was irrational.

"Excuse me, gentlemen!" Henri O's raised voice called. "I heard a child crying. It disturbed me greatly, and then, when a gunshot rang out, well, naturally, I came to investigate. Might any of you know something about that?" Her look was vague.

Gawking at Henri O' and her ludicrous question, Leslie blinked, not believing the whole scenario. This practical woman, unusual as she was, would surely not walk up in the middle of obvious danger, into a situation where men held guns in their hands, and ask such a question. What was she thinking? Why hadn't she gone for help?

Jonathon Hager instinctively stepped away from Gaetzi, backing into the shadows of the nearest stall. His gun came up sharply as he eyeed the woman with incredulity. Leslie heard him swear under his breath. He called, "Who are you?"

Henri O' squinted, peering first at Gaetzi, then to the shadowed little man. "I'm the Schillers' housekeeper. Miss Mona told me Miss Weldon would be coming for lunch today, and I drove over to fetch her. That's when I heard the child crying and the gunshot. Is everything okay in here? Are you all right, Miss Weldon?"

Leslie continued to gape at her. The bizarre scene escaped all reason. Gaetzi glared at Hager, his left hand maneuvering to extract his pistol. Swearing, Hager raised his eyes upward and muttered, "I don't believe this. A housekeeper in the middle of nowhere!"

Finding her voice, Leslie screamed, "Henri O', run!"

Hager stepped forward into the light, his unsteady gun aimed at Henri O'. "Stay where you are, housekeeper!" His black eyes batted furiously, frenzied, as if his brain had shorted out. Leslie could almost visualize the man's entire thinking process thrown into a blender—his well-thought out plans obliterated. Now his goal to remain anonymous was also in grave danger. No wonder the little man looked wild.

Gaetzi, with his gun now secured in his left hand, shifted to stand alongside Leslie, aligning his gun barrel at Henri O'. His ugly mood had morphed into a white blaze of fury. It was a toss-up which one of the men was more dangerous at the moment. "You aren't going anywhere, lady. Neither is she. Get inside. Stand over here next to Miss Weldon." He motioned with his gun barrel, his gestures clipped and erratic. Whether pain or impatience caused him to clench his teeth, Leslie couldn't tell.

"Listen, Hager," he slurred from the side of his mouth, "it's time to cut our losses. We shoot them and get out of here. You said yourself there's no evidence to tie you to anything, and I've had it. Once they're out of the way..."

Hager leaned against the edge of the stall, his gun hand still shaking. "Wait a minute. Wait! One minute. Let me think." His jaw worked back and forth "We've got to be smart about this." His breathing was labored. "We can't shoot them here; the shots will be heard by somebody. Every time you turn around in this wretched place, someone else jumps out of a hat like a magician's rabbit. No! I've got it. We'll take them out to Rocky Ridge. We'll have one last accident. Part of the population thinks it's haunted anyway. It's perfect."

Gaetzi's mouth twisted. "Whatever. Just get it done, and let's get out of here." Shifting his gun to the hand in a sling, he rummaged in his leather pocket. Lifting a bottle to his mouth, he drank deeply, then returned the bottle to his pocket as Henri O' made her slow, methodical way toward the small group.

Hager stood opposite Gaetzi. "Fine! We'll take them in your truck."

Leslie wilted in defeat, trying to think through the situation. Time was running out. She needed to keep them rattled. "What are you going to tell people, Hager? We walked all the way to Rocky Ridge and threw ourselves over the top? So much for your great plan!" Leslie knew she was playing a dangerous game. The man's emotional balance was already frayed.

Hager whirled, pushing his twisted face within inches of hers. "Shut up, witch! You're dead either way! You won't look so smug then." With marked difficulty, he ambled over to Gaetzi. His face wrenched in pain, he ordered, "Go down and get Riker's Jeep out of the garage and bring it up to the door. We'll tie their hands, and you'll take them over in the Jeep. I'll follow in your truck. Wayne always kept the keys on a board inside the rear entrance of the house."

As Henri O' moved up alongside, Leslie lowered her head to whisper, "What's wrong with you? Why in the world did you walk right into the middle of this?"

"Listen!" Henri O's dark eyes darted in the direction of the opening.

Frowning in confusion, Leslie followed her gaze, straining to hear. Could she dare to hope help might be coming? *Boris! Boris's bark sounds like he's right outside this barn. Is he loose and running to my rescue?*

At that instant the huge animal bounded around the corner of the opening, thundered across the expanse, and lunged airborne at Gaetzi's half-turned chest. Gaetzi staggered backwards, tripping over his own feet, and dropped to the barn floor, his free arm flailing to pull off the fierce beast. Hager stumbled to the side in shock. Recovering, he forced his pistol upward with a limp arm. His pallor was white. Though markedly unsteady, he waved the automatic back and forth, trying to get a bead on the dog.

Leslie panicked. Thinking he was going to shoot Boris, she looked around, made a quick sideways step to grab hold of a bucket with animal feed, and swung it toward Hager, sending him to the floor, where they grappled for the dropped gun. A shower of animal feed covered them both as she lunged for the weapon. Her fingers were curving around the handle until Hager surprised her with a sharp hit to the side of her head and yanked it back. He pushed himself to a kneeling position and breathlessly ordered Henri O' to lower the shovel she'd raised over him in a threatening position.

Gaetzi screamed from the floor for someone to pull the dog off him. Hager nudged Leslie with the gun. "Call your dog off, Miss Weldon, or I'll shoot him. I swear, I'll shoot him! Call him off!"

Leslie looked from the fierce scene on the floor to the little man with the gun. He waved it like an out-of-control conductor's wand. She doubted he could shoot good enough to hit the dog and not Gaetzi, but she didn't want to take that chance. She threw up her arms. "I can't! He's not trained. He's not even a pet. He's a wild dog! He won't listen to me. If you knew Wayne, you know about this dog."

Hager narrowed his eyes as if considering her truthfulness. "Then pull him off with your bare hands if you have to, or I'll shoot you." He pointed the gun at her.

When Henri O' gestured toward him with the shovel, Hager staggered to his feet, wobbled, and shifted the gun in her direction. "Stop! I said, put that shovel down!" His eyes were panicked. He was weak and out of his depth, and he knew it. Leslie was now afraid the gun would go off by sheer accident.

A sharp clank exploded behind them. Whipping their heads about, they witnessed the loft shutter open and a dozen bales of hay drop to the barn floor in rapid succession.

"Lower your weapon, Mr. Hager. My officers have orders to shoot."

The order thundered across the expanse. Everyone's attention swung to the big opening. Sergeant Ford stepped from the bright light of the doorway into the shadowed barn accompanied by three uniformed policemen. Ford raised his eyes toward the loft. "All clear, Masters. Thanks for the diversion."

Leslie saw Clive standing on the edge with a rifle in his hands, his expression grim. "You took your time, Ford. I was afraid that head-case down there was going to shoot one of the women before you got into place. Of course, I wasn't about to let that happen. I had a bead on his head," he added with a hard grin.

Leslie's nerves were shot; she couldn't control the trembling in her body. Seeing a policemen approach Boris with a long pole and rope, she called anxiously, "Come, Boris, come, Boy."

The wild-looking animal lifted his massive head and left Gaetzi bleeding on the floor to come to her side. Kneeling beside him, she looked around at Henri O' and back at the dog in utter disbelief. "He actually came when I called!" she said, laughing.

"I warned you that animal was turning into a pet," said Henri O', lowering the shovel. She rolled her eyes and walked over to stand it against the side of a stall.

Clive scrambled down the loft ladder. Cradling his rifle under his arm, he hurried over to Leslie and lifted her to her feet, placing a protective arm around her back.

"How and when did you manage to get up there?" she asked, puzzled.

"I sneaked inside the side door while those two were arguing down here…actually while Gaetzi was binding up Hager's gunshot arm. What'd he do? Shoot himself?" His smile was terse. "I wish I'd got here before that scumbag hit you." He touched her face tenderly. "Evan let Boris loose to cause mayhem, creating an extra distraction so I could climb up to the loft and release the hay. I had to wait until Ford was in place with his men before I could make my move. It was an impromptu plan. We had to keep him from using you as a human shield."

He sucked in a deep breath. "That's what Henri O' was doing when she ambled up to join the party. She was the first distraction, buying us time to put everything in place by keeping their attention away from you." Seeing Leslie's reaction, Clive shook his head. "Look! We protested—especially Evan, but Henri O' was adamant, saying she didn't think they'd shoot without first finding out if more were coming besides her.

"Ford was already on his way from the hospital. Still it was all I could do to wait it out. I was halfway up the hill when I heard the gun go off, afraid it was you who was shot. I came so close to shooting that weasel Hager more than once, especially when he started waving that fool gun around. I don't know which was worse, his mouth or his gun."

Clive paused gently wiped the blood from the cut on her lip. His chin tightened in anger. Her hand stayed his arm. "H-how did you all know to come? None of my calls got through." She stammered as her left hand rubbed the top of Boris's head to calm him. The dog's eyes darted nervously at all the intruders.

Clive studied Leslie's face, his hand gently caressing her bruised cheek. "They got through. I saw the missed incoming calls bearing your numbers. Your phone was busy when I tried to call back, so I called Henri O'. She'd come in the house from outside and listened to your message. We persevered until we got hold of Ford. By that time he'd checked his messages and knew the score, but it was up to Henri O', Evan, and me to stall until Ford could get out here. Apparently, there was some unexpected brouhaha at the hospital today."

Leslie nodded. "I know. It was a threat against Roger." Her knees still felt weak as she thought back on how Hager had staged the diversion to keep the police away from the ranch, and it had almost worked. "I know something else. I'm going to buy a texting phone and take the time to learn how to use one."

Clive grinned ruefully. "Wouldn't have done you any good. My phone doesn't text, and I don't have the time or patience to play around trying to hit tiny buttons with my large thumbs."

Leslie shook her head, turning at the sound of Ford giving orders in the throes of the ongoing action in the barn. While one officer was busy handcuffing Gaetzi, Jonathon Hager managed to wrest free from the officer. He braced his weakened body against a stall and attempted to straighten his tie, as if he was going to a formal dinner.

Running his uninjured hand over his mussed hair, he sneered at the sergeant. "You think you have this all sewed up, Ford? You got nothing! And I want to press charges against that woman. She shot me." Venom dripped from his lips.

Sergeant Ford stared at Leslie curiously. "Really? Well, considering you were on her property threatening her with a gun, I'd call it self-defense. As for the other, we'll talk about that. Your boy—Gortez here, alias Gaetzi—had his fingerprints all over the steering wheel of the truck that ran Miss Weldon and a certain logger off the road yesterday. And today I've got you and Gortez holding Miss Weldon and Miss Romero against their will at gunpoint. That's kidnapping, attempted murder, and trespassing for starters."

"My New York lawyer will have me out of jail by nightfall. I'm not without influence in this town!" His once pale face was red and strained. His head arched high as if he attempted to raise himself above the sergeant.

"I don't doubt your influence, but bail might prove difficult, Mr. Hager. Judge Harvey is out of town on a fishing trip for the next few days. After that, we'll have to see. Now cooperate and go along peacefully. I'm tired of looking at you."

When the tall officer moved in, pulling Hager toward the barn opening, the little banker screeched, "How dare you! I'll have my day. I have plans. I demand a doctor attend me, or I'll sue for abuse. I'm bleeding in case you haven't noticed."

Leslie walked up to face the arrogant, disgruntled man. He shook with rage. "I wouldn't dwell on your failed plans, Mr. Hager. You were fighting against God's plans and His never fail. Ask for a Bible at the jail and check it out." Whirling about, Leslie utilized every ounce of remaining energy to hold her head up while walking back to stand next to Clive and watch Hager taken from the barn.

Clive eyed her with curiosity. "You shot him?"

"Wayne's revolver. They'll find it in Gaetzi's pocket."

"You got him in the arm. Nice shot," he said with admiration.

She winced. "Actually I aimed at the gun in his hand."

He pressed his lips as if biting back a bemused smile. "I see. First you shoot him and then you share your faith with the scumbag? Are you the same girl who five weeks ago wasn't sure she still believed?"

"He is a scumbag, but I feel sorry for the man, too. He's connived, cheated, and probably had people killed just to be important—have people look up to him. I think that's sad. He of all people needs to know Jesus."

Probing Clive's altered expression, Leslie felt like she could stop time and bask forever in the warm look he sent her.

"True enough," he murmured.

The tiny group stood silently outside and watched the two men be led away down the lane to patrol cars and a waiting ambulance. Henri O's chin nodded in satisfied approval. "If it's all right with you, Sergeant Ford, I'll be at the Schillers finishing up dinner. I gave the officer my statement."

Ford smiled and waved her away before turning his attention toward Leslie. "Hager has a point, you know. He is a man of a great deal of influence in the area. A slick lawyer just might get him off. I wouldn't count on any of his men talking. And with Galbraith's files burned the way they were, there's no concrete evidence of Hager's involvement in the investment group that was pushing to buy the ranch. Without that, there's no paper trail connecting him to all the sabotaged accidents on the ranch."

"Roger said that was privileged information anyway," Leslie added.

Sergeant Ford placed his hands on his hips. "Maybe so, but it could have put us on the right track. If there was a paper trail in one area, it stands to reason there are other avenues we could freely pursue. If we only knew where to begin..."

"Maybe Roger will remember enough to direct us. Though, from what Hager said, I don't think he knew the man's involvement. Hager himself said Roger didn't know about the gold." A thought struck, and she brightened. "Hold on there! Roger called me this morning. He was talking better, but it was still hard to understand him." She strained to recall his words.

Clive turned her to face him. "What did he say?"

"That's just it. I was in a hurry, and it didn't make any sense. I remember that he told me to be careful. Yes, and he said something else. He mentioned keys. He said it twice." She looked over at Ford in confusion.

"Keys? Keys to what? Whose keys?"

She shrugged. Forcing her thoughts back to the last time they were together, she walked mentally through each movement. "We'd planned that picnic at the bottom of Rocky Ridge. Roger was edgy, seemed driven to climb up to the top of the ridge before eating. I forgot the pillows and needed to go back to the Jeep, only Roger still had my key on his key ring. I took his keys with me when I started for the Jeep..."

"Where are those keys now," asked Ford, walking toward her.

"I don't know. Let me think," she said, pressing her forehead.

Clive hovered. "Did you have them when you left the Ridge?"

Leslie blinked at Ford. "Yes. We went to the hospital; then Clive and I stopped by the Schillers before coming back to the ranch." She tried to visualize her actions after she arrived home that harried night. Looking from Clive to Ford, she drew in a deep breath. "We've got to get back to the ranch."

The wolf-like dog followed the group down the hill. Entering the breezeway, Leslie turned toward the coat hooks in the mudroom area. She lifted down the lined leather jacket and felt inside the pockets, withdrawing the heavy, elaborate keychain.

Clive moved up on her left, and the sergeant leaned over her shoulder. "Maybe he has a safety deposit key?" He ventured a guess.

Examining the keys in the palm of her hand, Leslie cocked her head. "Not exactly," she murmured, her finger lifting out a small slim-lined apparatus.

"A flash drive!" exclaimed Ford. "Maybe we've got a thread after all. I'll take custody of that if you don't mind."

"A thread?" Leslie questioned.

Sergeant Ford unhooked the flash drive from the keychain and handed the keys back to her. "I've found over the years that if you can find a single unraveled thread, the rest of the garment will eventually come apart. This, hopefully, will be our thread. My next stop is the hospital. Mr. Galbraith just might have remembered something useful."

Leslie sighed, as much from weariness as anything, and dropped the remaining keys back in her leather jacket before returning it to the hook. "Assuming Roger's files are all on the flash drive…I just wish we could use that information to put Hager where he belongs."

"Have faith, Leslie," Clive whispered.

"Things are just warming up, Miss Weldon," added Ford. "I'll get back to you, later. The most positive aspect of this whole day is that you should be able to rest safely in your beds tonight." Lifting his phone, he strode a few feet away. Pausing, he changed his stance. "I can't believe Hager went to such lengths just to gamble on an old gold mine. From all appearances and the selected digging, it's safe to assume that Rocky Ridge was the specified site. Wonder where he got the info?"

Leslie leaned against the washing machine and crossed her arms as she considered his words. "I've been researching and thinking on that a lot in the last few days, and I'd say Hager had to have gotten most of his information from Cousin Wayne. Probably while fishing." She walked the short distance into the kitchen, coming back with a fairly new appearing journal.

Lifting the book so both men could see, she continued, "Reading most of Wayne's journal gave me clearer insight to his thinking. And my best guess would be that somehow he purposely misdirected Hager's thinking to the Rocky Ridge area. Why else would all that digging have taken place?" She had Clive's and Ford's attention. "After Wayne caught on that the banker's real goal in pursuing friendship was to get his hands on the ranch, Wayne would have done his best to derail him. I think he gave him false information. My cousin was a crafty man. It took prayer and real concentration on my part to ferret out his clues. Remember the birthday photo? That was only one of his clues."

Clive stared at her, his jaw agape. "I'm a little vague about this birthday photo, but you can fill me in later. Are you saying you suspect an alternate area for the buried mine? That's quite a bombshell! What do you have to back up your suspicions?"

Pocketing his phone, Ford did a slow about-face from the door, walking back to face Leslie. "You're saying, you don't think the gold mine is buried under Rocky Ridge?" the sergeant challenged.

Leslie cradled the journal in her arms. "Clive, would you put on a pot of coffee, please?"

28

Uncertainty

WHEN EVERYONE WAS SEATED AT THE TABLE and the aroma of coffee strong in the air, Leslie placed Jamie Cohen's journal on her left and Wayne's on the right. "Bear with me…my thoughts are fragmented. Reading two journals written almost two hundred years apart is a little spacey." She raked her hand through her hair, pulling it behind her ears.

Her finger thumped Jamie's ragged yellow-paged book. "From Jamie's account of where he found gold, I had trouble equating it with the location at Rocky Ridge. Jamie's young son was able to walk to the location from the homestead. And, from what I've heard and read, the original homestead was closer to where the big barn is now. The small legs of a young child could never have walked to Rocky Ridge from the barn area." She leaned forward on her elbows.

Ford took a long drag of his coffee. "Considering those calculations, the mine location could be anywhere in the general area within a mile radius…unless those journals give a more precise indication."

"Jamie's descriptions gave good clues, once they were all assembled, but it was Boris that pinpointed the general area."

Clive had just taken a swig of coffee and part of it spewed from his mouth. "Boris pinpointed the area," he restated, frowning.

"Yes," Leslie said with mischief. "When Meg and I followed him over the hill to his private hideaway, where a very pregnant, female dog is holed up, I saw something that ignited my curiosity."

"What was that?" asked Ford, sleepy-eyed, seeming to savor the coffee.

"Sparkling dirt," said Leslie, smiling. "Gold dust!"

The men exchanged glances.

Leslie closed the journals. "I believe that's where Jamie's gold mine is buried."

The sergeant's mouth puckered, his distant gaze indicating deep thought. "In this area it would be wise to keep your speculations to yourself, Miss Weldon, at least for the time being."

Clive rubbed his chin. "Yes I agree, but I've got an idea brewing. Give me a few days to work it through." He downed the rest of his coffee and stood. "Right now, I've got some horses to round up before sunset. I'll walk you out, Ford."

Standing at the breezeway door, Leslie watched the two men separate in the driveway and walk to their vehicles. Leslie wondered if Clive would be back to stay in Wayne's room tonight, or if he'd return to his ranch now that Gaetzi and Hager were locked up and the danger was over.

It made sense, she told herself. Then why was she suddenly at loose ends and unsettled? Hearing Boris's small whimper, Leslie turned and picked up the dog dish.

"I think it's just you and me tonight, Old Boy," she murmured. Surprisingly, she felt a bit of a letdown now that the culprit had been unmasked. Maybe she'd feel more elated if she knew for sure that scheming man would get his just due, but too often that wasn't the case in real life.

The charges that Sergeant Ford listed today would surely send him to prison for a reasonable amount of time, she tried to tell herself, but the policeman's warning that a slick lawyer like Jack Criswell from New York might be able to get him off took the edge off any feelings of everything being settled. *Lord, I'll try to leave his judgment up to You, but it's hard!* She slowly carried the dirty coffee cups to the sink.

Daylight was quickly vanishing and with it Leslie's hopes of remaining on the ranch. It was a race between time and money, which would run out first, and she was still without visible means of support. Daily, she'd checked for job openings available around Dahlonega, only to be disappointed.

Leslie walked to the front windows to watch the partly cloudy sunset, filling her mind with the view. She'd come to love the land and the people. Some of the trees across the road were showing early signs of dropping their leaves. Clive's roof was more visible than she had ever seen it, and she felt a tug in her chest. *I'll miss him most of all, Lord.*

Wrapping her arms around herself, she allowed the sights and aromas of drying foliage and pine trees to saturate her senses. When the phone rang, she barely turned, allowing the message machine to pick it up. Mona's voice was warm and uplifting, encouraging her to come to dinner and talk over the day's events.

Leslie drew her shoulders tighter. The tension, the fear of dying, and God's presence were so large in her mind, there was no way she could sit and talk over a quiet meal. *What I really need is a good cry,* she told herself. Food was the furthest thing from her mind. "I need you, Dad. I wish you were here," she whispered. *I'm scared. I don't want to leave this ranch—my heart is here now.*

Thoughts of her father brought back the old hurts of how they parted with never a chance for her to say, "I was wrong, and I'm sorry." After wandering the rambling house, she found herself back at the table where the journals lay. Now was as good a time as ever to finish Wayne's journal. Leslie curled up on the couch and snuggled down, allowing the last light of day to send rainbow colors across the room.

She switched on one soft light on the end table and flipped through the journal to the end section where there was a picture of Dad, Wayne, and her on their last, most memorable visit. She was especially interested in Wayne's notes and journal entries related to her and Dad.

Apparently Wayne and her father exchanged letters and calls regularly after that visit. Had Dad mentioned that fact before he died and she'd never paid attention? From Wayne's notes it was clear their friendship became strong. Turning the page, she found a pocket containing letters her father had written to Wayne. When Leslie began reading those letters, she was surprised to find how often she was mentioned.

The date on the last letter was written after she and her father had their argument and she'd stormed off to meet Kevin in the Islands. She held the letter, reluctant to read its contents.

At that instant the phone rang, but she allowed it to go to voicemail again. "Leslie, Mona again. Call when you're ready. I'm here to listen. We've good news about Meg." Making a supreme effort, Leslie moved toward the phone.

Hitting the button, she replayed Mona's message: "Your suggestion was a good one, Leslie. I talked with Sergeant Ford and, by applying a little pressure on Cleary Norton, he was able to work a tradeoff. Cleary signed away his rights to Meg in order to wave pending charges of abuse. Ray and I are free to apply for temporary custody as foster parents. It's a beginning! Call!"

Leslie smiled, blinking to clear her misty vision. Family was a precious thing. She looked longingly at the letter in her hand. Would she be strong enough to bear what was written inside? Could she read about how she'd broken her father's heart? She'd been silently bleeding with guilt each day since her father's death. She knew her sin was forgiven. If only she could ask Dad's forgiveness.

Unfolding the two page letter, she bypassed the greetings and questions about the ranch to the place where Bill Weldon began talking about his own life and Leslie.

For some time now, Leslie's been wandering away from God's truth, truth hidden in her heart from childhood. Her pain has been so great since her mother's death I've wondered at times if she wasn't blaming God for the loss. I want you to pray every day for her, Wayne. Leslie is at a crossroads in her life. Pray God keeps her from great sin that would burden her heart for years to come. I love her so deeply and have given her over to the Lord's care, having faith she will come through, shining like the sun.

My girl's heart was angry when she left this morning, but I know she'll call to ask forgiveness—a forgiveness I've already granted. I've been having chest pains of late. Generally if I take it easy until they pass, I'm fine for months until they crop up again. But in case anything happens to me, remember Leslie in prayer. I wish she'd come down and stay at your ranch. Inside she's a country girl at heart. I personally hope to come for a visit soon, myself. As always,

In His Care, Bill

The words repeated over and over in her mind: *A forgiveness I've already granted.* Gradually Leslie allowed the words and their application to penetrate her soul. *Dad forgave me!* When the teardrops started, she couldn't stop them. This letter was like her father sending her a message of forgiveness from heaven. She found herself laughing and crying at the same time. "Thank You, Lord! God's grace!"

The ringing phone jarred her attention. If that was Mona, she needed to talk to her. Laying the letter aside, she rushed to grab the phone. "Mona."

"No, Clive. What's this business about you not answering your phone?"

Swiping at her tear-stained face, she laughed. "Sorry. I just needed some space."

"Yeah, well, that's understandable, but Mona was getting concerned."

"I—ah, thought with all of the danger passed that it wouldn't be a problem. Sorry if I alarmed anyone."

"With or without the presence of danger, friends still worry when they can't make contact, Leslie."

"I haven't been that close to friends in so long, I've forgotten. I'm afraid I've kept people at a distance. It's become a habit," she admitted.

"Habits can be broken," he said softly. "If everything is all right, I'll say good night. I'm bushed!"

Her memory kicked in. "Did you get all your horses back?"

"All of them. We found them grouped together about a mile away. It was like someone rounded them up for us. Pretty amazing, but it sure helped us."

"God's been busy today." Leslie chuckled.

*

After talking with Clive, Leslie called and conversed with Mona for almost an hour. Reading her dad's letter to Wayne had been liberating, as if a burden had been lifted. Mona was full of plans for Meg, and it was exciting to listen. The two had been talking and it was fun to hear the enthusiasm in her friend's voice. Leslie felt a catch in her throat as she thought of leaving the treasured friendships she'd found on Dunn Road.

She found eating a bowl of cereal to be as satisfying as a full meal. When she turned out the lights, Leslie sighed. She'd lived a century in a few short weeks. Boris's quiet fellowship guarded her bedroom door as she lay, wondering about her future.

*

Early the next morning Leslie was up tackling the laundry and housework with an eye on the clock. Precisely at 10:00 a.m. she changed clothes and locked the door. She found driving Wayne's Jeep to the hospital made her feel freer than she had in weeks. The stately old vehicle she'd named Ruby, with the new paint job and dents of valor, rolled into the parking lot with pride.

Before heading up to visit Roger, Leslie popped into to say hello to Mona in emergency.

"Look at you, bombing around without a bodyguard," said Mona, laughing.

"And loving every minute of it. I'm making a huge batch of Uncle Ferreno's celebrated recipe for spaghetti and meatballs, and I expect the Schillers and their new family member to be present. Shall we say 6:30 p.m.? Oh, that invite includes Henri O', Miguel, and Evan too. I'll call Clive myself."

When Mona's jaw dropped, Leslie laughed. "How flattering! Believe it or not I can cook a little, and what I do is good—take my word for it."

Riding up in the elevator, Leslie drummed her fingertips on her jeans. For some reason she found herself nervous to face Roger this morning. Would he be mad at her for handing over his flash drive to Sergeant Ford—like she had any choice? She drew in a deep breath and blew it out slowly as the elevator opened.

Roger was sitting straight up in bed when she walked through the doorway of his room, now conspicuously void of a police guard. She knew in an instant he was the old Roger. His eyes were sharp, clear, and probing as she approached the bed. "Good morning, Roger. You're looking great. When do you get out of here?"

"To-day, if the doc-tor ever ar-rives to sign the pa-pers. Steph-anie is com-ing in about an hour to pick me up."

There was a new softness when Roger spoke Stephanie's name. Perhaps a spark of romance was budding between the two.

"How wonderful!" she said much too quickly. "You'll be back to normal in no time." So much had happened, yet there were still so many unanswered questions. "Look, I'm sorry I wasn't able to visit you yesterday." She studied the folds of his hospital bedding.

A small smile formed. "Yes. I heard you had an ex-citing day."

"Sergeant Ford?"

He nodded. "It was hec-tic a-round here for a whi-le too." He sounded out the words.

Feeling suddenly tired, she reached for a nearby chair, drew it close to the left side of the bed, and eased her weight down. "I'm sorry about Jonathon Hager, Roger. I now know he was a friend. Well, not actually a friend." Her brow wrinkled, finding it awkward to express her thoughts.

"It's o-kay, Les-lie. Jona-thon and I had mu-tual reasons for form-ing a friendship. I-I thought I had an easy ride to a luc-ra-tive cli-en-tele, but I wasn't ex-pect-ing no-tor-ious con-nections," he said with a touch of acid.

"If you didn't cross the line or break the law, you should be fine," Leslie encouraged, amazed at how improved his speech had become.

"If you don't count the fact my spon-sor was a cheat and mo-most probably a mur-der-er several times over." His look held painful remorse. "You've almost died so many times. I didn't know what I was do-ing. I now find I-I was help-ing Hager. I told him things—things that almost got you killed." He leaned his head back and sighed, his physical weakness taking over.

Leslie didn't know what to say. "But I wasn't killed, Roger," she blurted out. "God gave me another chance at life, just like He's giving you one now."

Silence cloaked the entire room. Roger's expression grew darkly pensive.

Raising his eyes to hers, he appeared agitated. "I have to say this, so let me talk. I'm sor-ri-er than I can say! There are not enough words...I thought—I thought I was help-ing Hager purchase the ranch prop-er-ty on be-half of this group of rich in-vest-ors.

"The fact I was in line for a hef-ty fee cloud-ed my per-spec-tive and dimmed my a-ware-ness. I bought the whole spiel be-cause I want-ed it to be true. That makes me look pret-ty stu-pid, and a stu-pid law-yer isn't much in demand. I don't know how it will all play out," he said sadly. He moved his hand to emphasize. "But the im-por-tant thing is, you're alive." He looked spent, physically and emotionally.

"I forgive you, Roger. I understand, really. If there was only some way to make Hager account for what he has done. If there is any way you could help the sergeant with this? I realize you're limited, but if there is anything...?" she pleaded.

Roger lowered his eyes. "We'll see, Leslie. We'll see."

*

The dinner party was noisy, filled with light merriment—a new freedom.

"Pass the bread." Mona fanned her mouth. "Wow, girl. That sauce makes your mouth sing. It's loaded with fire—and flavor!" she added, smiling.

Ray leaned against the back of his chair. "No wonder I like it," he said, breathing in deeply like a satisfied dragon.

"Fabulous sauce! Whoever Uncle Ferreno is, he's one whale of a cook!" Clive chimed in.

"He's dead, Clive, he was my great uncle," said Leslie, laughing. "I made the sauce. I realize that's hard to accept, but..."

His eyes twinkled. "Really! I'm even more amazed. You actually cooked this?"

"The whole meal!" boasted Leslie, proud of her one culinary achievement.

Henri O' leaned forward. "I know for a fact that my father would've loved this recipe. I wish he could have been here tonight," she said soberly.

"I wish so too. Miguel certainly earned it. I'll package some up for you to take to him. Tell him I'll come by in the next couple of days," offered Leslie.

As Meg worked on her piled dish of spaghetti, her eyes followed the table chatter like a tennis tournament. She sat quietly with a look of contentment. Being a part of the group was seemingly enough to make her happy.

*

When Leslie walked back into the kitchen for a minute, Ray edged closer toward Clive. "I've everything lined up on my end for tomorrow morning, if you're set?"

Clive nodded and sipped his iced tea. "Then everything's good to go. How's 9:30 a.m.?"

"Fine. You really think this will work?"

"The time is so short. I decided to play a hunch. The outcome is in higher hands than mine. From what Mona says, Leslie has no time left to stay at the ranch. Her money is low, and she has no job opportunities. It's worth a try, Ray. I think she really wants to stay."

"What are you two plotting?" asked Leslie as she returned with a pitcher to fill their empty glasses.

"Hard work. We're discussing work." Clive reached again for the pasta bowl.

"What's for dessert?" asked Evan, looking around with expectancy.

"Bakery bought cheesecake is the best I can do," said Leslie.

"What happened to 'I cooked the whole meal,' " chided Clive.

"Well, I made the most important part," retorted Leslie.

While everyone laughed, Ray and Clive exchanged a nod of agreement.

*

Leslie was empting the dishwasher and sipping her morning coffee when massive engine noise drew her attention outside. She peered out the window, her jaw dropping as she watched heavy-duty machinery roll into her drive. After bolting through the breezeway and out the door, she stopped, her head pivoting like a bobble head doll.

When the machinery stopped in the entrance leading to the barn lane, Leslie ran up to the lead backhoe. "Excuse me. What's going on? Why are you here?"

"Orders, ma'am," a burly-chested man answered. "We were told to wait here for further orders."

"Who told you?" she called up to him.

Hearing a truck pull up in the drive behind her, Leslie whirled about in time to see Clive climb out of the cab and hurry toward her.

"Do you know what's going on?" she asked just as Boris barreled down the farm lane barking for all he was worth.

"Yes," Clive shouted over the sounds of the idling machinery and barking canine. He drew his hand across his neck, signaling the drivers to shut down their engines just as Leslie called Boris to her side, still amazed whenever the dog obeyed her. Suddenly it was stone quiet.

Clive and Leslie both began speaking at once.

Leslie raised her hand. "You go first." She was clearly puzzled.

"Show us where you suspect the old mine is buried." He spoke with authority.

Leslie's shoulders slumped. "Clive, I appreciate this, but I don't have money to pay for the mine to be dug out. Besides, what good will it do? Even if we find gold, there's nothing we can do about it. We don't have the resources or connections, and the red tape would go on forever. I don't have forever."

"Leslie, trust me. Can you do that?" His eyes probed deep inside her.

Her gaze locked on his. "Yes, Clive, I'll trust you. I think it's a waste of time, but if you want to look for it, fine. It will be my last decision as owner of the ranch."

"We'll see. Show us where the mine is."

"There's one more problem." Leslie bit her lip.

Clive turned without a word and opened the back of his truck, lifting out a large box stuffed with rag bedding. Reaching inside the box he grabbed a plump package and looked up with a grin. "I've got good ground chuck to coax that she-dog out of the hole. Once we get the dog situated safely in the barn, I'll feed her the rest of the food. Hopefully, we can count on Boris to help us with the project. At that point, Miss Weldon, the backhoe can commence work."

"Looks like you've thought of everything, Mr. Masters, but we'll see." She turned with a tilt to her head and headed up the lane.

*

Leslie and Clive stood off to the side watching the backhoe lift bucket load after bucket load into a waiting dump truck. "Sorry about that tear in your gloves, Clive. I guess that she-dog hadn't decided you were a friend yet."

His eyes never wavered from the working machinery. "Nevertheless, I got the job done. So this is where you saw the gold dust?" he added, changing the subject.

Nodding, Leslie shielded her eyes upward of the higher ledge. "Do you see those giant oaks set back about fifteen feet apart?" Not waiting for him to answer, she continued, "Jamie Cohen is buried up there. Between the oaks are two slate markers, mostly buried in the earth. One bears Jamie's name and the other is etched deep with the words, *In Memory of Clara and Little Gus Cohen.* I found them while walking up along the old path between the oaks."

"Is that the child that all the ghost stories have been woven about?" he asked.

"Yes. Jamie Cohen planted those trees in their honor, above the mine. He wrote it down in his journal—perhaps he wanted someone in later years to know. The grave markers are another reason I favored this spot over Rocky Ridge."

"Well, at some point, we're going to have to finish the digging in the old-fashioned way. One man, one shovel."

Shortly before noon, Clive waved off the machinery and thanked them heartily for their work. They saluted him and chugged off toward the barn lane. Leslie hoped Clive knew what he was doing because it looked like nothing more than one big sand and gravel pit to her. "What now?" she asked as the heavy-duty vehicles departed.

"Now I go home for lunch and get some of my work done," Clive said, grinning. "After supper, Ray, Evan, and possibly George, will join me with pickaxes and shovels, and then we'll start the real work." He leaned over and kissed her cheek and strode off, leaving her standing in a puddle of confusion and gravel dust.

On her way back to the ranch with Boris at her side, Leslie entered the big barn to look in on the box bed containing Boris's lady friend. Careful to approach slowly, she saw the Husky mixed-breed female curled up in the box. After a rocky start, Clive was able to coax her to her new home with the raw meat, but Leslie didn't know what to expect. The animal raised her head as Leslie approached, growling low.

Immediately, Boris moved between the two and growled at the female. "Ssshhh, Boris, it's all right." Leslie stepped back. "Your lady is protecting her nest. She doesn't know me yet. Come on, give her some space. I'll bring her some food later."

Backing out of the barn, Leslie argued with herself. *What am I doing? I'm getting ready to move back to New York, and I'm adopting a pregnant dog?* She continued to berate herself walking down the lane. How would it all work out?

While eating lunch, Leslie thought of Roger and went to the phone. Dialing the number he'd given her in the hospital, she waited, only mildly surprised to hear Stephanie's professional voice at the other end. The young woman's tone grew noticeably chillier when she discovered who was calling. Leslie sighed.

Though stronger, Roger's weakness was evident in his voice. His spirit brightened hearing Leslie's voice. She heard new hope as he excitedly shared how Sergeant Ford had given back his flash drive, and now he and Stephanie would begin reconstructing his files. "Stephanie has lined us up temporary office space until the fire damage is repaired. It's amazing what's been accomplished in so short a time."

"That's great," she said, hating to change the subject. "I heard Jonathon Hager will be out on bail by tomorrow. Do you think he will contact you?"

"I have no idea. Doubt it, though. At this point we have nothing to talk about. When a man tries to have me killed not once, but twice, I take that personally." His anger was pronounced.

"He'll probably deny it, Roger. From what I've read in Wayne's journal and what you've told me, he's quite good at explaining things to make them seem plausible." The quietness that followed left Leslie uncertain. There was no way to know all that Roger was experiencing, but betrayal must be at the top of his list.

Their field of conversation was growing thin, partly due to the fact Leslie found it difficult to keep from pressing the issue of Roger giving the police evidence for conviction. It somehow seemed all wrong for Roger to have the evidence at his disposal, yet not be able to use it. Still, she knew if, as a lawyer, he didn't handle it the right way, he could lose his license. It was a quandary for all concerned.

She cleared her throat. "I'm glad things are going better for you. You'll be up and running again in no time. Does Sergeant Ford believe you still need protection?"

"I think he's planning on sending a patrol car around to periodically check on me. He doesn't think Hager will try anything at this point."

Leslie remembered Morey Santana and how someone gained access into the jail and Santana was later found dead, but she was reluctant to mention the incident to Roger. *Surely the sergeant knows if Roger is in danger or not.* Yet the thought continued to nag at her long after they'd said good-bye.

In the afternoon, Leslie finished up with Wayne's office files. She looked at the phone. Common sense told her she needed to call a realtor and put the ranch on the market, but Clive had asked her to trust him and she would do that, though the odds of something happening to alter her situation and allow her to keep the ranch were slim.

She polished off a frozen dinner at suppertime without much enthusiasm. The leftover spaghetti would keep for a night when her appetite was better, and her stomach was less nervous. After feeding Boris, she took a second bowl up to the barn and found the white-faced husky mix curled in the box where Clive had situated her.

Though Leslie wasn't an expert in such matters, it appeared as if the dog could drop her pups at any time in the near future. Her salt-and-pepper-streaked fur was tightly stretched around her engorged abdomen, and it was clear she was uncomfortable.

The dog eyed Leslie with suspicion but didn't attempt to growl with Boris right beside her. After placing the dish of food within her reach, Leslie backed away, talking softly as she considered the striking markings on the she dog. "I think I'll call you *White Feather,* little lady." Turning to Boris, she asked the wild-haired animal. "What do you think about that, Boris? Does White Feather suit her?"

Glancing at her watch, Leslie turned restlessly toward the door, wondering when Clive and the others would arrive with their shovels. As she thought of Jamie's journals of tragedy, she fought a quiver of fear at disturbing the mine with its memories, but at the same time a gentle assurance settled in her heart that it was something that needed to be finished.

Hearing a rustling in the tree tops, she heard an uneasy wind stirring outside. Walking to the barn entrance, she looked up at the strange coloring in the sky. Weather was moving in, and there was an unusual feel to the air. Leslie felt an urgency to pray...for what or whom she wasn't sure, but she prayed for God's protection on all she knew.

29

From Tragedy to...?

THE GLOW OF THE LANTERNS AND FLASHLIGHTS created a clandestine aura around the small digging site. Mona and Henri O' had carried lawn chairs for the women to sit on the sidelines. Their faces shone with a mixture of nervous anticipation and electric tension—a tension drawn from the fast-changing atmosphere.

Darkness had cloaked the peculiar sky hues, disguising them in shadows, but the restless winds were wild and uncertain, threatening violent storms. The small group of searchers was vulnerable against the face of this jutting hillside. Lightning was known to seek out its prey in the midst of a storm. Leslie stared upward at the fast-moving clouds.

Boris's yellow eyes pierced the black night from his position behind Leslie, where he lay with his head on his outstretched legs. From time to time his eyes probed the areas beyond the reach of light where animal cries contributed to atmospheric sounds. A low growl would rumble from his expanded chest as if to warn off mammal or spirit.

Weather reports had predicted heavy turbulence expected from two different directions, yet the hope of a wind change could carry the brunt of the storm front on by them—if they were lucky. The weather bureau seemed unwilling to give a definite reading, so the men kept one eye on their shovels and one on the sky. The features of men and women alike were tinted red by lantern glow and distorted by windblown hair and tense uncertainty. Leslie knew this night would live forever in her memory.

While the women huddled inside sweatshirts, sharing blankets, Clive, Ray, Evan, and George Truitt, the Schillers' hired man, whom Leslie had not met until this night, shed extra coats, and in some cases, even long-sleeved shirts. Their arms moved in constant rhythm, scooping heavy shovel loads. The dirt they'd moved from the large jutting boulder mounted in a growing pile.

Sandwiches, water, and iced tea waited in baskets where the women sat. Leslie's cell phone went off around 10:30 p.m. during the men's short break.

All eyes focused on her as she raised the phone to her ear, trying to block out the wind interruption.

"Speak louder! Who is this?" she yelled.

The narrative on the opposite end of the phone was garbled, but Leslie heard enough to cause alarm; her jaw dropped in utter disbelief. "You're saying it's the same guy?" Closing her phone, she sat immobile, staring out into the night. "Unbelievable!"

"What's unbelievable?" Mona yelled at her.

"They caught a guy inside Roger's place tonight armed with a knife. It was the same guy who was jailed the night Santana was murdered, the supposed drunk!"

"He's from out of state and ready to make a deal by telling who hired him to kill Santana. Not only that, but Willie Gortez, alias Gaetzi, alias supposed investor—" she smiled at Mona—"is not only ready to make a deal but is anxious!" She paused to draw a breath.

Every eye remained focused on her, waiting for an explanation.

"Morey Santana was a relative of Gaetzi, a half-brother or something. As soon as he learned Hager had Santana killed, he was ready to spill everything. I heard them arguing in the barn. I think Gaetzi had suspicions even then. Our Mr. Hager is going be locked up for quite a while. They are picking him up now! Halleluiah!" she screamed. "That means Ford used Roger for bait!" she stated with sudden wide-eyed alarm.

Clive shrugged. "So, you've been bait ever since you arrived. At least they finally got the guy! Did Ford say how they set it up?"

"Yeah." She rubbed her head, trying to recall everything that was said. "Remember the flash drive? After they discovered a listening device planted in Roger's home phone, Ford made a copy of the flash drive and gave it back to him, intending for the information to get back to Hager. Then they set up a stakeout and waited. Ford figured that they'd not only come after the flash drive, but Roger too."

"Then Galbraith's testimony won't even be needed to convict Hager?" Clive downed a second glass of water and mopped his sweat-drenched face.

Leslie remembered how foolish Hager had made Roger feel. "No. But apparently Roger will testify. He can't say anything about Hager's business dealings, but there was a situation when Hager asked him to do something personal—as a 'friend.' Hager collected useful friends like jellybeans. He'd asked Roger to pay off the Vanook brothers for so-called 'construction work.' "

Grinning, she continued, "After it was noised about that Hager had a bad habit of killing off his employees, Zeke Vanook changed his no-talking venue and is now willing to confirm Roger paid them not for construction work but to dig on Riker land for gold! Hager's house of cards is tumbling down!"

The whipping wind carried the beginnings of the expected rain, and Clive grabbed his shovel. "Well, Ford has done his part; let's do ours. Back to work, guys. A little rain won't hurt us."

Henri O' pulled out an extra-large umbrella and the women inched their chairs closer so they could all fit under its protective arms, each helping to hold it secure.

As the weather worsened, the men shoveled faster. At the point Leslie was ready to call the evening a total bust and tell everyone to go home to their dry, comfortable homes, the wind whirled sideways, drenching them. Then everything settled and grew strangely silent. Except for a gentle whispering in the trees and occasional spits of moisture, the bulk of the storm had passed.

The silence itself was almost as loud as the roar of the wind. The men kept digging, and the women waited quietly—the talking had been spent. Only the striking of shovel against stone and earth and an uncertain hopefulness remained.

When the breakthrough occurred, it was George Truitt who lifted the important shovelful of earth. The short, burly man with white mustache and gray hair yelled in victory, "Here! I found the opening. Help me dig it out."

The other three men rushed to where George stood and, side by side, they dug furiously as a unit. Moments later Clive called for all to stand back and allow him to continue digging alone. It took only a few hefty shovelfuls before a gaping hole loomed before them. The opening was no more than five feet wide and four feet at its tallest point. The ground was embedded with decayed wooden beams and hardened clay.

Wiping his sweating brow on his shirt, Clive threw his shovel aside and called for a flashlight. "Back me up, Ray, I want to go in a few feet and look around."

Leslie was on her feet racing to Clive's side. "Hold up. It's late, you're tired, and it's really too dark to see clearly. Why don't we set up a time tomorrow when there's plenty of light?" she asked, suddenly apprehensive.

As Clive studied the hole in the side of the jutting cliff, Henri O' quietly emerged from the shadows to stand alongside Leslie. "I agree with Miss Leslie. Daylight would be a better time to investigate the entrance to the old mine."

Leslie and Henri O' exchanged a long knowing look, Leslie remembering that Henri O' knew as well as she what was written in Jamie Cohen's old journal. Miguel would most likely have told her the particulars of the ancient tragedy.

Clive searched their faces suspiciously. "You two know what's inside, don't you?"

Leslie moistened her parched lips. "Not completely, but..."

Clive cut her off. "I appreciate your reluctance, but time is of an essence here. I'm going in." He looked over at Ray and got the expected nod.

"Fine! Then I'm going too." Leslie drew out a flashlight from her large sheep-lined farm jacket. Refusing to acknowledge Clive's look of disapproval, she squared her shoulders and moved up to face him.

"Come on, Leslie, use your common sense and stay out here until Ray and I determine it is safe. We'll call you." He turned as if the matter was settled, proceeding toward the ominous opening.

Leslie moved quickly to position herself between Clive and Ray in the lineup to enter the mine. Ray started to open his mouth but closed it before uttering a word of protest.

When Clive paused to check behind him, Leslie's presence was not well received. Through a clenched jaw, he murmured, "I'm serious, Leslie. This is one time you need to wait until we check it out."

Lowering her head, Leslie replied, "I'm sorry, Clive. This is one time I can't stay behind. I need to go in first! Trust me!"

Clive grimaced, focusing on the lead inside the ancient mine. He moved slowly, shining his light on the timbers shoring up the entrance. Ducking, he cautiously moved forward a few feet. Leslie squeezed in beside him and Ray gently pushed by both of them to veer to the right. The three spotlights moved as specters across the walls, door, and floors.

When Leslie's light shone upon a low formation of rocks enclosing a small alcove, her breath caught in her throat. As if pulled by a magnet, she moved toward that alcove, her steps wary of decayed broken timbers. Standing on the outside of the rock formation, she moved her light slowly around the inside of the alcove. She wavered slightly at the onset of a light-headed sensation, breathing deeply. The scrawled words in the journal echoing Jamie's raw pain blazed across her memory.

"Clive, come here a minute, please?" Her voice sounded very small and breathy.

"In a minute, Leslie, I'm scratching off a sample of ore from this side."

Sucking in a long, slow breath, she called again, "Clive, please!"

Both Clive and Ray centered their beams on Leslie and moved carefully toward her. Leslie waited until they stood alongside before turning her light on the contents inside the formation.

"Dear God," gasped Ray. "Who are they?" He moved off to the far side.

Clive turned to Leslie. "Do you know?"

She nodded. "I believe we are in the presence of Clara and Gus Cohen, gentlemen. Jamie buried his family inside the mine before he closed it down. I-I was hoping they would be covered by dirt by now."

Clive inhaled. "Whew! That's my shock of the night. I believe in cases such as these the procedure is to call the police and not move any of the remains."

He solemnly stepped away from the enclosed graves. "I-I've got the ore sample I needed. I recommend we leave things as we found them. There isn't anything else here, and it's not safe to venture any deeper until the mine is shored up with new supports."

"Leslie, you might want to come see what's behind this side of the alcove. Clive, shine your light with mine," ordered Ray, his voice tight and slightly peculiar sounding.

Leslie and Clive tiptoed around the rock formation to see what Ray was talking about. All three beams lit up the niche behind the alcove. Broken pottery pieces lay on the ground like a large, loose puzzle. Shafts of light reflected the glitter of glass and dull brass coloring between pottery pieces. Ground in dirt and discolored algae formed on the multi semi-wrapped objects tucked inside the niche.

Clive's beam traveled to Leslie's face. "What is all this? Why ever would he leave these inside the mine…Leslie?"

"Oh. Glory!" Her dirty hands flew to her face in shock. All air sucked from her lungs, as every instinct warned her not to hope too deeply. She knelt, her shaking hand encasing one of several filthy jars, and gently lifted it to be examined.

"Are those what I think they are?" asked Ray, his voice higher than normal.

"Chancing a guess, I'd say these are discolored half-eagle coins," Leslie managed with breathy exertion. She struggled to form intelligent words.

*

There were almost half a dozen flashlights trained on the area of the recent reopening of Jamie Cohen's mine. Sergeant Ford yawned and leveled a critical gaze at Leslie, Clive, and the Schillers. His fringe scope didn't exclude Evan, Henri O', and George Pruitt. The sergeant's features were lined with fatigue and irritation.

"Why is it that you people never do your investigating during reasonable daylight hours?" he growled.

"As a matter of fact, I did suggest...," Leslie began but the sergeant waved her off. "Just tell me what we are dealing with here."

With hands in his pockets, Clive nodded for Leslie to go ahead.

"We've uncovered the remains of Clara and Gus Cohen. They died from tragic accidents in the early 1800s, and Jamie buried them inside the mine when he closed it down—their private tomb. Remember our conversation earlier about the possibility of gold being the motive for Hager's planned accidents?"

Ford blinked his eyes and rubbed the bridge of his nose. "Yes, I recall you mentioning the mine." He raised his head, piercing her with a no-nonsense look. "You're saying that you have documentation to back up the burial of the two skeleton remains inside the mine?"

"Yes. Jamie wrote about the accidents and burying the bodies of his family inside the mine along with the half-eagle gold coins."

Inhaling deeply, the sheriff's sergeant nodded. "After the examiner's done, I'll drive you back to the ranch for that documentation." His focus shifted to the two old jars lying on top of a tea towel. "Those would be the jars filled with half-eagle gold coins?"

Leslie nodded. "They're badly in need of a good shine, but that's them."

"How many are in there?"

She shrugged. "I have no idea; we didn't take the time to remove them. They were wrapped and stuffed with rags and paper, most of which has disintegrated. There are broken jars still inside the mine with scattered coins. We left them."

Hands on his hips, Ford looked down at his feet and nodded. "Well, I see no reason why those shouldn't remain in your care for now. You can extract the others later. They were all found on your property, by you, and it's recently been determined that you are the last remaining link to this family. But the bodies are another matter."

Leslie stiffened, ready to protest, but Clive's restraining hand held her in check as the policeman lifted his phone to the light and pressed a series of numbers. He turned away, covering his ear. Clicking off his phone, he shifted back to face them. "The medical examiner will be here in a little while. After he releases the remains, you will be free to make whatever burial plans you wish."

"How long will it take the coroner to get here?" asked Leslie, anxious for the long day to be over.

The sergeant eyed her narrowly. "Orin purposely mentioned the fact he had to get dressed, said it was his first sleep in two days. Don't expect a cheerful mood," said Ford, yawning. He raked his hair with his hands.

Leslie found herself wanting to apologize for waking everyone up, but she held her tongue. *It's not my fault,* she told herself, feeling weary and petulant. No one wanted to go to bed more than she did. As she thought about what her friends had given up and gone through in recent weeks to help her, she chided herself for any self-pity.

Ford dismissed all but one officer before shuffling back to sit alone in his patrol car and wait. Leslie saw him lift a large thermos from the floor of the front seat and pour a cup of coffee. She didn't get the feeling he was interested in congenial conversation with anyone, let alone any of them. Walking back to where Mona and Henri O' were sitting, she eased down in the wet lawn chair.

Mona leaned close to her. "Leslie, I remember a certain conversation we had a week or so ago when you mentioned contacting someone about coins. Did you know about the buried coins?"

"I did, but I didn't, if that makes any sense? I know what I read in Jamie's journal, but I had no way of knowing for sure whether the coins would still be inside the mine—or even if Jamie actually did as he said. It was truly a shock when I saw the jars lying there. The possibility of finding the remains of Clara and Gus Cohen so freaked me out, I didn't consider the coins."

Leslie looked up to find Clive and Ray standing alongside their chairs. Evan and Henri O' were talking low, off to the side of the boulder, and George Pruitt was busy wolfing down a sandwich and a bottle of water on the other side of the food baskets.

"I wonder what those coins might be worth today?" voiced Mona absently.

Leslie shivered and rubbed her arms as the cool night breeze penetrated her wet clothing. "It will depend on the condition of the coins when they are cleaned up. If they're worn, the most would be three to five thousand apiece, but if they are in average to good condition, anywhere from eight to ten thousand each."

Ray and Clive stared at her in disbelief and Mona's mouth gaped open like a baby bird. "No kidding?" she murmured.

"Those jars are filled with coins!" exclaimed Clive, huskily.

Leslie nodded. "I noticed. It's really incredible!" Her brain felt foggy.

"Do you realize what that means?" asked, Mona.

Rubbing her forehead, Leslie tried hard to answer Mona honestly, but she was too weary to think in terms of specifics or anything requiring an opinion. "When everything is sorted, it could be a lot of money."

"It's more than a lot of money, Leslie. It's your ticket to stay on the ranch, seed money to set up a working ranch again. Of course, that's considering you want to stay?"

Leslie was stunned, and almost too tired to smile. Her mind worked to connect the dots. "You really think there might be enough for that?"

"I'd say that might be an understatement, but we'll contact a few people in the next several days." Clive pulled out the bottle of sample ore he'd scraped off the inside of the mine. "Depending on what I find here, it's possible a deal could be made with those investors to work this mine using that experimental chemical process from Australia."

Leslie looked up at him incredulously. "Investors—Australian process? I thought those investors connected with Hager were all part of his illegal scheme."

Clive stooped down in front of her, his voice lowered so only Mona, Ray, and Leslie could hear. "I stopped by and talked with Galbraith today. He contacted a number Hager accidentally let slip one day in some of their dealings. Hager had kept all contacts between investors and Roger metered through him. That way, he remained solely in control and set things up to his advantage." He took a long breath.

"From what little Roger has been able to discover in the short time he's been home, the investors are all on the up and up. They confirmed that the deal they'd set up with Hager was contingent on ownership of a gold supply. They trusted Hager to be the go-between person because he convinced them it was better that way."

"What a con man!" exclaimed Mona.

"He was a lot more than that!" offered Leslie, feeling a new shiver run through her. "He'd been setting everything up for at least three years since he first came to town, like some kind of carnivorous predator," she added angrily.

All heads turned as a patrol car parked up on the farm lane and a tousle-headed, fiftyish man hustled down the incline toward the digging site. Sergeant Ford climbed out of his car and met him, explaining the situation as they walked toward the mine entrance. The medium-framed, slightly bent man cast a sharp glance in their direction.

Leslie wandered away from the group, staring up at the sky as the clouds parted and thousands of stars dotted the sky. She gazed up at the huge shadow of the big barn and all that it encompassed. *My ranch? Could it really work out for me to stay here and operate a working ranch?* The idea was staggering, bigger than anything she dared dream since her arrival! She'd never allowed herself to think beyond where she was.

Leslie knew from Wayne's journal how he'd come to the ranch a complete novice with only an invalid brother. Clive and the Schillers would be here to help and direct her. It was what Wayne wanted when he left her the ranch—it was what Dad wanted.

The excitement bubbling up inside her was swallowed by the fear of such an enormous undertaking. Shivering, Leslie drew her shoulders up against the night breezes until she felt Clive's arms encircle her.

"It's all pretty scary, isn't it?" he commented softly.

"It's petrifying!" She leaned back, absorbing strength from Clive's massive chest and drawing courage from his presence. She suddenly wanted all of the support she could grab hold of. "Would staying and making Riker Ranch a working ranch be the right choice for all of us?" she asked, lifting her face to probe deeper than his eyes. "I feel all of you might end up wishing I'd sold to someone who actually knew what they were doing. I've been a constant source of trouble, not even talking about the imposition to each of you since the moment I arrived."

Clive's arms tightened around her. "You're not an imposition. We've been working diligently to make it so you can stay here. We want you here! Wayne told us he was leaving the ranch to his only living family member, a daughter of someone he'd come to think of as a brother. He wanted you here. I want you to stay, Leslie."

"Why Clive?" she whispered. "Why do you want me to stay?" Her heart was racing. She needed to hear him say the words.

He lowered his gaze. "If you go back to New York, we'll never know—and I want to know."

"What?" She felt frustrated at his inability to speak clearly about his feelings.

"I-I think we could have something really good and important happening between us here. Look, I know we haven't known each other very long, but if we did have more time, who knows? The thing is… Oh, for crying out loud, Leslie, you know what I mean…" He bit his lip in obvious frustration.

Leslie smiled with a hint of sadness. "Thanks, Clive. I would love to stay, but the fact remains I need money to live on. There's not much but my slush fund left, and that won't last long. Finding the coins is great, but it will take time to see their benefit. There are so many processes to go through—and taxes. I have to find out about taxes. Then the possibility of the mine active again is still little more than a hopeful speculation that will take who knows how long to prove out—if it ever will?"

She gazed up to the distant stars. "I need money to come in now, and so far I haven't been able to find work anywhere in the area. I don't want to leave." Her voice caught in her throat, fighting her desire to turn back into his arms. She didn't trust her emotions. To have everything she could ever want so near ripped at her heart.

His lips brushed the back of her neck. "Something will work out, you'll see. If God wants you here, something will work out."

Clive's strong conviction made Leslie's faith feel small and ineffective. She wanted a faith like Clive's and Ray and Mona's—and that of her father's. Dad had always said that faith grew with seeing what little trust you have, honored. *"God wants you to be a strong woman of faith, Leslie. Commit your life to Him, read His Word, and your faith will grow. When you step out and trust Him, Jesus will be there!"*

The sharp call of the sergeant brought Leslie and Clive abruptly about. "Hey, you two, if you don't mind, I'd like to get home sometime this morning."

Exchanging glances, Clive and Leslie rushed back to the group.

It was agreed that the opening of the mine would be blocked off by tarps and braced timber after the ancient skeleton remains were removed. Until then, a police officer would remain on duty. Leslie phoned a mortuary in town. With that acceptable decision, Sergeant Ford nodded and bid the group good night. After a few steps he turned with a wry grin. "The very next phone call from you people better be during the day."

Clive chuckled, motioning for Ray and Evan toward the barn for the timbers and tarps. George Truitt trudged along, determined to do his part, as the women grouped together to keep warm, still awed and partially dazed over the mine discovery.

*

It was 3:00 a.m. before Leslie and Boris were back at the ranch. Thoroughly chilled by her damp clothing, she jumped in a hot shower before burrowing down in her bed to eek out as much sleep as possible. Surprisingly, Boris never roused her until almost 10:00 a.m. Sleep logged, she staggered back from the breezeway, pausing long enough to set up the coffee pot. Her sore body longed to head back to bed.

As Leslie passed the phone on the kitchen counter, she remembered the need to reconnect with the mortuary. Mona had recommended an old establishment in town. Based on prior dealings, she thought they would handle the unusual situation with discretion. Flipping through the local book, Leslie dialed and set up a time for a consultation.

She wasn't five steps from the phone when its shrill ring caught her midstride. She lifted the receiver, yawning sleepily. The booming voice of Hamilton Longworth bounced between her eardrums like a huge base drum. "Morning, Miss Weldon."

Leslie shook her head and held the phone away from her ear. "Oh, good morning, Mr. Longworth, how are you?" Her mind raced with possible reasons for him to be calling. She felt awkward, remembering how she'd first thought he might be the guilty one.

The banker cut right to the chase. "The thing is, Miss Weldon, I feel downright awkward about this whole situation concerning Johnny. No one had a clue what the man's objectives were when he arrived. He was so—" He swore, then said, "Excuse me. He was so darn good at arranging things for everyone—me included. I can't believe the things the police have told me. It's like another person entirely." Longworth coughed.

"What I'm getting to, Miss Weldon, is, I—I mean, the bank—feels some responsibility for all the pain and mental anguish Mr. Hager imposed upon you, seeing as he worked for our establishment. I'm sorrier than I am able to express. This is a close community, and goodwill is part of our image. If there is anything I could do to help make amends, I shall strive to do so. From what I hear, you are a woman of outstanding character and abilities. Too bad I didn't have you working for us instead of Hager." He paused for a breath.

Leslie rubbed her tousled hair. "Mr. Longworth, there is something you could do that would be a big help to me. Is it possible for us to talk sometime today? I'll be driving into town after lunch. If we could meet briefly..."

*

After lunch, Leslie headed for town in Wayne's Jeep. It was crazy the way she prayed for God to work out all the wild plans whirling in her mind. She smiled at her prideful thoughts. *My plans? Are they really mine, or did they initiate with the Lord? This God thing was unbelievable! He's worked out seemingly unsolvable situations.*

When Leslie was finished at the bank and mortuary, she headed down the familiar side street. Out of habit, Leslie pulled her car around the back of the row of shops. The charred debris from Roger's office was almost cleared away, but it gave her chills just to think what that horrid little man was willing to do to have money and power. Hurrying up to the back of The Christmas Shoppe, Leslie knocked hard before rushing inside.

"Georgie McCray, I have a proposition I want to talk to you about," Leslie said, her eyes twinkling with possibilities for the future. She placed a loving arm around the older woman's shoulders. "We have a lot to talk about, Mrs. McCray. Could be I just might have a future here in Dahlonega, and an idea that might work out for your good, too."

*

Slightly breathless, Leslie remembered less than twelve hours ago she'd told Clive she needed a job, and now she had two. Georgie had orders for a dozen bulbs for Christmas, expecting more. A verse sprang to mind: *"I have come that you might have life and have it more abundantly!"* She turned in the kitchen to smile at Clive.

His laughter rang lustily. "What did I tell you? If God wanted you to stay, He could work everything out. When do you start work at the bank?"

"I'm still reeling from the shock!" she said, excited. "I begin the first of next week. By that time I should be able to settle some business matters." She ran her fingers through her loose hair, pulling it up into a ponytail clip. "My head is swimming with a list of things. First, I have to call and cancel my lease on my apartment in New York and arrange for my things to be packed and shipped out to me.

"Tonight I'll call Bert in New York. Just pray she might be open to coming out to live in Dahlonega. This Tuesday, my boot cast comes off, and I'll need to finalize arrangements for Clara and Gus's remains." Leslie finished pouring Clive's coffee and carried it over to the table by the window, where she slid into the chair across from him.

Clive passed her a plate of inviting doughnuts. Picking a large cinnamon bun, Leslie grinned and licked her fingertips. "This isn't a bad arrangement. I offer late-morning coffee, and you bring bakery doughnuts."

"My privilege. It was safer than having you fix eggs." He chuckled lightly.

"It pains me to admit it, but I have to agree. Your omelets are much better than mine." Leslie savored her pastry and looked out the window. With her doughnut in mid-air, her head snapped back to stare at him.

"Leslie? What is it?"

"After everything that happened yesterday, I forgot to do half the things on my list. Right after we finish up here, I'll be driving back into town."

"Really! Were you planning on visiting Galbraith?" His brows narrowed.

Leslie looked surprised. "Roger? No, I mean, sure I will visit him sometime later this week, though I don't think he'll notice with his secretary around. Have you met that woman?" She shook her head and laughed.

Clive shrugged. "I just thought you might still be interested in him." His voice sounded strangely vulnerable.

Her features softened. "I admit I liked the attention he gave me and he certainly isn't bad looking, but, well..." Leslie lifted her coffee cup and enticed Clive with a smile. "You see, there was this other guy who owns a horse ranch..." She left the sentence unfinished, wadding the rest of the cinnamon bun in her mouth.

Clive reached for another doughnut, the hint of a smile playing on his mouth, too.

30

At Home

One week later

IT WAS A CLEAR FALL DAY, complete with a brisk breeze across the top of the ridge behind the big barn. They were all there—everyone close to Wayne who'd known what the ranch and its history had meant to him. Leslie brushed her flyaway hair from her face as Henri O' finished singing a haunting rendering of "Blessed Assurance."

"It was Wayne's favorite," whispered Mona. "He always said, 'A man needs to know where he's going to spend eternity. It helps him live his life with confidence.' "

Leslie nodded solemnly, now peaceful that she too possessed the same blessed assurance within her. She glanced at the faces gathered in a semi-circle around the burial hole next to Jamie Cohen's marker. Meg's eyes were like mournful saucers, as if she were reliving painful memories even while she stood in respectful silence.

As Henri O' took her place next to Evan Robinson and George Truitt, Clive stepped out and read verses about the dead in Christ being raised at the sound of the trumpet. He stepped back in line beside Leslie, and everyone waited for her to close the memorial service. "May this family be reunited with you in peace and love, and on that glorious day, Father, raised complete in Christ's glory."

Clive's strong hand took hold of hers. "Amen," he echoed.

The remains of Clara and Gus Cohen were ready to be lowered, and Evan and George stepped forward. Together they lowered the simple, resting box into the earth, not far from the marker bearing Jamie Cohen's name.

Leslie looked over at Henri O' and nodded. "I think any ghost worries can safely be put to rest as well."

Henri O' gazed at her through lidded dark eyes, her small smile hinting of mystery. "Ghosts only haunt the dreams and memories of the living, Miss Leslie." Her eyes traveled between Clive to Leslie, her meaning clear.

George picked up a shovel and slowly began covering two hundred years of history as each person passed respectfully, following the worn path leading down from the ridge. A soft hush seem to settle over the area between the two towering oaks.

Henri O' and Evan purposely walked ahead of the group. Henri O' promised a special lunch would be ready at the Schillers and seemed anxious to get back to her kitchen.

Leslie walked slowly, reluctant to leave. She'd felt something special here between the giant oaks reuniting the physical remains of a family torn apart by tragedy, especially when she was so blessed. Not only did this beautiful land belong to her, but these people surrounding her—people she would live amongst—were her new family.

Deep inside Leslie was this feeling that somehow Dad not only knew but was pleased. Inhaling deeply of balmy, fragrant air, she cast a long glance back to the top of the ridge. "I can't believe this ranch has its own cemetery," she murmured, discovering she was afraid to raise her voice.

Clive lowered his head so his voice wouldn't carry. "I think it is one of the coolest things I've ever heard of. Leslie, these are your ancestors, a part of the virgin ground they plowed and the life they forged out of the wilderness to make your ranch what it is today."

"Unfortunately it isn't all that much at this stage," said Leslie.

"It's a whale of a start, and it's going to be a great deal more. It's already several times the acreage that Jamie and Clara first started with. Acres added to by following generations through history. Now it's your turn to forge out a new life for yourself, Miss Weldon." He squeezed her hand, his look sending a hot rush to her face. She looked away so she could breathe.

"I've been thinking about something important, and I'd like to run it by you," said Clive, slowing his steps to turn and face her directly.

Leslie's heart beat like a frightened rabbit. *Surely Clive isn't going to propose! It's too soon!*

His eyes took in her reaction, a slow grin spreading across his face as if he knew her thoughts. "Now that you've made the decision to stay on at the ranch, I think a new sign should be hung out by the road. What would you like it to read? *Weldon Ranch?*"

Embarrassed, she pushed away an annoying twinge of disappointment. Were her emotions for Clive deeper than she realized?

"Leslie? What do you think about the sign?" he pressed.

She paused, remembering what she'd read of Wayne's dream for the ranch. "The sign is a great idea, Clive, but I think I'd like to keep it Riker

Ranch for a while longer, in memory of Wayne," she added thoughtfully.

His deep look warmed her. "Wayne would like that."

Smiling gently, she averted her face. But she could still see the twinkle in his eyes.

"Tell me, Leslie," he said in a husky, teasing tone, "what did you think I was going to ask?"

Aware of her flushed coloring, Leslie redirected his attention with an uplifted hand. She pointed across the lane where Mona walked close to Meg. It was evident that Mona had sensed Meg's difficulty at the gravesite and was now comforting the teenager.

"Isn't it amazing how everything worked out for them? The Lord rescued Meg and put a family together."

"The family was God's original idea," said Clive.

Leslie was suddenly very much aware of how physically close they walked together. Conscious of her heightened pulse, she was thankful when Clive's next question helped clear the air. "So when is your friend from New York arriving?"

Leslie scrambled to realign her thoughts. "Alberta is in a frenzy, making arrangements and trying to choose what she can and cannot live without, way out here in the wilds, as she calls them. She'll fly into Atlanta next week. Mona has agreed to pick her up. I can't afford to take off work so soon after taking the job at the bank."

"I heard you and Mona talking. Is she going to stay with that Christmas Shoppe lady in town?" They were nearing the lane leading up to the barn.

"Not at first. She'll stay with me until she and Georgie get better acquainted." Leslie paused to giggle, thinking of Georgie and Bert working and living together. "Their nicknames are so funny. They sound like a couple of old men, not women. They've been talking almost nightly on the phone since I suggested the plan, and they seem to be getting along fine, but Georgie wants some time before they make a firm decision. Personally, I think it would be a perfect arrangement. They've both been lonely and are hungry for companionship. And when Georgie found out Bert was a Christmas fanatic, she could hardly wait to meet her."

"My, aren't we the little social arranger," Clive said softly. His words were tender, clearly not meant to be cutting. "You have a very caring heart, Leslie Weldon. How would you feel about coffee and doughnuts tomorrow morning?"

"I'd like an omelet better," she said, batting her eyes.

The corners of his mouth tipped upward. "That can be arranged." His arm slipped around her and drew her close to his side. "Would you like to stop by the barn and see the puppies?"

"The puppies! When?" she asked excitedly.

"Sometime last night. I checked in on that husky mix when I put some things in the barn late last night. The pups couldn't have been more than a few minutes old."

"Oooh!" Leslie cooed. "I wish I could have been there." Her attention turned across the lane toward the troubled young girl. "Meg!" she called, pointing excitedly toward the barn. "Puppies!" she yelled.

Meg's dour countenance burst into a brilliant smile. Seconds later, she raced for the barn. Mona laughed and waved back at Leslie. Teenagers' emotions were easily distracted.

Feeling Clive's gentle squeeze on her arm, Leslie's heart was full, her thoughts brimming with possibilities for the days to come. She waved back to Mona and sent a "Thank You" toward heaven. All was right with her world. She had finally come home.

"Come on, Clive, Let's go see those puppies!"

"I choose the one that looks like Boris," Clive flung over his shoulder, sprinting ahead of her in the direction of the barn.

WATCHED!

PATRICIA L. STEBELTON

Ginger's nightmares are now coming more and more often.
But what if there's truth to her troubling dreams?

Ginger has lived in the small town of Collier all her life, where everybody knows everyone else. So why does mystery still surround the death of her aunt, and why was her house robbed after her mama's death? And why is someone stalking her now?

Then Ginger finds some mysterious old journals while helping out at a local book shop. She's convinced that Lisbeth, the owner of the shop, knows more than she's telling. But secrets swirl around Lisbeth, too. Why did she leave town, and then suddenly come back a short while ago?

Ginger is up to her ears in too many surprises…and her confusion over the handsome Houston, the first boy to ever be interested in her, isn't helping.

SUSPENSE. MYSTERY. ROMANCE.

A keep-you-on-the-edge-of-your-seat
mystery & detective thriller with a twist of satisfying romance

INHERITED DANGER

PATRICIA L. STEBELTON

The black Jag sped head-on toward Ginger and switched to her lane.
The driver was going to ram her.

Ginger thought her nightmares were over after she and her boyfriend, Houston, had explored Garnett Manor's long-hidden secret. But now, after visiting a controlling relative she's just discovered she had, things start happening to her. Crazy things, like two cars in one night trying to bump her off a dark stretch of highway into a deep ravine. Clearly, somebody is trying to kill her, but why?

Just as Ginger is starting to put the pieces of her life back together, the old, unanswered questions about her past and a potential large inheritance rear their heads. But all is not what it seems. Will Ginger be able to uncover the dark deception in time to save herself, and a dear friend, from their deadly enemies?

The exciting, not-to-be-missed sequel to Watched!

SUSPENSE. MYSTERY. ROMANCE.

A keep-you-on-the-edge-of-your-seat

mystery & detective thriller with a twist of satisfying romance

www.oaktara.com

The Sleeping Matchbook

Patricia L. Stebelton

A yellow Mustang.
A maroon and gray jacket.
A mysterious matchbook.
They all lead to murder.

Samantha Westhoff will never forget the night she waved good-bye to her crazy-in-love best friend, Amanda Griffin, as she jumped into her boyfriend's yellow Mustang to go to a birthday party. The next day Randy's gunshot body was discovered behind the wheel of his car in an empty parking lot. Amanda hasn't been seen since.

Now, four years later, as seventeen-year-old Sam is helping to sort out Amanda's room, she finds the jacket she's sure Amanda was wearing the night she disappeared. *But then, how could it be in her room now?* Sam wonders. When she discovers a matchbook hidden deep in the lining of the pocket, Sam knows she might be holding the one clue to what really happened that night....

About the Author

PATRICIA L. STEBELTON, a masterful romance-suspense and mystery-detective writer, began by writing poetry when she was young. Now she is the author of six not-to-be-missed novels: *The Sleeping Matchbook, Watched, Inherited Danger, Henri's Ghost, Uncharted Storm,* and *Forgotten Witness* (all OakTara).

She has also published numerous other writings, including a real-life love story "A Night of Destiny" in *Falling in Love with You* (OakTara); a devotional in *Love Is a Verb,* compiled by Gary Chapman with James Stuart Bell; a short story in *Angels, Miracles, and Heavenly Encounters,* compiled by James Stuart Bell; a short story in *Whisperings in God's Ear,* compiled by Wayne Holmes; and short stories in Guideposts book series *Unexpected Prayers* and *Desires of Your Heart.*

Patricia and her husband live outside a picturesque, small town in the heart of Michigan. They have three children and six grandchildren. In the midst of raising a busy family, Patricia took courses in writing and art, attending seminars whenever possible. Presently she works at her writing and commissioned art projects, enjoying activities with her family such as summer cookouts and camping trips.

Patricia enjoys hearing from her readers: **plstebelton@yahoo.com.**

www.oaktara.com